ROGUE'S POSSESSION

COVENANT OF THORNS #2

BY

JEFFE KENNEDY

One does not break an oath to the fae...

But I am getting much better at finding and exploiting the loopholes. I may have promised the ruthlessly sensual fae lord, Rogue, that he can sire my firstborn child—but I never said when. And I'm not giving into his will-eroding attempts to seduce me until he tells me what will happen to my child.

Which he refuses to do.

So, I'm holding out against his allure, no matter how he tantalizes me, because the one way to protect my child is to make sure they're never born. Unfortunately, Rogue is as wily as he is persistent, and soon I find myself in more bargains—I must give him a kiss every day and sleep by his side at night. Even as I travel through Faerie, perfecting my sorceress skills and seeking the answers to the questions Rogue won't—or can't—answer, he is constantly by my side, working his way through my defenses.

He refuses to let me go. Most terrifying of all, I'm finding I don't want him to...

DEDICATION

To Amazing Agent
Pam van Hylckama Vlieg
for loving *Rogue's Pawn* and for being the advocate for my
work I never expected another person to be.

ACKNOWLEDGEMENTS

I've developed the very useful habit of creating a list of acknowledgements when I start writing a new book. That way, every time a friend holds my hand or someone tweets something useful, I can note them down and then paste them in when it comes time. For a reason that escapes me, I didn't do that with *Rogue's Possession*. I keep looking for the list I surely must have somewhere, but no.

So, if I've forgotten you, feel free to send me a note to include in the next book. Seriously.

First and foremost, heartfelt thanks to all the fans of *Rogue's Pawn* who wrote and demanded the next book. It means more than you can guess to know you all love these people and this world as much as I do.

Many thanks to the reviewers at Thebookpushers.com, especially E and Has, for truly living up to their name. Your enthusiasm is a fine and rare thing.

Thanks to Amy Remus, for being the best fan ever. And for asking interesting questions.

Thanks and love to the gals (and two guys) of the Land of Enchantment Romance Authors—seeing you all is the highlight of every month.

Special thanks to Carien Ubink, for beta reading and giving me a crazy-check when I needed it most.

As always, thanks to the Cone Gang—Laura Bickle, Marcella Burnard and Carolyn Crane—for critique, hand-holding, cheerleading, brainstorming, conniving and other assorted clandestine conversations.

Thanks to my long-suffering editor, Deb Nemeth, for all the hard work making this the best book it could be.

And also thanks to Angela James and the rest of the Carina crew, for supporting this trilogy and all the many ways they cheer on their authors.

An official thank-you to Kev, for the light-up pillow. It is beyond awesome.

Finally, my love and gratitude to David, who keeps me going and makes it worth the trip.

A NOTE FROM THE AUTHOR

This book is a new edition, one I republished when I received the rights back to the Covenant of Thorns trilogy (and the seven other books I did with Carina Press) in 2022. As I noted in the new edition of book one, Rogue's Pawn, very little has changed *inside* the book.

I tweaked one reference I felt hadn't stood the test of time and I changed a conversation between Rogue and Gwynn ever so slightly.

I've left the original dedication and acknowledgements, as they reflect my personal history at the time. Some of those relationships have changed or faded away. Others remain strong. I'd like to add some thanks here, especially to my current agent, Sarah Younger of Nancy Yost Literary Agency, who helped me regain the rights to these books even though she won't benefit directly from them. Also, many thanks to my amazing assistant, Carien—who actually appears in the old acknowledgements, pre-assisting days!—and who commenced a re-read of these books for me, so I wouldn't have to. Finally, immense gratitude to my cover artist, Ravven, who came up with the concept for these covers. These are the covers I always wished for. Finally, I have them and they are everything.

Welcome to the second edition of Rogue's Possession! We can even call it the 10th Anniversary Edition.

ROGUE'S POSSESSION

PART 1

Tweaking the Experimental Design

CHAPTER 1

IN WHICH I ACCOMPLISH SEVERAL IMPOSSIBLE THINGS BEFORE BREAKFAST

Negotiation is the science of the fae culture, providing the guiding precepts for all actions. Virtually nothing is offered without a price attached. Conversely, nothing can be taken from you without appropriate payment. Pretty much.

~*Big Book of Fairyland*, "Rules of Bargaining"

WE WERE LATE to the battle.

As I'd been promised, the Promontory of Magic enjoyed a spectacular view, though I wasn't there to sightsee. The finger of rocks thrust well out into the ocean, the water the unnatural blue of a resort hotel pool, despite the thunderous surf and driving rain.

Below, two fleets of sailing ships exchanged fire. They were conveniently arrayed on each side of the promontory, flanking me as if I were a Wimbledon line judge sitting at the net, ready to call faults and points. Except my power was even greater.

I would decide who lived or died.

Whether I wanted to or not.

My hair lashed against my cheeks, stinging me, and I pulled up the hood of my cloak, grateful for its warmth. A gift from Rogue, the cloak magically repelled water. Despite all I'd learned about controlling and stabilizing magic, Rogue's abilities far exceeded mine. The scent of sandalwood teased me, bringing up warm and sensual memories of his devastating kisses. Rogue managed to be both the bane of my life and the addiction I couldn't seem to shake. My life had become irretrievably intertwined with the fae lord's, though I hadn't seen him in days. His absence made my heart that much more vulnerable to the longings he stirred in me. I tucked them away, where they wouldn't distract me.

"Which side is ours?" I asked.

My fae companion, Puck—a vision in celadon polka dots that clashed quite alarmingly with his strawberry blond locks— gave me a goggle-eyed stare, as if I'd asked which way was up, and pointed at the left side. Good thing I'd asked—I'd thought maybe it was the other. One of the many disadvantages of being a human in Faerie was missing out on their hive-mind shared understanding.

"It's a fine day for a battle!" Puck gazed out over the ships with a gleeful expression and I tried to fake the same enthusiasm, despite the dread in my heart.

Of course, every day in Faerie was fine, in a purely aesthetic sense. The sun, which shone most of the time, did so with lustrous brilliance in depthless skies. The grass glowed an emerald green Oz would have envied. Even the rain shimmered like effervescent and musical drops of platinum.

Beautiful, gorgeous, yes.

Don't wish you were here.

Seriously.

In a place like Faerie, the pretty merely masked the reality, which could be horrible indeed. I hadn't liked my university job as a neuroscientist in the physiology department back in Wyoming, but being employed as a war sorceress sucked far more. Forget the glam sound of it—killing people at someone else's whim whittled away your humanity in hateful bites. Compared to that, my old tenure committee seemed like amateurs.

"You recall your instructions?" Puck bobbed his head as he spoke, encouraging me to agree.

"Piece of cake."

Puck cocked his head, puzzled, and I knew my idiom hadn't quite translated. Usually my intended meaning got through just fine via the telepathic network, but sometimes, particularly if I didn't pay attention, my good old American English slang created strange images in the fae mind.

Some gaps could never be bridged.

"Yes. Darling will inform me of the moment and I will sink exactly half of the enemy ships." I sent a questioning thought to Darling, my cat Familiar, to make sure he was still on board with the plan, especially since he provided my only long-distance communication access. When he felt like it. Imagine a cell phone company run by kittens.

"It shall be a battle to go down in history! Victory shall be ours!" Puck galloped off, leaving me alone with Darling's grumbling narrative in my head, which roughly translated as *bored, bored, bored.*

Darling had become my Familiar largely in a quest for adventure, and being stuck with the generals at battle HQ so he could relay information to me annoyed him to no end. He wanted real action. Sometimes his thoughts came across with a disconcerting manly point of view—especially since he communicated mainly in pictures and feelings. He also suffered from delusions of grandeur.

I had bigger problems, however. The terms of my indentured servitude to General Falcon as pet sorceress in his war dictated that I do as he instructed. The arcane rules of bargaining in Faerie gave me something of an out—as long as I stuck to the letter of our agreements, I could skate around what he really wanted.

In this case, the drowning death of half the humans in the opposing army. Or navy, I guess.

I sure as hell couldn't drown a bunch of innocent humans. The fae might regard their lives as disposable, but I knew the men on those ships had no more choice—or stake—in Falcon's ridiculous war games than the wooden vessels themselves. Rogue had warned me I'd face this moment if I chose to honor my servitude instead of running off with him. Since I hadn't been eager to exchange my status for an even more questionable one with Rogue, I was well and truly stuck.

Don't think about him.

A white slice of anger at my current predicament flared in me. Something sharp and alien enough to take my breath away. I shuttered my mind, thinking it came from elsewhere, but it continued its headlong race through my heart and disappeared again, leaving me rattled. This wasn't the first time I'd felt it since the last battle—like the remnants of a fever dream after you've awakened. I wasn't sure what it meant, but I knew giving it attention was probably a bad idea.

Instead I concentrated on my goals for the day:

1. Do what you're told.
2. Keep to simple agreements.
3. Stay alive.
4. Try not to kill anyone.

The four habits of highly effective sorceresses.

I found a rock to sit on, tucked the cloak around me and watched the ships wheeling around, puffs of flame and smoke exchanged, and not much else.

Maybe it was just me, but I found battle to be incredibly dull. Especially from a distance. I had no doubt it didn't feel that way for the people actually fighting. As far as spectacles, however, it was terribly overrated. And then knowing that people were losing their lives for no good reason—it all made my stomach clench. There were few combinations worse than horrific monotony.

Darling had fallen asleep and I envied him the easy nap. To keep myself focused, I counted ships. Then counted again.

With a slowly dawning horror I realized there were nine enemy vessels. And I'd agreed in specific language to sink exactly half of them. No matter if I sank four or five, I'd be an oath breaker. My knotted stomach revolted as I thrust away the images of what I'd seen happen to those who violated their bargains. I couldn't let it happen to me.

Despite the chill air, a cold sweat broke out over my scalp.

Could I sink half a ship? And how would I make sure it was

exactly half? The sailors and fighters on board would certainly count, and they'd be in motion. It would be next to impossible to make sure exactly half of them—no more, no less—went into the drink. And then how to keep them from dying?

I tried to make good use of the downtime, planning a spell that might simulate drowning. Darling, clearly just catnapping, showed me a mermaid giggling and cuddling him against her plump naked bosom. I seriously doubted he'd really found any mermaids, but he insisted on the tale.

Though...didn't mermaids save drowning sailors? Maybe I could work that angle.

Darling yawned and stretched. *Uh-oh.* He sent me an image of General Falcon conferring with the fae noble in charge of the navy. It had to be nearly time, though the battle below looked much the same to me. The fae both looked upset, however, pointing at the sky and growing red-faced.

From my vantage point, I tried to discern which way they were looking. And then I saw them.

Dragons.

Heart thudding up into my throat, I stood, squinting at the V formation of giant reptiles flying through the roiling clouds. They sparkled like jewels despite the gloom, glorious, impossible and terrifying. I'd encountered them only once before, but that had been plenty to convince me to keep my distance. Immune to magic, they were the enemy's trump card.

Darling sent a pointed poke, like a claw-swipe to my mind. *"Now."*

I reached deep inside for the place my trainers had taught me to find, that cool and remote spot where I existed without attachment to the world. It came from nothingness. The nothing I had become when they destroyed me before rebuilding me in their image. Almost.

My skills had been hard-won, paid for with pain and the kind of loss of self that comes only from torture and sophisticated brainwashing. I was frankly lucky to still be sane. If I truly was.

Carefully I shaped the idea of what I wanted. Precision was crucial if you didn't want unpleasant side-results. Like with organic chemistry, a slight error turned sugar to poison. To keep it simple, I focused on sinking four of the ships, holding the images of those particular ones clearly in mind. They would come apart with slow grace, the planks becoming sieves. Gently, they would lower into the water, allowing the people on board time to swim away. I added mermaids, beautiful and solicitous, carrying the sailors and soldiers to the beach.

A lot could go wrong, but it was a key discipline to keep any of those thoughts from contaminating my idea. Only what I wanted. Exactly what I wanted.

Once I had it, perfect, shining and precise, I pulled on the energy. It seethed inside me like my own personal churning sea. In this way, Rogue had done me a favor, staying away these past few days. My desire for him raged hotter than ever before. Our torrid night together, dream world or not, had barely touched the roaring need he stoked in me. All I had to do was open the door to it and it poured through, setting fire to my idea and making it reality.

The world shimmered, shifted as the new reality settled in, and the four ships I'd selected began sinking into the waves, like ladies in fancy ball gowns dropping into a gracious curtsy and continuing forever.

The size of beetles from my perspective, men poured overboard, jumping into the water where mermaids popped up, drawing the swimmers to shore.

Sometimes I impressed even myself.

"Lady Sorceress!" My page, Larch, was shouting, his blue fists knotted in my cloak as high as he could reach to get my attention. He pointed to the dragons. Which were headed directly toward us.

They glittered in the sky, enormous lizards with leathery wings, the moisture in the air steaming off in streamers as they dove.

With a rumble like a 747 on takeoff, the lead dragon dropped, man-high talons outstretched. I flattened myself, and the claws whistled through the air over my head.

"We have to get down!" Larch shrieked over the dragon-thunder and the pounding surf. He practically dragged me over the side of the point, letting me go at my own pace only once he was sure I was following him through the slick, sharp-edged boulders.

Another dragon dive-bombed me, the wind of its passage rocking my tenuous grip on the rocks. Larch crawled under the shelter of one, but I kept going, working my way forward to where I could see the enemy ships again. Larch shouted incoherently after me, which I ignored. I'd rather get munched by a dragon than violate my oath. I still had half a ship to sink.

To get around the point of the promontory, I had to clamber up a bit. Going down wasn't an option. The surf boiled just below, the cold brine soaking my boots. It would have saturated the cloak if not for Rogue's spell.

A rumble of approaching dragon warned me and I dropped to the side. It barely missed me, the enormous talon snagging a rock just above and shattering it, the shards raining down on me. I really wished they'd go away—one wish that would do me absolutely no good whatsoever.

The hood of my cloak had fallen back, and my hair plastered to my head in the chill rain and surf splatter. As fast as I could before the next pass, I crawled up and over the point, spotting the five remaining enemy ships. I would just have to try for it.

The dragon caught me by surprise. No approaching thunder. It must have glided in somehow, because the tip of its talon caught my hood, lifting me into the air. I shrieked, a sound immediately cut off by the loss of air as the cloak strangled me. Before I could think to reach for the ties at my neck, a black object torpedoed through the air, knocking me off the point of the dragon's claw and dropping me into the cold waves.

The impact stunned me, knocking the breath from my body. Cold seemed to freeze my lungs, stopping me from drawing air immediately. Not sure which way was up, I thrashed in the water, tangling in the cloak and my own skirts. Pushing through the surface felt like a miracle, until I drew that longed-for breath and took in as much sea water as air.

I spluttered and coughed as a wave swamped me, carrying me toward the point. The cloak didn't drag me down, but it wasn't buoyant either. Remembering the riptide rules, I swam crosswise to the current that insisted on crashing toward the rocks. The water wasn't cold enough to induce hypothermia right away, but neither did it help. I let the next swell lift me a distance, then struck out again once it passed.

The rocks, however, were too close. The wave crashed on them with a boom. Another few minutes and that could be my body breaking. I frantically sorted through magical solutions. A flotation device wouldn't save me from the rocks. I couldn't just wish myself out of here without a specific plan or a dragon would get me. I did wish away the boots, which helped considerably. Maybe flippers?

Before I could form a clear image, a bigger wave caught me, throwing me sideways and into the sucking current around a looming boulder. Gasping as momentum scraped me against the sharp edges with bruising force, I choked on water that tasted oddly sweet and tried to hang on to the rock. But the force of the receding water sucked me back into the sea's mercurial grasp, pulling me under. I thrashed to the surface, tangled in the cloak.

This was not going well.

A black head popped up next to me, sleek as a seal but with a slavering mouth full of white teeth. The Black Dog seemed to grin at me, full of puppyish joy. It was he who'd knocked me out of the dragon's grip. He yipped at me and I reached for him, but lost the moment to another swell that pushed me down. Teeth fastened on my shoulder, yanking me from the water. I gritted my teeth against the pain and turned, wrapped my arms around the Dog and climbed on his back, anchoring my grip around his chest.

I'm not a big person, but the Dog is nearly as large— enough to lift me partially out of the water, all surging muscle beneath me as he swam for the sandy shore. In exhausted relief, I leaned my cheek against his wet fur, the heat of him burning through and warming me.

Most everyone was terrified of the Black Dog, but not me. For I knew his secret now.

He pulled me all the way through the tumbling surf, and I let go when we reached the sand, rolling off him onto my back. With enthusiastic affection, he licked my face, meaty breath washing over me.

Darling sent an urgent thought, an image of Falcon snarling in rage.

I sat up. "Jeez, I've been a little distracted, okay?"

A dragon wheeled overhead but kept its distance. The Black Dog fell outside a lot of the usual rules of magic—in ways I hadn't yet quantified—but it seemed the dragons were wary of him. I struggled to my feet, wishing my dress dry. An easy wish and that was so much better. The ships were farther out to sea now, sailing away, perhaps.

Down the beach, the soldiers and sailors who'd made it to shore seemed to have noticed my presence and were pointing in my direction, near as I could tell. They likely recognized me from previous battles. The tone of their shouting didn't sound like gratitude for the trouble I'd gone to in saving their miserable skins from drowning. Probably they were peeved about me sinking their ships in the first place. Some people.

And, of course, I'd foolishly left my weapon tied to my horse's saddle back on the promontory. My self-defense instructor would give me a tongue-lashing for that—and not the pleasurable kind.

At least I could do that. I wished for my dagger to be in my hand and it appeared. Not that it would do much good against

the mob making its way up the long curve of the beach, but it
gave me a bit of comfort. They had a good mile to go.

I concentrated on the ships, nearly out of sight, obscured
by the blustering rain. Now to sink half of one. I'd have to find
a way to seal up the opening, like a magician's trick when they
cut the lady in half, to keep it afloat. Dammit—I didn't know
enough about sailing ships, but surely that wouldn't be
aerodynamic, or whatever the nautical version of that concept
would be. The only real solution would be to keep it magically
buoyant.

"A pretty trick, even for me," a voice behind me drawled.
"Are you sure you can do it?"

CHAPTER 2

IN WHICH I ENCOUNTER
THE ANTI-APHRODITE

Faerie operates on a sliding scale of moral ambiguity. The Golden Rule is turned inside out to become "When others do unto you, weigh the cost to yourself and charge accordingly."

~*Big Book of Fairyland*, "Rules of Bargaining"

MY HEART—THE TRAITOR—LEAPED and my blood heated. Deciding not to give Rogue the satisfaction of knowing he'd startled me, I refused to turn and look at him. I shouldn't have been surprised. The Black Dog came from him. Or was him. Or was a manifestation of his subconscious nature somehow. The physics of it escaped me, but where there was one, the other followed. And, like Clark Kent and Superman, they were never in the same place at the same time.

"Howdy, stranger."

"Always a pleasure to see you, lovely Gwynn," he returned. "Though you look a bit worse for wear."

"Thanks for pulling me out of the water."

"Is that what happened? I wondered." He spoke from right

behind me, the scent of Stargazer lilies and sandalwood weaving through the rain.

I gave in and looked at him. Though I'd braced myself for it, his sensual impact took my breath away. His long black hair flowed loose, hanging in wet strands over his shoulders. Blue eyes like the sky just after sunset met mine, showing lingering anger tempered with amusement. And desire. My body reacted to it and he knew it, dark lips curving up on one side—the left side of his face, which was covered by a network of inky lines and thorny spikes that seemed to reach out from around his skull, fingers and vines splaying across his skin. At first I'd wondered if it was a tattoo, but now I knew they grew out of the same place the Black Dog did. The pattern continued back into his hairline and down past the black shirt he wore.

I happened to know they kept going from there.

Not an image I needed in my head right now. I channeled the flaring heat into banked energy. Should be plenty to keep half a boat afloat.

"I'll be interested to see if you can pull this off." Rogue gazed out at the disappearing ships. "You always seem to have inventive approaches, if amateurish ones."

"Don't bug me. You don't even know what I'm trying to do."

"Sink half a ship. Careless of you not to mind that aspect of the bargain."

"Eavesdropping, were you?"

"I don't have to," he retorted. "You still think far too loud. Anyone with a nugget of ability can hear your internal monologue."

"Sorry I disturbed you."

"Oh, you disturb me all right, passionate Gwynn. What will you give me to help you out?" He traced an unnaturally long finger down my cheek, the sensation sending currents of heat through my blood. "I have some suggestions."

"I'll bet you do." I sounded breathy. This was not good. "But the bargain is that I'd do it. So quit bothering me and let me figure this out."

He gestured grandly at the churning ocean, then folded his arms and watched me expectantly.

"Can't you go somewhere else?"

"I'm protecting you." He nodded his head at the mob of men who'd gotten significantly closer. "Yon angry humans seem to be headed this way."

"Yes. I know. Let me do this and I'm out of here." I tried to concentrate, straining my eyes to pick out one ship. Rogue's gaze felt like a caress on my skin. My cheek tingled where he'd touched me.

"Do I make you nervous?"

Yes. "No. Be quiet."

With a precise wish, I redistributed the people on board to an equal number on each side, trusting in the magic to handle the math. I called up the mermaids and cut the boat in half, letting one side sink. This was no gentle drop, but that couldn't be helped. Envisioning the half I wanted to keep afloat with the breach sealed over, I wished it buoyant. Then frowned out to sea. I really wanted to see if it worked.

"Change the material of the ship to something else." Rogue was looking out to the horizon. "It's the wrong shape to stay afloat long like that. It will just drain you. Then send it to shore."

"Can you see it?"

He glanced at me, fulminous blue eyes definitely amused under arched black brows. "There are many ways of seeing. Too bad you don't know them."

"Nice," I muttered. In my heart, though, I could admit that part of me enjoyed sparring with him. As much as he taunted me, he always seemed to consider me a worthy opponent.

Not sure why the image sprang to mind, I kept the sealed-up ship shape, but changed it into fiberglass. Strong enough to hold the people, light enough to float well. Hopefully I hadn't just thrown the whole ecosystem all to hell by introducing that. I wished up a current, to drag the ship to shore. Then let it all go.

Rogue waited, one eyebrow cocked. Nothing happened for a few minutes, then Darling sent me a purring compliment and showed me the nobles going home. Another victory. Yay me.

"Well done." Rogue smiled at me, gaze warm, and slid a hand around the back of my neck in a sensual caress. "Let's continue our discus—"

He broke off when the air seemed to shimmer and gel. A sound like a gong rang through the sand, and the waves quieted, peeling back from each other. Like a perverse Aphrodite rising on sea foam, Titania appeared in the breach.

Lovely, yes, like all of Faerie. Her naked body featureless as a Barbie doll's, colorless gleaming hair flowing around her, untouched by the surf or rain. Her pale eyes, long-lashed but unnervingly like a white rabbit's, fixed on us.

"Oh no." I choked on the words. It hadn't worked. I'd broken my vow and now here she was, my personal night-mare, come to take her pound of flesh from me. Which could be literal. Or worse.

Rogue edged in front of me, a protective gesture that moved me beyond measure. "This isn't about you." He pitched his voice so only I could hear him. "It's about me. She may not notice you."

Not likely, but for once I kept my mouth shut and stayed behind Rogue's tall form. I didn't know if he was a match for Titania, but I sure as hell wasn't.

"Lord Rogue, my handsome love," she cooed in a tinkling child's voice. "I've been looking for you. You left me so precipitously."

"How can I serve you, Titania?"

I'd never heard Rogue sound obsequious. It chilled me to the bone.

"Who's your little friend?" She peeked suddenly around Rogue's arm, quick as a striking snake. My heart skipped several beats and she blew me a little pink kiss. "Just being silly. I remember you, Sorceress—Rogue's new plaything. Are you enjoying it? He's a magnificent lover, isn't he?"

My thoughts fluttered, moths hitting a hot bulb and frying instantly. "Your Highness..." I curtseyed a little, hoping that might appease her. Rogue could say her name out loud, but I couldn't. With the fae hive mind, they could all refer obliquely to their insanely cruel goddess-queen, which I heard in my head as "Titania"—my internal association for queen of the faeries, thanks to AP English—but when I said it, they heard it as her actual name. Which could invoke her attention. Nasty attention. Like now.

Titania reached out to touch me, her extra-jointed fingers a nest of spider's legs. My grip tightened on the dagger still in my hand and I longed to slash at her. Rogue shifted slightly, enough to nudge her hand away, and her gaze flashed up to him, the air heating dangerously.

"That's not in the rules," he murmured to her, like the lover she claimed he was.

She pouted, smiling up at him coyly. "But I'm so bored," she complained, sounding like a petulant adolescent. "This is taking too long. Let's sweeten the pot."

"I decline," Rogue replied.

"What do you think, Sorceress?" Titania craned her neck around Rogue's arm again. "Can I entice you into a little wager?"

"Don't say a word, Gwynn. Don't think any, either."

Usually I balked at Rogue's high-handed orders, but I took his advice. I had absolutely no idea what Titania was needling Rogue about, but I knew better than to draw more attention to myself. I'd winkle it out of him later. If we survived this encounter. I clamped a stronger shield over my mind, quieting my thoughts as much as I knew how.

Titania's hopeful expression turned nasty. "Fine," she snarled, all sweetness gone from her voice. "But I grow weary of this game. I shall find a way to make things more interesting for us all, Lord Rogue, if you don't pick up the pace. Tick-tock, tick-tock. If you don't see to this business yourself, I'll take matters into my own hands."

She walked back down the sand, her feet leaving no mark. Her presence had emptied the beach of the mob of soldiers. No dragons in sight. No one went near the Queen Bitch if they could help it.

"Oh!" Titania glanced back at me, flipping her ankle-length

hair over one shoulder like a diabolical Marcia Brady. "I nearly forgot. I have something that belongs to you, Sorceress. What's left of it, that is." With a tinkling giggle, she waved a segmented hand and a crumpled heap appeared on the beach. She nudged it with a toe.

"Tick-tock!"

And she vanished.

I approached the pile on the sand, the awkward twist of pale limbs and shredded flesh. Even destroyed like this, without her wings, she was recognizable. Dragonfly, my erstwhile foolish maidservant. The waves teased at her, dragging the pieces of her broken girlish body into the surf. I swallowed, trying to master the surge of nausea, tossing aside my dagger and reaching out a hand to maybe grab her by the foot to keep her from washing out to sea.

Long fingers wrapped around my wrist. "Let her go," Rogue said, uncharacteristically gentle. "She's well past saving."

"I should bury her, at least. I owe her that much."

He waved a negligent hand and a wave crawled up, wrapped around the girl's corpse like a watery fist, and swept her away. "There. She's buried. Now, we have things to discuss."

"Okay." I throttled down my residual terror and rising annoyance at his callousness. "Let's start with where you've been and what the Queen Bitch was talking about. Were you with her?"

Rogue turned the hand holding my wrist to weave his fingers with mine. "Jealous? Did you miss me?"

"I did not." Not that I'd admit. "Now answer my question."

"Which? You asked three questions."

I stopped myself from growling at him. "What was that 'tick-tock' shit? What will she take into her own hands? Give me a straight answer."

"What will you give me in return?"

That white-cold feeling rose up again, a flash of silver claws raking my heart. The anger welled, cold and precise, a razor edge of rage. For Dragonfly's wasted life, for Titania's cruelty, for the fact that I had missed him and that I desperately feared he'd been with Titania, plotting about me, laughing with her about the ignorant human.

Abruptly, Rogue's head snapped around. He turned in a wary circle, searching for something I couldn't see. His cautious gaze finally settled on me. Was that a glimmer of fear? Surely not. He feared nothing. Except perhaps the Dog's power over him. Not that he'd admit it.

"Gwynn." He held palms out toward me, as if warming them at a flame. "What is that? What are you doing?"

"I—I don't know." I shifted, unsteady on the sand. His uncertainty put me off balance. Always he knew more than I did.

"What does it feel like? No games. This is deadly important." He'd moved into his professorial mode. "Describe it in the best detail you can."

"It's white. Kind of a ghost. And chill with it. It has curved claws, very sharp. Feline." I thought of the things I'd seen in his mind, images I associated with his feral brand of magic. And the Black Dog. "What is it, Rogue? Why are you looking at me like that?"

He dug his hands through his hair, scrubbing over his scalp in thought. In near desperation. Then he threw back his head and laughed at the sky, a bitter sound, throwing his arms out as if daring a bolt from above. Or from Titania. "Of course. How could it have been any other way?"

"What? Tell me." I fisted a hand in the wet black velvet of his shirt, demanding his attention, which he settled on me with such full intensity I had to steel myself not to flinch. "Is it the Black Dog? What is in me, Rogue? I have to know."

He laid his hand over mine, soothing, flattening it out to rest on his lean chest. The three-four beat of his heart thumped under my hand. Regret softened the fierce lines of his lips. "It may be best that you don't know. You cannot stop it."

"Knowledge is power," I insisted.

He shook his head, slowly. "Not always, my Gwynn. Sometimes it's just the wound that never heals, the ongoing torment of knowing there is part of you that defies containment. I did not wish this for you."

"It's not the Dog. It's…something else."

His fingers stroked my hand. "Yes. Feline, you said. It will find its way out of you and you will come to know it through the way the world reacts to it. It's stronger than you can ever be."

"Where did it come from?"

His mouth quirked. "From you, magical Gwynn. All from you. You carried the seeds already. Now they grow, a vine twisting in your soul. She's still a ghost to you now. She will eventually take flesh from yours."

I shuddered. I'd seen the Black Dog erupt from Rogue's body in a fountain of blood, leaving an empty skin behind. He must have suffered it many times. Floundering, I tried to understand how this could be possible. "But I am not immortal as you are. How can I survive such a thing?"

"I doubt you can." Though his words were blunt, even cruel, his voice, his face held a kind of compassion. His twisted, unfeeling brand of it. "I will help you. But this makes it even more crucial that you be by my side at all times. That you learn what I can teach you. Your very life and sanity may depend on it."

He poured it on just a titch too thick. *Tick-tock.* I pulled away again. "This is just another manipulation. You'll tell me whatever you think will get you your way."

He raised one silky eyebrow, on the left side, where the twining pattern of black lines, thorns and fangs shifted with the movement. *A vine twisting in your soul.* The hiss of white claws whispered through me. I touched my face, wet with cold rain. Would I soon bear a similar mark?

"You are not stupid, Gwynn." Rogue made the observation quietly. "It ill behooves you to play the fool."

Fear crept through me, ice riming a window with slow curlicues of frost. And I had no one to turn to for comfort. Only the offer of help from the man whose greatest desire was to lock me up so he could exploit me for his nefarious purposes and pleasures—or, it now appeared, for Titania's.

He stroked my cheek, gaze melting blue now. "Never would I lock you up. I swear that to you. I can taste your fear. Don't be afraid of me."

"I won't ever wear a leash again, Rogue."

"We all wear leashes—some are just more visible than others."

I took a deep shuddering breath. "This changes nothing. It's as if I found out I have cancer or something. I can't let it stop me from living. And you won't distract me with this. What does the Queen Bitch want from you and what does it have to do with me? Is she why you want me to have your baby? Tell me the truth."

He studied me, still stroking my cheek. I took an obscure comfort in it. Sometimes I longed to stop fighting him and just let him take me over. It would be so much easier in so many ways. But then, slavery always was. The Romans defeated the Britons not with warfare, but with steady food and hot baths.

"You fascinate me, Gwynn." Rogue murmured. "Have I ever told you that? The flow of your thoughts, the quicksilver of your mind, and that crimson passion boiling beneath. Even if I didn't need you, I would be unable to stay away."

His lips hovered near mine, wine-dark, so tempting.

"I will make you a deal. No, don't argue yet. I will visit you daily, for lessons. I'll teach you what you need to know about Titania. We can work together to track the evolution of your beast. Perhaps I can help you navigate the minefield of it. Working together, Gwynn. Partners. It's what you said you wanted. It's a good bargain."

As he spoke his lips had drifted over my skin, a whisper away from my cheek, my temple, my ear, jaw, throat. Desire shimmered through me.

"Won't you just tell me the truth?" My voice came out hoarse.

"This is how I can. Trust me on this."

"It sounds very expensive—what's the price for such generosity?"

"You know what I want."

Yes, my firstborn child. Talk about pricey.

His hand slid over my shoulder, down to the small of my back, pressing me to him, his heat and alien heartbeat infusing me. "You can live at the camp, if you insist, but I will visit you at night. I want to share your bed."

"That's it?" I tried to focus, searching out the loopholes. "The other rules remain in place? No hanky-panky under the clothes, etcetera." In one of my rare, proud moments, I'd managed to outwit Rogue. I'd let him think he'd maneuvered me into flirting with him, which meant acting like I was attracted to him—not difficult, unfortunately—and allowing one-handed physical contact over the clothes, to all publicly accessible skin. It strained my willpower, but prevented him from impregnating me. Apparently all of those religious groups who insisted on full-coverage clothing for women were on to something after all.

"That's it. I won't take you until you beg me to."

"That will never happen."

He smiled. "Never is a very long time, succulent Gwynn. Six years is much shorter."

I sighed for the truth of that. "Okay, I agree to the terms as stated."

"One more thing."

I braced myself. Here it came now.

"I want a kiss."

"Now?" The beach remained empty, cleared by Titania's fearsome presence.

"Now and at least once a day going forward, at the time of my choosing. Though you may always freely offer more."

"What's my incentive? We already have a deal."

"I have not put my agreement to it. I want this perk."

"What kind of a kiss? How long?" I knew better than to leave this to chance. He'd kissed me twice before, both passionate, long and completely devastating kisses. I would not be getting away with chaste pecks.

His eyes glittered. "Will you set parameters even on a kiss?"

"Absolutely. As you said, I'm not stupid."

"How do you propose to quantify it?"

"It's your kiss—give me some options."

"*Our* kiss," he qualified.

I squinted to keep from rolling my eyes. He hated when I did that, said it wasn't flirtatious, which I suppose was valid. "We will set a time limit."

He considered. "I will say when the time is up."

"Oh no, no, no." I poked him in the chest, but he only held me tighter to him. "I'll make a sand timer—" I barely caught myself in time to avoid saying *hourglass*, "—and we'll use that. Same length of kissing every time. Lips to lips, only."

His mouth quirked at that, making me relieved I'd caught that particular loophole. "I want my first kiss now."

"We don't have the timer yet."

"So make it." He let me go. "I will want to approve the length of time. I need to assess your level anyway, if I'm to teach you."

Making this thing was a small effort, but my faults include pride. I wanted Rogue to be, if not impressed, at least satisfied.

I created a perfectly clear image in my head of what I wanted, along with the most precise sense of five minutes I could produce. One minute would be better, but I doubted Rogue would go for it. I held out my hand, palm up, and wished the timer into being.

It appeared on my hand, looking suspiciously close to my grandmother's egg timer, with its cheerfully yellow plastic end caps. I would have modified them into a less-tacky natural wood, but I didn't want to give Rogue the impression that it hadn't turned out exactly how I wanted it to.

He took it from me, turned it so the sands slid the other direction, and nodded. "Agreed."

Showing off, he withdrew his long-fingered hand and left the glass hanging midair, the bottom full, the top empty, waiting to be overturned.

"My lady." He took my hand and laid it over his heart again, drawing me close. Thunder rumbled with the surf, the sound of drumbeats running through it, darkly musical, and the rain poured over us.

I trembled with anticipation, not wanting to contemplate whether I'd allowed him to maneuver me into this deal because I wanted to taste him, needed his lips on mine.

"Our kiss." The glass tumbled over and he leaned in.

I expected the wolf, the demanding, ravishing kiss, maximizing his time with the most he could take. Instead his mouth brushed mine, a slow seeking, tenderly exploring, urging me to open. A flower blooming in the warm sun, I unfurled, the desire he fulminated in me pouring forth. He kissed me like he loved me, a nourishing caress that stretched into infinity, drowning me in warm pleasure.

I was in seriously deep shit now.

CHAPTER 3

IN WHICH I SIGN UP FOR COURSES AT THE LOCAL COMMUNITY COLLEGE

꿈꿈

*In Faerie, life is not precious until evaluated and priced
according to the going market. Usually this evaluation is not
under the control of the person whose life it is.*

~Big Book of Fairyland, "Rules of Bargaining"

THE LAST GRAINS of sand slipped through the glass with a soft sigh. No—I couldn't possibly hear that over the rain and the drumming of the surf. That was me. Rogue still held my hand in his, looking into my eyes.

"Come away with me, Gwynn. Let me show you what we could have."

I wanted to say yes. Heavens help me, I did. This was why he wanted the kissing. Erotic teasing I could withstand—more or less—but these drugging kisses went straight to my foolish heart. Which clearly needed armoring. Teflon might work.

"Nice try, but no." The words came out with a satisfying edge. I stepped back and wiped the rain off my face, twisting my hopelessly tangled hair back behind my neck. "You can teach me what I need to know here, while I keep doing my job."

"You are an exceedingly stubborn woman."

"Please don't tell me you're just now figuring that out."

Rogue snapped the timer out of the air and pocketed it somewhere inside his cloak. He hid his irritation well, but I could scent it on the air, a tinge of impatience. Point for me. Good to know I got under his skin too.

A subtle movement and I glimpsed the ever-patient Larch making his way around from the point, leading my horse, Felicity. I had no idea how such a stolid fellow managed to move so gracefully. Brownie magic, no doubt.

"Well." I felt awkward. End of date, no more kissing allowed. Did we shake hands?

"Until tonight, lovely Gwynn." Rogue bent over my hand and brushed it with an air kiss. With a wink, he disappeared.

"Poof," I muttered to myself, suppressing my smile out of principle, then turned to make the short walk to Larch and Felicity.

Immediately upon returning to my tent on the fae side of General Falcon's sprawling war camp, I wished the brass tub in the corner full of hot water at my favorite temperature—if only all magic was so simple—and immersed myself, dunking my head, too, and savoring the burn. What I really missed at times were hot showers, just standing there and letting the water pound the headache out of your skull. I should try to make one.

But this was good. The hot water felt like heaven, warming my chilled extremities. My myriad scratches stung, especially over my scraped chest and my shoulder where the Dog had latched on. Bruised and battered, but nothing time wouldn't heal. As I soaked, I mulled over what had happened. *What did we learn today, kids?*

Starling came in and handed me a glass of wine without asking. She had managed to find a white that I liked and kept it in supply for me. One of her many thoughtful ways of making my life easier. I couldn't decide if the half-fae, half-human young woman was my friend, maid or babysitter. She and I had been through a rough spot recently. The whole being-looked-after-by-servants thing didn't always sit all that well with me. Particularly when it leaned toward feeling chaperoned.

But that was water under the bridge. For better or worse, I'd gotten myself bonded or something to Rogue, and there would be no more sneaking off and dallying with handsome human officers again.

Besides, it was really nice to have someone hand you a glass of wine after a hard day at work. And flirting.

She scooped my now-ragged dress off the floor and held it up, scowling at it. "What in the name of Titania happened to you?"

"Her," I replied in a sour tone, "among other things. But most of that damage came from being dropped in the ocean by a dragon. The rocks around here are sharp."

If I'd expected horrified sympathy, I was out of luck.

"I heard Lord Rogue rescued you from the sea monsters." Her caramel-brown eyes were wide and soft with romance. "I knew he'd come back for you. Does this mean we're moving to his castle now?"

Starling's fixation on my supposed happily-ever-after romance with Rogue had to come to an end. Clearly I needed her as my friend, if I was going to find my way through this tangle with Rogue and Titania. I set down my glass and grabbed the little vial of scented shampoo.

Starling moved to help me.

"No—stay there. I can soap myself. Pour yourself some wine. There are things I need to tell you." Closing my eyes against the suds, I lathered my scalp and thought about how to explain this to her. "I know you have ideas about me and Lord Rogue. Mostly things other people have told you. I don't know if you precisely understand the nature of the bargain between us." I squinched open an eye to see her interested look.

"Nobody really explains anything to me, you know?"

I sighed in agreement and dunked back to rinse. "I *do* know."

"So, here's the deal." I got out and dried off with one of the rosemary-scented towels Starling left stacked on a little table next to the tub. "It's a long story, but in essence, I owe Rogue a life debt."

"Ooh," Starling breathed.

"Exactly. When I first got here, I was badly hurt. Rogue saved my life and claimed my firstborn child in return. And, through a complicated trade involving Puck that I don't quite understand, Falcon ended up paying for my healing. So I owe him seven years of war service for *that*. Six and a half-ish now."

Starling nodded as if this was perfectly normal. Their version of medical and life insurance.

"Upshot is, after I perform my war service for Falcon, I'm to report for impregnation by Rogue. After which, I guess he gets the baby and I don't know what happens then."

"I guess I knew some of that."

I dried myself off and shrugged into a nightgown and then a red velvety robe with a high collar and full sleeves. "So, as much as staying here sucks, it's all that's keeping Rogue from starting the clock early. That, and a certain set of rules that keeps him from seducing me early." I plopped down on the pillows next to her and they lit up in rainbow colors at the impact. I smacked the one under my elbow into a softer glow. "Do you understand what I'm saying?"

A line formed in her smooth forehead. "Yes. But..."

"But what?"

"Why would that be so terrible? Don't you want a baby? Isn't Lord Rogue your one true love, destined to be yours until the end of time?"

She sounded like the sidekick girlfriend in the standard rom-com flick, asking the heroine to explain again what's so awful about the obviously delicious love interest. I rolled onto my back and studied the tent ceiling. Rain pattered on the silk in a steady pattern, making the interior cozy. Especially now that I was all warm and relaxed.

"Okay, explain this to me—why does Rogue want my firstborn child? Specifically one he's sired?"

"Well!" Starling opened her mouth and then slowly closed it again. Cocked her head to the side. "Maybe he needs an heir."

I turned onto my side and propped my head on my hand. "Okay. Let's take that as an operating hypothesis."

She giggled. "Sometimes you say the funniest things."

"No, really. Let's say that's true. Rogue needs an heir. In order to have an heir, he needs a female, preferably willing, cuz that makes everything easier. Now—does he lack for willing females?"

"Oh, Titania, no! Practically every female fae in the land has been throwing herself at Lord Rogue for centuries. You should just see…oh. I played the game wrong."

"No!" I sat up and punched the pillow in excitement, accidentally ramping it up to a sizzling citron that seared my eyes. I tapped it a couple more times to damp it down to a more soothing level, glad that I'd built this adjustable function into the magic fiber-optic light-up pillows. "You played it correctly. This guy demonstrably does not lack for potential wombs. Why mine?"

"Um…true love?"

I felt myself sag but persevered. "Let's entertain that variable. Assuming he and I share a true love—completely undefined at this point—why is that necessary for him to have an heir?"

"I don't know. Here, your hair will dry all snarled. Let me comb it." Starling staggered up and grabbed a comb, hair oils and another pitcher of wine, which she used to refill my glass.

To hell with it. I could really use a good drunk. "Okay, so we table that. Rogue and I share some kind of emotional/metaphysical connection that makes our hypothetical baby full of awesome. Ow."

"Sorry—but if you'd let me wash it properly, it wouldn't have tangled."

"Let's stick to the program here."

"Yes. Game of theories."

I snorted my wine uncomfortably into my nose at her translation. "So far we've set aside the theories that Rogue can't get laid without blackmail and that only a true-love baby will do. What other reasons are there?"

"Well, you're human."

"Yes. And, more specifically, a human not from here. Like your father."

Her hands slowed in my hair, combing thoughtfully. "Like Daddy, yes."

I turned to look at her. "Are you a firstborn child?"

She faltered then, her wide brown eyes full of shadows. "No." She whispered it. "I had a brother. But he…"

"What?" I clasped her hands, knotted together over the comb. "What happened to him?"

She pressed her lips together and leaned forward so our foreheads nearly touched. "Everybody always talks as if he died—except Mother, who won't talk about him at all. Ever. And sometimes, I think—I mean, I get this feeling that…"

"Yes?"

"That it's my brother Daddy's really looking for. His eternal quest." She laughed it out with bitterness. "Not to pass back through the Veil, but to find the son I'm not."

"It might not help, but if what I'm thinking is correct, it doesn't matter that he's a son. What was salient was that he was first. If you had been first, you might have been the one to disappear."

"But why?" She looked up, with tears running down her face. "Where did he go?"

"I don't know." And I didn't know how much I should say. "There are tales, back in my world, that the fairies would come and take human children, especially the firstborn, and swap them with fairy babies—changelings, the stories called them."

"What happened to the fairy babies?"

I paused, having to think. What happened to the change-lings was usually not the point of the story. Just the loss of the human child. Fragments came to me of the fate of changelings, boiled alive or exposed to wolves. None of it pretty. Neither were the changelings, though, and in the Faerie where I found myself, everything was pretty. At least on the surface. "I'm not sure. I don't think they survived in my world."

"That's so sad."

It was sad, when you thought of it that way.

"Sometimes, though, they disappeared too. Or maybe they just eventually grew up and learned to masquerade as regular humans. Blend in."

Starling nodded, solemn. "I think a lot of us do that. Figure out how not to be quite so weird to everyone else as we get older."

She had a point. Changelings, at some level, all of us.

"At any rate, my working theory is that these firstborn children—" hell, maybe they were all half-human/half-fae; entirely possible that this element would be left out of the tales, given that no one would want to 'fess up to cavorting with fae on the sly, "—hold some kind of intrinsic value."

"But what?"

"I can tell you who probably does know." I pointed a finger at Starling. "Our beloved Lord Rogue. And, possibly, your own mother."

Starling gaped at me. I suddenly understood why mothers were wont to tell their children to close their mouths so they didn't look like goldfish.

"Why would my mother know?"

"Think about it. If it's true your father is off searching for your brother, it's because he believes he's alive and not dead. And if your mother allows *you* to believe your brother is dead, rather than speak the truth, doesn't it follow that she knows what's become of him?

"Further, this desire for firstborn children belongs entirely to the fae, at least this mysterious version of it. It's not the humans seeking out fae for interbreeding and swapping out babies. Your mother is the fae in that relationship. Tell me—how did the two of them hook up? You said your dad got here 'the usual way'—what way is that?"

Starling busied herself with tidying up and I didn't stop her. I always preferred to be actively doing something while processing an unwieldy batch of information too.

"He called himself 'an Irish cliché.' He'd been out to the local pub, having a pint or two, and got drunked up, so much so that he forgot his horse and wandered home."

His horse? With a sinking feeling I wondered just how long ago this had happened.

"Daddy loves to tell a story." Starling sighed with affectionate impatience. "So it changes every time. But he usually says the stars were singing a sweet song that led him to a soft green hill. He lay down to rest his head a spell and woke up on the same hill, only here, instead."

How well I knew that particular hill. Only I had started out at Devils Tower. Many gates going to one place? It bore thinking about. Later.

"And then how did he meet your mother?"

Starling frowned, shaking out the cloak and hanging it up thoughtfully. "He had adventures. He's got no magic, like you have, but he's very good at quests and such. My mother was imprisoned in a tower in the Glass Mountains by a dragon and—"

I choked on my wine. "No way!" Her mother—the crisp, efficient Blackbird, my seneschal—did not match my mental image of a damsel in distress.

"Oh yes. She had very long, glossy black hair, dark as the River Styx, and the dragon loved to use it to floss his teeth. Also, she made excellent bait. The young lords would come to rescue her, the dragon would eat them and then—"

"Floss his teeth with her hair. Got it. Talk about needing extra-strength conditioner." I waved for her to continue when she cocked her head. Stopped myself. "Wait, how did the dragon eat the fae lords if they're immortal?"

She rolled her eyes. "Because dragons are above all magic."

"Ah, right." I needed to ask Larch where he'd packed my vial of dragon blood. Surely that would come in handy. "Keep going."

"There's not much more to tell. Daddy defeated the dragon, rescued Mother and they wed. Happily ever after."

"How did he defeat the dragon?"

"Oh, he's exceedingly bold and courageous."

"Uh-huh. So, you're telling me some mortal Irishman with a penchant for forgetfulness and Guinness succeeded where innumerable immortal fae nobles did not?"

"Well, and because he was her—"

"Let me guess. Her true love."

Starling nodded but lacked her usual beaming certainty on the topic.

"If they're such true-lovers living happily ever after, why is it that he's off questing and she's working in Rogue's castle, running the household?"

"I don't understand."

"Starling—in my world, people who love and marry then live together and work as a team, a partnership in life." Of course, half a dozen counter-examples popped into my head, but still, the concept was there. "The rescue and wedding shouldn't be the end of the story—it's the beginning."

She put her hands on her hips, a gesture very much her mother's. "Well then! If living together is the key to preserving True Love, why do you refuse to move into Rogue's castle?"

"Because—" I unclenched my jaw, "—he is not my true love, nor am I his. There is no such thing."

"But you just said—"

"I said love. Period. Plain, old boring love. Nothing magic about it. Love, as a verb, where you actually have to put some effort into it, not waltz around in a glittery cloud of happiness and light."

"Aha!" She pounced on my words. "So you *do* believe in love, the effort kind. Thus if you try to love Rogue, you will."

I put the cool wineglass to my forehead. "I should never have taught you logical thinking."

She giggled.

"No. Don't be all pleased with yourself. This is what I'm trying to explain here—I don't *want* to try to love him, because I don't believe he has my best interests at heart. Nor those of my potential child. If I love him, I'll lose the power to resist him. I can't ever be that again." My voice cracked, and unshed tears clogged my throat.

"I don't think that's how it works." Starling looked sympathetic, sat down and took my hand. "Don't cry, Gwynn. You're just tired is all."

"I'm not crying." I wiped my eyes, to be sure. "But I am tired."

"Rest, then. Larch is standing watch. You're safe."

"What I'd really like to do is talk to your father and get the straight story from him." I rubbed my aching temples. "But I don't see how that's possible if I'm stuck here."

"Well, that might be difficult with no one knowing where he is."

"Maybe Blackbird knows more than she's let on."

"If she does, you'd have to go to her, as well. I'm not asking her. And it's not like she'll come anywhere near Falcon, if you're thinking along those lines."

I had been contemplating that, wondering if I could summon her to attend me. I was getting as high-handed as Rogue. And, dammit, I'd forgotten to mention to Starling that he'd be showing up before long. "By the way, Rogue will be sleeping with me at night—new deal."

"Really?" Starling drew the question out with a suppressed squeal and plucked the empty glass from my hand.

"Don't get excited. I'll explain later." The emotional break had tipped the scales, and the need to sleep dragged at me. I barely heard her humming a happy tune and I fell into oblivion.

༧⚘

WHEN I AWOKE from the short nap, I blessedly had the tent to myself. The rain continued to fall in the same soothing pattern.

The light from outside that gleamed through the clever raised flaps remained the same steady silver. Outside, the camp noise continued at its usual level. Since the mixed fae population seemed to be constantly active—I suspected some species were nocturnal and others might not truly sleep at all, much like insects—music played and various groups cavorted, celebrating today's "victory." No telling how far nighttime might be.

I'd love to have a clock of some sort, but a few things stopped me from wishing one up. First, I wasn't entirely certain how a mechanical clock worked. Oh, I know—gears, cogs and springs and all, but how did you know what size to make them, so they kept the right time? There was a reason I hadn't become an engineer. Second, if I wished up a fully functioning clock, wouldn't it be the kind I knew, set to follow earth's rotation? I wasn't sure how time flowed in Faerie.

Which led to my third hesitation. Fear.

I had this sneaking suspicion that some days lasted longer than others, and that time here ebbed and flowed more like tides than going in an orderly progression. I thought sometimes of light-deprivation experiments, which caused sleep cycles to alter and fragment. Marquise and Scourge, the sadistic teachers who taught me to control my magic, had deliberately broken my sense of time and self. Sleep-deprived, then sleep-fragmented, starved—nothing of my old cycles remained after that nearly half a year in their tender care. If I conjured a clock to track time in Faerie, it would likely be something out of *Alice in Wonderland*, with spinning hands and random alarms ringing. Some things you just didn't want to know, really.

I wanted to believe that six years would proceed at a normal pace. We clung to our small bits of denial like life rafts.

So I foraged for food from the small buffet always laid out for me and carried the plate to my workbench. There seemed to be no point in getting dressed, since I was in for the evening and, especially given the nightgown beneath, the robe provided the best anti-Rogue coverage, should he pop up anytime soon.

I settled into recording my notes from the conversation with Starling into what I, more than a little sarcastically, called my *Big Book of Fairyland.* In particular, I wanted to note my new theories on firstborn children. Resolved to discard no avenue of investigation at this point, I even made a section for evidence toward Starling's "True Love" theory.

I still didn't believe in it, but I also hadn't believed wishes could come true in the blink of an eye, so I needed to be willing to entertain a paradigm shift.

Much more likely was that firstborn children tended to be strongest, with the best health. Nice, fresh body to gestate them and all. It wasn't my field, but I recalled some physiological studies along those lines. It was a particularly cruel joke that I'd always believed I'd have books and databases to access information I didn't care to memorize. Whatever my neurons had managed to store—which seemed disconcertingly random—was all I had.

A hungry demand invaded my head, along with an image of a mermaid on a plate, just before Darling pushed through the tent flaps. With a prodigious leap, he landed on my pages with wet and muddy paws, slapping me under the chin with a soggy—and somewhat fishy-smelling—tail.

"Hey! Not on my grimoire. This is super-special sorceress

work here." I snatched the book out from under him and set it safely aside.

He sent a disdainful image and purred invitingly, with a cat's patented combination of contempt and adorable charm. I stroked his tortoiseshell coat and he arched his back agreeably, blinking bright green eyes at me with more intelligence than a cat should have. Something Titania had tossed off the one other time we'd met led me to believe that Darling had once been a fae noble, who she'd trapped into this feline body. He seemed happy as a cat, though. Or maybe those were the limitations of his current brain. He head-butted my hand and sent an agreeable thought when I obediently scratched his ears.

"Did you really get close to one of the mermaids?"

He purred, arch and mysterious. Somehow I really doubted it. Darling insisted, showing me that same picture of a big-bosomed mermaid cuddling him to her naked breasts and cooing what a fierce fighter he must be. I snorted and he batted my hand with an indignant swipe.

I sat back and watched him start into a vigorous bathing session.

"What's your vote—should we move into Rogue's castle?"

He flattened his ears in disdain, splayed his legs to lick his butt, and sent me an image of him striding through a battle-field, tossing monsters aside. The cat had battles on the brain. Plus he wanted a new name. A battle name.

"What if we went on a quest instead?"

Darling paused in the butt-licking and fixed me with a bright green stare, flicking an ear tip in interest. He imagined himself on the prow of a sailing ship, his fur blowing nobly back in the breeze. Perhaps a pirate name?

"I have no idea if we'd need to sail, since I have no idea where we'd look."

"Well," Starling said from behind me, making me start, "if you're thinking of looking for my father, we should go to Castle Brightness first and ask my mother."

I turned sideways in my chair to better see her. She chewed on her lip, but held her chin high.

"Color me surprised. I got the impression you didn't care to confront Blackbird over this stuff."

Her gaze slid down and to the side, looking at something only she could see. "I've been thinking about what you said, that if I'd been firstborn, it might be me that…disappeared. And I think I'd want my brother to look for me."

"Good for you," I said softly, trailing my hand down Darling's arched spine. He approved of the plan.

"Yes." She nodded, a crisp echo of Blackbird. "We ask my mother, find my father and discover what happens to the children."

"He may not yet know."

"No, but you can work on Rogue, to find out what he knows too."

I picked at a sand burr in Darling's fur, focusing on that. Even it was pretty—a little jewel, with hooked spikes. "He already agreed to help me."

"He did?"

She sounded as if I'd said Rogue planned to dance naked under the full moon. Probably he already did that. "Yes, he did. Why else would I agree to let him sleep with me every night?"

A sly grin twisted her pretty mouth. "I figured that was his natural charm."

"Ha to that."

"Do you doubt my natural charm?" Rogue's smooth voice echoed in the tent a bare moment before he materialized before us. Sound preceding light in this case—interestingly reversed.

"Speak of the devil," I observed wryly.

"Lady Starling." Rogue took her hand and kissed it. "You're looking delightful. So grown-up. The hair suits you—Gwynn's work?"

"Yes," she simpered, tossing the blond locks flirtatiously. "Thank you for noticing, my lord Rogue."

"How did you know it was my work—does it show?"

He glanced at me, dark-blue gaze sweeping me from head to foot. Not for the first time I wondered what he saw when he studied me in that inscrutable way. My blood ran just a little faster, my skin warming. It wasn't easy to keep my face impassive.

"Your magic, lovely Gwynn, has a distinctive flavor. And yes, it clings to what you touch. No one would mistake but that Starling is your creature now."

"She is not my 'creature'—she's her own person."

"It's okay, I don't mind being your creature." Starling's hands flew up, as if she could pet us into being nice.

"It is not okay. That was an obnoxious thing to say."

"I withdraw the observation then." Rogue grinned at me and swept a bow to Starling. "Now, as your own person, can you still arrange for an intimate dinner for two?"

"Oh! Of course, Lord Rogue—"

"Wait. I didn't agree to dinner."

"Must you argue every little thing, stubborn Gwynn?"

I cocked my head at him, returning his assessing gaze, pretending to think about it. He looked good, of course, dressed in his standard black. But his current outfit looked more...romantic, dammit. A loose-sleeved shirt was tucked into tight pants, the collar open to reveal a tantalizing bit of golden skin, the swirling black lines of the fanged pattern from his face and throat continuing downward.

"Yes," I decided. "I do."

"I still owe you a lesson for the day. We can eat and talk. Afterward, bed." His tone made it sound like ever so much more.

"Isn't it early yet?" I glanced at the skyflaps to see the same persistent glittering gray.

"Yes—but I thought you might tire early, given your exertions today."

"That's surprisingly thoughtful."

"I'm making an effort." His voice held a wry tone that was new. Almost self-deprecating, if that were possible from the King of Megalomania.

Starling, with an apologetic look to me, slipped out of the tent, presumably to arrange dinner. I winced as Darling's paws sank into my shoulder, and the cat walked down my body, his personal ladder, into my lap.

"Don't mind me," I muttered and he flicked his tail, thankfully much drier now, under my nose.

Darling sent me an affectionate thought and, broadcasting the same image of the mermaid on a plate, he strolled out.

Rogue watched him go. "Do you suppose he really did get to taste one?"

"Don't you know?" I was genuinely surprised.

"I don't know everything. Would you like to change for dinner? I'd be happy to wait while you do. Or watch."

"Let me think. No way."

He smiled, in a very close to charming way. "Can't blame me for trying."

"Do you know what happens when the irresistible force meets the immoveable object?"

"Do you imagine that your powers equal mine?"

"I can imagine a lot of things."

Rogue brushed a lock of hair off my forehead, with an almost tender gesture. "Indeed you can, my Gwynn."

Larch, followed by several of his Brownie cohort, marched into the tent just then, carrying a small table, two chairs and an array of dishes. They set to moving the pillows—I swore the things multiplied like rabbits when I wasn't looking—to clear a space, then draped the table with a black cloth and set two crystal candlesticks with deep-blue candles on it.

I felt the flick of Rogue's thought when he lit the candles into dancing flames.

"Fire is against Falcon's rules," I reminded him.

Rogue raised an elegant inky eyebrow at me. "Falcon does not make rules for me."

"Must be nice."

"Indeed." He offered me a hand up from my seat. "Shall we, my lady?"

The food smelled enticing. Much more so than my usual fare. Clearly Starling had gone all out for Rogue's visit. I bit into fowl in a sort of tasty curried mushroom sauce, perfectly complemented by the flaky pastry, and closed my eyes to savor it.

"Do you like it?"

"Yes." I eyed him and broke off another bite. The fae had missed the concept of silverware somewhere along the way. "You brought this with you?"

"You'll like this too." He poured me a glass of honey-gold wine.

I tasted it cautiously, in case it turned out to be more of the Kool-Aid they called wine here. I sighed at the delicious flavor, true ambrosia. "This is all part of the seduction, isn't it?"

"Every weapon at my disposal, sweet Gwynn. Wearing away at your immovability."

"If you keep feeding me, I'll become an enormous object."

He laughed at that and allowed an image of a very pregnant me to drift my way.

"Now that was a miscalculation on your part. I do not find the idea of pregnancy even remotely attractive."

"Why is that, Gwynn?" His tone was conversational, as though wondering about my inclination for white wine over red.

"You're asking about my preferences, all of a sudden?"

"I am," he replied evenly. "I want to know your objections to having my child."

"Because you think you'll chip away at those too."

His blue eyes glittered in the candlelight. Even in this affable mien, the imperious dark side of him showed through, a glimpse behind the mask.

"Allow me the opportunity at least."

"Okay." I sat back, wiped my mouth and fingers with the black napkin. "Let me count the ways. One, it's my body and I decide about whether I want to have a baby. Two, I have never wanted children. Three, I'm not thrilled about giving birth in what amounts to a Third World country, even with the magical healing, since I likely can't afford it. Four, I am not the mistress of my own fate and thus have no ability to promise my child a secure life. And no, having you as the sugar baby-daddy does not count as security. Finally, I don't believe I'd even have the opportunity to raise the child because you'd take it away."

"To where?"

"Well, now. That's the question, isn't it? Why don't you tell me what would happen to our hypothetical child?"

Rogue drank from his wine, his mind very quiet. Carefully making sure I caught no glimpses of his true thoughts. "Why do you assume anything would 'happen' at all?"

"You're answering a question with a question. That means you're dodging."

"Maybe your thinking is foreign enough to me that I need more explanation."

Fencing. Time for a different attack.

"Let's try this question. Why do you want this child? Or is it really the Queen Bitch who wants it and that's what she meant with her tick-tocking?"

He started to push a hand into his hair, but he had it neatly tied back. Instead, he ran it over the glossy smooth surface and cast his gaze to the ceiling. The light had truly faded now and the rain had slowed to a soft patter. When he met my eyes again, his glimmered with that odd combination of regret and irritation that arose when I pushed him on his intentions toward me.

"I can't tell you," he finally said.

"*Can't* instead of *won't*."

He nodded, a bare dip of his pointed chin, and held out a hand to me, palm-up. Finding myself unable to refuse the invitation, I slid my hand into his, the unnaturally long fingers familiar to me now.

"Why can't you tell me?"

"All of us answer to someone, my Gwynn. None are free of all obligations."

"Is it her?"

He rubbed a thumb over my palm, lips curving when I shivered at the touch. "Now do you really think I'd tell you that, when I can't reveal anything else?"

I narrowed my eyes. "That was a *won't,* not a *can't.*"

A smile broke through his somber mien, the sun after rain. He squeezed my hand and released it, returning to his dinner.

"Fine. I'll find out for myself. I still have six years."

"Careful, bold and foolish Gwynn. You seek to pry into matters far beyond your abilities."

"You can't stop me."

"Can't I?" He raised that eyebrow at me, twisting the fanged lines on the left side of his face, and popped a bite into his sensuous mouth.

"I'm not without resources. I bested you once, didn't I?"

"But you couldn't restore the tree, when I could," he reminded me in a tone of cool silk.

"That was different."

"Why?" He took another bite and licked his fingers. I had to yank my gaze away from his glass-edged lips.

"Because..." I shrugged. "I don't know. You tell me."

"Your lesson for the day? So be it." He smiled, wolfish. "This will be fun."

CHAPTER 4

IN WHICH I SLEEP WITH ROGUE

Why do fairies in the stories always want human babies?
Possibilities: To raise as their own? To play with? To eat or
somehow consume (energy drain)? Consider in terms of
exchange—why leave one of their own in a human
child's place?

~Big Book of Fairyland, "Notes for Further Research"

"TELL ME HOW you felt, when you tried to use your magic."

Eesh, I really didn't want to do that. Even thinking about the wild arousal of that moment had me shifting in my chair. I took a cooling sip of wine. "I don't really recall."

"Playing coy? Not like you. What are you hoping to hide from me? I need honesty if you want me to teach you."

"Fine," I snapped, lacing my fingers together in my lap. I could face this. To learn and grow. "Because I had nothing left after."

Rogue rose, tossing his black napkin on the table, a flag signaling a new play in the game. He moved behind me and brushed my hair aside, tracing the line of my neck with sensuous fingers. That something in me purred and my nipples hardened under my robe. I sat as still as I could.

"After what?" he murmured, everything in his voice saying that he knew perfectly well.

"Weren't you there?" Hell if he'd get me to say it.

"Why had you nothing left?"

"Because I used too much power?"

"Try again." He traced the shell of my ear, sending fluttery petals of pleasure to my groin.

"Because…"

"Yes?"

"I can't think."

"A good lesson for you. You must learn to think, no matter what is being done to you. Remember that I can do plenty to you, lovely Gwynn, despite your little rules." Rogue slid a hand down to cup my breast through the robe, thumbing the stiff nipple, sharpening the pleasure. He'd bent down now, warm breath feathering against my ear.

"Please," I whispered.

"What are you begging me for?"

I clamped my lips together and closed my eyes. I also couldn't afford to ask for anything from Rogue, being fresh out of anything more to give.

I tried to think about the formula for the circumference of a circle. $2\pi R$. Diameter multiplied by pi. Too easy. The wet core of me ached. π was equal to 3.14 and what else?

3.14792. No that couldn't be because the 7 would round up to 3.15. So what was the fourth digit?

"Gwynn." Rogue sighed, the feel of it teasing my skin.

"You are meant to be thinking about magic, not numbers."

My eyes popped open. "You could hear me? I thought I was being quiet."

"When we're this close—" he squeezed my breast and I choked back a moan, "—I can hear you better. Also, I know you want me."

"Do you?"

"Your body doesn't lie." He inhaled. "You smell of sex. Like wine and roses, mixed."

"What I want and what my body wants are not the same thing, Rogue. Haven't we had this conversation?"

"But it's so entertaining to debate with you." He switched to the other breast. I thanked my foresight for insisting on one hand at a time. "Now, answer the question, like a good girl."

My head swam for a second. He wasn't asking about pi. I rewound the conversation, no, not what I was begging for—that was obviously rhetorical.

"Because of the..." Orgasm. Climax. Because I came. Just words to say.

"There you are," Rogue murmured, stroking my breast with a tender affection that undid me even more. "I'll allow the thought to answer, since you're shy to say it aloud."

He sounded satisfied in that and it reminded me that no one seemed to think it odd that Rogue essentially demanded sexual favors from me in exchange for saving my life.

"Now you learn the why of it."

"Only a superficial why." I rose also, moving out from under his devastating touch and needing to bleed off some of the tension. Surprisingly, he let me. "I already knew my magic comes from sex—Marquise and Scourge said as much when they thought I wasn't listening."

"Clever girl." Rogue waited, watching me pace. "Tell me—
how much did you manage to hide from them?"

"Wouldn't you like to know?" I stalked over to my workbench and fiddled with a rubber ducky I'd found in the tribute
tent. People here gave me so many gifts that Larch had finally
set up a separate tent, just to house all the shiny stuff. The
rubber ducky looked exactly like one from my world, a
conundrum that continued to puzzle me. And no, I didn't
know who'd given it to me. I didn't know who had given any
of that stuff to me.

"I would like to know." His hand stroked down the fall of
my hair, a caress meant to soothe, not stimulate. "Clearly their
claws did not sink so deeply as they'd hoped. How did you slip
the leash?"

"Are you asking so you can collar me more effectively?"
The words came out bitter. My time in that palace of torture
was not something I revisited easily. Probably I needed serious
therapy to deal with the PTSD. Not a casual chat about the
worst time of my life with one of the people who'd put me
there.

"I would comfort you, my Gwynn." Rogue's voice was
soft. Not at all like him.

I set the ducky back in its place and turned to search his
face. "Why now?"

"You never let me before."

"You put me there. I haven't forgotten."

"No," he corrected, his face icing into his more usual im-
placability. "I was simply unable to prevent it. I've told you—
even I am constrained. I did the best I could do to prevent the

worst for you."

"The worst?" I nearly choked on my gasp. "Do you have *any* idea what they did to me?"

"Yes." His midnight blue eyes were grave. "And I know it could have been worse. By staking my claim on you, I prevented them from having you in every way. Believe me, your teachers are quite effective at rape and all forms of sexual torture."

Oh.

I'd always been relieved that Marquise and Scourge hadn't gone any farther than they had. That they'd always stopped at a certain point, no matter that I was their naked and helpless slave, at some points so desperate to please them that I would have done anything for them. Nothing had been beyond me.

"Don't weep, lovely Gwynn." Rogue brushed the tears from my cheek and, after studying the fluid gleaming on his fingertips, tasted them. "I meant to reassure you."

"How do my tears taste to you?" The question came out of me from somewhere else, in the surreality of the moment. Of so many things to say to him, I asked this.

He smiled, a sorrowful twist of his perfect mouth. "Bitter."

I had no reply to that.

The silence between us spun and grew, fragile threads of unspoken thoughts. I could nearly sense the drift of his mind, the scent of a night-blooming flower, so faint you lost it with the next breeze.

"Finish the lesson," I finally said.

Rogue inclined his head, noblesse oblige. "Yes, bitter Gwynn. Sex is magic and vice-versa. As your passion waxes, so does your power."

"So sexual frustration is actually good for me, sorceress-wise. I knew that from experience."

He laughed. "It's not a direct relationship. An exchange of sex will not drain you. Rather the reverse."

"So why did that one drain me?"

"Because you took all that lovely energy that I stoked in you and made a lightning bolt from it."

Whoa. "That was all me?"

"Some from me too. It took me time to recover."

"But you were able to heal the tree."

"This is one of the things you must learn. I have resources outside myself. You do not."

"How do I get more resources?"

He held out a hand. "That will be a future lesson. For now, you are tired. It's time for bed."

In answer to some unheard call, Larch trooped in then, followed by a parade of cronies. He bowed to us both, but mainly to Rogue, and they cleared the table away. Others carried in pieces of what turned out to be a large four-poster bed, as they assembled it.

"I'm going to need a bigger tent," I observed, watching the thing came together. I recognized it from my dreams— alluring, dark fantasies of Rogue tying me to this bed with those green silk cords. The bedding they carried in, all of it gleamed black, though with various colored highlights from my lamp-pillows, like the rainbow shine on an oil slick.

"I don't care to sleep on that pad you call a bed."

"No problem. I'll sleep on my futon by myself."

He captured my hand in his and pulled me to his side, leaning in so his lips nearly brushed my temple. "No."

The simple word carried such menacing promise that I shuddered. Impossible the ways I responded to this so-alien man. And yet, he'd reminded me that he knew my secret terrors likely better than I did, since I could hardly bear to touch on some of them.

The Brownies left. I busied myself with slapping the pillows into dark mode. It felt oddly domestic to be preparing for bed with him there. I brushed out my hair, the nighttime ritual steadying me. I turned to find Rogue had unbound his own hair and taken off his shirt and was unlacing his boots.

His hair rained around him, a spill of ink across his golden skin. The lean muscles of his arms flexed as he pulled off the boot, leaving his long foot bare. The black pattern that dominated the left side of his face wound down that side of his body, forking over his pectoral muscles and flat abdomen, disappearing below the waist of his pants. He had no belly button, something simultaneously creepy and intriguing. I'd seen images of him as a boy—had he fruited on a vine? No, even that left a navel scar.

His skin gleamed, hairless and velvet smooth in the glow of the few pillows on his side of the tent. My fingers itched to touch him, to feel the contours of that body I'd experienced only in dreamscapes. His hands went to unfasten the clasp of his pants.

"Wait!"

He cocked an eyebrow at me.

"What are you doing?"

"Undressing for bed."

"Oh no. You're not sleeping naked with me."

"I always sleep naked."

I always had too, until I'd taken to wearing voluminous nightgowns to expose less publicly accessible skin to him. "This is not about comfort. I don't much like sleeping in these nightgowns, but I'm lumping it. You can too."

He frowned, but the playful gleam in his eyes gave him away. "This was not a part of the negotiation."

"Neither was you dragging this monstrous bed into my tent. I think that's a fair swap."

"These pants are tight."

Yes. Yes, I knew that. I also knew I really didn't want to see, in the flesh, the equipment so clearly delineated by the black velvet material. He strolled over to me, almost stalking, hair sliding over his bare skin.

"You're staring, Gwynn. Would you like to touch?"

I had to swallow to get the words out. "No, thank you."

He took my hand anyway and laid it on his chest, satin hot under my fingers. "Touch me. You've had other men. You could have me. I am no monster. Just a flesh-and-blood man."

"Your heartbeat says otherwise." I glanced up into his face, the inhuman eyes, the tangled pattern that was and was not part of him.

"Is that what bothers you? That I'm not human?" He left my hand where it was and snaked an arm around my waist, to press against the small of my back, pulling me closer. Not quite pressing against me. His hair fell around us in a cape when he lowered his head to whisper against my cheek. "I can promise we would fit."

"I've told you my objections."

His skin was inches from my lips and the scent of him made my mouth water, salt and cinnamon and man. The three-four rhythm of his alien heart soothed me even as his highly charged proximity sent fine tremors of arousal through every nerve. No, I had no doubt we would fit. Or that it would be phenomenal.

"I noticed," he murmured, holding us still in that position, as if he could sense how much I longed to close that distance, "that among your objections, you did not list the fear that I would lock you in a tower and make you into a 'Rapunzel fuck-toy,' I believe your words were."

I snorted with laughter at the English words coming out of his mouth. "I may or may not have been kind of pissed off when I said that."

"So you trust me that much, at least?"

I backed off enough to study his face, indulging myself by running my hand up his enticing chest, the strong line of his collarbone to his cheek, the edges of the black lines indiscernible from the normal skin. "Maybe I just trust that I could get myself out of it."

He smiled, a thin-lipped promise of dark delights. "Or that you would enjoy struggling against any bonds I put you in."

I ignored the heat that flared in me at the suggestion, but he smelled it in me—my thoughts perhaps too loud with this intimacy.

"Touch me, lovely Gwynn."

"I am."

"No. Touch me, here." Slowly he let go of my back and took my hand from his cheek. He held my gaze mesmerized and drew my hand back down his chest and abdomen, to his waistline and below. His ink-dark pupils dilated, nearly swallowing the fulminous blue of his eyes, as he laid my hand over his velvet-clad cock.

It jumped beneath my fingers, long and steel-hard. I should have known it would be long, as all his limbs were. Even in this upside-down world, some laws of physiognomy applied.

Rogue closed his eyes and shuddered, seeming overcome. Thrilled to have him at my mercy for a change, I stroked him. He fisted his hands by his sides, threw back his head, exposing the line of his throat, and hummed in pleasure, the sound becoming nearly a song of words.

"Ah, my lovely Gwynn, I need you so."

I stroked the hard line of him once more, memorizing the feel and shape, then let go and stepped back. His gaze snapped down to mine, hard and bright.

"Why did you stop?"

I folded my arms, felt too defensive and unwound them. "It doesn't seem wise to…encourage you."

He laughed. Not amused, but with a wild edge. In a flash, he closed the small space between us and grasped me with a hand cupping the back of my head. He liked to hold me like that when he kissed me, but for now—having already taken his kiss for the day—he only stared at me, a crazed look, ferocious and starving, tightening his face.

"There is nothing you do—*nothing*, enticing Gwynn—that does not make me burn for you more. I will not give up until I have you, in every way. In all ways. Do not mistake that."

I trembled, shaking with both longing and fear. Did I really believe I could escape him if I needed to? In many ways, it had ceased to matter. He already had me tied to him, binding me in invisible, subtle ways.

"Is this only about the child, Rogue? About whatever you

and the Queen Bitch have cooked up?" I asked softly, not really knowing where the plea came from. Probably Starling and all her silliness over true love. I didn't believe in that, but if I thought I might mean more to him than a means to an end, perhaps...what? I didn't know.

"I cannot divide out who I am and all the forces that drive me." His voice was as quiet as mine, but the grip was still hard, nearly lifting me to my toes. "You are not pieces of things to me, my Gwynn. You are the where all my roads lead. Where all the cords knot. Only you can untie them. Let me have you."

"I can't." I whispered.

"But you want to. Tell me that much."

I closed my eyes against the intensity of his gaze. How could I deny it, with my nipples so tight they hurt, my sex drenched and vulva aching. Even the pores of my skin felt hungry for him, as if only pressing my naked self against him would ever let me feel less than starved.

"I do."

The confession came out without sound. But he heard me. I felt it in the flare of heat from him. He set me gently down and splayed his hand over my throat, fingers toying with the high collar of the robe.

"Are you naked under this?"

My eyes flew open. "You wish!"

"I do wish." He replied, a deadly stillness about him. "And you know I can make my wishes come true."

My throat tightened. "That would be cheating. Against the bargain."

He looked thoughtful, undoing the catch of my robe. "Not necessarily. I might be able to skate by on a technicality."

"You wouldn't risk it."

He undid another clasp, revealing the equally high neck of my white nightgown. "You would never let Titania take me. You'd cry off the bargain first."

"I might not have time. Or be able to. Even if I wanted to. You wouldn't risk her wrath. It's too much of a gamble for you." I gasped a little as he undid another clasp and brushed the inner curve of my breast with the back of his hand. "What are you doing?"

He raised an eyebrow at me. "Undressing you for bed. Surely you don't plan to wear the robe too."

"No, but I'm still not going to…"

"Let me have my way with you? Take off this ridiculous thing and let me kiss every inch of your delicious skin? Part your legs for me so I can bury myself between your thighs and—"

"Just stop now."

"Why?" He slid the robe off my shoulders so it puddled at my feet and cupped my breast through the cotton nightgown, his hand so hot it nearly burned me. "Do my words make you want to give in?"

"I can't give in, Rogue!" I nearly shouted it at him and wrenched myself out of his grasp. "Not without answers to my questions."

"The main one being what would happen to this child."

"Yes. Though the other objections still stand. And I want to know what's up with the Queen Bitch and that tick-tock nonsense. Especially if it's the same answer."

He seemed to be thinking. Finding his way around the words. "Castle Brightness is as good a place for you to start as any—for a number of reasons."

"But you won't—or can't—tell me why."

"You're clever. I'm sure you'll figure out the whys."

"How am I supposed to get to Castle Brightness?"

"Now *that* I can arrange."

"How?" I pressed my thumbs over my eyebrows, the early morning and long day catching up with me despite the nap.

"Come to bed," he coaxed, taking me by the hand and drawing me toward it. "You'll see how well you sleep with me to care for you."

He sat on the edge of the downy mattress and slid back, pulling me with him. Reluctantly, I went, relieved at least that I didn't need to use the chamber pot. Magically disappearing waste or not, that would be just a bit too much intimacy. Rogue settled me under the covers with my back to him and he curved his body around me in a shell that did feel oddly safe.

He arranged my hair on the pillow, then slipped his arm around me to cup my breast, so my hard nipple pressed into his palm, making me shiver.

"Shh…" He hummed and I remembered how he'd soothed me the same way once before, even as he held a knife to my throat, ready to kill me if I slipped up. "All is well. Sleep now. Sleep deep, my Gwynn."

Surprisingly enough, I did.

৽⁊ৈ

I AWOKE FROM such a deep and dreamless sleep that, for a moment, I thought I was back home and that the furry weight nested against me was my cat, Isabel. Without conscious thought, I rubbed her belly fur and Darling rolled lasciviously under my touch, then sent a simultaneously salacious and jealous observation about me having two men in my bed, huffed off said bed and out of the tent. It helped ease the pang of sorrow and guilt I still felt over the cat I'd abandoned.

Opening my eyes and rolling my head on the pillow, I found Rogue's gaze on me, focused with blue consideration. Sunlight streamed in the skylight flaps and the tent had already grown warm and stuffy.

"It stopped raining."

"Yes. Good morning, my Gwynn."

"Hi."

I felt as morning-after shy as if we had done the deed. Except not nearly as sated. Rogue's hand rested on my belly, dangerously close to the juncture of my thighs, my nightgown tangled high around them. I wanted to tug it down, but that might draw his attention. Which seemed to be entirely on my mouth at the moment.

"What?" I finally asked.

"I'm deciding if I want our kiss now or if I want to save it for later."

"I probably have morning breath."

"Do you think I care for such things?" He caressed my belly, sliding in tantalizing strokes toward my vulnerable sex, clad only in the thin panties I'd wished up.

What I needed was something more like a chastity belt.

Rogue chuckled. "Always fascinating to listen to your mind run. From the quiet of sleep into full-on blazing chatter."

"You don't have to listen." A little stung, and grateful for the mood break, I pulled away and slid off the high bed to the floor, the voluminous gown modestly covering me. Besides, now I really did need that chamber pot. "Can I, um, have a little privacy to get dressed, prepare for the day, that kind of thing?"

With leisurely sensuality, Rogue sat up and stretched, the lean muscles of his arms flexing. His skin looked warm and soft in the morning light—different than in candle glow, but just as tempting. He combed his fingers through his long, inky hair and pulled it back to the nape of his neck, and suddenly it was tied back, sleek, no hair out of place.

"I don't know why you do things the long way," he observed. "It's quite limiting."

"Force of habit."

"Habits can be limiting, also." He slipped off the bed and I noticed he'd at some point changed the black pants into blue silky pajama-type bottoms. He grinned. "Do you like them?"

His morning erection tented the silk quite prominently—or maybe it was the same one from the night before—but I decided to refrain from comment on that.

"I didn't know it was possible for you wear something besides black."

"They match my eyes. I notice you like my eyes." He grinned at me, then pursed his lips at my nightgown. "I, however, do not enjoy that sleep garment. If I give you another, will you wear it?"

My mind went straight to a dream he'd once sent me, where I'd worn a blue lace gown for him—the kind that made you feel even more naked for the wearing it.

"That would be a no. This one serves its purpose."

"Mine would be more flirtatious."

I sighed at the reminder of our terms. "We'll discuss it tonight and negotiate one that's mutually satisfactory, okay?"

"Agreed."

His magic pulsed, a swirl of blue-black and a hint of mace, and he was fully dressed in black leather, dagger at his hip, black boots gleaming. It was half-court gear, half-armor.

"Got a formal occasion?"

"Yes. As do you."

"Gosh, I must have forgotten to check my Outlook calendar. Care to enlighten me?"

"Our meeting," he reminded me in a tone of infinite patience, "with Falcon."

I felt the little crease between my eyebrows and knew I must be frowning at him. "We have a meeting with Falcon today? Together?"

"You wish to begin your quest immediately, I should think. Even if you don't—I do." He sent me a searing look, an erotic reminder of last night's conversation that made me shiver. "I will help you secure an early departure from Falcon's service."

I laced my fingers together, really wishing I didn't have to pee so badly, and then sealing off that thought so it wouldn't come true. I was wary of doing anything that might modify the working physiology of my body. He'd outmaneuvered me, yet again. We'd come full circle so that I would be leaving Falcon's war, just as Rogue had wanted all along. Only now it was dressed up as my idea.

"I need a moment."

For once, he didn't argue. Instead he bowed gravely, perhaps acknowledging my realization that he'd neatly won this round.

"I'll wait for you outside. And I'll send Starling in. Formal gown, please."

"Before ten in the morning? I've never heard of such a thing!"

He ignored my remark and pushed through the flaps. I dashed for the magic chamber pot behind the screen.

Feeling more human but no less annoyed at myself for falling so neatly into Rogue's plans, I dressed in the gown Starling had hung up for me. She bustled about discreetly, humming a happy tune while she made up the bed. I brushed out my hair, watching her in the mirror as she smoothed the sheets and pillows affectionately.

"Nothing happened, you know."

She sent me a bright, beaming smile. "If you say so, Lady Sorceress."

I contemplated throwing the hairbrush at her. Instead I focused on my "makeup," magically enhancing the colors of my lips and around my eyes. I still liked the ritual of going back and forth between being made-up and being my natural self. Anything that helped ground me in my normal self was a good thing, I figured, despite Rogue's snide remarks on limiting habits. "It seems that we may be leaving on our quest sooner rather than later."

"So Lord Rogue informed me—I'll send a message to Mother that we'll be visiting."

"How do you do that?" The fae didn't seem to use writing at all, so the business of non-hive-mind communication still presented a mystery.

"Why, via Brownie, of course."

Of course.

I adjusted the neckline of the green dress so it didn't dip quite so low. Though Falcon had a weakness for cleavage, and it never hurt to keep him off balance. The scrapes from the rocks looked less angry now, but the bruises had purpled and were tender. Not exactly enticing. Though, given Falcon's proclivities, the sight of them might turn him on. I decided to leave it as is.

"We should put up your hair." Starling held out the little vanity chair for me. "Lord Rogue said formal."

And, of course, we just do everything Lord Rogue wants. I kept the grumpiness to myself, however, and used the time to settle my thoughts into careful blankness. I'd need all the cool serenity I could drum up to survive being in the same room with those two and not end up bargaining my life away.

Starling worked efficiently and soon my hair was in an elaborate coiled braid, like a crown. It also made my scalp ache and I reached up to loosen it a little. She slapped my hand away. "No. Be good."

I scowled at her. "This better not be a long meeting."

"It probably will be. Word is Lord Falcon has called for a formal lunch to be prepared."

"Charming. And here I haven't even had breakfast."

"Tomorrow, I'll bring you and Lord Rogue a romantic breakfast in bed."

"No! Don't do that. I—" I caught her impish grin and realized she was teasing me. "Wench."

She simpered, the picture of innocence. But she also patted my shoulder reassuringly. "I know nothing happened. Lord Rogue looks far too irritated. Good for you for holding out."

"He looks irritated?" That pleased me. I pulled on a pair of heels. Not as high as my come-fuck-me heels, but still power-sexy. Starling held back the tent flap for me and I stepped out into the bright sunshine to find Rogue lounging in a chair under a giant pink silk parasol, being hand-fed fruit by a cluster of dragonfly girls.

CHAPTER 5

IN WHICH I NEGOTIATE A SABBATICAL

ᘓᙏᘓ

It seems that the fae do not, or cannot, lie directly. There is, however, plenty of room for omission, obfuscation and all forms of equivocation.

~*Big Book of Fairyland,* "Rules of Bargaining"

REALLY, I WASN'T sure what else to call them. Poor Dragonfly had been this type of fae—a sort of petite adolescent girl with a bouncy personality and not a great deal of intelligence. I hadn't observed much variation in them. They seemed given to giggles and flirtation. None of them had the stiff, dragonfly-type wings—hence my name for her, since she seemed to have no other—but otherwise they were much like my erstwhile servant. All shades of hair, from golden to lilac tinsel, like a bouquet of frivolous flowers.

And they all just seemed to love Rogue.

My irritation was boiling up into a snide remark when Rogue glanced up, scooted the one who'd been perched on his lap off to the ground and stood, sweeping me a gallant bow.

"Good Titania—you look gorgeous, Gwynn."

I looked like a 1950s prom date, I thought, but the glowing admiration in his cobalt eyes gave me a certain flutter. Plus, it didn't hurt my ego to see him nearly toss the darling dragonfly girl aside for me without a second glance.

"You need something more." He held out a closed hand, and opened it to show glittering earrings perfectly arranged on his palm. They were dangling lilies, upside-down trumpet-shaped flowers, shimmering as blue as the live indigo Stargazer lilies he'd once tried to give me. Like those, these looked as alive as flesh. Probably with the same drowningly sweet scent.

I put my hands behind my back. "No. No gifts. You know that."

"But this isn't a gift. It's important that you go before Falcon with something of me on you. Proof."

"Of what?"

He trailed a finger along the upper curve of my breast. "Don't be coy." Then his gaze caught, held. His face whitened.

I sighed and batted the finger away. "I mean, what exactly does it prove? If I'm making some kind of public declaration, I want to know what it is."

But he was frowning, gaze still on my cleavage. "You were hurt yesterday. Why didn't you tell me?"

"What's to tell? You mess with the Black Dog, you get a little torn up." I meant it as a joke, but he had paled and now clenched his hands, as if he was stopping himself from grabbing me by sheer force of will. Even though I couldn't accept those lovely earrings, I hoped he hadn't crushed them. "Really it was mostly the rocks. A minor bite, maybe. I might be mortal, but I'll heal. Don't look so stricken."

"I believed that the Dog would not harm you." Rogue's voice was deadly quiet, nearly strained.

"Are you kidding me? The Dog nearly tore my throat out the second I set foot on your sacred lawns."

"That was before. And it was necessary."

"That's debatable, but these are just some bruises and scratches. Hardly a big deal. I just haven't worked on them yet."

He still looked profoundly perturbed. Off balance in a way I never saw him.

"Hey." I put my palm on his cheek. The dragonfly girls watched us with avid interest, but I tried to ignore their whispers and giggles. "You didn't do it on purpose. It's no big deal."

"*I* will decide what is and is not a big deal, Gwynn." He nearly hissed it and I took a step back. The black lines on his face seemed to snake, in the way they did that prefaced the Black Dog asserting itself. That slice of white inside my heart responded, a chill breath of foreboding.

Around us the war camp was dancing with carnival life, full of music and hilarity. A hand-to-foot wheel of lilac pages rolled past, chanting some incomprehensible tune. A miniature unicorn with what seemed to be a pair of pink panties in his teeth trotted by, muttering to itself about fairy sluts. I took a breath, released it and sought that calm place of control.

Rogue visibly did the same. "Falcon keeps no healer in camp?"

"No. He thinks it breaks the whole dying gloriously and painfully theme."

Rogue nodded, curt, his thoughts too wrapped up in whatever was eating at him to be amused at me. Then raised his hand and opened his palm, the lily earrings as lush and perfect as before. "You *will* wear these. And in return, you will allow me to do what I can to heal your wounds tonight."

Arguing with him in this mood would be clearly futile, but I still balked. "That sounds an awful lot like you giving me two things."

"It's not." He bit it out. "You will allow me this reparation. You owe me that much."

"Fine, fine." I held up my palms in a no-foul gesture. "I accept these earrings and, in even exchange, I'll let you heal these bruises and scratches.

I snatched the earrings from his palm and suddenly re-membered that the fae healer had closed up my pierced ears when she fixed up everything else following the infamous throat-rending incident. A little unnecessary surgery that had likely added months on to the time I owed Falcon. The ends of the earrings, which would have hooks in my world, had instead little fibrous hairs that waved slightly, as if reaching for something.

"Hold them against your earlobe. It will attach."

Creepy. But in for a penny, in for tentacles on my earlobes. The sensation was odd but kind of pleasant. They did smell of Stargazers, sweet with spice.

"There—happy?"

Rogue's eyes glittered, the centers cobra-black. "No. Far from it. But taking a bite out of Falcon shall go a long way. Shall we?"

He presented his arm and I slid my hand through it, grasp-ing his lean forearm through the black leather. Larch popped out from wherever he'd been lurking and began to precede us through the camp, demanding in his surprisingly booming voice that all make way for the High Lord Rogue and his lady, the sorceress Gwynn.

"Now I'm *your* lady?" I muttered.

"Don't be difficult, Gwynn. I'm not in the mood."

"All the better to sic you on Falcon, I say."

His lips twitched and I knew he suppressed a smile this time. "Hush. Look dignified."

I rolled my eyes but decided against baiting him further. Instead, I mentally rewound our conversation, parsing it for clues. I knew the Black Dog progressively escaped his control, so I suspected his anger stemmed from that. He'd also counted on the fact that the Dog, for whatever reason, seemed to have a fondness for me and so wouldn't, oh say, crush my skull with his jaws as I'd seen him do to others.

The thing about him having proof of our relationship on me, though, that was troubling. Especially with Larch announcing us as if we were a married couple. Not that I was hoping to date around or anything, but I really wondered what the undoubtedly complex rules were here about that sort of thing.

"Do you ever stop thinking?"

I sent Rogue a sunny smile. "Nope. Not so much. You'll want a different girl for that."

"You say that as if I have a choice in the matter."

"That's me—the old ball and chain." Still, the remark stung and I felt stupidly hurt—a response I took care to bury very deep. After all, I wasn't thrilled either about the metaphysical forces that tied us to each other. His life, and blue balls, would likely be far better off with one of those countless noble fae girls Starling mentioned.

Not that I was feeling sorry for myself or anything.

We climbed the rise toward Falcon's tent-complex. His people always seemed to find a high point for him to lord over the camp. Not easy here in these lowlands by the ocean. The tent sides were all tied back to the poles, creating a kind of open-air pavilion feel. Falcon sat on what amounted to a throne, built up high so he could glower down from it, yellow eyes bright, even from a distance.

He was another with a face-pattern, though on the right side of his face, and nowhere nearly as complex as Rogue's. I'd also never seen it seem to come alive and visibly grow as Rogue's did. But he had once shapeshifted into a falcon in front of me. Involuntarily, to all appearances, but he didn't seem as driven by his demons as Rogue did.

Or as I might be.

I shivered and Rogue glanced down at me, a warning in his eyes. Right. Dignified.

Larch led us up to the foot of Falcon's chair and stepped aside. Falcon glared at Rogue from above his harshly hooked nose, thick fingernails digging into the wooden arms.

"Lord Rogue. How is it possible that you are lurking around my camp?"

Rogue released my arm but slid his hand around to the back of my bare neck. Falcon watched the movement and I saw him take in the flower earrings with an inaudible hiss. I really hoped they didn't count as some kind of engagement ring.

"I came to claim my property."

I tensed and his hand flexed on my neck. Oh boy, this was so not going to be fun.

"Oh?" Falcon raised his brows and sat back in the chair, acting as if he'd just now noticed my existence. "I was under the impression that the Lady Sorceress Gwynn was *my* pet for the time being."

"That time has ended."

"No." Falcon propped an elbow on the throne and leaned his head in his hand, putting on a thoughtful face. "No, I'm quite sure I have six years left of her oh-so-valuable services. Why, we would never have won the Battle for the Shining Seas without her brilliant strategy the other day."

He beamed at me, like the fake-affectionate uncle who molests you at night and knows you don't dare tell. It turned my stomach and I lifted my lip in a sneer. Falcon knew perfectly well what I thought of him.

"Of course, her performance yesterday left something to be desired." His fingers flexed and I knew he longed to use those thick yellow nails on me, just as he'd used his teeth before. "Which part of drowning did you not understand?

I twisted my fingers together to keep from fussing with the elaborate updo. "In the final analysis, my instructions were to sink the ships. You know it's important to me to do exactly as I'm told."

His lips curled in a silent snarl as he turned his attention back to Rogue. "Regardless. The agreement is ironclad and nonnegotiable. I won her years of service fairly."

"Those years were a trade with the healer. They don't truly belong to you."

"On the contrary, I have performed considerable...services," he leered at me, "for the sensitive Lady Healer in return. She likes her pain in precise and unusual ways. How is your tit, by the way, Sorceress? Do you still bear my teeth marks? I'd be pleased to renew them, if you beg nicely."

Rogue glanced at a passing butterfly, lazily observing its bobbing, polka-dotted path. I expected him to yawn with boredom next. I smelled the seething beneath, though, and resigned myself to letting him fix those marks too, though I'd very nearly healed them on my own.

"I suppose then—" Rogue stroked the back of my neck, considering me, "—I could simply buy her from you."

I clenched my jaw against the protest. Rogue saw it, his lips twitching in amusement. Now who was baiting whom?

"Oh?" Falcon studied his thick curved nails, nearly talons. "I can't imagine what you could possibly offer that would interest me. No. I think I'll keep my pet sorceress." He held out a hand to me. "Come climb on papa's lap like a good girl."

I managed to not tell him to go fuck himself and held my tongue. No way I wanted to interfere in this battle between them.

"I'll offer my services in her stead."

Falcon's eyes glittered with true lust now and I recalled how, in the so-called war-planning sessions, he'd complained about wanting Rogue's abilities.

"You won't be as decorative, hanging about the camp, but I suppose you could take her place. Why you'd risk this juicy lamb wandering about by herself, however, for just anyone to take a taste of, is beyond me."

Rogue laughed, deliberately amused at the absurdity. "Don't be a fool, Falcon. I will win your war for you and the

Lady Gwynn and I shall go about our business."

"*General* Falcon!" Falcon screeched it, his nails splintering the wood of the arms as he strained forward. "You will show me due respect in this place, Rogue. This war is *my* project and I shall choose how to end it. We have at least five spectacular battles planned and you shall not cheat me of them. You do not dictate to me or I shall feed your little slut to the sea monsters—after I've pillaged her every orifice and perhaps some extras I choose to make."

"Have a care, Falcon." Rogue's voice was ice-quiet. "You risk your pledge to me. Perhaps I shall have to pay nothing, if you break your end."

Falcon writhed in his seat, as if gripped by DTs. None of the fae were exactly sane by human terms, but this behavior seemed especially neurotic. Was it Rogue's proximity? Now Falcon gripped his temples with clawed fingers, holding himself still.

"Then what?" He ground the words out.

Rogue smiled, ever calm and self-possessed. He stroked my neck and I relaxed a little, not realizing how tense I'd become.

"Five battles, you say? I could possibly assist with those. On an on-call basis."

"I said *at least* five." Falcon seemed calmer now, speculating. "I need to call a meeting of the generals, to determine our exact strategy."

"Of course." Rogue inclined his head.

As if this exchange had set off some sort of signal, a scurry of pages and Brownies dashed up the hill, rapidly setting up long tables draped with whimsical cloths. Their noble patrons followed behind at a more leisurely pace, though with no less fervent excitement. Falcon leaped off his throne with an excited click of his heels and went to play gracious host.

I frowned at their precipitous arrival, recalling Starling's prediction for an extended formal lunch, and realized this meeting had been planned all along.

"If this was a foregone conclusion, why the elaborate dance with Falcon?" I muttered to Rogue.

He toyed with my flower earring, stirring the sweet scent and sending a shiver through my sensitive lobe, a sly smile drifting across his lips. "Because, darling Gwynn, the dance is the important part. How can you not know this yet?"

"I'd say that should be my next lesson, but I don't believe you." No, I suspected it had all been an elaborate charade, staged for my benefit. The gullible audience of one.

"What reason would I have to mislead you?"

I made an O of mock surprise. "Gosh, let me think!"

He tapped me on the nose. "Such a pretty mouth. You've been doing a lovely job of keeping it shut. See that you continue to do so."

Taking my hand, he tugged me in the direction of the rapidly evolving feast. I dug in my high heels and resisted. When he turned to me this time, he wore a wary, questioning look. Good.

"I want to register a complaint."

"Not now. We must appear to be one in our objectives."

"I know, but I don't like this."

"You just don't like that you're not running the show."

"Exactly how you would feel, were our positions reversed. But that isn't all of it. I will not give you carte blanche to run my life, Rogue."

"Have I asked for it?" Impatience shimmered through him. Oh, how he hated to be thwarted in the least little way.

"Every time I give you an inch, you take miles and miles."

He cocked his head, not quite processing my metaphor.

"No—you have not asked for carte blanche. You simply assume it is yours."

Rogue fiddled with his dagger. Probably wishing he'd just cut my throat in the very beginning of all this. "You endanger us both with this little tantrum. What must I do so that I can trust that you'll behave?"

I laughed. Then stepped in and walked my fingers up his chest, looking flirtatious, I hoped. For the benefit of our observers. "You can stop manipulating me. Don't you understand that by now? You can never trust a person you've manipulated, because you never know if they're sincere or just doing what you programmed them to do."

I tapped him on the end of his elegant nose and walked away.

"Lord Puck!" I called out. The tall fae tossed his cascading curls and danced an impromptu jig at the sight of me, then took my hand and kissed it.

"Most Powerful Lady Sorceress Gwynn." He exclaimed with apparent delight, as if he hadn't seen me for months, then kissed my wrist. He kissed his way up my arm, pausing between each to praise my gown, my eyes, my hair. He wore a less searing shade than usual, nearly sedate in a peacock blue lounging outfit. With his mismatched eyes, one sparkling brown, the other glass green, he still clashed. A tall feather threaded through his locks, bobbing whimsically with each kiss.

Rogue's hand fell on the back of my neck again. I'd have to point out to him that it didn't necessarily allow him to operate my mouth as his puppet.

Puck paused at my elbow and grinned up my arm. "And the ever-terrifyingly enigmatic Lord Rogue. Such an unexpected pleasure to have you join our merry company."

"Oh, he's lurking about more than you'd think," I assured him breezily and those long fingers flexed on my neck. I glanced over my shoulder at Rogue. "Aren't you, sweetheart?"

His hand stroked down and caressed my shoulder. "Any opportunity to taste the pleasures of your bed, my Gwynn."

Touché.

In their standard mass-mind decision-making, everyone moved then to the tables, strewn with flowers and sparkling confetti. Rogue sat us at Falcon's right hand—far too close for comfort, in my opinion—but the apparent seat for the guest of honor.

The fae noble I thought of as Navy Man sat across from us. Not in his sailing ships uniform, he nevertheless declared himself a sailor, wearing an outfit reminiscent of Humphrey Bogart in a yachting flick from the golden era.

"Aha, Lord Rogue, so you capitulate at last. Our next battle—next several battles, I should hope—will be at sea. How do you propose to vanquish the enemy?"

"As expeditiously as possible." A flash of cobalt blue as Rogue glanced at me. "I have other interests to pursue."

"Lady Strawberry here is suggesting sea monsters, but I find that so trite. So last season—don't you agree?"

A sunset-orange page set a shallow bowl of tiny fish in front of me. Still swimming. I looked to see if Rogue was really going to eat it and found Falcon's beady yellow gaze on me. He grinned, baring sharply pointed teeth. Nobody else had received the dish. Under the tablecloth, Rogue placed a hand on my thigh in subtle warning. The last time we'd feasted side by side like this, he'd warned me not to refuse my host's food.

But a bowl of fish?

I wondered if it would be bad manners to convert them into rice. Or chicken nuggets. Surely puking up my host's food would be more insulting than not eating it.

A paw patted my other thigh and I looked down in to Darling's hopeful green gaze. I scooted my chair back enough for him to leap onto my lap and scratched between his ears.

"So thoughtful, Lord Falcon, to provide for my Familiar. He's been just craving fish."

Someone at the table giggled, and I figured more than one person had heard about Darling's exploits—imagined or otherwise—with the mermaids. Darling delicately perched on the table and lapped at the swimming soup eagerly. Rogue patted my leg. Hopefully in approval.

He set to arguing the pros and cons of sea monsters, sliding his own plate of the usual feast food of pastries and fruit between us, so I could share. In big groups, with lots of people chattering, the translation telepathy tended to fail me. The words became a wash of nonsensical sound and I received a kaleidoscope of images, most of them not correctly sequenced. Rogue's hand stayed hot on my upper thigh, distracting even through the full skirt of my dress.

I confess I tuned a lot of it out. Now that I knew how to screen thoughts better, I filtered most of the white noise and focused mainly on Rogue and Falcon.

That was when I caught Rogue saying "kill the rest of their mortal troops easily enough. With no humans to fight for them, they'll be crippled."

I swallowed hard on the crumbly pastry I'd been chewing. Once I would have blurted out my opinion. Once I had done that very thing and—though I wasn't superstitious—the lapse had in some ways precipitated this entire adventure. I'd learned some difficult, painful lessons since then, and one was definitely about keeping my mouth shut.

I was already sick to death of the practice.

There was no way I'd stand by and let them sacrifice my kind just because it was easy for them to do. The fae nobles had all the power, and the humans—and, to be fair, pretty much all the lesser fae—were merely disposable game pieces. The humans had no one with any ability on their side.

Except for me. The human ace in the hole. I'd gone to great lengths to find ways to perform magical feats that won the battles without causing death and destruction. It didn't matter that the human folk didn't ask for it or appreciate it. Call it genetic loyalty.

"Can I speak to you alone?" I asked it of Rogue as softly as I could.

He regarded me with cool surprise and a glint of clear warning. "You would insult our host?"

Okay, no. I considered telling him mind to mind, but he'd told me long ago that sort of communication was more easily overheard than verbal. I needed some kind of code. But with the translation telepathy in effect, everyone would likely hear what I intended to say regardless of the words I chose.

I ground my teeth in frustration. Nothing for it but the

direct route then. "I cannot stand by and allow the humans to be harmed."

"It doesn't concern you." Rogue started to turn back to the conversation, but I put my hand over his. The blue-black feral anger in him stirred and I stroked his skin. We really didn't need for the Dog to put in an appearance.

"It does." I kept my voice as quiet as I could, but he had to know I wouldn't budge on this. "Our objectives are the same, remember."

"Surely you don't claim those animals as kin, Lady Sorceress." Navy Man looked astonished and more than a little disgusted. "Though it would be anticlimactic to simply sink the rest of the ships. The naval battle would be over *far* too soon."

"Perhaps I could provide sea monsters," Lady Strawberry suggested, as if she'd never said it before, "to eat the sailors once the ships sink?"

"The Lady Gwynn has always displayed rather lowbrow tastes," Falcon nearly purred. "Should we be concerned about your loyalty, Sorceress? Or are we safe from you, now that Lord Rogue holds your leash?"

They all leered at me and Puck waggled his eyebrows. Darling stalked off down the center of the table, knocking goblets over with a swishing tail.

"The humans are not her people." Rogue appeared to be answering Falcon's question, but the words were directed at me. "She left her people behind, as a snake sheds its skin. Look at her face—even now the fae lines are showing."

I pulled my hand away, but he captured it, holding on fiercely, while the others murmured speculation among themselves.

"It's on the left side. Silver-white, faint, barely catching the light, but there—on your temple. You are not what you were."

The cold razor claw in me shifted, whispered, answering to the swirl in him.

I turned my hand, laced my fingers with Rogue's despite the queasy fear that undermined my thoughts. "I have a proposition then."

Rogue's lips tightened into a thin line.

As I knew he would, Falcon pounced. "What deal do you offer me?"

Rogue continued to study me, shifted so his thumb stroked my palm, sending warm shivers through me. Somehow soothing, stimulating and threatening all at once. Down the table someone chastised Darling for sitting in their plate of food. He hissed in reply and the someone yelped, no doubt at a clawed paw-swipe.

"A twofer."

Falcon's eyes blazed with yellow lust. I could hear his thoughts spinning with glee. Rogue had gone still. Waiting. It was a form of trust, I supposed, that he didn't stop me immediately for committing him to an unknown plan. Or the confidence that he could prevent that, with the least effort.

Keeping my thoughts as still and clear as possible, I crafted my phrasing.

"In exchange for my freedom, for a number of occasions, the exact number and duration to be determined in this negotiation, Rogue and I will work together to solve the problem posed for the specific battle. We shall arrive for those occasions and leave after they are complete." Had I forgotten anything? Darling trotted up the table, urgently reminding me about his military career. "Oh, and Darling will also return, to participate in those select battles."

Falcon looked suspicious. Rogue was downright steamed.

Only Darling seemed pleased with me, happily flopping himself into the empty soup bowl, which he overlapped so much that his head landed in Rogue's plate, offering me his belly for rubbing.

Navy Man, Puck and Lady Strawberry proclaimed it an excellent deal and urged Falcon to accept it. Falcon chewed on a thick nail, frowning.

He wasn't sure of the catch, I realized. I'd thrown a wrench into their careful choreography, altering whatever backroom deal they'd set up, and now Falcon suspected a trap. For his part, Rogue simply continued to stroke my palm with a sensual threat.

Well, hell. I'd tried to talk to him before it came to this. I widened my eyes and shrugged a little. A kind of apology, what-could-I-do sort of look.

"The deal is acceptable," Falcon said, slowly, sounding it out, and the table broke into cheering and, in one case, a jig. "We shall establish—"

"A moment." Rogue's icy voice silenced the room. Even Darling stopped purring and opened one sleepy eye to keep it on the man holding my hand in an increasingly fierce grip. Would he disagree? Falcon already knew I'd introduced something new. Though he likely thought Rogue had coached me to do it. "I have something to add that I believe Lady Sorceress Gwynn neglected to mention."

My blood ran cold at the look on his face. I'd pissed him off before, but not so much since our new level of intimacy. I suppose he hadn't expected me to dig in on this point, with the humans.

"I will perform all magics. Not Lady Gwynn."

I felt the frown knit my forehead. Why was that a big deal? On the surface it seemed just fine, but I hated feeling that I'd missed something here. Rogue released my hand and raised his to my earring, brushing my breast on the way up, making me catch my breath. The little clawed tendrils of the earring responded to the movement, sending another arousing tremor through me. Clouding my mind with desire.

"Agreed, my Gwynn?" Rogue purred, and the anger still seethed beneath the words, black and hot. "We decide together, but I perform the magic."

I nodded, tearing my gaze from his compelling eyes.

The others dived into the negotiations with renewed vigor, listing potential battles, debating the relative glory to be gained from each, and all seemed genuinely thrilled to speculate on what Lord Rogue might bring, in the way of spectacular magic.

As for me, I'd gotten what I'd hoped for—the opportunity to protect the humans from being treated as disposable toys. And he'd agreed to help me with both of my quests. I hoped it wasn't just cynicism in me that warned me that I'd just gotten exactly what I wished for.

Which never boded well.

CHAPTER 6

IN WHICH I AM MAGICALLY TRANSFORMED INTO A CONCUBINE

ᡩᠠᡝ

Dragon's blood appears to have anti-magical properties, to the point that at high concentrations it becomes repellent or toxic to magical beings. Humans, however, appear to be immune.

~Big Book of Fairyland, "Objects with Magical Properties"

THE FEAST DID indeed drag on for hours. That was one of the downsides of hanging around immortal fae types—they didn't get tired, and what they find fun could be on a whole other level of excruciatingly boring. There were so many more interesting things I could be doing with my time than listening to the Mad Hatter crowd spin stories of potential battles and retell previous ones with utter disregard for what actually happened.

It says something about me that I took comfort in Rogue's similarly seething restlessness. He had himself on a tight leash, speaking little and only occasionally fixing me with a molten blue gaze that revealed only that his anger hadn't subsided. My neck started to feel stiff and sore from holding up the elaborate hairstyle, and a headache threatened at the base of my skull.

Despite my stubborn nature, I really hated having Rogue mad at me. Or anyone, for that matter. I had to stop myself from reaching out to soothe him, to get him to smile at me again, with that affectionate charm. I had to keep reminding myself it wasn't wrong to adhere to my own standards.

Even if he was pouting.

By the time the feast ended, Rogue had negotiated the generals down to three pivotal battles, to be named. Everyone seemed pleased. Given that he bargained with the skill of a long-scam con artist, Rogue could elicit the best deal for him and make people delighted to give it to him. And I was happy to let him handle it.

Finally, he decorously assisted me to my feet and then ran a long-fingered hand down my back to rest on my hip. The sun was slanting to afternoon. We said cheery goodbyes—the truth in mine fueled by my intense relief at finally getting to leave—and strolled out on the acid-green grass with Larch in the lead. I'm sure we looked for all the world like a happy couple with their faithful page.

"I should take you away right this instant," Rogue said, in a silky tone, "tie you to my bed so you can't move and teach you better uses for that clever tongue."

"Now you sound like Falcon," I retorted. Larch gave no indication he'd overheard.

"Have a care, foolish Gwynn—you have pushed me far indeed."

No surprises there. I contemplated apologizing, but what

exactly would I be sorry for?

"I'm sorry I made you angry," I finally offered. "It was not my intention."

"You do realize those humans care nothing for your fate? They are not the people you left behind. These are little better than animals—grubbing among themselves for the least crumb of advantage. The soldiers here may admire you, but in the villages they would burn you alive for bearing the taint of Faerie magic."

"I'll take that under advisement."

"Which means you will ignore my cautions, as always." His own magic churned around him, sending out seeking tendrils, threads of cobalt edged in black. "I shall bid you farewell until tonight. I trust Larch will lead you back to your tent."

Since I was saved from having to explain, yet again, that I only disregarded Rogue's cautions because I couldn't tell them from his attempts to corral me, I did not point out that I could find my own damn tent and that maybe I had other places to go.

He faced me and cupped the back of my neck, rubbing it so that the tension there faded. His eyes had darkened to nearly black, and the pattern on his face seemed to pulse, a sign that the Dog welled near the surface.

"I shall ask you to make this up to me tonight, my rash and beautiful Gwynn. Be prepared for that." The words sparked a startling surge of lust, my sex suddenly aching. He smiled, knowingly. "Wine and roses."

He released my neck and flicked a flower earring, sending an extra pulse of sensation through my nerves. Then he dissolved into thin air.

"Dammit—he didn't tell me how to take these off again," I groused to no one, since Larch was waiting, patient as a garden gnome, a short distance away. Tugging at them, I found, only made them clamp tighter, changing their light tickle to outright pain. I calmed myself and wished them away. No change. Didn't that just figure. I headed toward the tent.

"Where are you going, Lady Sorceress?" Larch inquired, ever so politely.

Well, I had *thought* I could find my own tent. "Isn't it this way?"

"Yes, but you are late for your self-defense lesson."

"I'm pretty sure those are canceled now."

Larch's face fell, his features crushed with disappointment. "You would break your vow to me?"

Well, shit. One of these days I'd learn to quit carelessly promising things, like that I'd learn how to defend myself if Larch would just give me a moment's peace. Unfortunately, I'd nearly had a fling with my instructor, the handsome Officer Liam, which had come to a nasty end when Rogue found out. All I needed to round out this fabulous day would be an unpleasant encounter with the almost-lover scorned. No choice there.

"Okay, fine. But I'm not exactly dressed for it, I don't have my weapons and I'm quite certain Liam won't be there.

"You can alter your garments easily enough, powerful as you are, Lady Sorceress, and I shall send someone for your weapons." With that, he trotted in the lead, whistling such a merry tune that I suspected the crestfallen look had been an Oscar-worthy acting job.

To my great chagrin, Officer Liam was waiting at the practice ring and clearly had been for some time. He squinted at me and then at the sun, bronze curls gleaming. "You're late."

I gestured to my dress. "I was otherwise engaged. Command performance."

A gaggle of dragonfly girls dashed up, carrying my sun-and-moon wheels and my three-foot stick. It seemed I was doing this.

"You'll have to show more commitment than this, if you hope to accomplish anything." His tone was fine, but the words barbed. Seemed like an awful lot of people wanted to tell me what to do today.

"Aren't I paying you?" I asked him in my best lady-of-the-manor voice. If there was to be distance between us, I wanted it my way.

"Yes, Lady Sorceress." He bowed, irritation wafting off him.

"Fine." It might do me good to work off some energy—both the sexual and the mad. I concentrated on the image I wanted and converted my heels to a pair of cross-trainers and my dress into workout shorts and a sports bra. Liam's mouth dropped open, both for the display of magic and skin. A grin of satisfaction warmed me and I picked up my stick, swinging it in the figure eight I'd learned. "Let's do this."

I hadn't had a lot of lessons so far and little time to practice or build my arm muscles, but I was improving. I swung the stick, blocking Liam's attacks, spinning my way through the practice movements. The spiky sun-and-moon wheels were more difficult to manage. Nevertheless, I didn't clonk or slice myself the way I had the first few times.

And it felt good. Muscles working, sweat running down my body, no time to think about all the things that consumed my waking thoughts. No complex negotiating. Just movement. Thrust. Parry. Spin. Lunge. The silver wheels flashed in the sunlight and I drove hard into Liam, backing him up as the knife-edges drew closer and his blocks grew more desperate.

I felt supple, elastic, closing in on my helpless prey.

"Hold!" he yelled, the sound penetrating my mind enough for it to inform me it wasn't the first time he'd said it.

I pulled back and the man bent over, panting, hands braced on his knees. My hair had long since fallen out of Starling's elaborate headdress, and now it hung long, plastered to my neck and arms with sweat. My body sang with power and strength. I could take him now, while he was weak. Claws flexing, I closed the distance between us.

The man's head rose and his eyes flared with fear. He froze. Wise. He couldn't escape me.

"Lady Sorceress," a blue page intoned behind me. "Your next appointment awaits."

I frowned at him, not entirely certain who the little guy was. Though he smelled good. Would he taste of blueberries or flesh?

"Lady Sorceress Gwynn," he said steadily, no fear in his face. Larch. This was Larch and I was...

Predator. The cat ghost, silver-white, flashed through my mind and disappeared into the hot course of my bloodstream. And here I'd thought Rogue's and Falcon's strength came from the leverage of their long limbs. I hadn't imagined that it was fueled by these animal natures. My left temple itched and I scratched at it. Wondering if the lines were visible.

Liam watched, wary, though looking less like a deer in the headlights than before. Behind him, a fair distance off, nearly shrouded by the tall coastal grasses and the lengthening shadows of evening, the Black Dog sat. Waiting for me.

"I beg your pardon, Officer Liam. I can't say what came over me." I sounded like Rogue. It was an effort, to keep my gaze on Liam and not stray to the Dog.

"It seems that you've...progressed, Lady Sorceress." Liam still hadn't caught his breath.

"Yes. It does seem that way."

I bit my tongue on thanking him, said farewell for now instead, asked Larch to take my weapons back to my tent, and strode off to meet the Dog. As I walked through the grasses, each blade a different citrus color that made a sound of chimes when they rustled together, I wished my shorts and sports bra into a long, flowing white dress. It suited my mood. I kept the cross-trainers though—all the better for squelching through the increasingly marshy stuff.

He'd been sitting on his haunches, as if carved from a block of obsidian, glossy black and unnaturally still, but now the Dog stood, wagging his tail, tongue lolling out. It would be a happy dog look, if not for the white fangs inside the massive jaws. They were tinged with blood and I resolved not to wonder whose it was. He nudged his broad head under my hand and I stroked the short silky fur.

Of all the denizens of Faerie, the Dog seemed unconditionally devoted to me. He required no payment from me and followed no rules himself.

Something similar grew out of me now and somehow I knew the Dog understood. More, was attracted to it.

Restless, I kept walking and the Dog paced by my side, waist-high so I easily rested my hand on his muscular shoulder. Though I now knew for certain that Rogue lurked somewhere inside this beast, he felt no more present to me than ever before. Rogue wasn't aware of the Dog's actions, couldn't remember them, so where did his consciousness go? Maybe he was less inside than temporarily suspended elsewhere for a time.

Where had mine gone, for that matter, when the feline-ghost in me decided to take over the physical fight? I didn't remember being anywhere. The lost time was the only evidence. That and Liam's dramatic reaction.

At least it seemed I didn't need to be concerned about self-defense anymore.

A breeze blew in off the ocean, scented with salt, lifting my drying hair. I skirted the human camp, giving them a wide berth. Together the Dog and I walked up a bluff that over-looked the beach. The sea glowed a nearly fluorescent blue now, in the late day sunlight, flashes of orange in the foaming surf. I didn't see any sign of my fiberglass half boat, but huge wooden scaffolds had been constructed and already frames of new sailing ships sat in them. Made of fine golden floss, the ships seemed to be woven instead of built and the sails seemed made of the petals of orchids, vivid, ruffled pastel.

As if they could sail into the sunset and become one with it. Part of me longed to go with them.

The Dog bumped my hand and I crouched in front of him, scratching his ears. "Rogue? Are you in there?" I asked it anyway, though I felt sure he wouldn't answer. The Dog never did—never communicated even in images. He cocked his head and gave me a canine grin. Then he slurped my hand with his tongue and took off down the bluff, fae and humans alike scattering with shrieks of terror.

I watched long enough to make sure he didn't eat anyone—though what I'd do about it, I didn't know—and saw him leap into the water, dog-paddling out toward the horizon. No doubt Rogue would make an appearance before long then.

I turned to walk back and found Larch waiting just behind me.

"My lady." He bowed. Said nothing more.

"Something you wanted, Larch?"

His stolid face puckered as he considered. "The Black Dog is not evil. You should know that."

This surprised me, not because I disagreed, but because Larch was rarely forthcoming. Especially about anything to do with Rogue. "I do know that."

"There is such a thing. Evil."

I never had really believed in the concept. All was shades of gray. There was cruelty and self-absorption to the point of being destructive to others. I suppose I thought everyone believed they were doing what they needed to do. But evil? "Perhaps. But no, not evil—the Dog is simply what it is. Elemental."

Larch inclined his head, part agreement, part tribute. "I thought that might be something you needed to remember, Lady Gwynn."

"I see."

We walked back in silence and now my thoughts creaked back into life, parsing what had happened. The cat thing in me had taken over, briefly, but with a stealth and power I couldn't resist. It wasn't evil though—that much I knew. It simply operated as the Dog did, without rules or boundaries, as purely itself. That was what Larch wanted me to know, offering me reassurance in his funny, oblique way. For surely he'd witnessed it, had seen clearly through his blueberry eyes that I had temporarily become something else.

At least it hadn't torn my mortal body to limp shreds of flesh. Yet.

"Do you come with us to Castle Brightness tomorrow?"

"Yes, Lady Sorceress. Your tribute stores have been packed for storage. I assumed you would wish to travel light for now."

"I assumed Rogue would have given you instructions."

He snorted, a most un-Larchlike sound. "Lord Rogue is not speaking to me at this time. I believe he's still angry that you slipped past me the other night."

"Ah." I took that in. "So, you are my prison guard then."

"No, Lady Sorceress." He blinked up at me with a sly smile. "That's why you were able to escape so easily."

I revised my assessment of Larch then. One more player for Team Gwynn. That should be rewarded.

"How much am I paying you, anyway?"

"As your seneschal, Lady Blackbird takes care of that."

Well, yes—I knew that much. It still didn't answer the question.

"How about a bonus then? Pick something from the Tribute Tent. Which I imagine is now the Tribute Self-Storage Unit."

"Anything?" He sounded aghast at my cavalier generosity. Frankly, though, the vast majority of the things that had been given in tribute to me was stuff that I had *no* idea how to evaluate. If I did want to know the relative value of something, I just ended up asking Larch or Starling anyway. Given Starling's tendency for hyperbole, I didn't quite trust her take. Certainly Rogue couldn't be counted on for a straight answer, particularly if another would give him more power over me.

"Yes, anything you want. One thing." All I needed was to be embezzled of my entire fortune, such as it was. "And while you're at it, could you dig out that vial of distilled dragon's blood I concocted?"

"I will pack it in your bags for you."

"No. I want it close to hand. Call me paranoid."

He didn't call me anything, but the disapproval wafted off him. Whether for my unladylike behavior or the risk-taking, I wasn't sure and didn't care.

"Um…" We were closing in on the tent. "You won't say anything about…today?"

"Your secrets are always safe with me, Lady Gwynn."

That, I did believe.

Starling was busily packing up the contents of the tent, a manic Mary Poppins with her singing and flinging about of dresses. She gave my dress the hairy eyeball and sighed.

"Did you just poof away the other one? It was expensive, you know."

Oops.

"I could maybe recreate it?"

"Did you pay enough attention to the fabric and the lines to do that? It was woven by pixies—not easy to replicate."

"Oh. Probably not. Sorry?"

She snorted at me. "No, you're not. But next time, could you maybe send the expensive dresses back to the tent and make your new getups out of something else?"

I looked down at my white dress and tennies. It wasn't *that* bad. I'd been feeling kind of Jane Eyre-ish and tragic. And it wasn't like there were phone booths for me to slip into to change into my superhero costume while I dutifully teleported cocktail gowns back and forth.

"I'll see what I can do. Meanwhile I suppose I'd better get ready for Rogue's visit. He probably wants dinner again."

"He does," Starling confirmed. "It's all arranged. Night-gown and robe then?"

"I wish. Somehow I agreed to wear a nightgown of his choice." Sure seemed as if I'd agreed to an awful lot lately. I must be slipping. "So I might as well wear a decent dress."

"You mean—not like whatever it is that you're wearing?"

"Hey! Leave my tragic Jane Eyre outfit alone."

She cocked her head at me. "Does that mean anything at all?"

"No." I sighed and plunked myself down in front of the mirror and started brushing my tangled hair. Starling took the brush out of my hand and did it for me, with considerably more soothing care than I gave myself. "I had a self-defense lesson with Officer Liam and some other stuff happened. Plus Falcon is a right bastard. It's been a day."

Starling raised an eyebrow, catching my eye in the mirror. "What else happened?"

I realized I didn't want to tell her about the ghost-cat. Turning my head to the right, I could maybe see a faint gleam of white-silver on my left temple. Just a hint, a minor capillary breaking. I resisted the urge to lean forward to study it more closely. *What are you looking at, Gwynn? Oh, just signs that I'm turning into a monster.*

"Gwynn?"

I started, for a moment thinking we were having the conversation out loud.

"Oh, nothing. Just Rogue being high-handed and Falcon being the nasty dictator he is. Is there anyone here not grabbing for power?"

It was a rhetorical question, of course, but she screwed up her face, thinking hard. "No. I don't think so. After all, what else is there?"

What else indeed?

Starling left my hair down and helped me into a pretty blue gown that matched my new earrings.

"Do you know how I can take these off, by chance?"

She shook her head without looking. "They're very beautiful."

"But?"

Starling shrugged, not meeting my eyes. "But I'm surprised you accepted them."

"Why? What do they mean?"

"You don't know?"

I reined in my impatience. "How would I know, Starling? I'm not *from* here."

"Oh," she said in a small voice. "Well, you might not like the answer."

Color me oh-so-surprised. I kicked some pillows aside, sending them blinking into different jewel-tone shades, and padded barefoot over to the food table. Pouring myself a full glass of wine, I took a long, grateful sip, and braced myself.

"Okay, tell me."

"Well—they kind of mark you."

"Yeah. That's what Rogue said. Proof."

"Exactly!" She nodded vigorously in relief. "So you *do* know."

"Not so fast. Proof of what?"

"Um." She pursed her lips and raised her eyebrows in what should have been a cheerful, innocent look, but instead gave her a manic chipmunk cast. "I don't know how things worked in your old world. But here there's married—which is official and all—and then there's, well, other kinds of relationships."

"So, you're saying that these earrings mark me as, what, Rogue's concubine? Mistress—that kind of thing?"

She clasped her hands together. "Um. Yeah."

I savored the wine—so much better than the alcoholic Kool-Aid Falcon served—and considered. "I don't think I care."

"You don't? It's not an, um, flattering status. Not as if you were his lady."

"Yeah. That much is parallel in my old world. But I imagine marrying Rogue would bring a whole raft of obligations and rules, yes? Whereas, if the analogy continues, being a mistressy sort gives you social freedoms that wives don't enjoy. This place is so feudal in some ways, I'm betting that's true here too." I raised my glass in a little toast. "Here's to being Rogue's official concubine—much good may it do him."

"Oh, it may do me more good than you think."

CHAPTER 7

IN WHICH I EMBARK UPON A QUEST WITH MY BRAVE COMPANIONS

༃

It's an inescapable conclusion that Rogue and the Black Dog
are one and the same. But somehow it runs deeper than
simple shapeshifting. If shapeshifting can be called simple.
~*Big Book of Fairyland,* "The Black Dog"

I WHIRLED AROUND to find Rogue lounging on his silken nest
of a bed, boots crossed at the heels and his hair loose,
spread enticingly over the pillows.

"You just love to do that, don't you?"

His lips curved in a satisfied smile. "I do, yes. Taking you
by surprise, Concubine Gwynn, is always rewarding."

He infused the words with sexual intent, embarrassing
Starling into a flutter of activity. She stammered something
about sending dinner in later and dashed out. I studied Rogue.
He was relaxed now in a way he hadn't been before. The
restless anger had dissipated, leaving behind the playful version
of himself. Sated, rested. Refueled.

I moved over to the workbench and flipped open my grimoire. The pen I'd made lurked somewhere under a few trinkets—undoubtedly batted there by Darling. I flipped to the section on the Black Dog and made a note.

"What are you doing?" Rogue's hand stroked down my arm with warm affection, his voice amused as he peered over my shoulder.

"Special human magic," I replied in a lofty tone. "You wouldn't understand."

"May I?"

I obligingly moved aside and let him bend over the page, nearly full of notes and comments about the Dog. I'd had proper note-keeping rammed into my head by an OCD chemistry professor once upon a time, and my handwriting was as neat as an engineer's. Rogue absently pushed the fall of his hair over his shoulder and touched the page with a careful finger, following the line of the characters, as if he expected the texture to change. It put me in mind of the way I touched his skin, searching for the boundaries of the black lines and thorns embedded within.

"This is strange indeed. Yet, I don't feel your magic, beyond what you used to create it. What does it do?"

It still boggled me that their whole society had no concept of books or writing. Perhaps the hive mind made it unnecessary. But why hadn't the humans developed something? Too busy slaving away for their overlords, probably.

"It's a way of...leaving messages for myself. Things I want to remember and think about."

He turned his head, midnight-blue eyes sparkling. "I doubt you need to remember to think about things, saucy Gwynn."

"You'd be surprised," I answered in a dry tone, lacing my

fingers together to resist the urge to run them through the silky black hair spilling over his shoulder.

"Would I?" He straightened and touched one of the lily earrings, setting it swinging. "I thought you'd be angry when you found out."

"If you thought I'd be angry, why did you do it?"

"Besides that it was necessary for dealing with Falcon and his cronies? Because I thought you would not agree to a formal mating."

"Insightful of you."

"Though the offer stands."

"No, thank you."

"A thousand girls would kill to be my lady."

"Don't let me get in the way."

He laughed, took my hand and set it on his hair. "Why don't you touch me when you want to? It's your right."

"Because," I whispered past the dryness in my mouth, unable to resist winding my fingers through the silk of it, watery soft as ink, "it's dangerous."

He raised an eyebrow. "How so?"

"Each time I give in to temptation, it makes it easier to give in the next time, to yield a little more."

"Yield a little more, lovely Gwynn," he coaxed, turning me so he had me boxed against the bench, one hand clinging to his hair like a lifeline. "Shall we have our kiss now?"

"I thought we'd have the lesson first." But my eyes were glued to his mouth, the dark-blood lips. My body thrummed in anticipation.

"So orderly." His mouth hovered a breath away from mine. "Work before pleasure. Do you want me to kiss you now?"

I did. I didn't say so.

He smiled, knowing anyway. "But I think you're right. Lesson first. When I kiss you next, I want it to be in my bed with you wearing the nightgown I made specially for you."

"Remember I get consultation on that."

"I need no magic to remind me. Now, shall the subject of the lesson be how your cat took you over this afternoon?" He stroked a finger over my left temple, eyes intent on the spot.

"Are the lines more pronounced now?" I asked, though I was afraid of the answer.

His gaze returned to mine, the deep blue thoughtful. "Than at midday? No. But they will be. You won't be able to control this, clever Gwynn."

"How do you know what happened? I thought you didn't remember things when you were the Dog?"

His lips twisted in a wry grimace and he pulled away. With reluctance, I let his hair slide through my fingers, leaving them bereft. He tucked his hands behind his back and paced the tent. This was what he often did, pacing as he taught. I smiled to myself, that he was so familiar to me in some ways, and scooted back to sit on the bench.

"Answer me this—do you recall what occurred when the cat took over?"

I started to say no, but that wasn't precisely true. "It's like a dream. Flashes of images. Not vivid, like your dreamscape—whatever that is—but more an ordinary dream. Jumbled and nonsensical."

He nodded. "You'll find that the cat will have its own agenda. One that will likely grow more defined over time. But it will retain something of your interests too. You may remember more of the things that the cat witnesses because you are interested."

"Thus the Dog arriving to witness my practice. Because you wanted to know what I was doing."

"Yes." He flashed me a wicked grin, full of teeth. "We are both interested in you."

"Fuck me if I know why," I groused.

"That too."

I wrinkled my nose at him. "So, does the Dog take you over? Just inside?"

Rogue shook his head, abruptly somber. "Not since it took flesh. I can sense its rise, but that internal-only possession only occurs until it gains enough power to take flesh. Once it can have that, it rarely settles for less."

I shivered, queasy. "What gives it power?"

He raised his eyebrow, on the left side, making the thorns of black shift and realign. "Among other things, you do."

"How?"

"If I knew that, my Gwynn, I would not be in the position I'm in."

"What position is that?"

He stalked over to me and wrapped his hand around my throat. Gentle, but implacable. My pulse suddenly pounded, in fear or arousal, I wasn't certain. "Enslaved to you, powerful Gwynn."

"I thought you wanted me to be your slave."

"Is there a difference?"

"Yes."

"Are you sure?"

Was I? Once I had been. Once I'd thought the world fell into orderly patterns.

"Is that enough for you to think about for now?"

"Definitely," I breathed.

"Thus endeth the lesson."

In response to an invisible signal, Larch and his assistants trotted in, assembling the little dining table and feast for two. Rogue handed me into my chair with a courtly gesture and settled himself opposite me.

The food was again delicious—all of my favorites—and I ate voraciously, surprised at my hunger. Though, upon reflection, I hadn't eaten much at Falcon's awful luncheon, and my cat-induced workout had been more intense than I'd ever do alone. We ate in silence, aside from comments about the meal, each absorbed with our own thoughts. That companionable, domestic feel returned. I could become accustomed to this schedule, the intimate evening ritual Rogue was slowly creating.

And this, my friends, was how water wore down rock.

He'd even arranged for dessert—a confection that tasted amazingly close to chocolate. I gobbled it up, humming my approval and licking my fingers to enjoy the last bits of it. I felt Rogue's gaze on me and glanced up to see his eyes hot, molten chromium. My breath caught in my throat as the longing throbbed between us.

I looked away first. Then stood, for once wishing I could fiddle with the dishes.

"Gwynn—"

"No." I stopped him. "Don't even ask again. Where's this damn nightgown? Let's get this over with."

"On the bed."

It hadn't been before, but that meant nothing. Knowing what I'd see, feeling that sense of dreamlike haze settle over me, I moved over to it.

And there it was, draped over the black coverlet, streaming pale lace, nearly white, but with icy blue hints of highlights. I remembered it well from my dreams. Even though Rogue had watched me, in that dream I'd stripped naked and slipped on the confection of lace. The bodice had dropped low over my breasts, hugging the curves so that the lacy swirls just barely covered my nipples, the lace falling in streamers down my legs, tantalizing with what it revealed and hid.

"Will you put it on?" Rogue asked, from just behind me.

In the dream he'd ordered me to and I'd obeyed, trembling with desire for more. It was notable that this time he asked. Maybe. No sign of the green silk sash either—the one for tying my wrists to the headboard. I knew full well that he'd sent the dream to me, knew every detail. Perhaps he didn't know I'd woken in such a state of arousal that I'd masturbated with his blazing visage in my mind, coming within moments.

"I really don't think so." But my voice trembled.

He stroked a hand down my arm. "It would greatly please me."

"It doesn't meet the criteria." I grasped at logical straws, alarmed at how much I wanted to please him. "One slip of those streamers of skirt and all my bits are publicly accessible. No way. There are no panties."

"No. No panties. But I can make a concession."

The gown shimmered and the skirt was full silk. No slits or see-through lace. From probably about the pubic bone down.

It would still cling to my torso and hips revealingly.

"More silk. Less lace. In fact—no lace."

He obliged and now the nightgown shimmered in all-translucent silk. It would still be low-cut as all hell, but at least I would be less exposed. The fabric was awfully thin, but he could touch me through the cotton nearly as easily.

"I suppose I can live with that," I allowed, hoping this wasn't a mistake.

"Agreed, with one condition."

Here it came.

"I want to see you in the nightgown as it originally was— only to look. Then I'll change it to this."

I stared fixedly at the gown, which now drifted back to its initial lacy, streamerish state. "Why torment yourself?"

He bushed my hair over my shoulder and traced the nape of my neck with a warm caress. "If I can't have you, I can at least look. And there are other benefits to finding ways to enjoy this privation you are determined to put us through."

"You could go elsewhere."

"Alas—that is not true."

"Why not?"

"Perhaps I simply don't wish to. Put on the gown as it is, lovely Gwynn. Let me see you," he coaxed, sending liquid pulls down my spine with each stroked of his hand on my nape.

I snatched up the gown, turned to face him and brandished it. "You better to hope to hell I don't regret this."

He held up his hands in mock surrender, smiling in vast amusement. "I don't have to hope. I'll make certain of it."

"Okay. I agree—*if* I can change into it behind the screen,

which means no peeking, and you change it when I ask you to."

"I need it in this form to see well enough to do the repairs on your wounds. Particularly Falcon's mark. After that, I'll change it when you say."

I agreed to that and went behind the screen, wondering where the hell my spine had gone. I found this charming and teasing Rogue ever so much more difficult to resist. Resolutely, trying very hard not to be the giddy bride on her wedding night, I yanked off the dress and slid on the nightgown.

It was heaven, fitting me perfectly, like a second skin of sex. I looked down at myself knowing what I'd see, what I'd already seen in that dream—my breasts, nearly naked, with the hard pink nipples pushing at the lace.

And marked with unsightly bruises and scabs. No wonder Rogue was so het up to fix me up.

I wouldn't be sorry, frankly, to lose the vestiges of Falcon's teeth, faint though they were. They still worried at me, a harsh reminder of a number of things I'd prefer to forget.

"My Gwynn—are you coming out?"

I sighed. Braced myself. Walked out.

He'd surrounded the bed with brightly lit candles—*all the better to see you with*—and lounged back against the headboard, clad only in his navy silk pajama trousers. The hungry wolf, indeed. His hair spilled over his naked chest and shoulders, a cape of night, and his eyes were the blue of that last moment of twilight before true darkness. They consumed me, ravenous, covetous.

Unaccountably, I blushed, the hot flush rising from my breasts to my cheeks.

"Turn around." His voice sounded gruff, nearly inhuman. "Slowly."

Though that hadn't really been part of the deal, I did, obliging him.

"Lift up your hair and do it again."

Mesmerized by the moment, I did, gathering up the heavy fall of my hair from the back of my neck, and raising it, my nipples high and tight against the lace. When I faced him again, he'd gone eerily still, a snake in the coiled moment before it strikes. I froze, as any prey animal will.

"Oh, devastating Gwynn," he finally breathed, coming to life again. "You undo me. Come to me."

I hesitated.

"Just for the healing," he offered, gentle, harmless. He stood up from the bed and gestured for me to lie on it. "Healing first."

I skirted him, sensing his amusement at my cowardice, and settled myself on the coverlet, resisting the urge to yank up the lace higher over my bosom. I tensed when Rogue climbed over me, straddling me without touching, on all fours. His hair slid down to tickle my exposed skin in sundry places.

"Hold on to the headboard."

"Why?"

He tsked. "So suspicious. I need you to hold still. Shall I tie you?"

Suddenly green silk ribbons appeared, wrapped around the carved slats of the bed, ends dangling invitingly. The sight of them drove a hot spike into my groin and I closed my eyes.

Rogue stroked my cheek. "You want me to."

I opened my eyes to find him studying me, inhaling me.

Seeing things in me I never wanted anyone to see. But it didn't matter that he accepted this about me, embraced it. I couldn't allow myself to be helpless with him. Maybe ever. "I can't."

"Not yet."

I didn't answer, but I couldn't look away.

He nodded, understanding. "Grasp the headboard then. And hold still."

I reached up and held on, willing myself to be still. This, too, had been part of my lessons. I possessed a self-control my previous self would have envied. Never mind the price to my sanity.

With a mischievous glint in his eyes, Rogue sucked a finger into his mouth and set it on one of the bruises. I steeled myself from responding to the touch, clamping down on a moan of pleasure. One after another, he erased the scabs and bruises, as if Photoshopping me. Each time he touched my skin, it was as if an electric spark passed between us. My whole body throbbed for more.

For the last, he cupped my left breast, eyes unfocused and intent. My flesh tingled, rousing to his magic moving deep in the tissues, bringing them to snapping life. His thumb passed over my excruciatingly tight nipple and I couldn't hold back my moaning response.

"There." He said it quietly, with satisfaction and a hint of something deeper. He met my eyes. "Perfect."

"If you can heal, why didn't you do it before, back at your castle. Why did you bring in Lady Healer?"

"It's not my forte." He trailed a hand down my waist, his gaze following. "I can only do small things."

"Who knew there were limits to your many powers?"

With a rueful smile, he caressed my hip. "Lately it seems there are too many limits."

His hand touched my naked thigh, where a barely-there streamer had fallen away. My sex pulsed, hot and desperate to be touched. Dangerous.

"Change the gown. Now."

He smiled, but didn't move. His fingers were no longer hot on my skin, however, but were shielded by the slight barrier of silk. "As you wish, my Gwynn. The fabric is not as soft as your skin, but I can feel you through it. Touch you as I wish. And now, let's have our kiss."

"Oh no." I whispered it, mainly to myself. He had me so on edge, I felt like I could come from just the touch of his lips.

"Oh yes." His hand moved on my thigh, sliding up. "I've been waiting for this moment since midnight last night. That is my torment."

The little egg timer, absurd in its perkiness, appeared to hang in midair.

"And this, passionate Gwynn, is yours."

The timer flipped over and his mouth descended on mine.

His hand splayed over my sex, pushing the fragile silk into my folds and drenching it instantly. I cried out and he drank it in, deftly stoking my arousal to unbearable heights. Knowing full well he could touch me all night if he desired, I gave myself up to it, drowning in the kiss, spreading my thighs so he could push those long, silk-sheathed fingers into me.

With a skull-shattering crash, I climaxed, even in my frenzy of desire, careful to feed it back into him. No lightning. No wayward magic.

Only the ferocious outpouring of longing I could not allow

myself to release in any other way.

He drank my cries of pleasure like a man dying of thirst, coaxing out every last drop as the final sands slipped to signal time over.

₷⁊₷

IN THE MORNING, he was gone when I awoke. I should have been relieved, but found I kind of missed him. I might have touched the sheets to feel for his warmth. At least I was able to use my magic chamber pot in peace and pull a robe over my stained nightgown before Starling saw it and got ideas.

Oddly, Rogue hadn't pressed me for more, following our interlude. He'd simply doused the candles with a thought and bid me to sleep well, stroking my hair until I fell asleep.

And now I started to feel selfish for not returning the pleasure he gave me. Which felt all twisted and wrong, because I hadn't asked for this, or for him to be exclusive to me. I supposed that was why I was willing to put on that sexy gown and let him look. Throw the guy a bone or something. Nothing to do with the fact that no one had ever looked at me with that kind of desire. It was a heady thing.

I hadn't missed, though, that he said that perhaps he didn't wish to go elsewhere. "Perhaps," indeed. Somehow that, along with that tantalizing remark about being enslaved to me, made me think he didn't have much choice either.

Automatically, I drifted over to my workbench to record some of these very interesting findings but was thwarted by the empty space. Oh, right.

"Everything is packed." Starling said, bustling cheerfully in.

"The horses are ready and your riding habit is laid out there. As soon as you change, I'll pack up your nightclothes and we can get going!"

I glanced at Rogue's massive bed.

"Oh, Lord Rogue said he'd take care of that."

Ha. I was just sure he would.

"He'll meet us tonight."

"Are we camping? Or staying somewhere?" Snuggling with Rogue in the equivalent of the Faerie sleeping bag might be a little much for my steadily eroding self-control.

Starling shrugged and handed me my hairbrush. "I don't know. Larch has the direction. Apparently Lord Rogue has something for you to see. Do you want me to braid your hair or will you leave it loose?"

I took the brush and obediently set to work. "I'll leave it loose. How did, um, Rogue seem this morning?"

"*Seem?*" she teased me. "He seemed his usual imperious, irritable self. You, however, you *seem* all kinds of satisfied and happy."

I threw the hairbrush at her and she caught it neatly.

"Except for that lingering bit of temper," she remarked.

I quickly changed clothes into the emerald green riding habit that was part of the original wardrobe Blackbird and Starling had outfitted me with. Attempts to poof away the nightgown got me as far as I had with the earrings—absolutely nowhere. How he managed to make this stuff resistant to my magic was a mystery. And something I would really love to know how to do.

Instead, I folded up the gown inside the robe and handed it to Starling in a pile neat enough that hopefully she wouldn't feel the need to redo it.

I looked all satisfied and happy, huh? Go figure.

Outside the tent, they all waited for me. And by *all*, I mean Felicity, with Darling perched atop his riding pad, tail high with anticipation, fat mice rolling in his thoughts, plus Starling, Larch, and about forty human soldiers mounted on horses too, and a solid contingent of Brownies and dragonfly girls, all on foot. Never mind the baggage train.

"Geez—suddenly I have a massive entourage?"

"Lord Rogue provides for your protection, Lady Sorceress," Larch informed me in a formal tone. I glanced over the ranks of human men and saw that Officer Liam led them. He saluted me but did not meet my eyes. Was this some new game of Rogue's? Time would tell on that. "And here is the item my lady sorceress requested."

Larch handed me a velvet bag. I knew from the feel of it that it must be the dragon's blood. It almost pulled on my magic, the way endothermic reactions create cold by drawing energy from the substrate around them. I wished a deep pocket into my skirt and tucked it in there.

"Ever efficient, Larch." I studied him. "Did you take something for yourself?"

I swore he flushed, which looked odd on blueberry skin. He purpled.

"I did, my lady sorceress. Would you like to see?"

"Not necessarily. I'm just curious what the stolid and serious Larch would take from that great collage of knickknacks."

He didn't tease well. Just glowered at me, brows furrowed while he dug in his little tunic. The thing fit closely enough over his little round body that I would have said he carried nothing. But he fished out an object bigger than his fist and held it up for me to see. One of those jeweled pear thingies. There had been a number of them, piled in a cauldron. They were pretty, but it surprised me that the practical Brownie had selected something so…frivolous.

"A gift for a pretty Brownie back home?"

He cocked his head at me. "She would have to be lovely indeed, to rate a dragon's egg."

I peered at it. "Is that a euphemism or can this actually hatch a dragon?" It didn't look organic in the least. Of course, dragons seemed the exception to many of the magical rules, so what did I know?

"Whether it hatches or no is up to the bearer, the legends say."

"And you're going to take a crack at it." I grinned at him. "I love that."

He shuffled his feet.

"I have more, right?"

"Yes, my lady sorceress—three more."

"When you get a chance, would you get one out for me? I want to experi—play with it."

He bowed.

I swung up into Felicity's simple saddle, suffering grumbles from Darling about being crowded and the nasty bag smelling like ass. A fine comment from someone who regularly licked his, I thought back at him, which shut him up. But I also added a buffer envelope of air around the bag.

"Lady Gwynn!" Puck managed to make his somewhat hasty arrival seem like a grand entrance. "You've forgotten something important." With a wink and a shuffle step, he affixed a set of bells to Felicity's mane. She shook her head and they jingled merrily. "So you won't forget to find the joy, also. I shall miss you, my brilliantly powerful sorceress."

"Why don't you come with us?" I asked on impulse.

His cheerful expression crumpled like celadon tissue paper in the rain. "Alas, I cannot."

"Why stay with Falcon? You can't possibly like him."

Puck tossed his strawberry blond curls, using the movement to see if anyone was close enough to have overheard, then produced a sunny smile. "I can't possibly leave the war! So much glamour and excitement! You go. Success in your quest, Lady Sorceress."

He danced off, singing a song about pigs in the rain. Everyone watched me expectantly.

"All right, let's head out then."

My word their command, everyone sprang into motion and we rode away from the war camp and the sea.

PART 11

EARLY FAILURES

CHAPTER 8

THE CRYSTAL CAVE

*Fairy stories tend to leave one with the impression that travel
between the realms is solely the provenance of the fairies—
but is that truly the case?*
~*Big Book of Fairyland*, "Magic"

I ENJOYED THE ride more than I had any others up to this
point. I noted everything with an eye for sorting out this
strange land, wishing up a little notepad to write on. Starling
shook her head at me when she saw it, but remarked that at
least it kept me from asking her questions about everything,
which was likely true. Instead she wisely used her time to flirt
with some of the human soldiers, who seemed to find her
quite attractive. Not Liam—he remained stoic, with an alert
eye on the countryside. He might avoid being in my company,
but he never failed in his duty.

Darling, at least, provided interesting commentary, sending me images of what could be stalked, chased or eaten—
usually all three, in that order—in the various meadows and
copses we passed. Some of the creatures he pictured looked

exactly like familiar rodents, others like something out of anime, badly drawn with complete disregard for the laws of bilateral symmetry.

Never any birds though.

We rode along at a fairly good clip, Larch and the other Brownies jogging alongside and the dragonfly girls doing this kind of skipping/dancing movement that moved them inexplicably along at the same speed.

In the dazzling sunshine, Faerie appeared to be a landscape of such improbable beauty and iridescent colors that it seemed to be something created in a Disney film—and then brutally twisted sideways. I half expected elephants in pink tutus to pirouette past, though I fortunately possessed enough control now that they didn't pop into sight from my visualizing.

Some of the hills and fields looked as civilized as the English countryside, which made no sense, since there were no farms. No settlements of any kind, as far as the eye could see, though Liam had mentioned there were human villages somewhere. I'd ask him about it, but I felt sure he wouldn't be wanting to chat.

I was no ecologist, but I'd had to study the basics. Nothing about the landscape we traveled through followed the ecological laws. Apparently wild forests dripped with bright, heavy fruit or panicles of iridescent blossoms suited to tropical climes then gave way to groomed lawns with no border succession areas between. Lakes were crystal clear or bright blue, never swampy or remotely oligotrophic. Simply put, the ecology should not be sustainable. So why was it?

Once I was even certain I spotted a stream flowing uphill, but when I wanted to ride closer to see it, everyone protested about being late to meet Rogue.

We moved at a pretty good clip, away from the flatter coastal lands and into rockier foothills. When we stopped at midday, Larch gave me some traveling biscuits—like having cookies for lunch—and we remounted without much delay. Toward late afternoon we reached a glen nestled at the foot of some craggy hills and the group, as one, began to set up camp just as a gentle rain started to fall.

Of course, I didn't get a job. Lady of leisure and all that. One thing I'd learned was not to get in the way. So, since there was no sign of Rogue yet, I grabbed my grimoire from the bags and found a relatively dry spot under a tree. Starling hastened up, handed me my cloak to keep me warm and dry, along with a little velvety pouch. Then, seeming terribly busy, she dashed off again.

I tucked my cloak and skirts around me and pulled a dragon's egg out of the pouch. Larch never missed a beat. It filled my palm, glittering with intricate facets and colors, a fae Fabergé egg. But, now that I examined it closely, it became clear that this was not something created by human—or inhuman—hands. The spirals and hash marks marched across the surface with the internal precision of a nautilus shell. If I measured them, I'd bet they'd follow the proportions of the Golden Rectangle. Which meant, more like the natural world whose laws I understood than the sideways tangents of Faerie.

Unlike the eggs I knew of, however, this one did have a distinct pear shape, bulging more at one end than the other. As far as I recalled, eggs were always spherical or ovoid, never uneven. Likely that came from them being soft and watery when laid, so the rules of surface tension applied. Perhaps this egg was already hardened when produced?

I focused on the metallic shell, then dipped into it, feeling for life. The odd deadness of it to my mind reminded me of the dragon's blood. Not surprising. Still, it neither repelled nor drew the magic energy in me—aside from that cool, endothermic quality. In some ways, it was almost as if it didn't exist to my magical senses. If I set it on the grass next to me and closed my eyes, I couldn't detect it at all. When I held it cupped in my palm, my mind registered the weight and feel, but with my eyes closed, I could no longer remember exactly what it looked like. Interesting.

When a long-fingered hand dropped on my shoulder, I started almost out of my skin and very nearly dropped the egg.

Rogue knelt on one knee next to me, sleek as a cobra, shining with raindrops. He slid the sphere from my unresisting fingers. The eyebrow on the clear side of his face arched, Rogue held it up to the misty light, turning it to see the raised lines shimmer with prismatic color.

"Where did you get this?" His dark blue eyes glittered like mica as they ran over my face and I felt uneasy.

"I don't know—it was in my tribute stuff."

"A grand tribute indeed. Be careful who you accept gifts from."

"How can I when this stuff just appears? I don't mind giving it back, if I knew who to return it to. It's not as if these things come with gift tags."

Rogue inclined his head, black hair gleaming with cobalt and silver highlights in the rain, and moved to hand it back to me. I raised my hand and he laid it in my palm, wrapping my fingers around it. "Just...be careful."

"Thanks for that ominously vague warning."

The egg felt curiously much warmer now, more than simple contact with Rogue's skin should have made it. I tucked it back in the velvet carrying pouch and pushed it into my pocket with the vial of dragon's blood, wondering if I should mention I had that too. For some reason, I didn't want to. It remained one of my few secret weapons. A girl needed to keep something in reserve. Just in case.

Besides, the blood hadn't been a gift. I'd extracted it myself and so I should carry no obligations for it.

"Are you ready?" He stood, offering me a hand up.

"For what—new lesson?"

"Yes. Something you'll enjoy. Walk with me."

I left the grimoire sitting under the tree, knowing someone would pick it up and put it with my things. How did I ever live without an army of servants? One wondered.

We climbed the muddy trail up the hill, the trees dripping in counterpoint to the greeting rain, the air filled with pine resin, moss and petrichor. The misty weather colored all the world in sage greens and sliding grays of liquid mercury, so the raven silhouette of Rogue's long back cloak stood in sharp relief. He moved easily, striding up the hill on long legs. I straggled ungracefully behind on the narrow path. What I wouldn't have given for my Levi's and Keens at that moment. The cute little riding boots were definitely NOT for hiking.

Fix it, dummy. Taking a moment, I paused, concentrating, and wished the riding gown and boots into a neat pile beside my grimoire under the tree—Starling would be pleased I'd thought to save them—and replaced them with my favorite pair of old jeans, a sweatshirt and my lime-green Keens. That kind of swap-out is a little tricky, requiring attention to detail and a deliberate disregard for the conservation of mass, but I pulled it off. I wiggled my toes in the comfortable shoes. The sight of my old-world clothes in this landscape made me giggle. Find the joy, indeed.

I caught up to Rogue, who stood on a bit of level moss in front of a cave. He looked me over, eyes alight with interest, focusing on my hips and thighs.

"Most alluring," he commented.

"The cowboys always thought so."

He snorted out a laugh, making me wonder what image he'd gotten from my quip. I'd meant more as a general thing, cowboys liking girls in jeans, not me in particular.

With a courtly wave of his hand, he gestured for me to go in. Now, I was from mountain country where one just didn't wander into inviting dark caves unless you were really excited to see a grizzly or cougar up close and personal.

"Afraid?"

"Justifiably cautious."

He chuckled and preceded me into the cave. I followed close behind, suppressing the urge to wind my fingers into the back of his cloak. I clutched my own instead. The meager light from outside barely filtered in, then diminished into black as we turned a corner.

"Hold on to my cloak," Rogue said quietly, "unless those cat's eyes of yours see in the dark."

I wished. Rogue's cloak, though damp, felt soft as angora in my hands. Only the rain clinging to it kept me from burrowing in. We walked for some while this way. I'd always been terrible at judging the passage of time, but it seemed we walked for ten or fifteen minutes. How Rogue could keep us from clonking into a rock wall I didn't know. The cave was completely lightless. More of that magic vision, most likely.

Rogue finally slowed, then stopped. We stood in the lightless space. Just as I was about to make a smart remark about how incredibly *uninteresting* this was, the room came ablaze.

"Ack!" I covered my eyes, cringing from the sudden onslaught. My eyes adjusted, slowly, to the crash of bright light. We stood in a chamber about as big as my tent but entirely rimmed with crystal. It was as if we stood inside an enormous, diamond-bright geode. Light shards ricocheted and repeated, mirroring and amplifying.

"It's like Merlin's cave," I whispered in awe.

"He uses it from time to time," Rogue answered.

I narrowed my eyes at him, unsure if he was teasing me. He returned my gaze with bland indifference. Maybe we weren't talking about the same person. Who knew how that translated?

"Where's the original source of the light?"

He shrugged out of his cloak and tossed it on a rock outcropping just outside the entrance, a lightless and narrow opening in the blazing radiance of the cave. "Does it matter? It's a good place for focusing and intensifying magic. Crucial for certain kinds of magic."

"Like what?"

"Do you want to discuss or learn?"

"Both."

Rogue tipped the hood off my head, running a hand over my hair in affection. "Take off your cloak. We'll be here for a bit."

Obediently I draped my cloak next to Rogue's. He settled himself into a smooth glassy spot on the floor and gestured me to sit opposite. I plopped down with far less grace, cross-legged, as we did in elementary school, ever so grateful I'd changed into the Levi's. Rogue raised that supercilious eyebrow but refrained from commenting.

The crystal we sat on echoed infinitely clear, with facets running deep within. It reminded me of being on a glass-bottom boat, only instead of fish, below us stretched what seemed to be endless depths of shining crystal. Was the entire inside of the small mountain made of it?

Rogue watched me, navy-dark eyes somehow just as brilliant as the blazing crystal around him. He held out a hand, so I scooted closer to lay mine in his. He tugged a bit, so I got closer, until our knees touched. Or more precisely, my knees lay over his lower legs, which lay flat against the floor, flexible as any yogi. I had become accustomed to the inhuman length of the fae's limbs and noted it far less, until something jarred me—like Rogue's knees extending a good half a foot on either side of mine. It seemed almost insectile.

"It would be better if we held both hands," he said with careful quiet and I could understand why. Now that we sat in the middle of the domed room, his voice amplified, running over the crystal and returning in echoing murmurs. "Can I have a two-hand dispensation for this room only?"

"Okay," I agreed, only realizing when I saw the flash in his eyes that I'd been too dazzled to remember to limit the time frame. I gave myself a swift mental kick and gave Rogue my other hand.

"Close your eyes." The cave whispered the words back at

me. "Quiet your mind."

I allowed my eyes to close, shutting out the fantastic prismatic radiance. And found Rogue in my head. Startled, I nearly opened my eyes again, but he soothed me, almost like a hand against my cheek.

"I will show you three things, curious Gwynn. Pay attention."

He rarely spoke directly mind-to-mind. In this chamber, though, I imagined we were sealed in, the mental energy reverberating back as the sourceless light did. Funny, too—I'd long become accustomed to his habit of prefacing the name he'd given me with various adjectives. Hearing it directly from his thoughts, it became more clear that these words were simply my interpretation. I'd never quite understood why he picked "Gwynn" except that it was an old Celtic variation of my name. But it was me who put that spin on it. Rogue simply called me "you," colored with however he was thinking of me.

"True. You named yourself, clever Gwynn. I simply gave voice to it."

I did feel clever. My mind, Rogue's thoughts, it all seemed defined and clear. I felt smarter than I had in years, as if my brain were twenty years old again, full of fresh neurons and infinite capacity.

"That's the crystal—it intensifies and clarifies thought."

So cool.

"Create something."

"Anything?"

"Something you like. You'll have it for a long time."

Excitement thrilled through me. He was showing me how to make a permanent spell! What should I make? Damn, the performance pressure was killing me. I knew there had to be things I really wanted to keep around, but I couldn't think of any of them right that second.

"*Something. Anything.*" He mentally yawned. "*You will have other opportunities.*"

Right, right, right. Umm. Okay. I took a piece of my sweatshirt and wished it into a little gold horseshoe. Why? I didn't know. Thinking about cowboys and ol' Wyoming, I supposed. It lay next to us on the smooth glass floor, shining in my mind.

"*Now hold it in your head. The shape, the feel. How it's infused with your magic.*"

"Okay."

"*Good. Now feel how the crystal is echoing your magic—how it's bouncing back to you, only more clear, more sharp, more lasting?*"

"*I do!*" I wanted to gush about it, but he mentally winced so I hauled it back. Quiet.

"*Better. Layer that in. Just add...more.*"

He kind of shrugged but I followed his meaning. I poured more in, layering the magic into the little horseshoe, like electroplating tungsten probes for neurophysiological experiments. Feeling full of power as endless as the echoing crystal layers, I crammed more into the gold, making it dense and full.

"*Stopstopstop!*" But Rogue was laughing.

In chagrin I pulled back. The poor little horseshoe shone with a beacon of magic. Like a cockroach, it would likely outlast a nuclear blast now.

"*That's the first thing. Follow my mind for the second.*"

He wrapped himself around me and I rode with him. We rose up, toward the cavernous crystal ceiling and into it. I looked down to see our bodies, hands clasped, far below and felt a pang of fear.

"No. You are safe. I will take care of you, sweet Gwynn. Never fear. And never look back."

Lots of old stories about that kind of thing—Lot's wife, Orpheus, the guy in the movie who just *had* to look down while crossing the dissolving rope bridge over the chasm while cannibals raged at his heels.

Always good to pay attention to the cautionary tales.

Disembodied, we flew over to the camp, looking for all the world now as if it had been there for weeks instead of hours. Smoke billowed from damp wood, but the fires sparked merrily and my entourage all seemed to be happily eating and dancing—the former for the soldiers' side and the latter for the fae side.

"Pick someone."

"For what?"

"One of your experiments."

That gave me pause. *"You don't just experiment on living beings, especially sentient ones. Even a lab animal I wouldn't sacrifice without a strong purpose and a clear experimental design."*

His exasperation washed over me, tinged with impatience. I refused to apologize. I might be slowly losing my humanity, becoming some cat monster, but I wouldn't willingly throw all ethics to the wind. Particularly ones ground into me by NIH.

"Pick someone or I will." His mental voice was metallic. Tasted like it too. *"You must learn that this is a different place. Your cultural ethics don't apply. The lower orders of fae are numerous because they are mortal and expendable. Easily replaced."*

"How can life mean so little to you people?"

"I would ask you why you think it should have meaning. Never

mind—*charming as it is to debate with you, this is not the time. I promise no harm. Just a minor mental change, so you can see how it's done. In case you decide your own mortality is more important than someone else's."*

"Fine." I mentally pointed at one of the dragonfly girls, a particularly silly one with powder-blue ringlets. *"Make her smarter."*

He seemed surprised, amused arrogance flickering through his thoughts while he contemplated. Likely he'd only played this game to make people dumber or more obedient—as he'd probably done with those uncanny drudge servants in his castle.

"Not the same thing at all." He sounded a little absent now. Only half paying attention. *"It is you who should be paying attention. Watch."*

We descended into the girl's...presence. That was the only way I could think of it. Almost a magical representation of her. That echo of herself on this other plane of existence, the one where the dragon's egg did not exist.

Rogue formed a thought and showed me, the girl being alert and interested, absorbing information. He kept it very low-key, just a smidge of amplified energy, and fed it into her, a gentle shower.

"That's as light as I'm capable of. Satisfactory?"

"Yes."

"Now you do it."

He guided my mental "hands," showing me how to layer in just a hint more. I wished her good memory and critical thinking skills. *May they serve her well.*

"That's part two. Now for three."

"Is this mental travel gig how you poof yourself about the countryside?"

His dry amusement rippled around me. *"Something like it."*

"Do I get to learn that?"

"Maybe someday, once I'm certain you won't accidentally knock yourself out of existence."

Yeah. That would suck. Maybe I'd emulate Dr. McCoy and stick to shuttlecraft.

We spiraled up, high into the misty twilight sky, into the looming clouds and then into deep darkness. Abruptly I became aware of sensory deprivation—no light, no sound, nothingness. I flailed in panic and Rogue caught me, wrapping tight.

"I'm here, I'm here, I'm here." He chanted it in my mind, folding tendrils of his presence around me, much as I'd layered my magic into that little horseshoe. It steadied me.

Then we burst into light and reality again.

Different entirely. I no longer seemed to float above, observing my fae companions. Instead, I was walking through a pine forest again, but not the one on the hillside around the camp and the cave. This one smelled dry. Normal colors, nothing intensely surreal. My world.

Through the bright, high-altitude light filtering through the needles, Devils Tower loomed above. Rogue and I walked hand in hand on the path, just past where I'd left the trail that fateful day.

"Are we really in Wyoming?" My articulated thought spun away into nothingness. Though Rogue's presence still intertwined with mine, in much the same way as he walked beside me, long fingers interlaced with mine, we couldn't

communicate that way. It was as if I wore a puppet body, only looking through the eyes, hearing through the ears, but otherwise unable to affect the world.

Most disconcerting.

Then I saw myself—the old me. Strange to see myself as I had been then, with my dirty blond hair and tight expression. It seemed so long ago now that my petty problems had loomed so large. Breaking up with awful Clive, in retrospect, had been such an obvious, easy thing to do. But no—I couldn't do the easy thing.

I—I mean the old me—was walking briskly, glancing over her shoulder with fear on her face. I remembered that moment, feeling watched. Had I felt my own eyes upon me? The eternal conundrum of time travel, if that was truly what this was. The old me plunged off the path.

And there was the Black Dog, melting out of the deep shadows of the dark face of the tower. It had been there, all along—just as my inner alarms had warned.

Now I saw what had been invisible to me then, the shimmer of black-and-blue magic runneling down the deep grooves of rock, focusing through the Dog, a living lens, traveler between worlds. As the old me worked her ritual—one I could never have consciously known—the rays' fae magic connected her to the Dog, to the tower and beyond.

She swayed on her feet, and I wanted to reach out but could not. The Dog could. It moved in a flash, through and into her.

And they both were gone.

We shot up into the air, rising above Devils Tower, the early spring country spreading below, still more brown than green. It suddenly hit me that Isabel would be in this time, very close to this place, and I struggled in Rogue's folds, trying to tell him about my cat. He resisted, holding tighter.

"Isabel!" I shouted it into our combined minds.

But he didn't listen, just clamped tight and plunged us into blackness.

I mourned all over again. My heart broke a little more for this one foolish connection. Something Rogue could never understand when he dismissed even most fae as worthless and expendable. What would one nonsentient cat matter? Not at all.

Except to me. And to her.

Back in my body, I opened my eyes to the welcome blaze of crystalline light and yanked my hands out of Rogue's grip.

He'd reached mad ahead of me, though, glaring at me from under lowered brows, the snaking black lines on the left side of his face sharp and full of thorns.

"Do you have *any* idea what would have happened to you if you'd managed to break away from me?" His voice hissed back in sibilant echoes, building uncomfortably though he'd kept it low.

"Of course I don't!" My clenched tones wound with his, reverberating. "Do you have any idea what it is to love someone who's dependent on you? A creature totally vulnerable to the world, who implicitly trusts the promise you gave her that you'd care for her? And then to know that you abandoned that trust, however unwillingly? This is not an idle whim for me, Rogue. If there is any chance at all that I can rescue her, I want it."

He raked a hand through his hair, beyond aggravated with

me. "I can't replace everything you've lost."

"I'm not asking you to. I'll do it myself." I folded my arms. "I want to go back. Show me how to get back there."

"Absolutely not." Louder now.

"Then I'll do it on my own."

"I showed you a fraction of what you need to know to cross the Veil. You may or may not have noticed, foolish Gwynn, that not even I was physically present. How in the name of Titania's cursed womb do you imagine you'd bring something *physical* back through—especially a living being?"

I cringed at the decibel level, but he just glowered at me in righteous fury.

"The Dog could! Isn't that what you wanted to show me?"

He reached out to touch me. Dropped his hand and sighed.

"I thought to answer some of your questions, in a gesture of good faith, so that you'll understand both my part and yours in you being here. If I could give you this companion you so long for, don't you think I would? You think that because more things are possible than you knew before, that everything is possible. But it's not, my Gwynn. I promise you, it's not."

He sounded world-weary, an edge of defeat in his voice. What had he wanted that was simply not possible for the omnipotent Rogue? I leaned my elbows on my knees and studied the scuffed toes of my shoes, the knotted cords I'd faithfully reproduced from my last memory.

"I can't give up wanting this."

Now he did touch me, cupping my face in his hands so I had to look at him. "You are a passionate woman. Your wanting, the strength of it, makes you who you are. I would never change that. Just...have a care with how you go about satisfying it."

"You're not usually on the side of urging me to hold back."

The left side of his mouth quirked into a smile, the lines around it coiling. "The irony has not escaped me."

The little horseshoe winked golden next to me and I picked it up, stood, then offered Rogue a hand up, as he so often did for me.

He quirked an eyebrow, took my hand and uncoiled to his feet, watching me study the horseshoe.

"Where I come from, this is meant to be good luck."

"Is it?" A wealth of meaning in that simple question.

I shrugged, the earrings swinging from my earlobes, a not-so-gentle reminder of our connection. "So now I know how you make these stay on me—a kind of persistence spell."

"Yes."

"You always say you're mine as much as I am yours."

"Very well then," he replied, understanding the train of my thoughts. "I'm honored to be marked as yours."

The statement stirred me. I had never said anything like it to him and it occurred to me that it might bother him that I hadn't.

I pressed the horseshoe to his left earlobe—U-shape up, of course—wishing it to attach and drawing on the streaming crystal amplification to make it stay there. He moved under my touch and I thought perhaps it felt as sensual to him as it did to me.

When he opened his eyes to meet mine, they burned with feeling. That edgy, part-hopeful, part-desperate desire. The egg timer popped into the air next to us, which didn't surprise me in the least. Two-hand dispensation, after all.

He pulled me into his embrace, hands roaming over my body while he kissed me with long, gentle pulls of his lips. He cupped my bottom, palming my curves in the close-fitting jeans. For my part, I buried my hands in his hair, holding to the back of his neck and returning the kiss with a fervent longing that did surprise me. Where had this hunger come from, when I had been so angry with him?

I just couldn't think about it, any of it. Only touching and being touched made any sense.

Much too soon, he broke the kiss and pulled back, hands still on my body. I must have made a little sound of protest, because he cocked his head a little.

"Are you offering more than one kiss, delicious Gwynn?"

His dianthus-edge lips were dark and moist in light. The cave had amplified our desire for each other too, I realized. I throbbed for him and marveled at his self-control.

"I'd better not," I whispered.

Those lips twisted in a cynical half smile.

"Of course you think that." He shook his head but grinned. "For now, it's enough that you want this too."

CHAPTER 9

AT THE INN OF SEVEN MOONS

*Time slips between realms do not appear to follow any
mathematical progression I can determine. The worlds
appear to mesh randomly. Perhaps a chaos theoretician
would have insight.*

~Big Book of Fairyland, "Magic"

B Y THE TIME we made it back to camp, it had grown late
enough for all the human soldiers to be asleep. Starling
was waiting up for us but looked so bleary I sent her off to bed.
I had barely enough energy to gobble some sort of roasted
fowl before I began nodding off myself. Rogue explained that
the cave could do that—you felt supercharged while you were
in it, then drained after.

Part of the price you paid for its services.

I would have been fine with him leaving that part out.
Now I felt uncomfortably as if I'd been in the gullet of a
gorgeous, crystalline Venus flytrap. Rogue was tired enough
not to correct my image, which told you something right
there.

Consequently we slept with no further hanky-panky. Which was just as well as I didn't think my heart could withstand another onslaught. It was a bad sign that I couldn't stay mad at him. Lust I could withstand. This slow-growing regard for him…this craving to be with him…bad, bad, bad.

Worse, in the morning when I woke and he wasn't there, I missed him. Again. Still. Rogue had become my crack and I needed regular hits or…or what? *Nothing. Get up, get dressed, eat your breakfast, mount the horse.* Why Rogue couldn't be bothered to ride along with us, I didn't know. Too pedestrian, I supposed.

Starling muttered some caustic remarks about cranky sorceresses and, promising that lunch would put me in a better mood, left me to my own devices while she rode beside her new love-interest.

At least Darling kept me company, though he seemed uncommonly excited about the midday meal also. I mulled over what I'd learned the night before. More important, I wondered why he'd shown me so much, given me such powerful tools. To organize my thoughts, I made a little list of possible reasons.

1. Out of the goodness of his heart (ha!)
2. To equip me with skills to protect myself
3. To lull me into trusting him
4. To deceive me with partial information
5. All of the above

This was why multiple choice never worked. You could almost always make an argument for "all of the above." With a sigh I tucked my notepad in the pocket with the dragon's egg and vial. I'd think about it more after lunch. Which, it turned out, was waiting for us around the next bend. At a classically styled pub.

It could have been imported from the U.K., every stone and beam faithfully relocated and reassembled, just like the London Bridge moving to Arizona to span Lake Havasu. And with the same sort of startling dissonance.

The building sat in a curve of the road, as if it had been there hundreds of years, with posts for horses and extensive stables. A cottage garden thrived on one side, flowers nodding in the light breeze. The peaked gables likely housed cozy little rooms with fireplaces, and the wide doors stood open, inviting passersby into the common room. A young boy with coppery bright hair began pumping water for the horses.

Liam led the soldiers to the horse troughs, where they joked heartily, dismounting and edging the horses aside to splash their faces with water. Darling made a prodigious leap off his riding pad and daintily jumped onto the narrow rim, swiping at a horse that snorted at him. The dragonfly girls danced inside, giggling, and Larch stood at my stirrup, ready to help me down and take Felicity for her own refreshment.

"The Inn of Seven Moons," Starling told me, finger-combing her hair, her eyes bright and cheeks a becoming pink. "I love this place."

"You've been here before?"

She nodded with enthusiasm. "They brew the best lager this side of the Glass Mountains."

"These would be the same Glass Mountains where your mother was imprisoned by a dragon?"

Starling laughed. "Of course! It's not as if there are two sets of Glass Mountains."

"No—of course not. So what's on the other side of them?" I followed Starling into the cool interior, Darling trotting beside us, sniffing the air. The mullioned windows were thrown open to the lovely day, and window boxes of flowers in all shades of violet and crimson showed through. Starling made a big deal of picking the best table and held a chair for me. Darling settled himself at another, peering expectantly at the empty space of table in front of him.

"The other side of what?"

"The Glass Mountains."

She looked puzzled. "How would I know? Why do you think there's something on the other side?"

"Because," I explained, in my most patient tone, "you said this is the best lager on *this* side, which implies there's another lager—possibly even a better one—on the other side."

She pursed her lips and wrinkled her nose at me. "This is that critical thinking thing again, isn't it?"

"Pretty much, yes."

"Can't it just be good beer? Try it!"

One of the dragonfly girls—with a striking shade of hair a romance novel would call titian—set mugs in front of us and burst into a fit of giggles. The mugs were glass, white with frost, and foam spilled over the sides. Darling got a bowl of it, which he began lapping like milk.

Starling lifted hers and gave me an encouraging look with her wide brown eyes, waiting for me to lift mine. I did, tapping my mug to hers. "Happy days, as my grandmother would say."

Okay, the lager was delicious. Reminiscent of Harp, maybe, but with a deep resonance of flavor. They'd chilled it just enough to be refreshing, but not enough to kill any of the rounder notes. The scent, pleasantly yeasty with hints of cinnamon and something of chicory, filled my head along with the pleasant buzz of alcohol hitting my bloodstream on an empty stomach. Once again I'd managed to skip the most important meal of the day. Maybe that wasn't true in Faerie, since so much else wasn't.

"See?" Starling nodded, answering her own question. "Best ever—on either side of the Glass Mountains. So there!"

I drank deeply, savoring the lager that might, indeed, be the best ever. Another dragonfly girl brought us a basket of honest-to-god chips—the homemade style potato chips like the Welsh pub I frequented in college used to serve—and a vial of what could only be balsamic vinegar.

"You sprinkle the vinegar on the chips and—"

"Actually, I know the drill on this one."

Bemused, I dashed a little onto one chip and bit in. Absolutely, bizarrely, exactly right. Darling meowed impatiently and I gave him a little pile of his own. He did not want the vinegar, however.

"How long has this place been here?"

Starling shrugged, her mouth full of chips. "Forever, I guess."

We were the only ones in there. Liam and his men crowded onto long benches at one side of the room, while the Brownies and dragonfly girls sat mostly on the tables by the door. Everyone had chips and beer. No one else was in evidence.

"Who owns the place?"

"Oh, Mistress Nancy. You'll meet her when she brings out the bangers and mash."

"Bangers and mash. Really?"

"With applesauce. It's the—"

"Best ever," I finished with her and she beamed at me.

"So, where are the Glass Mountains from here?"

A dragonfly girl brought us new mugs, to replace our drained ones. She gave me a quizzical look and I noticed the powder-blue ringlets. Frowning, she seemed about to say something, but Starling spoke and she wandered off.

"I don't know. Past the Black Bogs, for sure. Somewhere near the Plain of Fire. Why are you wondering?"

"Everything I can learn about this world could be vital information."

She giggle-snorted into her beer. "I really don't think knowing where the Glass Mountains are could be vital to anyone."

"Knowledge is power."

"I thought power is power."

I parsed through the image I got from her, trying to decide if she'd used two different concepts that I received as the same word, but I didn't think so. "Knowledge is a way of gaining power then."

She pointed a finger at me. "No. Magic is a way of gaining power. That's the fast road to the top."

"Are you drunk? Already?"

"'S really good beer. Best ever." Starling stared dreamily into her mug. The soldiers laughed uproariously and broke into a drinking song. One of the dragonfly girls fell off the table and was upside down, giggling with her skirts over her head.

Larch appeared to be passed out with his face in a basket of chips. No sign of blue ringlets.

I felt fine and Darling seemed his usual self. He waved his tail in contentment and asked for more chips.

Sipping my beer—and empty stomach or no, it wasn't hitting me anywhere near as much as the others—I stretched out my thoughts, listening for what might be going on. It just felt wrong. Like some sort of ambush. Clearly Liam and his men were in no state to defend me, should something happen.

Some magic glittered here and there—mostly fixed spells of the kind Rogue could make and I couldn't. One tangled nest of magic carried an interesting signature I didn't recognize, but was almost mathematically constructed to convert heat to cold. Thus the unexpected refrigeration. So interesting.

Beyond the human men and Starling, who now had her mug upended over her face, waiting for the last few drops to run down, there seemed to be only two other minds in the vicinity and the thoughts of both were curiously obscure. Not muted like Rogue when he didn't want me to hear what he was thinking, but…almost like they were in another language? Which couldn't be right.

"Don't fret—none of them others can read my mind either."

The near-Cockney accent, speaking English, no less, started me out of my near trance. A cheerful woman stood next to the table with an enormous platter. I scooted our chips aside to make room for her to set it down. "Mistress Nancy, I presume?"

"The one and only. Welcome to the Inn of Seven Moons, dearie."

The advent of the promised bangers and mash sent increased excitement through the room, waking the sleepy and stimulating those in fits of hilarity to get serious about their plates. The dragonfly girls staggered only a little while bringing more platters and additional mugs of beer. Starling seized hers and took a deep drink, burping happily.

Meanwhile Nancy served me a generous plate, adding a dollop of enticing chunky applesauce.

"Now taste that and tell me if it's not just like home." She fixed me with a keen eye.

I speared a piece of sausage, swirled it in some of the gravied mashed potatoes and dipped it in the applesauce. She nodded at my technique, then grinned when I groaned at the flavor.

"This is amazing! It does taste totally authentic." I glanced around the place and sized her up again. "Everything here is. Why do I think there's a story?"

She chuckled and set her ample rear end in the chair next to me. "Where did you come though?"

The question didn't surprise me at all. Clearly she was several steps ahead of me.

"Devils Tower. Big rock monument in Wyoming, in the U.S. New world," I added, just in case.

"Your kitty want a sausage?"

"Undoubtedly."

She tossed a banger to Darling, who pinned it with one set of flexed claws and started enthusiastically gnawing on the end.

"What year was it when you left?"

"2012. You? And where did you come through?"

"1867. Time flies, don't it? And somewhere in the English

Channel. I tell you, dearie, I was ever so happy to wake up here instead of in my maker's arms. Got tossed overboard." She winked. "Never tell a drunk ship's mate that you're carrying his child. Doesn't go over well."

I remembered the boy out by the horse troughs and the thought electrified me. Surely he couldn't be the same kid.

"What happened to the child?"

"Oh he's hereabouts. Billy!"

The red-headed lad came racing into the room, covered in mud and carrying some kind of froglike creature—with eight legs. "What, Ma? Look what I found!"

But Nancy had her eyes on me, nodding as I assimilated the shock. "I should say time flies in some places. Not in others."

"You weren't surprised by my time."

"Nah. I heard tell of you and took a guess. Go on then, lad. Take that critter outside again. Last immigrant I met was 1927 and that was a while back, so I figured the next would be a jump. Tell me—do you all have ships that fly to the stars?"

"Who wants to go there?" Starling demanded, then hic-cupped. The soldiers must have finished their meal, because they once again broke into a drinking song.

"It's not important," I told her, raising an eyebrow when she gulped more beer to stop the hiccups. She grinned, foam on her lips. "We do," I answered Nancy, "but mainly to the moon and Mars."

"So, this isn't Mars then?" Nancy asked this so earnestly, with such urgency that I managed not to laugh out loud.

Starling listened with a puzzled frown. I could just imagine the images she might be getting.

"No. You thought maybe Faerie was on another planet?"

She made a face, sad now. "I remember hearing tell of such things. This place—I don't think it's connected to home, you know?"

"I do know."

"I thought maybe as the people come through who are smarter. You know, with more technology, you all might have more answers. That's why I arranged for you all to stop here—so I could ask."

"I suspect that the old stories your granny told were closer to the truth."

Nancy cast a jaundiced eye toward the Brownies and dragonfly girls, who'd now pushed the tables back so they could conduct an intricate, weaving dance while several Brownies played fiddle and pipe. "The Little People are real. Who'd have believed it?"

One of the soldiers Starling had been flirting with showed up at the table and, giggling, she accepted his offer of a dance and stumbled off to join in. Darling, however, stayed, to all appearances listening intently to our conversation.

"How did you do that—arrange for us to stop here?"

She winked at me with broad good humor. "I may not have been graced with a gift like yours when I landed here, but I have my ways. A gal learns to make careful bargains, yes? A little magic to make life easier. A little help to make a normal life for my boy."

"So—he's all human? Came over with you in the womb? And he's your firstborn?"

"Aye. Why should you ask such things?" But she didn't look puzzled. Instead she leaned forward, intrigued.

"Have any of the fae...courted you?"

She laughed, a hearty, booming sound. "No, dearie. They take a look at me and turn up their elegant noses." She patted her rounded belly. "None of them have wanted to plant another bairn in me, if that's what you're getting at."

"It is, yes."

Nodding sagely, she leaned in and lowered her voice. "I steer clear of politics and keep to myself and my inn—but I hear tell you're Lord Rogue's consort these days. I do hope you're watching yourself with that one."

I glanced at Darling, who blinked at me, smug, unhelpful.

"In what way?" I tried to keep the question neutral, so as not to bias such a good source of information.

Nancy cocked her head at my own belly. "If you end up in the family way, you might end up wishing yours had tossed you overboard, if you get my meaning."

"Can you be specific?"

"Do you want a tour, dearie? Of the kitchens and such like? I'll show you my little brewery too."

Okay then. I followed her into the kitchen while the others danced and drank. Darling trotted along at my heels, waving his tail with interest. I considered making him stay behind but he gave me an owlish glare and I figured he might as well know all my secrets. He was my Familiar, after all.

The kitchen astonished me, with all the fittings she'd managed to cobble together. A small room served as the refrigerator/freezer—cool on one end and icy on the other. "Magic, you know," she explained cheerfully. "This was my most expensive bargain, but well worth it."

"What did you trade for it—do you mind saying?"

"Oh, quite a few things. Let's just see." She strode over to a little desk under the kitchen window and opened a sort of ledger of accounts. In it were listed names, items and exchanges, marked complete or not. "They can't read, see. Had you figured that out?"

I was frankly surprised that she could and wondered who she'd been. Probably a housekeeper, with her management skills.

"Beer. Beer and food. Aha!" Her finger pinned the page. "Sixty-seven instances of beer and food for parties of no more than ten."

"That is expensive."

"This party—" she jerked her head at the revelry in the other room, "—is on the house for Lord Rogue. In exchange for the opportunity to meet you." She closed her accounts book with a snap. "Come see the brewery."

And here I'd contemplated what it was that Rogue did all day—apparently he got around. "They all seem unduly drunk on your beer."

Nancy widened her cornflower-blue eyes in innocence. "Such a surprise that my brew affects those with fairy blood differently that pure humans. How was I to know?"

"But the soldiers—aren't they human?"

She pressed her lips together and shook her head tightly. "More like us, yes, but never think it. The magic, it's a pestilence. It infects everything, after a time."

I might have imagined it, but for a moment her gaze touched on my temple and skittered away. The brewery equipment was housed in another building out back, taking us farther away from the others. "You should know, dearie. Lord

Rogue drove a hard bargain. He only agreed if I promised to tell you that you should have his child as soon as possible. So, here I am, telling you so." She nodded crisply, checking the obligation off in her mind.

I let the irritation burn a little, to clear my mind.

"But I have another story to tell you." She led me through the warren of tanks and supplies, pointing to things, as if explaining the brewing process, but speaking of something else entirely. "Some years back, when Billy was still toddling about, a grand lady stopped to stay the night with her party. She was nigh to bursting with child and said she traveled to her lord's castle, for the lie-in."

"The woman from 1927?"

"You're a smart cookie. You pay attention. I like that. Yes, Lady Cecily—cute thing she was. Saucy with it. Had a handmaid with her as you do. Nasty piece of work. Lady Incandescence. You know her?"

I did indeed. Though I usually thought of her as Nasty Tinker Bell. "And her lord—who was that?" I found myself hoping and praying that it wouldn't be Rogue. Please not Rogue.

"A Lord Fafnir—know of him?"

I breathed a sigh of relief and shook my head.

"Well, you wouldn't, given what happened."

At the dark warning in her voice, my stomach congealed. This would be the moment in the horror movie when I couldn't bear to watch. The dread became too much to face. "Tell me she lived."

Nancy pressed her lips together. "No, dearie. I'm sorry. You would have liked her too."

"What happened?" Feeling a little faint, I sat on a bench. Darling sprang up next to me and bumped his head under my hand.

"She went into labor early. I tried to help—I've done a bit of midwifing in my day—but that Incandescence locked me out of the room. Then Fafnir appears on my doorstep, sword in hand, and nearly tramples little Billy in his stampede to Cecily's room. I hear her screaming, begging him not to. Just bloodcurdling, I tell you, I—" She took a look at my face and stopped herself. "Well never you mind that bit.

"Next thing I know, all goes quiet. I mean, bad quiet. And them two come down with the baby all wrapped up in a blanket. I didn't stop them." Nancy shook her head, anger at herself written all over her.

"You couldn't have. And then Billy would have been or-phaned."

"Aye, so I tell myself. But that poor bairn. They take it out to the courtyard and the Queen Bi—You know who I mean? Yes, that one. She shows up. Bolts of lightning everywhere. Billy is wailing away, but that little baby never made a peep. She takes it up, pulls the blanket off and examines it. It's still bloody from its mama's womb. Then—maybe I should stop there."

"No." I buried my fingers in Darling's fur, the image of Titania holding the newborn in her cruel hands burning in my head. "I need to know this."

"Well, I wouldn't tell you otherwise. It's not a tale for idle telling."

"I understand."

"She looked that little baby over and then, well, her mouth got all big, like a gopher snake's will, and she swallowed it down. Whole."

I really hoped the food wouldn't come back up. I wiped my brow and found it clammy.

"You should know the rest." At my nod, she continued. "The queen then looks at Fafnir and Incandescence, all disappointed-like and says that the child was no good. Fafnir starts raging and she gives him this look. And then she melts him."

"Melts him?"

"Yes. Like he was a piece of ice in the sun."

"Good riddance."

"I thought so too. Then the queen, she tells Incandescence that it's Lord Rogue's turn to try now. That's the part I thought you should know."

I nodded, my throat tight. "And Cecily?"

"They'd cut her open. Left her to die like a gutted pig. Sorriest thing I ever saw."

We were both quiet for a bit.

"I appreciate you telling me." I finally managed.

Darling purred, comforting.

"That's why, when I heard you were Lord Rogue's consort, I thought I should tell you."

"I see."

"And one more thing."

I laughed a little bitter. "How can there be more?"

"An important thing. Cecily—she told me she was in love. That Fafnir had married her and desperately wanted this child. She couldn't wait to see him again. She was ever so happy."

The earrings clung to my ears, taunting me.

"I didn't stop what happened to Cecily. But maybe I can keep it from happening to you, Lady Gwynn."

CHAPTER 10

In Which I Return to the Scene of One Crime

୧ᐱᐟ

Rogue is somehow obligated to see this game through as much as I am, and he obeys the rules with utmost care. I often wonder who is on the other end of his strings.

~Big Book of Fairyland, "Rogue"

W E RODE OUT to Castle Brightness in a merry string of song and shouts of drunken glee. Except for me. I lagged behind the festive group, and Starling eventually gave up trying to tease information from me and moved up the line looking for more interesting company. Nothing could distract me from the image of Titania's jaw unhinging and that monstrous maw swallowing the newborn while Cecily lay upstairs, gutted by the sword of the man who'd sworn devotion.

The silver flash of Rogue's sword as he dueled with Liam stabbed through my thoughts, sickening my stomach.

It didn't help that the afternoon sun beat against my scalp, curdling into a headache. Maybe the beer had gotten me more than I thought. Magic creeping into my blood. A pestilence, Nancy had called it. Or a kind of radioactivity, mutating my genomes, changing me into something else.

And yet, Nancy remained immune in a way that I was not. Stolidly human and cheerfully unmagical. Why was I so vulnerable? Why had I been able to work magic—huge, potent magic—from the moment I arrived and not her or poor, doomed Cecily? Or perhaps since before that and I just hadn't known it. But I'd seen it, hadn't I? The blue sparkling magic running down the dark face of the tower and into me. My stomach shifted greasily. Whatever it was that connected me to Rogue, that led me to Devils Tower and those fateful steps that brought me here in the first place, it lurked within, as surely as the white claw of the cat that would likely tear me apart from the inside out.

If Rogue didn't kill me first.

In a few hours, I would see Rogue again. I'd have to kiss him, share his bed, keep to all our bargains, big and small. All the while wondering if Cecily's fate would eventually be mine.

I had no idea what I'd say to him.

Except I wanted the fucking earrings *off right now*.

I fought the urge to tear at them, knowing it would lead nowhere. Perhaps if I cut off the entire lobe? I would be like Van Gogh, cutting off my ear to send my lover, to express my great anguish. With as much effect, most likely. Still, the drama held a certain appeal.

For a while I tried reversing what I'd done in the cave, making the attachment un-permanent. But I couldn't dig my nails into it. What Rogue had put into place stayed neatly sealed, smooth as glass, far beyond my strength to reach.

He'd well and truly trapped me.

Darling leaned against my back, sending sleepy thoughts of affection—and the image of him, horse-sized, and me riding his back to glorious safety. The addition of Rogue running after and flailing his arms in the air made me smile.

"If only I could escape these ties that easily, Darling."

Felicity topped the rise and, though we'd been riding no more than an hour or two, it appeared that the company had decided upon naptime. The soldiers had doffed their packs and lolled in the shade of some trees. The Brownies and dragonfly girls had piled together like happy puppies and were already snoring musically. Starling had curled up in a tight little ball, cheek pillowed on her folded hands.

I would have griped about the apparent total lack of concern for me, the person they were all purportedly protecting, but the reason for their abandonment—and likely their sudden desire to sleep, stood waiting in the middle of the road, arms folded, black hair loose in a shining cape around him, dark blue eyes steady on me.

I reined up and Rogue took Felicity's bridle, holding up a hand to assist me down.

"Fancy meeting you here." I raised an eyebrow at him, declining to dismount for the moment.

"I'm not in the mood for games," he replied, cool and remote. "You and I need to talk."

"I thought you once said talk is the death of romance?"

He studied me and I quickly quieted my thoughts. Too late, it seemed.

"In this case, what you are already thinking can cause us a far deadlier wound. Get down, Gwynn."

Ignoring his hand, I did, taking a moment to straighten my skirts and brush them off—and plan my strategy. Darling leaped from his saddle pad to my shoulder, sinking in his claws and making me huff out a breath at his sudden weight. His teeth fastened on one of the dangling earrings, reminding me. Rogue narrowed his eyes at the cat in glittering threat.

"You want to talk?" I gave Rogue my sweetest smile. "I want these earrings off."

I'd surprised him with that. How interesting.

"After we talk, we'll discuss the earrings. They look so lovely on you, my Gwynn."

"Cut the crap, Rogue. I want them off and I want them off now. Nonnegotiable."

He tucked his hair behind his ear, letting the golden horse-shoe I'd affixed there wink in the afternoon sun.

"And will you take back your gift as well?"

"If you like. Fair's fair."

"Fine." He nodded once, in curt agreement and held out an imperious hand. "Come with me."

Unwilling to fight another battle just yet, I took his hand this time. Darling swiped a claw at him.

"You—" he pointed at Darling, "—are not invited."

Darling hissed.

"Control your Familiar, Lady Sorceress. If you can."

I mentally nudged Darling along and allowed Rogue to draw me into the woods. Okay, that was understating it. He practically dragged me and I stumbled after. Maybe I was still in a bit of emotional shock over Nancy's story, because I didn't really feel anger over his pisser of a mood or his snotty remarks about Darling.

In fact, I felt remote. Walled off. As I'd done back under Marquise and Scourge's torturous training. Really not charming at all if any emotional shock would send me reeling back into my mental PTSD cell.

It was protecting me, I supposed—and the world. For me, strong emotion had become high-octane gasoline. That deep subconscious training had likely kicked in, isolating my wishes from that explosive fuel, icing it down, separating the trigger from the dynamite. Maybe the rage in me had reached such a level of heat, then was forced down under extreme pressure, so that it had sublimated into another emotion entirely.

That explained the fine hissing sound in my ears. Steam escaping.

Rogue stopped suddenly, so that I nearly crashed into him. We stood at a break in the forest, a stream babbling past, golden sunshine pouring through the leaves to land on the emerald moss with sparkling motes of light. He pushed my back against a massive tree and raised our joined hands above my head, commanding my attention.

I observed the cracks in his composure with detached interest. Something vicious, nearly desperate roiled in him. His fingers drifted near my cheek, as if he wanted to cup it.

"I can't lose you now." He said the words more to himself than to me, but I answered anyway.

"You can't lose what you never had in the first place."

It was cruel, yes. I felt cruel saying it, a sharp claw, slicing. But I also couldn't shake the image of Cecily, her flapper's body splayed obscenely open, bleeding out while her lover strode away to sacrifice her infant to a monster. I wanted to take Fafnir and Incandescence apart with my bare hands. I struck at Rogue in their stead.

"You condemn me for a crime I didn't commit."

"Yet. If I waited for empirical evidence I might find myself shit out of luck to take precautionary steps."

"Had I known what that slattern intended to tell you…" Rogue's jaw clenched on the rest.

"What? You would have prevented me from knowing? You would keep me wrapped up, imprisoned and impregnated in happy ignorance so that I can't ruin all your carefully laid plans?"

"It would be infinitely easier," he snapped back. "Have you considered why I haven't done so?"

"All. The. Time."

The blue in his eyes seemed to boil and we stared at each other, forever at our impasse, never quite communicating what we needed to.

With a growl of frustration, Rogue gestured and the little egg timer, absurd in its perkiness, appeared to hang in midair. I glanced at it, shocked.

"You have got to be kidding."

"No. I'm not. I need this, so shut up."

I couldn't have spoken if I wanted to, because his mouth descended on mine, feral, demanding, full of that desperate seeking that had shot over his face like a night creature ducking the light of day. Though I thought I'd become accustomed to his kisses, this one affected me in a different way. The sheer heat of him thawed that icy shell that had clamped over me. With an animal cry of longing, I kissed him back, twining my fingers with his. I was utterly lost to him and he was the only one who didn't know it. If only it could work between us. I truly wished for that.

I didn't dare wish for that.

Carefully, I eased off the mental trigger and let those feelings flow away. *Be oh so careful what you wish for.*

The final grain of sand fell with an inaudible ping that nevertheless resonated through us both. Rogue pulled back just enough so that our lips no longer touched. He paused there, regaining his breath, gathering himself.

"I am not Fafnir," he finally said, so quietly that someone standing next to us would not have heard.

"But you play the same game."

His gaze flicked up to mine. "The game, as you call it, changes. I do not make the rules."

"I don't know what to believe." My words came out as a plea. "I'm not this person who just rolls with the magic and the pretty stories. I rely on facts, on empirical evidence. The past does not lie, and a keen observer of what has already occurred can reliably predict the future. Numbers add up. Demonstrable evidence leads to reliable hypotheses, which assemble into theories."

"Very little of what you just said made sense to me." He breathed out a laugh that fluttered over my lips. We'd stayed close, as if the physical proximity might bridge the gulf between us.

"That's because here, none of that is true. The physical laws of the universe I've always known no longer apply. I'm adrift, with no framework to base decisions on."

"Then trust me, doubting Gwynn. Give me that. Believe in that reality."

"How did you know what Mistress Nancy said to me?"

He leaned back a little, grimaced and lifted the hand he'd fisted against the tree beside my head, flicked one of the earrings.

"I thought so. You ask me to trust you, but you reveal your own lack of trust by spying on me. Forever trying to control me."

"Protecting you."

"So says every abuser that ever lived."

"The stakes are high. Far higher than you know."

"Then tell me."

"If only I could."

"Can you tell me why you can't?" This felt like playing Twenty Questions. I nearly asked "animal, vegetable or mineral?" Flip, but better than cruel. Asking him to play warmer or colder would be just asking for trouble.

Rogue considered the question, lowering our hands and rubbing mine with one thumb, thoughtfully. For the first time I considered that how he abided by these unknown rules was entirely up to him. I'd imagined some sort of geas that bound him from speaking, like the character who couldn't tell what happened, but could nod yes or no, or write it out.

Instead, he navigated his way through a complex set of regulations, perhaps accruing points here and losing them elsewhere. Every move that skirted a certain line put him in danger of losing. Though I often felt we were opposed—after all, he'd clearly told me that he was not my friend—I could most likely rely on his loss being mine also.

It was also tremendously likely, given the evidence, that my ignorance of the rules was one of the factors he dealt with. At least he gave me glimpses into what I didn't know, where

Fafnir had played it another way with poor, blissful Cecily.

I hadn't tried to keep these thoughts quiet and he watched my face, clearly listening. He didn't nod or tell me that I was warmer. But, deep inside, on this level where those coils between us intertwined, I knew.

It wasn't logical. I had no evidence to support it.

I had nothing else to go on.

"Fine." I stopped short of saying I'd trust him, but the tension shuddered out of him and he smiled, with just a trace of his usual insouciance. I thought he might embrace me, but he restrained himself. Always the utmost care to observe the boundaries I set. I wondered if Cecily had even known she could do that. In a way, Rogue himself had led me toward that understanding. That and my astonishing introduction to my own magic.

"Did you know that I would be a sorceress when I arrived here? I mean, I know you don't control the Dog, and he's the one who brought me through the Veil. Who showed me how to connect my subconscious wish for a different life to the power he brought with him. But if he's part of your subconscious, did you somehow direct him to find someone like me? Not a Nancy or a Cecily, but…"

"Gwynn." Rogue released my hand and stroked my cheek with long fingers. "You should know by now that I stack the deck whenever I can."

I laughed and laid my hand over his. "I do know that."

He sobered. "Do you still want the earrings off?"

"Yes."

To his credit, he did not flinch, but reached up and pulled them gently, one by one, from my earlobes. They released my flesh with a tingle of regret, a faint sigh of loss. I held out my hand, palm up, and he raised a sharp eyebrow, the thorns around it spiking.

"I'll keep them."

Bemused—how I loved to take him by surprise—he laid them in my hand, iridescent and lovely, glowing as blue as his midnight eyes.

"I'll be angry if you lose them," he warned, which told me this was a measure of trust from him. It might be taking me a while, but I was learning to understand his coded messages to me. I tucked them in my pocket, the bag holding the dragon's blood bumping my fingertips. Good thing I'd shielded that puppy or Rogue would surely have sensed it.

"I'll keep them close. And if I need you, I'll put them on again."

"Be sure to do that, my Gwynn. You are more vulnerable than you know."

I should have been chilled by his words, but the sheer delight in feeling that I'd cracked part of the puzzle—and that the PTSD had released its dreadful grip—gave me a bright and cheerful confidence.

Any scientist could tell you that this was always the sign of a false breakthrough. Those promising first results just never seemed to pan out.

I put my hand up to take back the horseshoe and he gripped my wrist. "Will you let me keep it, my Gwynn?"

"If that's what you want."

"I can think of only three things I want more."

OF COURSE HE wouldn't—or couldn't—tell me what the three things were, though I teased him about it as we walked. It turned out we were quite close to Castle Brightness. Which didn't seem possible, given what I thought I knew about the landscape, but I was going to have to give up some of my attachment to the physical laws that had governed my previous world. A leap of faith into the absurd had to be full immersion. No picking and choosing. Accept the precepts of the new working hypothesis. Anything less was counterproductive.

Rogue led me along the banks of the stream, assuring me the others would meet up with us. Gradually what appeared to be old-growth forest gave way to younger trees, and then to the ordered apple orchard I recognized as the one I'd seen from my room at the castle when I'd stayed there.

I pointed to the round fruits that hung glowing with rosy gold allure, heavy on the branches. "What do you call these fruits?"

Rogue barely glanced at them. "They're poisonous—don't touch them."

Astonished, I surveyed the rows upon rows of the trees, clearly tended, yielding a bountiful harvest. "Why grow poisonous fruit—and so much of it?"

He shrugged, uninterested. "I don't spend *my* time doing it. Blackbird comes from a strange family. They've long dabbled in odd practices."

"You don't wonder at all?"

Rogue snorted, squeezing our interlaced fingers. "You have more than enough curiosity to get us both destroyed, my Gwynn. I endeavor not to add to it."

"I thought you couldn't die."

"There are worse things that death."

A sudden thought occurred to me. "Is Fafnir still alive?"

He went deadly still. Without looking at me, he spoke. "I will say this once. Don't go there."

Funny how my mind translated the expression he used. It carried all the unutterable implications of a curse. Doomed all ye who enter here.

Without another word, he resumed walking through the idyllic grove of deadly fruit.

We emerged from the orchard to find Castle Brightness rearing above us, in all its alabaster gilded magnificence, colorful pennants flapping gaily in the breeze. Looking up, I spotted what had been my room and a frisson passed over me. I was circling back upon myself, it seemed and a small, endlessly terrified part of myself quailed at the thought that my prison might be next.

Rogue released my hand and pushed his under my hair to grasp the base of my neck, steadying me.

I nodded in answer to his unasked question and looped my hand through his arm for our grand entrance. Blackbird, along with her staff, waited for us with grand formality. They all sank into deep obeisances that likely said more about Rogue's status than mine. Still, I was struck by how much I'd come up in the world since my last visit. At least I looked a hell of a lot better, which was something.

"Greetings, Lord Rogue, Lady Sorceress Gwynn. You honor Castle Brightness with your presence." Blackbird looked the same as always, dark hair drawn back into a smooth knot, black eyes keen, hands folded neatly under her maternal bosom. I couldn't quite picture her as the sultry trophy princess languishing in a tower.

"It's good to see you too, Blackbird. Has everyone else arrived?" I felt blunt for asking, but it bothered me that none of the party was in sight.

"Oh yes, Starling is having a bit of a lie down. Lord Darling is, I believe, hunting mice." That seemed likely, as I recalled his penchant for the castle's fat and lazy rodent population. "And your servants are either preparing your suite or pitching in for the feast."

"The feast?" I echoed.

"Of course." She beamed at me. "To celebrate your betroth—" She cut herself off, though I didn't hear or feel Rogue warn her in anyway. Her thoughts skittered on insect legs and her gaze flicked to my empty earlobes and away again. "—surprise visit!"

"We're just here to talk."

"And talk we shall!" She clapped her hands as gaily as the pennants fluttered, and abruptly I saw through her elaborate dance. Fear resonated from her, a tuning fork of high emotion. "But for now, let's get you tucked in."

Her butler, a type of fae I hadn't seen before, led us to our rooms. He seemed to be a gray broomstick with a long head and spindly limbs. My fingers itched for my grimoire, or my lowly notepad, so I could add him to my list. But I was being polite and gracious Lady Arm Candy for the moment. A limiting role, indeed.

We could have found the rooms on our own, because the Brownie/dragonfly girl song echoed down the halls to nearly the front doors. The butler never spoke, simply gazed at us with cobwebby eyes and gestured to the grand brass double doors that led apparently to our suite.

"We're sharing?"

"Are you ashamed of our arrangement?"

"Some seem to think I should be."

"And you?"

"No, no—perish the thought."

The rooms, which seemed to go on and on with one sitting area leading to an opulent bedroom leading to a decadent bathing chamber, were full of life and spinning color as the Brownies and dragonfly girls made short work of the unpacking—despite the amazing volume of stuff. I explored while they worked, returning to the main sitting room to find Rogue sitting in a fussy chair, long legs splayed out. In a breath, all the servants disappeared, leaving us alone.

Uncertain what to do with myself, I stepped over to the windows that looked out over the front entrance, with the fanciful drawbridge crossing the sparkling moat and pointing to the winding road beyond. Rogue drew up beside me, gazing out the crystal mullioned panes, then tucked my hair behind my ear in an affectionately absent gesture and handed me a glass of wine.

He rarely seemed this relaxed. Perversely, it unsettled me. I knew where I stood with him as my opponent.

I probably needed to break this habit of thinking that any time it seemed that things were going his way, it boded ill for me. I sipped at the wine and grimaced. Way too sweet. Alas.

"Why does there *always* have to be a feast?" I complained.

He laughed and leaned against the window ledge, all enticing indolence. The sun set behind him, setting fire to the horizon in a display worthy of a sweeping soundtrack and a grand dramatic scene. Crimson and gold shone on his midnight black hair, lighting the unmarked right side of his face so that he looked like some noble prince, the marked side in shadow, so none of the dark fae lines that revealed his inner nature showed. The gold earring gleamed, a spot of light on the sinister face. For a moment I glimpsed him as he might have been before the Black Dog started growing in his heart.

Unaccountably moved, I laid my palm on that smooth, bright skin. He stilled, something vulnerable shadowing through the depths of his gaze. I rarely touched him of my own accord, and I wondered if his taunting me to do so was more than just goading. It might mask some sincere desire to be close to me. It would be lovely to think so.

My heart shifted, losing another layer of the cynical Teflon I'd tried to coat it with. I stroked his skin, breathing in that scent of mace.

He smiled, clearly amused by me. "Would you rather set up an interrogation, fierce Gwynn? Browbeat Blackbird into revealing her secrets?"

Rather than face another interminable feast? Why, yes. Yes, I would. "I suppose that would be rude. Why is she afraid?"

He raised an eyebrow at me. "She knows you come seeking her secrets. Wouldn't you be afraid?"

"No." I considered it. "I might be wary or defensive, but not afraid."

"Perhaps the consequences for revealing yours are not so heinous."

"Strong word."

"You must decide what is more important to you—your

goals or hers."

I didn't want to contemplate that much. I sighed, indulging myself by tracing his elegant ear, while I thought. No elfin spike, but his auricular helix twisted with intriguing other-worldly spirals, tempting me to taste them with my tongue. Would he shiver under my touch as I did with his? The visceral bond between us tightened, sending a darker thread of pleasure through my groin.

"Taste me and find out," he whispered.

I tsked. "Listening in?"

He didn't smile this time, just smoldered, a burning coal, the sunset colors gleaming sparks against his banked darkness. "I would know what you're thinking without reading your thoughts, passionate Gwynn. Did you think I don't pay attention to the way you look at me?"

"I didn't think I was that obvious." My mouth was dry.

"To me, you are like looking into a mirror. I see my desires reflected back. Magnified. Enhanced and sharpened. We could skip the feast, remain closeted in these rooms." He inhaled and whispered as he breathed out. "Wine and roses."

"Tonight will be soon enough."

"Will it?" He slid a hand against the small of my back, urging me closer. "What if something occurs to tear us apart before tonight? Or what if you continue to deny what we should share and then it's too late—will you forever regret not tasting the dark delights I offer you?"

I trailed a fingernail down the curve of his ear, behind to the velvety hollow beneath the lobe. "Playing the regret card? So far I haven't managed to shake you. I don't see it happening soon."

"Be careful what you wish for," he murmured, our lips a

breath apart. I knew he wouldn't strain our relationship by kissing me, but he tempted me to break my own rules. Each time he gave in, coaxed me into special dispensations, gave me fewer reasons to stand by them. *I can change the rules for this moment and then get them back into place.* But the victory that kept him from seducing me entirely had been hard-won. I'd tricked him—which was excessively difficult—and I was unlikely to do it ever again. Especially when it came to this arena.

Still.

I leaned in closer.

"I have *the* most splitting headache!" Starling declared from the other room, the level of her voice unlikely for a headache sufferer. I nearly fell into Rogue. Would have, if he hadn't steadied me with that firm grip on my waist. Starling rounded the corner. "Oops!"

She smiled an impish grin and curtseyed. "Excuse me, Lord Rogue. I didn't expect to find you here."

She was a terrible liar and I glared at her. She beamed innocently at me in return. "Mama—Lady Blackbird—sent me to ask if you require anything. And to see if you needed help getting cleaned up and dressed, which clearly you do, since you haven't done it yet."

"I'll just excuse myself, shall I? Since you insist on attending this feast, though I'd just as soon have meals sent up so we could stay...closeted." Rogue winked at me and slid a casual hand from my hip to my bottom. "I picked out a dress for you."

"I might not wear it."

He smiled knowingly. "Yes, you will."

CHAPTER II

In Which I Obtain a Clue

ቻ

The flora and fauna appear to be a conglomeration of the life forms recognizable from my world, that generally follow the same laws of form and function, and then wild variations that should be physically impossible. Certainly they do not seem to proceed from the same evolutionary path. It's as if natural law here has been subverted by another, more powerful, force.

~Big Book of Fairyland, "Rules of Magic"

S TARLING WATCHED HIM leave the room with a little lustful sigh.

"You are the worst lady—in-waiting ever."

She grinned at me. "I love you too, Gwynn."

I snorted, oddly flustered by her affectionate rejoinder. Or maybe by her knowing leer.

"It's lovely to see you two canoodling."

"I really don't want to know what image you had in your head for me to get the word that I did."

She giggled. "Was it dirty?"

"Are you still drunk?"

"Gah—maybe a little. That beer knocked me on my ass. Tell me, did I promise Officer Sean to meet him later?"

"I have no earthly idea. I was busy while you were canoodling."

She blanched. "Ooh—that *is* dirty. I most assuredly was not doing that!"

"Neither was I."

"You have to be either the most obstinate or the most disciplined woman in all the world."

"Possibly both," I agreed. "So? Bathing room, yes?"

"Bathing room, yes." She wrinkled her nose. "You smell more like Felicity than she does."

I followed her lead, realizing this whole quest wasn't about just me and my goals. Starling had a stake in this, and Nancy and poor perished Cecily. And perhaps all the other women— and fae—who'd been caught in this web. I figured I knew what fat spider I'd find perched in the center. I just needed to find ways to untangle her prey without bringing her down upon us.

꿎

ONCE I SAW the promised dress, I knew why Rogue was so certain I'd wear it. First of all, it wasn't black, as I'd been so certain he'd try to pull on me. And second—it was indescribably lovely. It seemed to be made of starlight and moonlight at once, formed of gauzy draping trails of cloth that shimmered and glittered. Starling couldn't speak for a full five minutes after seeing it. When she poured it over my head—because, duh, of course I wanted to wear it—it clung to my skin with light whispers.

No zippers or ties. Magic. Made especially for me.

Rogue's signature feral glow ran all through it, sensual and intimate.

Darling, who'd appeared early on in the process to loll on the edge of the sunken tub and sending me alternating thoughts of mermaids in bubble baths and mouse innards—a most disconcerting combination—approved of it, especially the dangly bits.

Starling let me leave my hair down, brushing it into a gleaming straight fall of black, agreeing that the contrast was striking. And that my hair helped cover up what the scandalous dress failed to. I ignored that last comment. The glory of magic made sure the dress clung to all the important bits and made me feel, wow, almost beautiful. It was the polar opposite of how Rogue had made me dress for my first feast and I knew that this, too, held a message.

We played a different game and in a different way now.

He confirmed it, waiting in the main room to escort me for dinner, wearing the same shades. I'd never seen him in anything but black and the contrast, the sheen of sliver threads, brought out the warm gold of his skin and unexpected shimmers of moonlight in his midnight eyes. The shirt he wore was so sheer that his lean chest showed through the cloth nearly as much as where it fell open.

He smiled at my approval and raised an eyebrow when I walked behind him. With one hand, I undid the jeweled clip he'd used to tie back his hair and let it fall free. I might have also indulged myself in stroking the thick silk of it, inhaling the scent of mace and man. I felt in harmony with him in a way we'd never before achieved.

Maybe he really was trying.

Or I was getting soft.

At the moment, I didn't care.

"I'm tempted to say we should stay in the rooms after all, but I want to show off my pretty dress."

"Alas, how my plan has backfired." He touched my cheek, a fleeting caress. "I'm pleased you like it."

"I do."

"Will you wear my earrings with it?"

The request did not surprise me. "Do you promise to take them off if I ask you to?"

"I promise," he returned gravely.

I fetched them from the table, where I'd tucked them in a little box that I'd wished locked to anyone but me. I had the dragon's blood safely hidden elsewhere. "See? High security measures."

He didn't comment, simply lifted the downward-turning lilies to my earlobes, his magic shivering through me as stimulating as his boldest touch. The little claws sank in with a brief flash of pain that settled into a wash of desire that made me gasp aloud. The left side of his mouth curved up in a half smile of satisfied pleasure.

"It makes you happy to see me wearing them."

His gaze moved from the jewel flowers and caught mine, intent, predatory. He paused so long I thought he wouldn't answer. "Yes."

The single word held a wealth of meaning. A meaning that made the cat deep inside stir, an answering wildness. I wanted to dig into him with my claws, nip him with my teeth.

"We'd better go."

"Indeed." He said the word in all blandness, but I felt the hum of excitement beneath.

We joined the feast in progress, seated together at the head of the table and feted like visiting royalty. Which I supposed we were. Unlike so many of the other events, this party was actually fun, with delicious food and performing acrobats. The other guests, who I presumed to be vassals of various kinds, lined the table. I still didn't quite understand the political structure.

I whispered to Rogue that Faerie Government and History 101 should be my next lesson.

"No," he replied, watching a trio of birdlike boys bend themselves into a complicated pretzel.

"Why not?"

"It's boring."

"Not to me—and they're my lessons."

He turned his gaze to me, amused. "I already have your lesson planned."

"Why does that sound kinky?"

He slid his palm along my thigh under the table. "We could do that too. I'm certain you'd be an apt pupil for some of the games I have in mind."

"No, thank you." I tried to sound prim, but my breath accelerated.

"You break my heart, cruel Gwynn."

"Or something lower," I retorted. "So what's the lesson?"

"Observe and learn, young student of mine."

He laid his hand palm up on the table, clearly expecting me to take it. As soon as I did, his magic began looping out of him, in great swirling waves of blue and black. I expected astonished comments, but no one else noticed. Except Darling, sprawled by my plate, tail draped affectionately over my wrist, who watched the tendrils as he would a tasty bird. His claws flexed in preparation.

"*Don't touch*," I warned him, and he flicked innocent eyes at me. Rogue seemed to be deep in concentration as the room filled, with the blue-black miasma settling over everyone but our little trio.

"There." He murmured it in satisfaction.

People still talked, laughed, enjoyed their dinners, but something had shifted in their voices. The room looked like we were underwater. Sparkling fish in a crazed aquarium of Rogue's making.

"What did you do?" It was both like and unlike what he'd done to the dragonfly girl. Only this was somehow general, where that had been specific and immaculately precise.

He smiled inscrutably and released my hand to drink from his goblet, spoke for my ears alone. "Wait. Watch. I'm interested to see if you can detect it."

Feeling like a grad student being grilled by one of my professors again, I studied the room, the conversations. Despite the whole underwater thing, it all seemed as before.

Then I noticed it. All the conversations were crystal clear. None of what they said carried the muddiness that social interactions usually did—the polite nonsense, the veiled insults, the sly innuendo. Instead they all said exactly what they meant.

"A truth spell?" I whispered into his ear, vaguely disappointed. "Isn't that kind of...prosaic?"

He snorted. "And how would you do it?"

He had a point. Wishing a physical thing into a different form required fairly straightforward visualization. Requiring a person to speak the truth—arguably a very subjective thing—would be quite a bit more convoluted.

"How did you do it?"

"You can grill me later. You'd best ask your questions now, before the party falls apart."

There were several arguments brewing. One pair of ladies looked daggers at each other and I wondered who had made the snarky remark first.

"I really only needed to talk to Blackbird—you needn't have bespelled the entire room."

He grinned. "I like showing off for my pretty consort."

Now I snorted, but the remark pleased me. *Sucker.* Fortunately Blackbird sat just to the other side of Rogue, well within conversational distance.

"I'd hoped to meet your husband tonight, Lady Blackbird." I pretended to scan the table. "Is he here?"

Starling, on my right, across from her mother, looked up, eyes wide. Hopefully she wouldn't blow it by chickening out.

"Oh no, Lady Sorceress Gwynn. He's—" She stopped herself, frowning. Likely puzzled at what she'd been about to blurt out. "He's off on a quest."

"Oh yes? And what is he looking for?"

"I—" She cocked her head at me, robin-black eyes snapping with suspicion. "I don't want to tell you."

The women down the table began shrieking at one another. I decided to skip a few steps.

"I'm sorry to do this to you, Blackbird. But I need to know what you can tell me. I think I know what he's looking for. I need to know what clues he's following. Where to find him."

Blackbird's gaze slid from my face to Rogue's and back again. She pressed her lips together. The women's escorts had gotten involved, one now standing up and poking a long finger at the other's chest.

"I told her, Mom." Starling broke in, leaning across the table, speaking fast and intensely. "All about little Brody."

Blackbird paled and I thought she might faint. She seized a goblet and drank it empty, staring into it for a long space of time. One of the men down the table punched the other and their neighbors stood, protesting and cheering, depending on the person.

"How can you possibly know anything about that?" she demanded. "You weren't even born when I gave him to—" Completely aghast, she whirled on me. "This is a horrible, nasty trick to play on me, Gwynn! I thought you might be a different sort than this ilk, but now you've become just like *him*." Blackbird clapped both hands over her mouth and moaned.

When I'd first arrived, Blackbird had been living in Rogue's castle as his servant and I'd despised him for doing that to her, using his hold on her. She was right, I'd become the same.

"Rogue—lift the spell."

"But you haven't dredged up all of her secrets."

"I don't want to do it this way. She's right. I'll take what Blackbird is willing to tell me, all right?" I asked it of her and she, hands still over her mouth, hesitated, then nodded. "Starling, pour your mother some wine, would you? Or something stronger, if you know her preference."

The room cleared with a ping that sizzled up my spine. It

seemed I was growing more sensitive to Rogue's magic all the time, as much a part of his allure as his gorgeous looks and enticing scent. Here was me, a fish flopping on a hook. Just waiting to be pan-seared and served up.

Blackbird beckoned to several pages and sent them scurrying to break up the fight and send the other guests on to the ballroom. She turned to us, all gracious hostess in place. "Shall we repair to the drawing room, then?"

She led the way and Rogue, Starling and I followed. Darling trotted off after the dancers, thinking happy thoughts about the tribute he'd receive for easing the sore feet of those determined to waltz all night. As a rare magical anesthetist, he was always popular at balls.

We entered a little parlor done entirely in aqua-blue velvet. To my surprise, several of my light-up pillows, in various shades of light blue, decorated the sofa. I should see if some could be sent to Mistress Nancy—as a thank-you, since I'd been too discombobulated at the time to think of it.

Blackbird folded her hands neatly and addressed us. "I'd like to apologize for the terrible, insulting and ungrateful things I said. In recompense, I—"

"Stop right there," I cut her off. "It was my fault. I did play a nasty trick on you. It's forgotten. It never happened."

Her eyes gleamed with unshed tears and she nodded. Now I saw her, the young woman who'd been trapped in a tower countless years ago. Always a chess piece in someone else's game. Starling edged up and handed her a tumbler of something and kissed her mother. Blackbird looked momentarily startled, then smiled and patted her daughter on the cheek.

"Look. I'm going to be straight with you, Blackbird. I think you understand why it's important to me to understand what's happening to firstborn children."

Blackbird flicked a wary glance at Rogue.

"Rogue has agreed to help me as he can. I know you're both—maybe every last one of you—restricted from discussing certain things." It occurred to me that I didn't seem to be. Was it that my foreign origin exempted me, or did I just fail to get the warning messages, as I missed all their hive-mind alerts? *Never mind that now.* "But I think your husband is looking for the same thing I am, more or less."

"I'll tell you the same thing I tell him. Don't go. Give it up. This is an endeavor that can lead only to disappointment, sorrow…and far, far worse."

"He comes back here from time to time, you said. When was the last time he was here?"

She shrugged. "A while."

Kill me now.

"It was the last blue moon," Starling inserted. "Before the apple-picking."

Blackbird glared at her. Not that the information was all that helpful to me, given that time and distance didn't necessarily stay in proportion to each other.

"Did he say what he'd found out? Where he was going next?"

"Fergus and I don't discuss *it*." Blackbird snapped. "We try to enjoy our time together, when and where we can, and then he takes off again driven by this stupid idea that our baby…"

Abruptly she dissolved into sobs. Looking stricken, Starling embraced her mother. Rogue put a warm hand on the small of my back.

I didn't know what to do. I hated to press. I had to. "Is what? Still alive, maybe?"

Hands pressed to her face, she made a strangled sound. "He's never forgiven me. Never. How could he?" She dropped her hands and glared at Rogue through tear-filled eyes. "They can't understand and we can never explain."

"No," Rogue replied quietly, stroking my back. "This is true."

She hiccupped and nodded, vindicated in this, at least.

We were going in circles, accomplishing nothing more than dredging up pain. Her emotional turmoil leaked out of her in waves, flavoring the air with the bitterness of regret and broken dreams. I pressed my fingertips to my temples, trying to think past it. The gesture jogged my memory.

"Lady Blackbird, would you let me listen in on your thoughts?"

Her emotions shut down, a steel security door slamming down on an invaded museum vault.

"Just a memory of Fergus's last visit. I can eavesdrop on what he said, glean something from that. Something, maybe, that you can't tell me."

She exchanged looks with Starling, then sat stiffly on a chair, still clutching her glass of untasted whiskey. "Fine."

I hesitated. "Are you sure?"

She pinned me with her bright robin eyes, reminding me that, for all that she seemed softer, more maternal and human than the other fae, she was alien to me. I might taste her thoughts and emotions, but she would forever be fundamentally *other* to me.

Just like Rogue.

"Lady Sorceress—do not toy with me. I'm perfectly aware you could scrape out and empty my mind as easily as I clear the ashes from a fireplace. I would only grieve myself resisting you."

I bit my lip against the urge to argue with her. I doubted I could do such a thing, even if my own moral code let me. And yet, in a world where I needed every advantage I could muster, being overestimated had become one of my most valuable commodities. I didn't need her to think I was a nice person.

Straightening my spine, I moved from under Rogue's touch and approached her, offering my open hands. Blackbird closed her eyes and I laid my fingertips on her temples, as I had done to Rogue so long ago, in those first chaotic days. He'd thought to convince me of his good intentions. Now, no longer an untrained bumbler, I understood a great deal more of what he had and had not let me see in his mind.

Starling perched nearby, anxious worry darkening the blond in her hair. Though I'd done the magic to change the color, I'd tied it to her self-image, to help it stick when we were apart. It tended to lose its luster when she lost that certainty.

"I won't hurt her, Starling. Don't hover."

"I'll hover if I want to," she retorted, but moved out of my line of sight. Rogue murmured something to her, but then they fell silent.

I concentrated on dipping into Blackbird's mind, wondering briefly how her brain was structured, if the sulci and lobes were like mine or wholly different. It might be similar to Rogue's auricle—same basic design, but with elaborations. Her cortical layers might spiral and wind with more intricate folds. It didn't matter. This wasn't about the physical structure, but the ebb and flow of the electrical gestalt. The metaphorical mind generated from the activity of millions of neurons. Rogue had explained it once as a lake, where thoughts swim at shallower or deeper levels. Marquise and Scourge, with their twisted, cruel aggression, had taught me to see a mind as a labyrinth, guarded by various doors and gatekeepers who could be circumvented or destroyed.

Since I left their keeping, I hadn't used the skills much, but I found my own approach forming, shaped by what I knew of the structure and function beneath. The brain was a kind of maze, wrapped in layers over itself. In the cortical regions, near the top and front, higher processing blazed along, synthesizing all the sensory information gathered by the peripheral systems and reported up through the various way stations and combined with memory, both short- and long-term, to create a constantly evolving understanding of the world.

I brushed past all that, the chattering creation and reformation of this moment and the ones that just occurred. What I wanted was deeper, stored in long-term memory, some of it consciously accessible, but the meat of it, the juicy bits I needed most, locked away, whether by her own wishes or some compulsion.

Trying not to invade her privacy more than I had to, I searched the vaults of her memory, scanning back through time, looking for images of the apple orchard. The trees hung ripe with fruit now, so I skimmed for impressions of them in blossom and, before that, bare limbs devoid of leaves, preceded by harvest.

Then I looked for pain. And love.

They radiated out, ribbons tied into a knot, attaching to

newer memories and older ones. One dark and shredded connection reached back and I knew where it would lead—to a place she hadn't given me permission to see.

Instead, I delved into this knot, letting the scenes from her husband's visit play for me like a movie. Only this one would be an IMAX in 360 degrees, with full sensory surround. I witnessed not just their conversations, but how she felt and the flashes of other memories that came and went with kaleido-scopic bursts of light and color.

More, I gleaned hints of what she hadn't fully realized at the time. Clues from him that she subconsciously understood but didn't consciously consider. It was truly amazing what we observed and understood but refused to contemplate.

Having what I needed, I started to withdraw, but that blackened cord leading to the deeper past beckoned me. Would I find a scene like the one in the courtyard of the Inn of Seven Moons? I didn't have permission to look, but this might be a vital clue. And an unparalleled opportunity to witness for myself what really occurred.

I followed the thread of it, coiling through dark and dismal emotions, clusters of ideas, like cancerous complexes growing off it. I imagined my own PTSD might appear this way, the wires short-circuited to kick in certain thoughts, prescribed reactions. Perhaps I could perform a kind of mental surgery on myself, to remove the scar tissue and speed healing.

The cord grew thicker as I closed in on the origin memory. Slimier too, coated with a repellant substance, necrotic and infected. I tried to delve in, but it shifted away, both dodging and sucking at me, a mire of quicksand. Even Blackbird herself could not reach into this. It shimmered, not with magic like mine or Rogue's, but with the mind-to-mind manipulation Lady Healer had once tried to explain to me. The kind that she'd said was not magic, not subject to the same laws and principles.

More like what I used now. And possibly, what connected all their minds together, flowers drawn into a bouquet tied with one noxious thread. One that trailed out into the universe and that ended, I was sure, with Titania.

CHAPTER 12

IN WHICH I INDULGE MYSELF

ぐ宅

The laws of entropy hold that the universe proceeds toward greater randomness—or "shit falls apart" as my physics prof would say.

~*Big Book of Fairyland*, "Incidental Notes"

RECOVERING MYSELF, I withdrew from Blackbird's mind and rubbed my hands together. Her bright black eyes opened, sharp with suspicion. She wondered what all I'd seen—and if there were things she herself did not know. Her mind had clearly been messed with, but suggesting that to her might plant seeds that could lead to mental instability.

If you couldn't trust your own thoughts, what was left?

"Well then, missy." She lapsed into familiar address in her snapping concern. "Did you find out all my deep, dark secrets?"

She'd meant it to be light, but the jest fell on a somber room. I paced away, to put a bit of distance between me and her anxious thoughts. Rogue sprawled on a pretty settee, all indolent disinterest, except for the bright sparks in his indigo eyes. He could have piggybacked along, without me knowing. Seen much of what I'd seen. Starling perched on the edge of a fancy scrolled chair, the thick paintbrush swing of her hair looking dull. She didn't look at her mother, but watched me.

"Well?" She demanded.

"I have an idea of where Fergus has gone, yes. And the trail he's following."

Blackbird frowned at me. "How is that possible when I don't know?"

My gaze fell on the magic cocktail cart and I glanced at Blackbird for permission, then went to help myself. It seemed to be an ordinary tea cart, but had been a reward to Fergus for "the usual heroics," Blackbird had told me on my previous visit. It never ran out of alcohol, always had just what you wanted, with enough glasses for everyone. Fergus had called himself an Irish cliché and that he'd chosen this sort of reward just confirmed it. I felt sure I'd like him. If I ever found him.

"The way the brain works—at least the human brain and I'm working on the assumption that fae brains are more or less the same—is that the lower areas of the brain collect much more information than gets relayed to the upper areas, where thinking occurs."

I poured myself some brandy—surprised that it was exactly what I wanted. A bottle of antifreeze-green liquor sat front and center, next to a very tall, thin, cylindrical glass. I raised an eyebrow at Rogue. "Is this for you?"

"Yes. Lovely."

It smelled of vanilla and apples and gasoline fumes. I hand-ed him a glass, not in the least tempted to try it, and continued.

"It's like—harvesting all of the apples, but you keep the

best ones for certain purposes." This might not be the best analogy, since it wasn't clear to me what one *did* with a poisonous crop, but Blackbird nodded. "If you thought about every little thing your senses reported, you'd go crazy trying to keep track of it all. Plus you people have at least one, possibly several more avenues of input, being able to detect thoughts, emotions and...whatever it is that tells you all what time things start."

Starling snickered and I wrinkled my nose at her, glad to see her less worried now.

"So, you're saying that my senses recorded things about Fergus when he visited that I never thought about—and you could see them and draw conclusions?" Blackbird's brow furrowed. "What if you're wrong? It doesn't sound very reliable."

I warmed the glass in my hands, still unsure what to say. Rogue gazed at me, expression bland. Didn't fool me for a second. But he was letting me run my own show.

I sat next to him on the settee and he moved over to give me room, so I sat in the curl of his body. It comforted me and I no longer cared to examine why.

"Lady Blackbird..." I hesitated. Sipped the brandy to stall.

"Just out with it. I'm a big girl."

True. I would want to know.

"He flat out told you. You had several conversations about where he'd been, what he'd discovered and where he planned to go next."

Her face went to ice. "Why don't I remember that? Surely if we had a conversation, I would have had to think about such things."

I nodded. Rogue stroked my hair.

"So something made me forget."

"Someone, I think."

"It explains so much," she spoke softly to her white hands, folded like birds around the glass in her lap. "He's always so angry with me. No wonder, if he thinks I don't listen."

My heart bled for her a little. After the prince rescued the princess, the happily ever after wasn't supposed to include infanticide and marital disharmony. Nobody brought up the subject of who might be running interference. Nobody needed to.

"Well then!" Blackbird stood, brushing off her dress with crisp movements, setting the whiskey aside. "I have guests to see to. Starling, are you with me or your mistress?"

Starling shot me a hopeful look and I tipped my head toward the ballroom or, at least, toward the general direction of the music. She danced off happily, already shedding the somber mood.

"And you, my lady Gwynn?" Rogue asked, sliding sensual fingers through my hair. "Are you for dancing?"

I really wasn't in the mood for partying. Divining my unspoken wish, Rogue uncoiled his long body from the settee and offered me his hand, lacing his fingers with mine. We walked through the empty castle, the music growing fainter behind us as we headed up to our shared rooms.

"Any observations?" I finally asked.

"Interesting."

"That's all?"

He smiled down at me. "I thought it was your favorite word."

"You eavesdrop too much."

"Ah, but Gwynn, you are an endless source of fascination."

"Did you see the bit at the end—that kind of cord around her memory of the baby and how it went off elsewhere?"

He shook his head. "I couldn't follow you there."

"You were prevented."

He shrugged and that confirmed it. Rogue should have more than enough ability to do anything that I did, and more. He'd seen enough to know what I was asking about, but had less luck than I penetrating that oily murk.

We'd reached our rooms and Rogue took the brandy glass from my hand and set it on the table next to the nearly empty cylinder of green gack.

"What was that stuff anyway?

"Ambrosia."

"You could have fooled me."

"Could I?" He caressed my cheek and ran warm fingers down my throat and over my collarbone. "It seems you are exceedingly difficult to fool."

"Well, shame on me and all that..." I caught my breath when he stroked the exposed upper curves of my breasts. "This isn't really the right time for seduction."

"Of course it is. We can hardly sail over the Endless Sea right this moment. Even for me, that takes time to arrange."

"Aha—you saw that much."

"I did," he confirmed, then took my hand and drew me toward the bedroom. "I have a brilliant idea."

Somehow I knew this inspiration had nothing to do with following Fergus on his quest.

Though the bedchamber was airy, high-ceilinged and

ringed with arched windows, the bed still predominated. Not black like Rogue's, it nevertheless sported four posts, made of spiraling gold vines. The bedclothes shimmered bronze and copper in the low torchlight. Then dark green silk ribbons appeared on each post and I groaned.

"No, Rogue. Just...no."

"Not for you—not unless you beg sweetly. For me." He toed off his boots and sprawled on the bed, arms and legs spread. "Tie me up, lovely Gwynn. Have your way with me."

"Don't be silly. You could easily break or wish away any knot I make."

"So could you, for that matter," he replied, blue eyes somber. "No one is using silver."

I flinched a little at the memory of the silver bands that had turned my skin black and made me into Marquise and Scourge's unwilling and helpless toy.

"You know you want to."

"I don't know that," I nearly snapped. Though I was tempted. Very tempted.

"I'll give you dispensation."

"What kind of dispensation?"

"You can touch me however you like, do whatever you like to me, without forfeiting any of your rules. Indulge yourself with no fear of pregnancy."

Did I mention tempting?

"Come tie me up and have your way with me. It'll be fun."

"I'm not here to have fun," I countered, but I did drift over to the bed and fingered one of the ribbons.

"Fun is part of being alive, serious Gwynn. If you're not having fun, you might as well be dead."

"Easily said by an immortal."

He just wiggled his bare foot at me, invitingly. Hmm. So, I looped the long ribbon around his narrow ankle, wrapping it around a few times and tying the ends together in a bow.

"Tighter than that."

"Really?"

His blue eyes had deepened with arousal, putting a lie to the playfulness of his game. "You don't want me to get away, do you?"

Now, while I'd had a reasonably eclectic liberal arts education, it had never involved the finer points of rope tying. And they only taught the Boy Scouts things like knots. In Girl Scouts we embroidered pillows or decoupaged magazine pictures onto cuts of wood. You know—life skills.

"Tie me tight. Make me your captive." His voice became a hypnotic murmur, burning in my blood.

I experimented, rewrapping his ankle, the dark green silk vivid against his golden skin. I didn't want to restrict the blood flow to his foot—since he had a heart and other bodily fluids, I presumed he had blood—so I needed to strike a balance. At last, satisfied with my knot, I moved to the other foot, stretching his legs wide to give myself enough ribbon to tie with.

With a bit more trepidation, I approached the head of the bed to tie his right wrist. Rogue rolled his head on the pillow, gloss-black hair streaming beneath him, and watched me with fulminous eyes under heavy lids. Desire burned through him so hot and sweet I nearly tasted it in the air. When I finished with the other wrist, pulling his body taut between the four posts, he hummed deep in his throat, transported.

"Now what?" My voice came out in a hoarse whisper.

"Whatever you want, fierce Gwynn."

"You don't have any limitations you want to put on me?"

He shook his head, holding my gaze. "I trust you. Whatever you wish. No repercussions. I won't attempt to free myself. Until dawn," he added and I laughed.

"There we are."

"Wouldn't want you to give me the slip."

"Like you couldn't find me anywhere." I trailed a finger down the bare skin exposed by his open shirt and he didn't reply. Not that it had been a question. "You're wearing too many clothes."

They vanished and he was naked. Like a schoolgirl, I gasped. I couldn't possibly be blushing, but my cheeks felt hot. Thankfully, he didn't tease me for it. Just lay still, a bounty of male beauty spread before me to do whatever I liked with.

And it wasn't even my birthday.

Actually—it could have been. I was born in late August and so the season would match. Disorientation washed over me. I might never again know when my birthday was. Why it was that these small things—the ordinary milestones of life, the aching guilt that I'd left Isabel behind, that she'd never understand why I abandoned her—these were the wounds that continued to bleed. Just when I thought they'd scabbed over, something would carelessly rub against them, sending fresh sparks of pain through my system.

"Stay with me, lovely Gwynn. Tonight is for indulgence. Save your grief for tomorrow."

He was right. Carpe diem and all that. With determination, I marched into the sitting room, then returned with our glasses. They'd helpfully refilled themselves—a trick I hadn't realized the magic cocktail cart could do. This place would be a fantasyland for some.

Rogue watched me with glittering interest. I took my time, sipping the excellent brandy and filling my eyes with him. His uncannily long body looked spectacular this way, his wiry muscles tight under that velvety skin. The black pattern on the left side of his face repeated all down that side of his body, thorny loops and swirls over his chest, belly, groin and thigh.

No hair dusted his chest or groin. His cock, long in proportion to the rest of him, but not freakishly so, lay upthrust on his lean belly, heavy scrotum beneath. I'd read that giving head to guys who waxed was nicer. My chance to find out, should I wish.

He had nipples, vestigial, as a human male would have. I stroked a curious hand over the unblemished surface of his abdomen, careful not to brush the weeping head of his cock.

"How can you not have a belly button? Did you not grow in your mother's womb?"

He sighed, gazing steadfastly at the ceiling. "You must be the only creature ever who would be examining me like a specimen instead of having your way with me."

"Sorry—package deal. You're the one who made me your consort." I shook my head so the earrings swung, sending pleasant shivers down my spine. "Besides, you agreed I could do whatever I liked."

"I had imagined something more salacious."

I raised an eyebrow at him. "Such as?"

"Such as the brush of your lips on my skin. Taste me, Gwynn. Please." He undulated a little in his bonds, enticingly.

Leaning over, I kissed the hollow under his collarbone. He tasted as hot and sweet as the sensual haze filling the air. "Like this?"

"Ah, yes," he breathed, a thirsty man tasting a drop of water. "More."

"Maybe I should just torment you—let you lie here hoping I'll touch you."

His feverish gaze held mine. "You could, my cruel mistress. I'm at your mercy."

Though I knew it for just another game, something about this freed me from worry. I trusted that he would keep to the bargain and stay bound and let me do as I liked. For now, I thought I wanted more brandy.

Upending the snifter, I poured a trail over his skin, from throat to groin, not caring that rivulets ran over his sides to the glorious bronze coverlet below. He hissed in pleasure, then groaned aloud when I followed the trail with my tongue.

Rogue tipped his chin back, exposing his throat and allowing me to kiss and nibble all those delightful lines and hollows. I licked down his chest, splaying my hands over his warm skin, feeling like I could consume him. The cat deep inside purred in feral agreement and for once I didn't mind feeling her there, prowling in my heart.

Hunger rose in me, liquid and rapacious. I feasted on the feel of Rogue's ethereal skin, his body moving under my touch. It seemed he loved everything I tried, humming and groaning in masculine satisfaction, his breathing deep and uneven. His thoughts swirled up, teasing mine, dark caresses of sensual emotion, pricking me here, enticing me further there, exciting me to higher levels. Urging me on.

I needed no urging. With hands and mouth, I draped my-self over him, soaking up the wild magic that was as much part of him as his bones and sinews. It filled me, winding with my own magic and fizzing together, black and gold bubbles sizzling against my skin from the inside with nearly unbearable pressure.

When I pressed my mouth to the pulse where his femoral artery should be, that waltz-beat throbbed strong and true. Only this orchestra had picked up the pace, the cellos and bass thrumming with driving urgency, dark notes of utter abandon. I bit him there and he convulsed, calling my name and crying out for more.

Crazed, I gave him more, took more. I tasted every inch of him, from the fragile blue-veined skin over his long-boned feet to the graceful points of his hip bones to the shadowed hollows of his collarbone to the winking horseshoe that marked him as mine. I took it in my teeth, sucking on his ear and relishing the way it made him tremble while he panted, now murmuring my name, then imploring me with wordless entreaties.

I straddled him on all fours, as he'd done me. He gazed at me in a delirium of sensuous pleasure, and power zinged through me to know I'd brought him to this extreme.

"What do you want?" I asked him softly, taunting. We both knew I would decide whether to give it to him. He licked his dry lips, blue eyes nearly black with the passion raging through him. I snagged the little vial of green ambrosia, held it to his mouth and he drank greedily. "Three things, my gorgeous Rogue. Ask for them and maybe I'll give them to you."

His face set into rigid lines, his fingers flexing. For a moment I thought he might sever the bonds that held him, but he didn't. After all, he'd promised.

"Why should I ask with no hope of receiving, my cruel mistress?"

"What can you hope to gain, if you do not ask for it?"

He bared his teeth at me. "I take. I do not ask."

I toyed with one of his nipples and he groaned, dropping his head back on the pillow. "You do not appear to be in a position to take just now, my Lord Rogue. Perhaps if you beg nicely for your three things, I might give you one."

He laughed. "Never let it be said that you are not tenacious. I'll name three—and not *those* three—and you will give me two."

"You know there is one thing I cannot give."

"Will not."

"Semantics."

"Is it, my lady?" He sobered abruptly, no longer drunk with lovemaking but purely lucid, staring into my eyes as if he could penetrate my thoughts. "I don't think so."

Nervous, I sat back on my heels. As that was between his spread and gloriously naked thighs, the regrouping did not give me much peace.

"Three things then, fair Gwynn, and you decide whether to give any or all to your helpless servant."

I nearly laughed, but it caught in my throat at the intense blue of his gaze.

"You, naked. Your mouth, on my cock. Your loyalty and trust, pledged forever."

He raised an eyebrow at me, a dare. An acknowledgment that I would refuse him all of this as I had refused him so much else. I climbed off the bed and took up my brandy glass—full again. One really had to track one's refills. Rogue's disappointment at my withdrawal tinged the air like the scent of burnt toast. He stared steadfastly at the ceiling again, visibly restraining himself.

"Rogue." I called his name softly and his indigo eyes snapped to me. I dropped the gown and stood there naked while he drank me in, his gaze clawing over me with near physical force. Arousal swamped me, drenching and heating me. Without him asking, I pivoted, gratified by the admiration and desire in his face.

He said nothing when I climbed back up on the high bed and took his cock in my hand for the first time in naked reality. Strong and hot, it thrummed in my grip, velvet soft as the rest of him, corded iron beneath. I held it up, my mouth just over the reddened tip. Rogue seemed transfixed.

"My people have a saying," I told him, running my tongue over my lips to wet them. "Two out of three ain't bad."

And I took him in my mouth.

LATER IN THE night, some sound woke me and I flung out an arm to find empty space where Rogue should be, the sheets cool where he'd lain. I sat up, my hair whispering over my bare shoulders, and scanned the midnight room. Nothing and no one.

Still, the hairs on my arms stood up, pricking my nerves.

"Rogue?" My voice whispered in the chamber, hissing back from the cold marble. I slid out of bed, the nightgown Rogue had made for me untangling from my legs and falling around me in a slide of silk. When had I put that on? The door to the bedroom stood closed, but light shone underneath.

I went out into the warm light of the sitting room to find it equally empty. A sudden fancy took me and I imagine that everyone in the castle had vanished and I alone remained, a tortured ghost to roam alone forever.

"Rogue? Are you here?" I called out, more loudly. One of outer doors opened and a human soldier—I think the one Starling had flirted with, popped his head in. I hastily wrapped my arms over my revealing lace-covered bosom.

"Is there a problem, milady?"

"Ah, no." Suddenly my midnight fears seemed childish and foolish. "I just wondered where Lord Rogue had gone."

"Said he had something to take care of, mum. I imagine he'll see you for breakfast."

"Oh."

"Good night, milady. Sleep well."

Just before he closed it, Darling squeezed through the cracked-open door, broadcasting cheerful thoughts of dancing and sugar-coated mice. I let him coax me back to bed and soothe me to sleep with his special gifts.

But the feeling of foreboding never completely faded.

CHAPTER 13

IN WHICH I MISPLACE
SOMETHING IMPORTANT

These notes attempt to quantify something which is possibly,
by its very nature, unquantifiable.
~Big Book of Fairyland, "True Love"

WHEN I WOKE the next morning, the worry crashed in on me with my first waking thought. Darling confirmed that Rogue had never returned—and added some sarcastic thoughts about not caring if he ever did.

"Don't say that, it's bad luck."

Starling hadn't turned up yet. The morning light still slant-ed low and dim, and nobody stirred outside that I could see. My fretfulness had awakened me early. Early enough that Darling had curled up and gone back to sleep. Or pretended to, in his huffiness. Not at all sleepy now, I found my velvet dressing robe and shrugged into its warmth.

I rarely missed coffee, but now I wished for a latte, which amusingly popped up in a Starbucks cup, so ingrained was that image in my mind. The sweet creaminess came very close to my memory of the pumpkin spice flavors, and seemed appropriate for the cooler air, the apple orchards waiting for harvest. Cupping it in my hands, I tried to mentally trace the source of my unease.

Rogue hadn't been there the past few mornings when I awakened, so this should be no different. Still, after what had passed between us last night...

My face heated, partly in embarrassment over my unusually wanton behavior and the rest in pleasure. Bringing the powerful and cagey Lord Rogue to excruciating climax with my mouth and hands had been a rush like no other. I wasn't young enough to still confuse the emotions of such intimacy with love, but I'd thought we'd found a new understanding, a deeper connection.

I wasn't the first woman, by any stretch, to wake up alone after giving herself to a man, thinking to find a new beginning only to find that sex had meant the end. Besides which, I knew full well Rogue didn't have everything he wanted from me. He might think I had given him the third thing as well.

He might be right.

I sighed for that uncomfortable truth and fingered the green silk ribbons still attached to the bedposts. I had vague memories of untying him. Of cuddling after. I had a nostalgic feeling of lying next to him, my head on his shoulder, breathing in his scent and touch, not wanting any more than that.

And then what?

I frowned at the incongruous paper cup, drained it and wished it away again. Had I fallen asleep then? Why didn't I remember? Maybe I'd passed out from too much brandy—a daunting thought—but I hadn't felt drunk. Just a little...wilder than usual.

Acting on impulse, I untied the ribbons from the bedposts, carefully coiling them into neat spools. I made a little pouch, like the ones for the dragon artifacts, and stored them inside. There had been a kind of magic between us last night, and the ribbons could carry part of that still. Or I was being all romantic and sentimental. Oh well, Starling didn't need to see what we'd been up to anyway.

Going to the big armchairs by the windows, I curled up in one and settled my thoughts. Once upon a time, I could never have done this, being the kind of person who really sucked at meditation. Now that silent space my trainers had forced me to create waited for me. I had only to reach into it to find it again. The place where I barely existed to myself. Where I stepped out of my own being.

As I had with Blackbird, I traced the patterns of my own brain. This time, I knew where the various cortical and subcortical areas should be. Every person's brain is different, shaped by our experiences, but the structure is generally consistent. I wound my way through my own memories— quite the starburst of emotion around the events of last night. Oh, and connecting to the turbulence of the day's activities. All my terror and doubt, transforming, turning into new avenues of thought.

Something to consider.

I dug deeper, knowing what I was looking for, but trying to set that thought aside, to keep objective. The diligent scientist built in objectivity as much as possible, because there was an insidious tendency to find what you hoped you would. Whether it came from ignoring contradictory evidence or massaging data outliers to fit the trend—if you were invested in a particular outcome, it was more likely to come about. Add the untamed variability of magic to that equation and it became that much worse.

Aha. And there it was. Black and oily and slick—a dark ribbon attached to my memories of last night, and I could no more sink my claws of understanding into it than I had been able to with Blackbird. Or than I would have been able to with Rogue, for surely he had one too, if I'd looked instead of being distracted with his enticing offer. There was also no knowing how long it had been there. I'd never known to look before. Possibly Marquise and Scourge put it there. Or Lady Healer.

Somehow, I doubted that, however.

I left it alone for now. Casting about, I looked for the cat, that other self growing like a mushroom in the dark of my subconscious, but found no trace. I didn't really think I would. Seeing into my own unknowable mind would be useful—and probably unprecedented. Slowly, I let myself rise up from my deep brain, a diver being careful of getting the bends.

But I couldn't shake that greasy foreboding, that sense that I'd taken another step into a morass from which I could never escape.

I opened my eyes to the cheery light of midday and blinked, further unsettled by the contrast and the passage of time.

With uncanny prescience, Starling came in. "All done then?"

"Ah. Yes."

She cocked her head at me, looking a bit weary. "Are you all right?"

"I'm fine. How was the dancing?"

"Titania, I'm tired!" She flopped into the chair opposite. "What a fun night, but I'm glad we have today to rest before we head to the Port of Blue Mermaids."

"To catch a sailing ship?"

"Of course! Lord Rogue didn't tell you?"

"No." I frowned, searching my memory. We had talked about sailing somewhere, right? "Maybe so."

"Something *is* wrong. Tell me."

"Eh. It's just…" I shrugged. "Did you notice anything odd last night?"

"Not really and I was up until nearly dawn."

"Funny—I woke up once and didn't hear any music."

"Magical soundproofing," she explained. "Most of the bedrooms at Castle Brightness have it."

Curiouser and curiouser.

Alarm tightened Starling's dreamy expression. "What happened? Do I need to call the guards?"

"No, no. It's nothing like that. I had a restless night and now I haven't seen Rogue yet today."

"Lord Rogue generally turns up in the evening, doesn't he?"

"Yes—exactly. So there's no need to worry."

"I'm surprised you'd even think to be concerned about him. I thought you were just as happy not to have him underfoot. Besides, he can take care of himself."

Of course she was right.

"Or—" she tucked her toes up under her and leaned forward, brown eyes sparkling with avid interest, "—have you changed your mind about him? The earrings look great on you and you looked very snuggly with him last night."

"Speaking of which—how is your mom doing today?"

Starling wrinkled her nose at me. "Fine—don't tell me. Mom is good. She's kind of over being mad and upset. Getting packed up for the trip is keeping her occupied."

"Packed? Blackbird is coming?"

"Did you think we could stop her? She's all determined to find Dad now, to explain and all." She pulled a lock of hair around and nibbled on the ends. "Kind of crazy about my brother, huh?"

"That's one word for it."

"Gwynn—" She paused, chewed. "What do you think happened to him?"

I thought of Nancy's horrific story and knew I could never tell Starling about it. A similar scene might be there, buried in Blackbird's locked-away memories. Infant Brody might be dead all these years and poor misguided Fergus on a fool's quest to find something that had passed out of this world entirely.

Starling, for all her flirty fun, possessed her mother's perceptive nature. She narrowed her eyes at me. "You're thinking up a lie to tell me. Don't. If you can't tell me everything, then fine. But I think you owe me whatever truth you can tell me. This is my family. My quest too."

"It doesn't have to be, Starling." I pointed a finger at her when she took a breath. "It doesn't. You have your own life to lead. You could stay here, maybe canoodle with that guy you like. Be happy. This drama belongs to your parents. I can understand Blackbird's need to do this, but frankly I don't think any of you should come along. You for sure could let it go—do your own thing and not play out this role in someone else's tragedy."

"It's not your drama either."

I sighed and raked my hair back from my face, aware in midmovement that it was one of Rogue's gestures. Where the hell had he gone? Hell, he never told me where he regularly went, so why did this feel any different?

It just did. I knew it in my bones.

"I don't understand the why of it, but I am wrapped up in this. So many threads tie me to this strange game that I don't see how I could extricate myself."

"A game? Is that what you think it is?" Starling pounced on my careless words.

"Isn't every damn thing in Faerie a game? Always about the trick, the sleight of hand, winning a prize of no value."

"I think," Starling replied slowly, with uncharacteristic seriousness, "that it only seems like a game to you because you don't understand the rules—or the value of what's being sought."

"Do you?"

"I don't know. But I do know I never will if you don't fill me in. Please, Gwynn." She bit down on her hair, making a disturbing crunching sound.

"Okay. You can't discuss this with anyone, and don't take it as gospel truth because I don't have much evidence to support my ideas. A lot of this is conjecture. And you shouldn't chew on your hair like that—you'll mess it up."

Guiltily she dropped the hair and fidgeted with her pretty yellow dress instead. "I promise not to talk about it with anyone but you."

Good enough. "What I think is that, yes, the Queen Bitch is running some kind of game. A competition, perhaps, where various fae—noble fae—have the opportunity to produce a child with someone from my world. For some reason, she wants this half-breed, firstborn child. So far, I think no one has succeeded in birthing the child with the quality she wants, so the game then moves to someone else."

"Why do you think no one has succeeded? If this is right, then she has Brody."

"Good point!" I said brightly, tucking away the image of Titania thoughtfully masticating doomed Cecily's baby and pronouncing it insufficient. "Maybe she needs a lot of them." Like bonbons.

"So you think Rogue is the one playing the game now. And you."

I nodded, my throat a little tight to have it put so bluntly, though they were my own thoughts, echoed back to me.

Starling reached for the lock of hair, then deliberately folded her hands and sat up straight. "See, this is what I think. I serve you—and I like to think we're friends too. If you're caught up in this thing, this game, and it's the same thing that wrecked my parents' lives, then I figure it involves me too. I could choose to stay behind and pick apples and dance all night, but maybe I want to be someone better than that. Someone more like you."

It took me by surprise, her bald statement. I couldn't remember anyone wanting to be like me and it moved me in some deep way. Frightened me too.

"Oh, Starling. We *are* friends, but I don't think you want to be like me. I'm stubborn and arrogant and not at all better in any way. Plus the magic is doing weird things to me. I don't know who I am half the time anymore."

"I know who you are," she replied with staunch loyalty. I remembered Rogue saying the same thing to me, back when we made our first bargain. *I know who you are, far better than you know who I am.* "Give me the credit to recognize the truly admirable in you. I'm going with you, Gwynn. You can't stop me."

"I *can.*"

"But you won't because you know I won't give up."

"Well, you've got the stubborn part down all right."

She squealed and clapped her hands. "Hooray—a quest! Now get dressed. They're picking apples today."

"They are?" I dragged myself out of the armchair, my body creaking with stiffness. Starling followed me to the bathing room. I poked my head into the bedroom along the way and saw Darling had abandoned the rumpled bed. Off hunting mice probably. A cheerful purr filled my mind, along with a vision of mouse guts. Just what I wanted to see.

"Yes." Starling groaned theatrically. "Mother decided it has to happen before we go, so she's rousting everybody out to get busy. You know how she is when she decides there's a task to be done. So everybody will be coming to help pick, then there will be feasting and dancing afterward."

"I think I would fall over dead of shock if there *wasn't* a feast and dancing."

"Ha-ha."

Geez, she was even starting to sound like me.

"Why not just use magic to harvest the apples? Seems that it would be a lot faster."

Starling was shaking her head, her blond hair swinging. "Can't. They're magic-resistant."

"I thought they were poisonous."

"That too."

"So why grow them? What use is there for so many poisonous apples that require so much effort to harvest?"

She looked at me in surprise. "Well, what else would the dragons eat?"

Aha! Now I liked the logic of that. Which came first—did the dragons' magic resistance come from the apples? And were the apples "poisonous" because they affected the inherent magic of the fae? Maybe Nancy and her son could eat them just fine. *Must note that down.*

After I dressed in a russet gown that seemed appropriate for an autumn harvest party and Starling fixed my hair into a simple, loose braid to keep it out of my face, we headed downstairs.

"There you girls are!" Blackbird called out. "I thought I would have to send someone after you, lest you sleep all day." She frowned at me and clucked. "You look peaked, Lady Gwynn. Are you entirely all right?"

"I didn't sleep well, but I'm fine. I'm a bit concerned about Lord Rogue—have you seen him?"

"Oh no, but I don't expect to. I wouldn't worry about that one. He comes and goes as he likes. He'll no doubt turn up this evening, as is his habit."

I was beginning to feel like the distressed spouse who has to wait twenty-four hours before filing a missing-persons report. They were all correct that none of this was out of Rogue's usual pattern of behavior. Only the nagging sense of wrongness led me to think otherwise. That and the ugly coil of knotted memory loss that lurked beneath my thoughts, a bad taste at the back of my throat.

The afternoon stretched out in a glorious golden haze, Faerie at its cliché best. The sky arched in perfect crisp blue, the apples shining bright, piled into baskets. Music played and everyone, fae and human alike, sang as they picked.

No one ate the fruit, of course. They had a slightly dead feel in my hands, though nowhere near the null-existence of the dragon-related items.

As evening closed in, bonfires sprang to life and people crowded around, pressing mugs of warm cider into my hands—presumably not made from the poisonous variety of apple—and loaded their plates from the tables piled high with food. I refrained from drinking the cider all the same. Call me paranoid. I refused offers to dance too, holding vigil at the edge of the festivities, searching the dark for a glint of amber eyes, perhaps.

No sign of the Dog. Or Rogue.

I alternated between the hollow certainty that he had abandoned me for some arcane reason and the deeper alarm that his absence had a more sinister implication. After all, the day was drawing to a close and he had not given me a lesson nor a kiss. What would happen if he failed to meet his bargains with me? Worse, what if Falcon called us in to do our promised service and I was unable to produce Rogue? The worry ate at me, a looming thunderhead of dread with flickers of panic lighting the edges.

Time seemed to accelerate. The dancing around the bonfire became frenetic, a video played on fast-forward. People whirled, human and fae, in a strobe pattern of phantasmagoric glee. Once, I thought I saw Liam across the crowd, staring at me sitting alone at my table. But when the dancers parted again, he had disappeared from view.

For my part, I waited. It wasn't like I could go walk the woods, calling for a lost pet. If midnight came and went, then Rogue would have violated two promises to me—something I felt sure he'd never do willingly. I only had to wait to find out. Midnight.

I reached for Darling and he popped out of the swirl of bodies and leaped, graceful as thistledown onto my table. For once he didn't tease, simply rubbed his head under my chin and inserted the image of fifty-three topazes into my head. His way of communicating fifty-three minutes to me. Less than an hour left, by my handy kitty clock.

He stayed with me, sitting in Egyptian cat pose, a sphinx overseeing the increasingly wild festivities. Thanks to his magic, the revelries continued without pause, one dance blending into the next with full abandon. No one tired. None of the ladies kicked off their uncomfortable high heels—neither did the gentlemen for that matter. Even Blackbird whirled past, her ample white bosom pushed into high curves by a tight corset, her dark glossy hair swinging free nearly to her ankles.

Darling sat up when the moment arrived, wrapping his tail around my arm.

Midnight.

And nothing.

I half expected a tolling bell in the distance, the lonely clang of the clock tower warning that the witching hour had commenced. It would fit the dread gathering in my chest.

But the frenzied music only played louder, with no pause, no mass-mind acknowledgment of a vow broken.

Somewhere, deep inside, that connection to Rogue, the something that breathed blue-black wild magic through me, shifted. It didn't quite go away, but it thinned, moved farther away. My earlobes tingled as the earrings swayed. I reached up, but they didn't come off in my fingers as I'd thought they might. It seemed they would be permanently attached until, and if, Rogue ever returned.

I should have kicked myself for not making him take them off before we fell asleep, but perversely, I was glad for them. I closed my eyes against the wild harvest party and sent a message to Rogue, wherever he might be. Not vocalized. Just a feeling. A vow.

I was coming after him.

PART III

RECALIBRATING

CHAPTER 14

IN WHICH I AM TREATED
AS A FRAGILE VESSEL

$\xi\rightleftarrows\zeta$

*The residue of memory removal feels less like a locked door or
vacant space and more as if that place in the mind is
connected to a wormhole that pulls it away to another place
entirely. And I can't believe I just wrote that down as
an observation.*

~Big Book of Fairyland, "Memory ~~Interference~~
Inconsistency"

I N THE MORNING, there was much marshaling of the
entourage, now exponentially multiplied by the addition of
Blackbird and all the things she seemed to feel we had been
doing without and shouldn't be.

I found her, to tell her Rogue had never returned, but
stopped midsentence at the grave sympathy in her eyes.

"There, there, dearie." She folded her white hands under
her bosom. "You know how men are—always off chasing
some new idea. Lord Rogue will turn up soon enough." Her
gaze flicked to my belly and up to the earrings. "He knows

how to find you when it's time."

"Lady Blackbird. I don't think Rogue is gone of his own free will. The night before last, I—"

She tutted and shook her head to stop me. "No need to explain a thing to me, Lady Gwynn. I know the ways of these things. It's no fault of your own. Men will be men, after all."

"That's not what happened."

"No worries. Worrying isn't good for you in your condition. Lord Rogue will be back for you. Have no doubt. When the time is right. Now if you'll just wait a bit, we'll all be ready to leave. Unless I can get you something?"

Dismissed and wishing I'd just lingered in my rooms longer, I stood by and seethed over Blackbird's assumptions. My "condition" indeed. By the way they all—fae and human, alike—cast sideways glances at me, then looked quickly away, word had gotten around. I should stitch a scarlet P to my dress, just to make them all happy.

To my eye it would be an hour yet before the many carts had been loaded. Whatever an hour was in Faerie time—no way could I stand here and be Object of Pity. I found Starling supervising the loading of a standing mirror.

"I'm going for a walk."

A flash of sympathy and guilt crossed her face. Yeah, no one knew what to say to the jilted girl, the bride left at the altar. Women could be sympathetic friends, but also ruthless competitors. When one of us failed to successfully hook the man, there was always a bit of wondering. A little judgment that she must have done something wrong to blow the deal.

I heard it too easily in her, what all the speaking glances implied. She felt sure we'd done the deed and she had me figured for knocked up from Rogue's magically potent seed and him run off to parts unknown.

"Maybe you should just sit and rest," she suggested, confirming the shadow of her thoughts.

It was on my tongue to tell her that even Rogue's magically potent sperm couldn't impregnate me if it never got near my magically fertile hoo-haw, but I bit down on it. She didn't deserve my anger and, right at that moment, I couldn't say much without giving vent to it.

"I'll be back."

Darling trotted alongside me, waving his tail. I didn't care to stroll through the orchards, now entirely denuded of fruit, as if a flock of apple-eating locusts had passed through, leaving only a few shredded leaves behind. The air held cooler moisture, a breeze blowing that carried an edge of wildness to it. It reminded me of the autumn winds that heralded the frozen death of winter. Once again glad of the cloak Rogue had given me, I wrapped it around myself and indulged in full-out worrying.

A footstep grated on a rock behind me and I spun, abruptly aware I'd forgotten my dagger, much less a longer fighting stick. Larch gazed at me with placid blueberry eyes, holding out the offending dagger.

I took it from him with a sigh. "I apologize. I forgot I'd left it on Felicity's saddle."

"Unlike you, my lady sorceress, to be so careless."

"Yeah. I'm out of sorts. I need to get my head together."

"Lord Rogue would never have broken his pledges to you. The rest are fools to think it."

Something inside me steadied. He regarded me solemnly,

Darling sitting beside him with an equally grave look in his light green eyes.

"I'm not pregnant."

"As you say, my lady sorceress."

Darling mentally sniggered.

"I'm afraid for him."

If I thought Larch would allay my fears, I was sadly mistaken. His brow creased. "Me also."

"Everyone says how amazingly powerful Rogue is and no one could stop him."

"This is true. For the most part."

"So what's the other part? Who's more powerful than Rogue—*her?*"

"Sometimes, my lady sorceress, it does not take more power to defeat someone, but simply the correct leverage against a known vulnerability."

"What does that mean? Don't give me riddles."

"But you're the one who can answer the riddle. I cannot."

"Because you think I know his vulnerabilities."

"As you say, my lady sorceress."

Darling chirruped and blinked, a slow lazy look.

"I thought you and Rogue weren't getting along," I told the cat.

He shook himself, the feline equivalent of a shrug, and sent me a burst of affection. I scratched his back in return and he purred in his low grumbly way. It helped, to have at least these two on my side.

"Do you suppose they're ready yet?"

Larch's gaze unfocused a little, as if he looked into the distance. "By the time we get there, yes."

Darling stretched himself up against my leg, delicately pricking me with hopeful claws. I swooped him up and carried him like a baby while he happily batted at one of the lily earrings.

"What I don't get is, why would *she* snatch Rogue if he's still playing her game? If she wanted him to lose, there are easier ways to foil him." Had she moved up the timetable, as she'd taunted him with? That seemed like an alteration of the rules. *Tick-tock*.

I had been kind of talking out loud to myself, but Larch cocked his head thoughtfully.

"Titania would not cause a deal to be broken. She is bound by her rules as surely as we are."

I stopped in my tracks and Darling bit down on the earring, tugging hard. "Ow. Stop. But you're right, Larch. She wouldn't. Maybe can't. Something else caused Rogue to fail."

Larch nodded. "So I believe.

"Someone discovered a vulnerability of his and played on it."

Darling patted my cheek with his paw, showing me an image of Rogue running down the road after me. Me. Was I the chink in his otherwise immaculate Teflon armor? Not pleasant to contemplate. But his various vague and dire warnings could be interpreted that way. Perhaps I'd done something that opened a door to him.

I, myself, could have been the door, since I didn't remember a damn thing.

Darling squirmed, his message conveyed, and scampered down the hill, tail banner high. The traveling caravan appeared ready to go, indeed, queued up like a many-segmented colorful snake, poised to strike down the road.

Starling waited for me next to a carriage that could have been created by Cinderella's fairy godmother—a sequined fishbowl for all intents and purposes. Hopefully they'd punched some airholes in it. Darling perched on top of the glass globe, looking immensely pleased with himself, and likely to slide off at any moment. Felicity, bestowed with a great sparkling plume, led a brace of four other horses, prancing in place happily.

"I'm riding in this?"

"Yes! Both of us." She patted my arm in sympathy. "So you won't tire yourself out."

"Starling." I scrubbed my face with my hands. "I want you to listen to me very carefully. I am not pregnant. I know this for a fact, because it is physically impossible for me to be pregnant since I *have never had sexual intercourse with Rogue.* Or anyone else since I got here, for that matter," I added, just to be clear.

And—*kill me now*—she looked indulgent, patting me on the arm again. "Don't worry about it now. We're here to take care of you. Just leave everything to us. I put your grimoire in there so you can work in it," she coaxed.

Because everyone was now waiting on me, and they all seemed so excited about the carriage, I climbed inside. Fortunately the blue velvet bench seats were remarkably soft and cozy. Also, what had appeared to be clear glass were window openings here and there, between the sparkly swirling decorations. Above, Darling peered down at us through the curved roof, eyes bright with superiority. An expression that vanished as the carriage lurch forward and he desperately scrabbled for purchase on the smooth surface, pink jelly-bean toes mooshing against the glass, paws splaying in all directions.

Starling giggled. I snorted. Darling glared at us, but—furry brown belly pressed tight against the carriage and all four legs akimbo—he began a slow, relentless slide down the back. Starling fell to her side, helpless with laughter. I nearly couldn't catch my breath long enough to make the wish, but I managed to create a pillow affixed to the top and scooted him up to it.

He sank his claws in and lifted whiskers to the crisp blue sky, at last in his rightful place.

Yawning mightily, Starling stretched out on her seat and promptly fell asleep. Taking my cue from her, I turned sideways on mine and, propping my back against the curved rest, opened my grimoire to review and add notes.

I created a new section by wishing in some new pages— way better than having to grab a package at the hobby store and wrestle the blanks into the binding—and contemplated how to categorize these recent phenomena. Blackbird's memories, mine—they weren't really lost. It was more as if they'd been interfered with somehow. I wrote down Memory Interference, but frowned at it. I didn't want to create an immediate bias by assuming some kind of outside agency at work. Memory Inconsistency, then.

I wrote down as many observations as I could recall of the oily rope in Blackbird's mind and in my own. Then I turned to the Rogue section and recorded every detail possible about our last night together, along with Larch's speculations about vulnerability. I'd never been much for personal journaling, and I felt my face heat as I remembered how I kissed and touched him. A naked feast just for me. In the bright light of day, the way I'd gladly—no, voraciously—gone down on him and sucked him to violent climax seemed...wow. Okay, it aroused me again just remembering.

Funny how I kind of wanted to hide the page, though I knew perfectly well no one could read writing at all, much less this. Still, I glanced at the peacefully snoozing Starling before I continued.

The whole interlude had been so wildly exciting I'd even swallowed, not usually my favorite thing. That part stood out vividly though, because I hadn't minded at all, hadn't felt choked by the mucous fluid as sometimes happens. I'd drunk him in with as much hunger as the rest, reveling in his gasps of pleasure, the wildly triumphant utter delight emanating from him.

With a sinking feeling, I made myself contemplate it. Had that been the joy of a final victory? Of course it was completely impossible for a human woman to become pregnant from ingesting sperm, but my own snarky thoughts came back...*Rogue's magically potent sperm.*

No no no.

Just because a lot of biology here didn't work according to my physical laws didn't mean that this could change too. There had been entirely too much superstitious nonsense and misinformation surrounding pregnancy back in my old world. Things here might work differently, but they still followed definable rules—if I could just find them.

Except Rogue had no belly button, so that implied he hadn't grown in a womb, not in the usual way. How had the egg and sperm united to form him? With fish, the male salmon distributed milt over the red of eggs—no male/female interaction necessary. If the fae formed in eggs, they wouldn't have navels.

It would explain why they all seem so convinced you're pregnant, if you are, my objective self relentlessly pointed out. Of its own volition, my hand fell to my flat belly. Surely not.

"Did the baby move?" Starling's eyes had popped open, bright with interest.

"No." I snapped the grimoire closed and set it on the floor. "The baby—which does not exist to begin with—would barely be a division of cells at this point. Microscopic bits of tissue do not move in any discernible way."

"Oh." She pouted. "I'm just excited for you."

"Starling…" I sighed. Started over. "Do you know much about how babies are made?"

This sounded like a condescending question to a twenty-something-looking person like her, but it had occurred to me that this wasn't such an obvious thing here. Cecily had been clearly pregnant to Nancy and seemed to be giving birth in a human way. I hadn't meant to question the extent of Starling's sexual knowledge.

But, unaccountably, across from me, Starling had turned bright red and was picking at the blue velvet upholstery.

"Some," she muttered.

Oh my God.

"See, I know that when a man and a woman love each other very much—"

"You can stop there. We're not having *that* conversation."

"But you asked." She thrust her lower lip out and I rolled my eyes at her.

"Tell me this—do you have a belly button?"

She nodded and lifted her dress, revealing pretty lace pantaloons that matched her skirts.

"Glass coach, remember?"

"Oh, they can't see in. Magic glass coach."

Of course. So I took the opportunity she offered and moved over to sit next to her on her bench. Her navel looked perfectly normal to me. A dainty little innie. But Starling was half-human, so not unexpected.

"And you grew in Blackbird's womb, right? She gave birth to you?" I asked this, just to be sure to cover all bases. The word niggled at me and I remembered something Rogue had said that last night, about Titania's cursed womb. I needed to add that to my notes.

"Yes, but they had to cut me out."

Interesting. Might not mean anything though.

"How about Blackbird—was she…cut out too?"

Starling frowned at me, puzzled.

"Let's try this. Do you have a grandmother?"

She cocked her head, not quite understanding the concept.

"Your mother's mother? Who Blackbird lived with before she was imprisoned in the tower in the Glass Mountains and so forth?"

"Well…I think she lived in that tower for a really long time."

"Right. But before that?"

"I mean, a *really* long time."

"Gotcha." I moved back to my bench and picked up the grimoire.

"The fae nobles are like that." She sat up and tucked her feet under her. "All immortal—*you* know. So you can pretty much lock one up in a tower and leave her there for a long time."

"And you?"

She shrugged. "I'd starve and die. Or at least, grow old and die. I think. It's not like I have a lot of half-breed friends to ask."

That got my attention. "How many do you have?"

"Um, none?" She gave me an impish grin, which faded as she looked out the carriage window, the breeze ruffling her sunny bangs. "I wanted it to sound good. You're my only friend, Gwynn. Before you I had no one."

"I'm sure that's not true."

"'Tis true." She blew me a kiss. "Except for Mom, who doesn't count."

"Have you heard of a Lord Fafnir?" I thought the seeming change of subject might be too abrupt, but Starling nodded.

"Lady Incandescence's old lover, before she became Lord Rogue's. I never met him though."

"Why not?"

"Before my time. I guess he was all the thing, back in the day, but then he met his final comeuppance."

"What happened?"

"He was defeated and went over to the enemy."

"Falcon's enemy in the war?"

"Is there another?" She sounded all irritated and flopped onto her back, staring up at the sky through the glass ceiling. "What do you care? Lord Rogue is a far better catch."

I didn't point out the obvious, that Rogue wasn't around. And certainly not caught. At least not by me, at the moment.

"I care," I explained with great patience, I hoped, "because

I'm thinking about our quest and the pattern of missing firstborn children, not about romance. There are more important things in life than figuring out which man you want to land." I added a couple of notes about Fafnir to his section in Flora and Fauna.

"Easy for you to say—you have them panting after you. You're not a tainted half-breed who'll end up a virgin spinster and laughingstock of the entire countryside."

"Isn't that a little dramatic?"

When she didn't answer, I glanced over at her in time to see her wipe a tear from her cheek.

"Ah, I'm sorry. What happened? Officer Sean?"

She looked miserable. "He has girls at home. *Human* girls. He'd never soil himself with a dirty half-breed."

I put down my pen. "He said that?"

"He wanted to, you know, do the deed, and I said, 'No! I'm a good girl and I'm saving myself for true love' and he says, 'Maybe I am your true love' and I say, 'Maybe you are but I don't know for sure yet but we have time to find out' and then—" She paused to draw in a breath and wipe her nose with the back of her hand. "And *then*, he laughs at me! He laughed and said I wasn't worth the wait. That he has his pick of human girls and I'd saved him from contaminating himself with fae twat."

I flinched at the ugly word. "That was a horrible, ugly thing to say to you."

"But it's true."

"No. It isn't."

She sighed and rolled her eyes at the blue sky. "It is, Gwynn. You don't know. The fae won't have me either. Who wants a wife who'll just die? And the humans—they're all afraid the magic will rub off on them, change them."

Interesting how that paralleled what I'd been thinking. "Yeah—but he was happy enough to dip his wick in it until you brought up true love."

"What? Oh!" She wrinkled her nose. "And ick!"

"But my point stands."

"I still don't understand," she whined. "I'm not as smart as you are."

"Oh, stop it. Yes, you are. My point is that he was not telling you the truth. This is a human thing and—I'm sorry to say it—not unusual for a human man when getting laid is on the line. He was happy enough to do the deed, as you say, until you scared him with the Oh My God lifetime and beyond commitment of True Love."

"But I *want* to fall in love!"

"Fine. But don't go looking for someone to pop into that role. Figure out who you are first. Make your life what you want it to be. You are not trapped in a tower waiting for rescue. When you find someone you like enough, who thinks you—the woman, Starling, regardless of your parentage—is wonderful also, then you can try on loving them. Love as an active verb, not some fairy-tale idea of this magical state of True Love that somehow descends on you from beyond."

"But everyone wants true love."

"It's a fantasy. It doesn't exist."

"You have it."

"No. Especially not me."

When we stopped for lunch, I left Starling to help Larch set out our colorful blankets, flasks of chilled wine and trays of leftover feast food. With the current size of our company, it took me a few minutes to find the human soldiers. The men had gathered around a small fire and were heating some kind of meat over it. Officer Liam spotted me and, wiping the grease from his cheek, rose from his crouch to meet me.

"Lady Sorceress." He inclined his head in apparent respect, but I heard the unhappiness in his thoughts, the sweet scent of desire forever tainted with the bitter metal of fear. Great. "How may I serve you?"

"A private word, please." I walked away, making him tag along after. Small pleasures. When we were out of earshot, I stopped. "You have an Officer Sean among your men?"

"He's a good man."

"I don't care. I want him gone. Send him home."

Liam's face darkened under the sunny bronze curls. "Is that Lord Rogue's order?"

"Lord Rogue isn't here. It's my order."

"Why do you want Sean to go?"

"It doesn't matter why—make it happen. Tell you what, you can go with him." I turned to leave.

"No, I can't."

I glanced over my shoulder at him. A handsome man, for sure, though not as tall as Rogue. "No?"

"Some of us hold our honor highly. I can't just gallivant off because the whim takes me. Not like himself."

"Excuse me?"

He scratched his bristly chin. "Seems I heard something about that—how you're knocked up with Lord Rogue's bastard and now he's off to greener pastures." He was pleased to needle me, his thoughts full of satisfaction at scoring a point.

I'd been screwed, just as he had.

"Really?" I said to him. "That's really where you want to go?" I stared him in the eye, letting the cat well up in me. She wanted out, frustrated from my worrying and with the lack of action in the past few days, ready for a little fight.

He held up open palms to placate me, but he smelled more of spitefulness than fear. "Just seems that I warned you of what would happen if you cavorted with the fae. 'Tis unnatural. No good can come of it." His gazed drifted down to my midsection and I resisted the urge to wrap my arms around myself in protection.

"You have no fucking clue what kind of choices I've had to make."

"No, but I know he left you. He said he didn't care what happened to you. How can you choose him?"

The cat crouched in my heart. "When did he say that?"

"The night before the harvest party."

Now he had my complete and utter attention.

"Tell me what happened."

He shrugged, putting me off, back to his insouciant self. "Nothing you need to fret about, Lady Sorceress. Something between men."

The cat's need to act, already so close to the surface, flared and melded with my own high emotional state. "Fuck that shit," I muttered to myself and lashed out a silver-white lasso of thought around Liam's, holding him in place with the merest wish.

This became easier each time. I sifted through his memories of the past few days with careless ease, quickly finding the one I wanted. There. Rogue waking him from slumber, imperious, demanding—and on edge. Was that fear or anger? Making Liam swear to protect me with his last gasp and laying the onus on him. And giving him a goddamn message for me.

"Tell her not to look for me. If Falcon calls, she should ignore him. I'll handle him. I don't care what she does, as long as she stays safe—and well away from me. Tell her to remember what I warned her about. Protect my lady, Liam, or I'll skin you and keep you alive that way."

So odd to see Rogue through Liam's eyes, the shine of wild magic around him, the flare of his cloak as he left again. I didn't have to ask Liam why he hadn't passed along the message. It stood in his thoughts—the disgust at my sluttish behavior, a bit of pity at me being cast aside, and the prurient hope that he might be the one to fuck me next.

I shook my head at Liam and let him go. He staggered a little, but I didn't care. With nothing further to say to him, I turned my back and left him there.

CHAPTER 15

JUVENILE DELINQUENTS AND UNEXPECTED AIRLIFTS

Magic seems to operate almost like a radioactive substance or other mutating agent. Which begs the question, who or what were the fae before they mutated?

~*Big Book of Fairyland*, "Rules of Magic"

I N THE BACK of my mind, I registered the fact that I'd taken another step past whatever ethical code remained to me. The cat, however, didn't care and she filled my head enough that the thought remained a minor note. Mostly we were thinking about Rogue's blunt message.

Tell her not to look for me.

I brushed my fingers against one dangling lily earring. It was all I wanted to do. I plopped myself on the blanket and Starling handed me a plate and a glass of wine.

"I can have wine even though you think I'm pregnant?"

"What does that have to do with anything?"

"Good enough for me." I pondered while I ate. Remember what he warned me about? I could have devoted an entire chapter to Rogue's ominously vague warnings, there had been so many. *Which* damn warning? The dragon's egg weighed, null and lifeless in my pocket, complimented by the vial of blood on the other side. He'd warned me to be careful of who I received tributes from. A place to start, anyway.

"Larch—would the dragonfly girls know who gave me which tributes?"

He screwed up one side of his face in thought. "Might be. Most of 'em are pretty silly though."

"You don't know, right?"

"No, Lady Gwynn. I have no head for accounting."

"When you're done eating, would you find me one who might—wait, Larch, when you're done—" But he'd already trotted off.

"Where did you go just now?" Starling eyed me with suspicious curiosity.

"Call of nature."

"Hmph. I needed to go too."

"Something I feel confident you can do entirely on your own."

"Mean."

"That's me," I agreed in a cheerful tone. Hopefully she wouldn't be miffed that I'd sent Sean packing. In an ideal world, she'd be so glad not to see him about that she wouldn't care why he wasn't. Even if she did find out and get annoyed, I didn't regret the move for an instant. Life was too short to risk conversations with boneheads.

Larch returned with the blue-ringletted dragonfly girl. Her round lavender eyes dominated her heart-shaped pixie face. With anxiety giving them a dewy sheen and pinching her little bow-shaped lips, she could be right out of anime. She crumpled into a heap at my knee, begging to know how she'd displeased me.

"What did you say to the poor thing?" I asked Larch and he sighed, stoic as ever.

"That you wanted to ask her some questions, my lady sorceress—nothing more than that."

"Why did you pick this one?" I peered dubiously at the pile of shivering ringlets and ostentatious weeping.

"Do you doubt my judgment, my lady?"

Frankly, at the moment, I did. But he had a point. I tugged one of the long powder-blue curls. "You haven't displeased me, girlie. Sit up. I just want to ask you some things about the tributes."

She obeyed immediately, tucking her slim little legs together and shaking her head so her hair tumbled around her girlish frame, Thumbelina come to life. I caught a flash of calculation from her, before she opened her eyes wider—more lilac than lavender—and gazed at me soulfully. Something about the deliberate guilelessness of her expression reminded me of Rogue when he worked to sucker me into one of his tricky bargains. A subtle flavor of his magic about her too. What had he said? That my magic had marked Starling as mine.

"What's your name?"

"What you called me is fine, your magical powerful highness."

"Yeah...not so much. How come none of you girls have names?"

"We don't really need them until we serve a grand person

like yourself. Until then we're like blossoms in the field—all more or less alike."

An astute explanation for a brainless blossom. Surely this was the one I'd pointed to, who Rogue and I had wished smarter. And now, as if one of his by-blows had come looking for him, here she sat, looking at me with much-too-canny lilac eyes and talking like me.

"So, Thumbelina, what do you know about my tribute collection? I'm looking to find out the origin of particular items."

She slid a sideways look at Larch, who remained impassive. "I would never take anything, Lady Sorceress." She said this with the tone of a vow, with a titch of guilt.

"Thank you, Larch. I think she'll do nicely," I told Larch, who bowed and discreetly withdrew. "You've been through it, haven't you? There's a reason Larch thought you might know where things came from."

"I like to look. To see the pretty things. I always put them back."

I caught an image from her mind, of looking through all the strange things and dreaming about their origins, while the other dragonfly girls giggled and danced. It had been a disservice, to make her smarter than the others. I'd thought improvement couldn't cause too much harm, but our whim had yanked her, a lily of the field, from a life of blissful idiocy to one where a newly restless mind sought stimulation.

"Do you have a way of knowing where the things come from?"

"How would I?" She looked down, cagey.

"Starling—would you mind getting my grimoire from the

carriage?"

Starling, who'd been listening to the conversation with great interest, jumped up much too quickly. "Sure! Actually I have to answer the call of nature—" she gave the phrase great significance, "—and will fetch it on my way back." She walked off slowly, making a great show of whistling as if she had all the time in the world.

"Okay," I told the petite fairy, "spill."

She tilted her head and gave me that innocent wide-eyed look, then, assessing me, she cast it off like a mask. Her expression sharpened. Gone was the sweet waif, replaced by a shrewd and sharp miniature woman. Fluffy kitten to spitting alley cat in an imperceptible, instantaneous shift.

"I hold things in my hands and I just know." She said it quietly for my ears only.

"Have you always been able to do this?"

"No. My kind—we don't *do* magic like that."

"How did you find out you could?"

"The other night, I got tired of dancing. It's just the same thing over and over, you know? And the singing—kill me now." She shook her head, as if perplexed by these thoughts. "So I wandered around, but that was boring too. I started looking through the tribute wagon, just for something to do and..."

She trailed off and I finished for her. "And you found something you liked and played with it for a while." So were juvenile delinquents made—restless energy plus curiosity and a dollop of bored rebellion.

"I wasn't going to keep it!" She threw the words at me defiantly.

I shrugged. Most of that stuff held such abstract value to me that I didn't really care. Still, I imagined stealing from a noble carried a pretty serious penalty. "So how did Larch find out?"

She grimaced. "I was an idiot. The first time that thing—and it was just a glass apple, you have twenty-two of them—reached out and showed me where it came from, well...I screamed."

I snorted out a laugh, more at how much she hated admitting her stereotypical dragonfly girl behavior than anything else. "Can't say as how I blame you. That must have been startling as all hell."

She looked pissed, a funny expression on her lovely face. "Yes. Larch gave me a set-down and told me I could stay if I put it back. I really thought he'd never tell you."

"He only did because I asked him who could tell me where some of the stuff comes from. And because he knew I'd be more interested in your help than in punishing you. I need an inventory. Do you know what I mean?"

Pushing the tumbling ringlets back with impatience, she thought about it. "Like, list out everything that's there."

"Yes. Can you do that? Look at each thing and say who gave it to me."

She shrugged and started counting off on her fingers. "One gray wolf hide, Lord Bristleberry. Twenty-two glass apples, Lord Ming. One monster harness, Lady Strawberry. Fourteen..."

"Wait," I interrupted. "You already identified and memorized everything?"

"No. Just some."

"I thought you said it frightened you when the glass apple told you where it came from."

She flushed, the pink a pretty contrast to her hair. "I wanted to practice. Seems stupid to be able to do something and not, you know, figure it out."

"Good thinking. You think you can remember everything?"

"I don't know. I never remembered things before, but now I do. It's kind of creepy."

I considered telling her the truth. Normally I'd said that I'd want to know, but the worry that something had changed in my own mind ate at me. I might have been happier not knowing after all. I could always tell her later. The magical ability must have come sideways from one of us too. Or we had awakened something dormant in her. Since her unexpected gift just happened to fit exactly what I needed, it was likely my fault.

"I don't remember everything so I'm going to write down what you tell me."

Right on cue, Starling ambled up and put the grimoire in my lap. Thumbelina watched with fascination as I pulled a pen from my pocket, flipped to a few pages from the end and titled it "Inventory." I filled in the items she had recited. "...wolf hide..." I muttered to myself.

"Gray wolf," Thumbelina corrected. I frowned at her. "Do you want it to be right or not?" She asked in a sweet tone that didn't fool me for a second.

"Fine, fine," I added *gray* with a caret between 1 and *wolf.* "Glass apples...guess I get to decide how to spell people's names—not like anyone is going to correct me. Is a monster harness what I think it is? To hitch up the monsters I don't have?" I blinked at them in sudden alarm. "Tell me I don't have any pet monsters!"

Thumbelina snickered and Starling gave me one of her mother's exasperated looks. "A monster would never fit in a wagon. And who takes monsters on a sailing journey?"

"Who takes wagonloads of glass apples and gray wolf hides everywhere they go?"

Starling sighed and rolled her eyes. "I don't know how you were planning to buy a ship—they're expensive, you know."

I didn't point out that this had never been my plan at all. Rogue had set it all up and I'd cruised along for the ride. Now my sugar daddy had left me high and dry. "I'm buying a whole ship? We can't just…hitch a ride?"

"No. And it's time to go."

"Ride with us, Thumbelina? That way I can get down what you've seen so far."

She sprang to her feet with a little hip swing and a cocky attitude. "Want me to carry the thing?"

"Lady Sorceress." Starling reminded her.

"I know who she is."

I laughed, handing her the grimoire and she walked toward the carriage, flipping through the pages.

"She should show you more respect," Starling fumed.

"Oh, she's fine."

"I hope she's sitting on your side," Starling muttered. "I don't think I should have to share."

"Jealous?"

"No. I just don't see why you need her when you have me. Plus she's impertinent."

"Because she can tell me what all is in the tribute wagons and you can't."

"I don't see why you need to know that."

"I'm chasing a clue."

"Oh!" Starling seized my arm. "That's so exciting!" Thumbelina glanced over her shoulder at us in startlement at the squeal. "What is it?"

I didn't really want to tell her about Rogue's message. Why had he left it with Liam, of all people? Starling would have told me immediately.

Maybe that was the point.

"Gwynn—you said I could help and here you are thinking up how to put me off."

She was right.

"That's the thing. I don't know yet. So I want Thumbelina to tell me what all tributes I've received and from whom, and maybe something will jump out at me."

"You want something that jumps?" Starling shook her head, blond hair shimmering in the sun, the same color as the leaves in the grove nearby. Fall colors.

"Sorry. Bad phrasing. I want to listen for something significant. You listen too."

"Ah." Starling nodded, assuming a wise expression. Then yawned.

Sure enough, once she sprawled on her bench in the carriage—since I asked Thumbelina to sit next to me—Starling started nodding off again. I didn't blame her really. The recitation of bizarre items and even odder names became a monotonous drone. Mainly I hoped the little fairy would mention the dragon's eggs, since I suspected that was what

Rogue had referenced.

After fifty-three items on my list, Thumbelina stopped. "That's all so far. I can look more when we stop tonight."

No dragon's eggs. Dammit.

I considered showing her the one in my pocket, but that would bias the experiment. So we rode on from then in silence. I busied myself with transferring names to the Flora and Fauna section. Some of them were people I'd met, if only glancingly. On those I added notes of what I could remember about them and my guess as to their position in fae society. Most I had no idea who they were. The light-up pillows I'd invented continued to sell like hotcakes, providing me with a tidy income. If one liked having seventeen vials of crushed alabaster shell.

"If you don't mind, that would be great."

"No. It's good to have...something to do."

When I asked Thumbelina who some of the people were, she said she didn't know necessarily—the names just came to her. Starling wasn't much more help. When she snuffled awake, I grilled her, but she claimed ignorance on most.

"My mother's the one who knows all that. Besides that's her job as your seneschal anyway. Not mine."

"Just what is your job, Starling?" I teased her.

"Stalwart companion and best friend," she replied, prim, giving Thumbelina the hairy eyeball. The blue-haired fairy didn't notice, entranced as she was in studying the characters I'd written on the pages. She ran her fingers over them, as if they might grow out of the page they were written on.

We camped that night, with me on my own in my travel tent on the futon bed I'd made, which Rogue so disdained.

Anxiety for him plagued me like a tooth with a cavity. Sometimes the ache faded into the background, but then flared with unexpected pain when I carelessly bit down. It didn't help that I missed him more than ever. The earrings swinging in my lobes reminded me of his touch on my skin, part comfort, part torment.

When I finally fell asleep—alone, since Darling had gone off hunting—I found myself searching in my dreams. I walked along the beach. The sand shifted under my bare feet, sliding away so I sank into it up to my knees, my skirts snarling around my thighs and dragging wet. I tried wishing them away, but nothing happened.

In frustration, I yanked at them, trying to climb out of the sand, but only sinking deeper in. The surf pounded up and a mermaid missing a piece of her tail pointed and laughed. I begged her for help, but she flipped her long powder-blue ringlets over her shoulder, giggling like a madwoman. The waves reached me and poured, icy cold into the sandy hole around me. I'd sunk up to my waist now, but I kept trying to struggle forward.

Down the coast, a sailing ship waited, flags flying. Rogue waited for me on that ship. I needed to get to him, but the water and sand filled my nose, suffocating me, drowning me.

"Rogue!" I cried, though the ship was too impossibly far. He'd never hear me, even without sand pouring down my throat. Yet I kept calling for him.

The ship set sail without me, serenely cutting through the waves, leaving me behind as the sand closed over my head.

I woke with a choking sound to the still-dark tent. Outside firelight glowed while the fae sang and danced. Some never seemed to sleep, like sharks that swam in endless circles to keep oxygen moving through their bodies. Thumbelina might be crawling through the tribute wagons even now, her restless mind and magical gift recording it all. A whiff of sandalwood and Stargazer lilies drifted past.

"Rogue?" I whispered, afraid to hope. My throat felt raw and I wondered if I had been screaming aloud.

"Stop looking for me."

The thought ran weak and pale in the back of my mind. I stilled, listening. Was that him and not me? Nothing more.

"I'm not looking," I thought back. *"I got your message."*

"Stop looking for me. Save yourself."

"I can't not dream."

But the voice—Rogue—did not reply.

When I dreamed again, there sat the sailing ship at the dock in the distance. The soft sand sucked at my bare feet. With renewed determination, I started walking. Maybe this time, I'd get there before it sailed.

⚞⚟

IN THE MORNING, I asked Blackbird to ride in the carriage with us, so I could quiz her on the people and politics. With the barest hesitation, she agreed.

Thumbelina and Starling waited in the carriage, arguing with each other about something. They snapped their mouths closed when we approached and I decided I didn't want to know. Blackbird raised a perfectly arched eyebrow at me, sizing Thumbelina up and down.

"Really, Lady Gwynn?" She asked softly.

"She's helping me with a project."

"It's not seemly to have such as she in your company."

I turned so my back was to the carriage, speaking only for Blackbird's ears. "'Such as she'—all the dragonfly girls or what? And why not?"

"Her kind are for service. Not companionship. Surely you've noticed they're not much for conversation."

"That doesn't mean they're not people too."

"Well, dear—actually they're not. They're more like...barely intelligent fruit."

I laughed, but her serious expression didn't change. Here I'd wondered if Rogue had grown on a vine. "Give Thumbelina a chance. You'll see. She's special."

Once we got rolling, Thumbelina got over her reticence at having Blackbird present, and regaled us with the list of her overnight findings. Feeling flirtatious, Darling decided to join us inside the carriage, making a nuisance of himself playing with Thumbelina's ringlets. She fussed over him, calling him a handsome young man, which he loved. He finally abandoned himself to a nap, completely overflowing her tiny lap while she scratched his furry belly and I took notes.

Despite herself, Blackbird became fascinated by the list of tributes and the people who'd given them to me—and in the magic of me recording the information into the grimoire. I caught her more than once eyeing Thumbelina with specula-tion. Intelligent fruit, indeed. She added in bits of information here and there, but was unable to tell me as much as I'd hoped.

The fae upper echelons seemed to be more or less flat. The nobles—and so far I'd recorded about a hundred names—all held equivalent titles. Tributes came from more than those people, however. I'd received gifts from Brownie tribes other than Larch's and from heads of various fae groups. There also seemed to be a group of second-tier lordlings, to which Blackbird belonged, for reasons that escaped me.

"Aren't you a princess?" I interrupted one of her explanations.

"Not anymore, dear. Not since I married my Fergus."

"Because he's not a fae noble?"

"Well, not exactly. But it makes no never mind. I'm happy to live a quiet life."

Starling had her head tipped back on the back of the seat, staring up at the sky. "And it's not like you can marry me off to gain status, either."

Blackbird patted her hand. "Not that you'd want that anyway. You wouldn't be happy with that life."

"How do you know?"

"I know my own daughter, don't I? And I see myself when I look at you."

Thumbelina looked back and forth between them, envy in her wide lilac eyes. If the dragonfly girls did grow as fruit, then she'd have no mother, no family to speak of. More and more I wondered if the intelligence we'd capriciously dumped on her wasn't more of a curse. Self-awareness could be painful.

"If you were a princess, though," I persisted, "does that mean your mother was the queen?"

If Blackbird were another woman—me, for instance—she would have rolled her eyes. Instead she gave me a *look*. "It doesn't work like that."

"How does it work?"

"It's more like a kind of special status, being a princess. It has nothing to do with ruling."

"That makes no sense to me."

"Then perhaps you ought to examine what the concept of princess means to you—you're the one hearing what we're saying that way."

Oh.

"What is that?" Starling pointed at the sky beyond the glass ceiling.

A vivid spot of scarlet winged through the sky, glittering with jeweled light, growing larger as it swooped toward us. I'd seen that exact sight before, back in battle. "That's a dragon. Coming this way too."

"Titania save us." Blackbird paled.

"Somehow I doubt she's inclined to do that." I grabbed hold of a decorative curlicue as the dragon dropped over us, a stained-glass bomber, great talons outstretched. "Hang tight. This might get ugly."

The carriage halted with a jolt that threw Darling off Thumbelina's lap as the horses reared, neighing in terror, their thrashing sending us tumbling, sea monkeys in a goldfish bowl. A cacophony of shouts rang out and our company came running, the human soldiers firing arrows that bounced harmlessly off the dragon's hide. With a swift wish, I cut the horses loose just before the magic-blocking claws the height of a house wrapped around the glass coach, shutting out daylight and our guards' terrified faces.

We lifted into the air, the enormous wings creating a tornado of sound while the dragon labored, lungs working with steam-engine noise.

It carried us away, trapped in our glass cage, while our helpless retainers scurried like ants below.

CHAPTER 16

IN WHICH I MEET THE ENEMY AND HE IS WALTER

୧⭑୨

Barbarism is in the eye of the beholder.
~Big Book of Fairyland, "Falcon's War"

"DO SOMETHING!" THUMBELINA'S rounded little nails dug into my arm with surprising sharpness. "Aren't you supposed to be all powerful or something? Get us out of here!"

"Leave her alone," Starling snarled, dragging the little fairy girl off me and dumping her on the floor, then braced herself against the swaying wall and blanched at the drop beneath the glass she stood on.

"Don't look down," I advised, practicing what I preached. Darling had crawled up my shoulder and buried himself between me and the bench seat, shivering in terror—and shredding my skin with his claws where he could find purchase. "And I can't do more than any of you right now. That dragon's magic-dampening field is canceling everything out. Look at Starling's hair."

The shining blond color had reverted to her natural brown. I put a hand up to my own hair, to find it barely grown out from the shearing I'd been given. The lily earrings fell from my ears and dropped into my lap. Now I knew one way to remove them. With a pang, I folded them in my palm. The grimoire had reverted to the wooden box it had started out as, sliding across the floor and banging into things until Thumbelina grabbed it.

"You look better as a blonde," she informed Starling.

"Gee, thanks." Starling eased back into her seat, steadfastly closing her eyes as Blackbird had done.

Thumbelina, still on the floor, placed her back against the curved glass wall and raised a pale blue eyebrow at me. "I like your do, though. Kinda punk."

I had no idea what a Faerie punk movement might entail, but surely Thumbelina would be in the forefront, with piercings and tattoos to reflect the newly fierce personality behind her pastel prettiness. As for me, it was sobering—and not a little painful—to be reminded of the shorn slave that still lurked under my illusory image. Once we got out of this, I resolved to permanently fix my hair and the grimoire—if any of the information I'd painstakingly recorded survived.

And if we got out of this.

"Now what?" Thumbelina asked us, looking pointedly from one to another.

"I think we wait," I replied in a dry tone.

"That seems awfully passive. Shouldn't we fight or something? Make a plan?"

"Any suggestions?" I managed to extract Darling from my shoulders and let him bury his face in my lap. The thoughts, if you could call them that, coming from him were all frightened kitty with none of his usual intelligence. Hopefully he wasn't severed from that self forever. Interesting, in a ghoulish way, that he hadn't reverted to human-form fae, but instead became more entirely cat, which meant the spell that actively bound him let him retain his higher nature even though he'd become a permanent animal. A daunting thought.

"We could break the glass." Thumbelina rapped her fist on it thoughtfully.

Blackbird opened one glittering eye. "Don't you dare."

We were flying over water now—likely the ocean we'd been traveling toward.

"Even if we could break the glass, which I doubt we could do without magic, I don't know that I could stop our fall in time to keep the impact from killing us. It might depend on how far the dragon's field extends. Something I'm not excited to test with our lives."

Thumbelina pushed her ringlets back with a little snarl. "We can't just sit here and do nothing at all."

I petted Darling, who trembled, and remembered all the days I spent starving in that cell, waiting for something to happen. "Sometimes that's all you can do. Our time to act will come. Quite soon, I suspect."

We rapidly closed on an island outcropping in the midst of the ocean. Waves dashed themselves on jagged rocks and dissolved into sprays of water. Rising out of the rock itself, a fortress crowned the island in an array of towers, walls and fantastic walkways.

Where the hell did the dragon plan to land?

The dragon stooped, dropping in a dizzying spiral distinctly reminiscent of the near-vertical drop in a roller-coaster ride, dragging involuntary screams out of everyone but Blackbird. I'd just be happy if no one puked. The drop slowed, steadied and I risked looking down.

We hovered just over a circular tower roof. The dragon set the carriage down with jaw-dropping precision, the glass wheels making the barest clink against the stone. As soon as the talons released us, the magic rushed back in with an audible rush, like air filling a vacuum. My ears even popped.

Ready for it, I put my hair back how I liked it and Starling's too. I decided to leave the grimoire as it was, for safekeeping. I'd find out soon enough if I'd lost all those notes. I placed the earrings against my lobes and they thankfully clicked into place with the now-familiar zing that made me think in totally inappropriate ways about Rogue's nipping teeth. Distracting, yes—but any protection I could get would help, and being sexually revved would only increase my magic. I fervently wished for Rogue, knowing full well this one would not come true. At least Darling's awareness seemed to be coming back. He blinked green eyes at me, wondering muzzily what had happened and where he was.

"Do you know where we are?" I asked Blackbird.

She smoothed her hair into place, giving me a sharp look. "Not for certain, but I believe this might be Castle Terra Incognita."

I wanted to slap myself on the forehead. Starling gasped and peered outside. "Really? I thought that was only in stories."

Thumbelina snorted and pushed her charming curls out of her face again. "Does anyone have a hair tie? And a knife?

I winked at her and drew up my skirt, showing her the dagger I kept strapped to my thigh as Liam had taught me.

"Nice. But what about me?"

With a wish, I dropped both at her feet. "Anyone else?"

Starling watched Thumbelina fit the dagger into her tiny fist and flash it experimentally through the air. "I don't know how to use one."

"What's to know?" Thumbelina looked disgusted. "You stick the pointy end in people you don't like."

Hearing my words come out of her pretty pixie lips was beginning to unnerve me.

I dropped knives at Starling and Blackbird's feet too. "Can't hurt."

"Make mine a sword, dearie." Blackbird flexed her fingers. "It's been some time, but I used to be quite handy with a rapier."

Starling gaped at her. "You never told me that."

"It never came up."

Darling demanded some body armor and I quickly gave him a plain set, telling him I didn't have time to give him anything more elaborate, so he could suck up the grumbles.

A door in the wall bordering the roof opened and a train of mossy-green gremlin-type creatures marched out, carrying spears three times their height and arranging themselves in a loose circle around the tower roof. "Okay, look sharp. I think we're better off out of the carriage. Stick close to me, okay? Starling, would you carry this?" Box or no, I didn't want to leave the grimoire behind.

"Can't you just wish us back to where we were?" Thumbelina grumbled.

"I'm not good at the poofing thing—sorry."

We climbed out, Darling bristling his fur irritably against the sea mist. He stayed right by my ankle, promising to defend me to the death. Unfortunately he imagined himself twice the size of the gremlins and I worried he'd get himself into trouble. Starling and Blackbird gathered behind me and Thumbelina arranged herself square in front of me, hair tied back in a tight ponytail, her petite figure in an attack crouch, dagger held out with surprisingly effective menace. I appreciated the thought but still invoked a kind of force field around us. I should have practiced with this concept—making something impervious to attack that would still be permeable to oxygen and carbon dioxide. Note to self.

A pudgy figure waddled out of the doorway, draped in misty rainbow robes that appeared to have food stains on them. He carried a staff with a crystal globe topping it. He paused, planting the staff so he could lean against it, and beamed at me, a fatuous smile puffing out his chubby cheeks.

"Gwynn!" He opened arms wide. "Come give us a hug! I'm so excited you're finally visiting."

"And you are?" I stayed right where I was, not trusting this for a moment—even if I had been able to get past my dainty blue-haired warrior. *Please don't say Gandalf. Or Merlin.*

"I'm Walter, Wizard of the Western Keep."

"Walter?" I repeated, like an idiot. But really—*Walter?*

He thumped his staff on the stone. "You can call me Walt. Come on inside. We have so much to discuss."

"Actually we'd prefer to go back to what we were doing before you kidnapped us."

"Would you?" He gestured to his gremlin guards. "Unfortunately being captives means you don't get to make decisions like that. You leave if and when I decide you do."

I'd had enough. I reached out to his mind, fully ready to twist his thoughts until he let us go.

And hit a blank wall of gray.

"Uh-uh-uh." He beamed at me with jovial indulgence and bounced the crystal staff a little more. "No fair starting a magic duel without setting up the rules first."

"What are the rules?"

"Come inside and we'll discuss. Hot cocoa for everyone!"

The gremlin guards closed ranks around us. Darling hissed and Thumbelina stabbed her little dagger at one. It danced back, making the sound of an agitated beetle. Another ran at Darling, but bounced off the force field like a rubber ball.

"Now, now. We don't need any of that!" Walt called over his shoulder, turning a little sideways to wedge himself through the doorway and pointing the staff at me. My force field collapsed in a puff of pink sparks. Just like that. Even Rogue hadn't dissolved my spells that easily. Or hadn't tried.

The fear I'd been holding at arm's length tried to rush in. I pulled on the center of quiet. If we were as screwed as it appeared, I'd need all my wits.

"Thoughts?" I asked Blackbird as they escorted us inside.

"Not many," she answered. "I've never met him before. We've been at war for so long, you know."

"War? This is one of Falcon's opponents? Is that what this is about?"

Blackbird twirled the tip of her rapier thoughtfully, staring hard at Walter's back. "Hard to say."

"I doubt it," Starling added darkly, then looked abashed at

my questioning glance. "I just think that if this was about the war, Falcon would have called you in. This isn't the way the war is conducted."

She had a point.

We wound our way down a spiraling set of stairs that protruded from the stone walls, a seemingly endless black drop down the center of the tower. All of us, except Darling, clung close to the outsides of the steps, away from that daunting abyss. The gremlin guards swarmed over the walls, clinging like locusts with spiny feet and hands and waving their spears, chittering.

For once, the noises made no sense to me. If the dragonfly girls—with the dramatic exceptions of Thumbelina and Dragonfly herself—were the mental equivalent of intelligent fruit, then these fell several levels below that.

Starling, descending right in front of me, hunched her shoulders. "I hate those things."

"No kidding."

The air grew warmer as we descended, becoming downright hot when we finally reached a level surface. We entered a great hall, enormous columns of the same gray stone rising up out of sight, into cavernous shadows. No furniture or anything else to designate what the room was meant to do. We had to be in the heart of the castle, deep inside the craggy island. Walter waved his arms expansively.

"Biggest throne room in all of Faerie. Those nobles can stuff it!"

So big it swallowed the throne, apparently, but I held my tongue. The floor burned through my soles and Darling trotted faster, then asked to be picked up. The gremlins crawled up the pillars and on the walls, watching us and staying off the floor.

"Why is it so hot?" Starling muttered.

"Dragons!" Walter shouted, still marching onward through the unending room. "Screw geothermal heat when you can have dragon heat."

"I don't suppose he's one of your apple customers?" I asked Blackbird and she shook her head, uncertain.

"But I mean to find out," she answered.

"Thumbelina—are your feet okay?"

She grimaced at her bare toes. "Hurts like a son of a bitch. Can you give me boots or something?"

"Sure."

"Actually—" she waved a hand at her silky fairy frock, "—how about pants too? Something less...silly."

I took a moment to concentrate, ignoring the wilder suggestions Darling inserted into my thoughts, and dressed her in a fighting outfit of dark blue leather, worthy of Angelina Jolie in her scariest roles.

Thumbelina surveyed herself and gave me the thumbs-up. "Awesome, Lady Sorceress Gwynn."

"Just hope Walter doesn't pop that spell too and leave you naked."

"Better naked than silly."

Words to live by. It occurred to me that she'd never lost her enhanced intelligence even when all the other spells failed—undoubtedly because of the permanence conveyed by the crystal cave.

"Oh, sweet Gwynn and entourage, where aaaaarrre yooo-ouuu?" Walter's call echoed uncannily off the stones.

We picked up pace and found him perched on a huge throne. Of course, to be truly in scale with the room, the chair would have to be the size of a blimp, but Walter had clearly gone to great effort. Unfortunately, it dwarfed him, making him seem to be an overfed toddler perched in his dad's armchair.

He frowned at Thumbelina, sniffing the air. "No fair, Gwynnie. No more magic without permission."

At least I was smart enough not to ask "or what?" The answer to that could be gruesome and I didn't dare risk my companions.

"All right, Walter. Thank you for explaining that rule. What are the others?"

A gremlin skittered up to me with silver bracelets on a platter. It danced from foot to foot impatiently, waiting for me to take them.

"You'll wear these so you can't do magic until the duel."

Involuntarily, my fingers went to my pulse. At least I managed not to touch my throat, as I remembered the silver collar my trainers had made me wear. Silver prevented me from using my magic, taking away my only real weapon. I'd never be that helpless again. "Absolutely not."

"But you have to." He frowned, petulant, then brightened. "I'll kill you if you don't."

"Fine. The only way you'll get those on me is on my dead body."

"Well, what then? You'll just promise not to use magic until the duel starts?"

"I agree."

"Hmm. That was easy, pretty Gwynnie." He flicked a hand

and the gremlin raced off again. Walt laid the staff across his lap, caressing the crystal globe in a way that seemed almost obscene and leering at me. "You're so pretty." His gray eyes wandered with affection over the group. "All of you. Pretty little flowers for my garden."

Oh great. Totally insane too.

"I'm so looking forward to your hot cocoa," Lady Blackbird fluttered at him, as if we were honored guests. "It's quite famous throughout the realm. Lord Falcon will be so jealous that I had the opportunity to try it."

Walter beamed at her and I took advantage of the distraction to touch the crystal globe with the barest brush of my thoughts. It felt like the crystal in the cave had, resonant and clear. He didn't seem to notice my poking around, though he'd been unusually sensitive to any more overt magic.

"Falcon is crazy for my cocoa—and my dragons. He shall have neither!"

"I'm impressed that you control them." I used my best suck-up-to-the-eccentric-senior-scientist attitude and Walter laughed.

"See, at the Western Keep, here there be dragons." He waggled his eyebrows at me. "Gwynnie gets the joke."

Though he'd been speaking in the fae tongue—or one of them, since I sometimes suspected there were different dialects for the various tribes and species—I finally got the clue.

"You're another immigrant. Like me."

And another sorcerer.

Walter belly laughed and pointed a finger at me. "You didn't know. You're such a babe in the woods." He fell to the side in the too-big throne, laughing hysterically.

"Nuttier than a drunk pig in a henhouse," Starling whispered sideways to me. One of Puck's many sayings that never made a bit of sense.

"The 'mighty sorceress Gwynn.'" Walter made air quotes with his fingers and pounded his feet against the throne, he was laughing so hard.

"When and where are you from?" I had to raise my voice so he could hear me and he abruptly sobered, sitting up straight.

"Wouldn't you like to know?" he crooned, taunting. "But you don't get to. No. No, you don't."

"Why did you bring us here, if not to talk?"

"I only meant to bring you, Gwynnie sweet. Your companions were unexpected."

"Then send them back. Sounds like this is just between you and me."

"No!" Starling whirled on me, but Blackbird put a restraining hand on her arm. Darling vowed his protection. And apologized that the floor was too hot for his paws. I did feel a little bit like Dorothy, holding Toto in my arms while facing the great and terrible Wizard of Oz.

Who turned out to be a humbug.

Important insight.

Walter was drumming his fingers on the crystal globe. "What's in the box?"

Starling clutched it to her chest. "Nothing."

"Show me."

She opened the lid to show him the empty interior and he snorted. "You people are nuts! But maybe I want to keep all of you."

"Maybe we don't want to be kept."

"No?" He waved the staff at the empty room. "Do you expect to be rescued? Nobody knows you're here. Not even your precious Lord Rogue. But he is, ah, otherwise occupied, isn't that right?"

I tensed, though I tried not to show it. "What do you know of it?"

He went back to stroking the globe, peering into it with affection. "I know all kinds of things. I am so much more powerful than you are. I really can't believe the press you get. It's so not fair."

"Maybe living out in the middle of the ocean has something to do with that."

He scowled. "I'm a hermit! It's meant to be glamorous and mysterious."

Thumbelina snickered and he pointed the staff at her. "Shut your face, little fairy girl. Or I'll make you be the prize for the duel."

"So, this duel," I prompted him, shifting Darling in my arms. "What's the plan for that? You and me, I take it?"

Walter continued to glower at Thumbelina, who was twirling her dagger and smiling sweetly. "I don't like her."

"Then she won't be the prize. We'll pick something else."

He stroked the globe. "I choose. It's my prize."

"Not unless you win."

"Oh," he chuckled. "I'll win all right. And then, when you're dead, all of Faerie will know that I am the most powerful sorcerer!"

The group went still around me and Starling edged closer. But it was Blackbird who spoke up. "There are many with vested interests in Lady Gwynn's continued good health who would take it much amiss if she were to die."

"Who? I don't give a rat's ass about Falcon. Puck is a puppet. And—as little Gwynnie knows, even if the rest of you don't—Rogue is quite out of the equation at the moment."

"I would be interested in your information about Lord Rogue," I told him. "Enough to engage in a duel for it."

"What is this? You're in no position to bargain. I brought you here to duel to the death and that's exactly what you're going to do. I've invited people!"

I shrugged, deliberately nonchalant. "Why bother? You've already said I'm going to die and you want to keep my companions. I have no incentive to fight."

"But you have to," he whined. "It won't work if I just assassinate you. There has to be a lot more juice to it or it won't make a good story."

He absolutely reminded me of a guy from my era, a computer nerd type. But Blackbird said the war had been going on for a long time—whatever that meant to her.

"How long have you been in Faerie?"

Walter gave me a canny look. "Long time, honey pie. Not everyone comes through at the same point in the time continuum. Yeah, I've been here, I'm guessing, something like a couple hundred years. It gets hard to keep track, you know?"

"I do know." Abruptly and absurdly, I felt sorry for the guy. At least I'd found more of a place here. He lived out this extended, isolated life while the magic worked to unbalance him more and more. "Who trained you?"

Squinching his face in suspicion, he glowered at me, tapping his fingers on the globe. "I didn't need training. Entirely self-taught."

As I'd suspected, which I felt sure meant he wasn't truly more powerful or the fae would never have let him roam about unsupervised. He'd developed some neat tricks, but that was all they were. It would be nice to see past that gray barrier in his mind. Getting that staff away from him would show me a great deal.

"Which is why I'll defeat you," he continued. "See—you're stuck in your ivory-tower interpretation of magic and I'm an entrepreneur. Innovate or die, Gwynnie!" He chortled over his joke, the sloppy sound combining with the squeaking of wheels. "Aha—the cocoa is here!"

A team of gremlins, hotfooting it over the floor, dragged a wagon with a great silver samovar on it. I flinched at the sight of so much silver and Thumbelina edged away. Steam hissed out of the top of it, bringing the delicious aroma of heated chocolate, rich, warm and enveloping.

Walter rubbed his hands together and raised his unkempt eyebrows at me. "At least the food is good, huh?"

The gremlins skittered off and Walter climbed—literally—down from his throne and grabbed a flagon, filling it from a spigot on the side of the samovar. "Help yourselves! I would offer you chairs, but ha! I have the only one."

He hefted himself back onto the throne by dint of crawling up the front, not easy with the staff in one hand and the overfull flagon spilling cocoa in the other. And not a pleasant sight with his robes hefting up over his wide behind to reveal his chubby thighs. I quickly averted my eyes to find Starling giving me such a horrified look that I nearly started giggling.

"Is it safe to drink from the silver?" I whispered and Blackbird caught my eye, giving me a small shake of her head.

"Okay, Walt. Let's talk about the terms of this duel."

"You don't want any hot cocoa?"

"I'm allergic to chocolate."

"Oh." He looked childishly disappointed. "Bad luck, that."

"You said you invited people—when is this duel?"

"Tomorrow. You'll fight then, put on a good show?"

"If you meet my terms, yes."

He slurped from the flagon, blinking at me owlishly over the rim. "You think you can outwit me?"

"You're the one who said we needed to discuss rules."

"True." He wiggled back farther in the deep seat, oblivious to his robes bunching up. "So here's the deal, Gwynnie. You don't do any magic between now and the duel tomorrow at high noon. Then we fight and you can use magic again. For my prize, I get to keep your Familiar and the rest of these idiots can go."

"All the resources at my disposal?"

"Such as they are, yes."

"And for my prize?"

"You won't win."

"I need at least the possibility of victory or I won't fight as hard."

He pouted. "You can go free too."

"We all go free. But if you want me to fight, I want your information on Rogue's whereabouts."

"Stubborn little twat, aren't you? Fiiine," he sighed, drawing out the sound, then farting loudly. "Blah blah blah, if, by some miracle you defeat me, I'll give you that information."

"What if I kill you—how will you deliver?"

He harrumphed at me. "It won't do you any good. It's not like you can rescue him."

"That will be my problem."

He drained the flagon and tossed it aside with a clatter. "Deal. But for your eyes only. Show our guests to their rooms! Except for Gwynnie here. She's earned a special private meeting."

The gremlins swarmed in, rearmed with their spears and poked at the others to go. Starling gave me a worried look and I smiled to reassure her, handing Darling to Thumbelina.

"Look sharp," she whispered to me.

I intended to.

CHAPTER 17

IN WHICH I EMPLOY SMOKE, MIRRORS AND SLEIGHTS OF HAND

*One of the tricks of magic is to remember that the possibilities
are as varied as the imagination. Never do the
expected thing.*

~Big Book of Fairyland, "Rules of Magic"

WALTER WATCHED THEM go. "Kind of a wacky bunch of sidekicks you've got there, Gwynnie. I take it back—the little fairy chick is kind of hot. You want to throw her in too. Sweeten the pot?"

"What do I get if I do?" I suppressed my reaction to him using Titania's term.

"I'll tell you a secret."

"About what?"

"Well, if I tell you then you'll know the secret!"

"How do I know it's any good?"

"Oh." He snorted. "It's good all right."

"Okay then." Since I had no intention of losing, I might as well go for all the prizes possible. Fortunately his bargain had given me exactly what I needed to defeat him—if what I suspected was true.

"Come sit up here with me." Walter wiggled over, making enough room for me to sit beside him. My stomach frankly turned at the prospect, but it would probably pay off for me to keep him pacified. I wedged my boot onto a jeweled leg of the throne and pulled myself up, scooting in next to him without actually making physical contact.

"Pretty good view, huh?"

We sat side by side, surveying the enormous room. You could see the whole thing from his perch—not that there was anything to see.

"It's big so the dragons can visit," he explained. "They like the floor hot, so they keep it that way. Really, you should get a castle of your own. Of course, you'll be dead, so it's a moot point."

"How do you control the dragons?"

"Aha!" He waggled his eyebrows. "I don't."

"No?"

"No. They like to help me because I know what they like best. That's the secret."

"And what do they like best?"

"You can't tell anyone—none of your little friends."

"Agreed." I really hoped the answer wasn't going to be babies.

"Human magic. Our kind. You and me, baby. We're like a drug to them."

"I thought dragons are impervious to magic."

He fiddled with the staff. "It's a conundrum, all right. I just know it works. They gave me this castle and do me favors and all I have to do is let them hang out with me."

"So you communicate with them?"

"If you call it that. I tell them stuff. They don't talk back."

"Did they give you that?" I pointed at the staff with the crystal globe and he moved it out of my reach.

"No touching." He caressed it, with a fond expression. "It's mine."

"Is that how you saw Rogue?" I could see it being a similar iteration of the cave, amplifying reach and vision.

Walter looked surprised. "Not such a babe in the woods, after all, huh, Gwynnie? Not that you aren't a babe." He leered at me. "Hey—wanna do it? Might as well have a last hurrah before you die!"

"Tempting, but no thank you."

"Yeah." He elbowed me knowingly. "Gotta keep that game edge, right?"

"So, you're going to show me Rogue?"

"Yeah, yeah, yeah. Okay—looky, no touchy." He hiked his rainbow robes up higher and wedged the globe between his pudgy knees, the long wooden staff end propped on the floor. He rubbed his hands over the surface, whispering magical-sounding words that came across as so much nonsense. How could he not know his show didn't work on me? I wondered if he'd learned the fae tongue because he didn't have the telepathic mind magic. I hadn't been able to read Nancy's mind either, come to think of it.

Interesting.

Images floated up in the globe and I watched, utterly fasci-nated, at the movie play of them. Icy peaks, with sharp edges, rolled past, as though we soared above them. Not ice—glass.

The infamous Glass Mountains, ridge after ridge of them. I'd flown over the Rocky Mountains more than once and these had to be twice as tall.

In the distance, one peak rose above them all, crowned with a fantastical castle made entirely of glass. It glowed with a beacon of light. The walls peeled away as the images unfurled, taking us inside to a fabulous throne room, this one crowded with fae of all shapes and sizes, glittering with color, while the sky outside glowed like the northern lights.

Perched on the throne sat Titania, in all her naked loveliness, her body featureless as a Barbie doll's, colorless gleaming hair flowing around her. Her pale eyes surveyed the crowd. Beside Titania, in an identical throne and devastatingly handsome in black, was Rogue.

She smiled at him and he took her hand, interlacing his fingers with her many-segmented ones, as he had so often with me, and then kissed her pale skin. Leaning over the joined arms of their thrones, she threaded her free hand into Rogue's glossy loose hair, tugging him down for a deep and sultry kiss, which he seemed to greatly enjoy. She whispered something against his lips and he threw back his head, laughing.

Sitting next to the awful, stinking Walter, who sniggered like a twelve-year-old at the kiss, I felt like I was back in seventh grade, certain that the kids laughing at the next table over were making fun of me.

"She's a babe too—in a creepy, preteen kind of way," Walter observed, rubbing a greasy finger over the smooth crystal as if he could touch her that way. "But you can see that your mighty Lord Rogue has moved on to greener pastures. Pretty sucky of him to leave you unprotected, but all the better for me."

"Right. Our duel to the death."

He nodded, then put his hand on my leg. I had to stiffen all my resolve not to knock it off like a poisonous insect. "You know, maybe it doesn't have to be that way. We could be partners—combine powers. I can teach you all kinds of stuff. We could challenge Rogue and Titania to a duel! Like Masters of the Universe stuff!"

"Gee, Walter." I affixed a sadly hopeful look to my face. "Would you really do that for me? I'd hate to drag down your reputation and make you look weak."

"Hmm." He pursed his lips, looking uncomfortably like a duck about to barf. "I do have that to think of. Sorry, Gwynnie—no can do. Gremlins!" He shouted, right next to my ear and I flinched. "Take Lady Gwynn to her rooms. Tomorrow, we duel."

⁊⁊⁊

I'D BEEN CONCERNED that he would have separated us—which would have been the smart thing to do—and that I'd have to go looking around for the rest of the crew. Fortunately, despite the great size of the castle, there didn't seem to be many actual bedchambers, and we'd all been stowed in the same tower.

Starling shrieked my name and ran up to embrace me, tears in her eyes. "I was afraid we'd never see you again!"

"Silly." I tugged a lock of her hair. "This would change color if anything happened to me, right? Besides, ol' Walter is all about the big duel tomorrow."

Darling, Blackbird and Thumbelina all came trotting in

from their various rooms, greeting me according to their natures. Darling complained that the battle armor itched and, with an apology and deciding that undoing wasn't the same as doing, I poofed it and used my nails to give him a good scratching.

"Please tell us you have a plan for tomorrow and you know what you're doing," Blackbird said.

"Hey guys—I have a plan for tomorrow and I know what I'm doing."

Thumbelina snorted and Starling rolled her eyes.

Blackbird did not look amused and instead regarded me with a stern look and a tapping foot. "This is hardly a joking matter, Lady Gwynn."

"No." I stood up and found a chair to sit in. Darling followed and immediately leaped into my lap, dragging his tail under my nose. "But I really do have a plan that I feel 98 percent sure will work and then we have much bigger fish to fry."

"And that 2 percent chance that it won't work?" Thumbelina turned her dagger in her hands.

"Then I'm dead and you all have to figure out your own way out of here—something you might want to put thought into, Thumbelina, since Walt added you into the bargain as his girl toy."

"I'll cut his tallywhacker off first."

"I figured. I was very careful not to promise that you or Darling would be compliant. You owe him nothing except that he thinks he gets to keep you. He's really quite dreadful at bargaining—I don't know how he's made it this long."

"He has been out here alone," Blackbird mused.

"But he's allied with the other fae, right? Falcon's enemies?"

"True. Still there's no telling how that relationship works."

I frowned at her, but this wasn't the time to pursue that avenue of questioning. "At any rate, we need to discuss the plan for tomorrow. And is there anything to eat?"

Blackbird sighed and Starling pointed to yet another samovar of hot chocolate and a platter of cupcakes, cookies and other sugary treats. And a bowl of popcorn. No wonder Walt looked so out of shape. I took a handful of popcorn to soothe my growling stomach, feeling cranky that my promise kept me from turning the food into something more decent.

"You're really certain you can defeat him? He seems so powerful." Starling twisted her fingers together.

"Yeah, *seems* is the key word there. And I'm not going to defeat him, we are."

Later that evening as I prepared for bed, Darling already crashed out on the one pillow, Thumbelina came in. "Can I ask you something?"

"Sure—what's up?"

"A couple of things. First, why do you call me Thumbelina?" She pronounced the English word pretty well, all things considered.

"Well, because you didn't have a name and I didn't want to call you 'Hey Girlie' all the time. And you reminded me of this fairy girl character from when I was young. Why—do you get a funny image?"

She screwed up her nose. "Yes. I see this tiny fairy with blue hair sitting in a flower cup looking all pretty and cute."

I sat on the side of the bed. "That about sums it up all

right."

"I don't want to be that."

"Okay. What name do you want? I'm happy to call you whatever you like."

She shook her head. "I don't know. You choose." She pointed her dagger at me. "But this time, choose someone smart. And tough."

"You don't need to carry that knife around, you know. I don't think anyone will bother us tonight."

"That's the other thing." She tugged her hair tie loose, the powder blue ringlets springing around her head and falling to her waist. "I want you to cut this off for me."

"Really? There was a time in my life I would have killed for curls like that."

"But not now, right?" She gave me a keen-eyed look. "It's not what you choose for yourself, I notice."

"Perceptive."

She plopped herself down on chair in front of the cold stone fireplace and handed me the dagger over her shoulder. "Cut it short and spiky. Like the outfit looks."

I took a long, shining ringlet in my hand. "You're sure?"

She clenched her hands into little fists against her slim, leather-clad thighs. "Yes. Get rid of it."

Deciding not to point out that Blackbird or Starling could have done this and likely done a better job, I sawed through the curls one by one. Deprived of the weight, the couple inches of hair left behind stood up in tufts. With grim satisfaction she eyed the blue corkscrews falling to the floor. Darling even roused himself to bat one across the stones. "Good riddance," she muttered, making me smile.

When I finished, she looked punk all right. With the short, wildly chopped hair, her lilac eyes looked even more enormous in her face. But she'd lost that flower-blossom innocence. Something of her shrewdness showed through, making her eyes clear and sharp instead of dewy.

"And a name?" She demanded.

"You sure you don't want to pick one yourself?" I asked, but she was already shaking her head.

"No. You choose. You're the one who knows."

I wondered what she meant by that, how she saw me. Of course, I'd carelessly bestowed her with the silly Thumbelina moniker, I could make up for that now.

"Athena," I decided. "The clear-eyed goddess of both craft and war strategy. It's a big name. I think you'll wear it well."

"Athena." She tasted the word and held out her hand for the dagger. "Yes. I like that. It will do nicely. Until tomorrow, Lady Gwynn. I can't wait to see Walter's face when you pull the rug out from under him."

She left, still a bit of that skipping to her stride, Darling following after. We'd left the doors between our warren of interconnected rooms open, for the comfort of each others' company, and I heard Starling exclaiming over the new hair while Blackbird tutted.

It didn't surprise me that, when I dreamed that night, instead of slogging through the sand, I climbed glassy slick slopes instead. Over and over, I climbed, reaching the ridge only to slice my hands to ribbons when I grasped the sharp edge. My blood ran crimson and hot, steaming like the hot cocoa, pouring down the clear glass.

Above, Rogue sat in a chair, watching me and laughing. He

kept shaking his head at me, as if he found my efforts ridiculous. When I slid, once again, all the way to the bottom of the blood-slicked surface, he peered down at me from his lofty heights and sighed, exasperated.

"Don't look for me, stupid Gwynn. When will you learn?"

"Never!" I shouted defiantly. "You're mine!"

Titania appeared, wrapping her naked self around him, pale eyes full of pity. "No, he's not." The intense musicality of her voice wrapped around me. "He never was."

"He's mine!" I cried, but I slid farther down, unnoticed as they kissed.

$\mathcal{E}\tau\xi$

STARLING SHOOK ME awake and I blinked blearily at the pity in her brown eyes. "Gwynn—you're dreaming. You were yelling out—" She bit her lip on saying anything more, but her thoughts were clear. Poor jilted me.

I sat up and scrubbed my face with my hands. The sunlight shone bright through the windows. "How long until high noon?"

"A while yet. Walter sent us outfits to wear." Her lips twitched in amusement. "But the party apparently begins soon. The duel is to be the culmination."

"He came by and talked to you?"

"Yes. And brought more hot cocoa, along with cinnamon rolls. He wanted to talk to you, but we told him you were preparing for the duel and couldn't be disturbed. It sounded better than sleeping in."

"Yeah. Thanks. Let's see this outfit."

Starling went to get it and I took the time to steady myself and clear out the last dregs of the nightmare. These were like and yet unlike the dreams I'd had before with Rogue. Unlike because, in many ways, I could trace the fragments of memory and the day's events flowing through them, the normal dreaming mechanism of my brain washing away the flotsam and jetsam of my experiences. But, as with the dreams I had before with him, these felt guided, as if they occurred in that semi-real plane where we'd first come together. That was the part that really ate at me. That he—or worse, Titania—were present and cognizant in these semi-dreams where I cried and pleaded for him. Him, the man I'd never wanted in the first place.

And now couldn't bear it that he'd been torn from me.

It wasn't as if I didn't have anything better to do than moon over some guy. Such as, say, win an impossibly stacked magical duel, rescue my companions and get us the hell out of here and back on track. "Stop being such a pitiful fucking loser," I muttered, forcing myself out from under the covers.

"What?" Starling looked a little shocked.

"I said I hope I won't be the loser today."

"Geez, me too. Please don't make me spend an eternity with Walt the Weird Boy."

"And here I thought you were bemoaning your fate as a virgin spinster. Walt could be your ticket out of that dreadful future."

"Suddenly the virgin spinster fate is sounding much more appealing."

"No doubt." I picked up what she'd tossed on the bed. It was a Princess Leia slave costume. If Walt wanted to be coy about his origins, he was doing a lousy job of it. "Never mind, I'll just wear what I had on yesterday."

"He was pretty insistent."

I shook my head. "Not part of the bargain—no dice."

I'd slept in my underwear, so pulling on my traveling dress didn't take much effort. Walt hadn't thought to give us things like hairbrushes, so Starling did the best she could to make me look presentable. Finally I stopped her. "That's just gonna have to do."

"If you say so," she fretted. "Why don't I have a task, like the others?"

"It's nothing personal—just how it worked out this time."

She fingered her hair and I knew she was resisting chewing on it. "I have no skills."

"That's not true. You do an amazing job of keeping me organized." As I said it, I realized how lame that sounded.

"Gee thanks. I wanted to go on an adventure so I could be something more than an efficient housekeeper."

"You will. You just haven't found your thing yet."

"Think so?" She sounded so wistful.

"I know so."

The gremlins came to fetch us not long after and we all trooped down together, nobody wearing their new Walt outfits, which had all turned out to be either obscene or humiliating or both. Particularly the pink bunny ears for Darling that now lay shredded on the floor.

Instead of taking us to the great hall, our insectile escort led us upward, not as high as our original landing pad, but into a great bowl in the center of the circling towers. I had to hand it to Walt, it was an impressive arena. We walked out from a tunnel like Roman gladiators of old. Two pedestals faced each other across the center. A festive audience of fae nobles filled a grandstand box at one end, the languid preying-mantis length of their limbs setting them apart from all the lower fae ranged in tiers behind them.

"Not exactly a full house," Starling observed and Blackbird sent her a quelling look. It was true, though—many of the seats were empty. Either all of Walter's guests hadn't arrived or the turnout disappointed expectations.

I suspected the latter, confirmed by the disgruntled look on Walt's face as he trotted across the sand to meet us. He wore flowing crimson robes, tall platform boots and a towering headdress.

"You're not wearing your costumes," he complained.

I just shrugged. "We forgot. Oops."

He dug the blunt end of the staff in the sand, the crystal globe on top catching the sun and sending rays of light in blinding shards, and squinted at me.

"You don't seem very concerned that you're about to suffer a horrible death at my hands."

"It's a good day to die." I replied, with Klingon gravity.

Walter grinned, the sincere pleasure making his homely face almost attractive. "Yes—exactly! Okay, your, um, guests have special seats over there. I don't know what you want to do about your Familiar. Do you need a kennel for it?"

Darling sent me an image of Walt on his back, disemboweled. I frowned to keep from smiling. "The cat stays with me."

"Well, I don't know if that's fair…"

"Okay, then you can give up the staff."

His shrewd gaze fixed on Darling, who started cleaning his

toes. "What does it do for you?"

"Darling?" I looked at him as if I wasn't sure. "Mostly he gets underfoot. But he sulks if I send him away." Darling swiped his freshly cleaned claws at my ankle and I yelped. "See?"

Walt chortled. "He'll learn manners when he's my Familiar. I think he'll look good riding with me on a dragon."

Darling, drat his egotistical soul, had the gall to look really interested in that. I reminded him how he'd reverted into a regular cat in proximity to the dragon and it deflated him so much that I felt sorry. Not the direction we needed to go. Time to start psyching up the troops. I reminded Darling of the plan and he perked right up. And let me know that the time for the duel approached.

"Is it noon yet?"

Excitement shivered over Walt and he drew himself up. "Nearly. Wait for the trumpets to signal—and then we duel until one of us is dead. Do you wish to say goodbye to your friends?"

"Bye, guys. See you in a bit."

They strolled off with casual waves. Walt scowled after them. "None of you has much sense of ceremony. And something happened to that girl's hair."

I smothered a fake yawn. "Yeah, she's like that."

He turned the black look on me and thumped the staff in the sand again. "You're not taking this seriously, Gwynnie. I don't think you have any idea of what terrible magics I can wreak upon you!"

"Guess you'll show me, huh?"

I stoked my anger now, carefully brewing it up, letting the

silver-white feline stir and stretch. This was really the only part I wasn't sure of—if I could keep her contained. Well, that and whether Walter's dragons would come to his rescue. That was my biggest gamble, that they wouldn't. I resisted touching the dragon's egg in my pocket, hoping I wouldn't need to use it.

Five topazes, Darling let me know.

"All welcome!" A page with a booming voice entirely out of proportion with his body stepped out onto the sand. The crowd—clearly bored and never tremendously noisy to begin with—settled. "All welcome to the Grand Duel between the Wizard of the Western Keep and the Most Powerful Lady Sorceress Gwynn!"

A polite smattering of golf claps.

"Go, Most Powerful Lady Gwynn!" Starling's voice hooted out.

"Will the contestants take their pedestals?"

I stepped up on mine, Darling on the sand beside me. Walter was screwing around with his headdress.

Three minutes.

The waves crashing on the rocks outside the castle sounded like thunder, but the sun shone bright in the cerulean sky. In my heart, I fomented energy, the cat rising with interest. I shook my head and the lily earrings swung, reminding me of Rogue and his dark kisses, the lust swirling up, sparking red and black. Ruthlessly I cut aside the worry, the sorrow, the bitter sense of betrayal, and instead concentrated entirely on the sexual desire that fueled so much of my magic, blending it with the cat's slicing physical edge.

One minute.

I drew the quiet around me. The dead silence Marquise

and Scourge had ground into me at such a dear price. I wrapped all my feral anger, my unrequited desire, in a seamless container, ready to be directed.

Walter sensed it, leaving his outfit alone and stared at me, nostrils flaring.

Ten seconds.

Five seconds.

"Go."

Darling took off running, straight for Walter. He was lifting the staff, ready to level it at me.

Noon.

My wish hit Darling with an instantaneous boom—all the more powerful for echoing his own wish. Suddenly he stood two stories tall, his paws the size of sports cars. More than halfway to Walter when he changed, it took only one stride for him to reach the wizard, seize him in his great mouth and shake him so the staff fell from his nerveless hand.

A bolt of sky blue and Thumbel—Athena—using her dragonfly girl magical speed, caught the staff and brought it to me. I took it and she whirled, dagger ready to defend me if need be.

The staff resonated in my grip like a tuning fork and suddenly the entire arena lit up in radiating lines, a shifting topographical map of magic. Darling, supernova bright, shook his head and Walter wailed.

A gong sounded and one of the fae nobles, Blackbird serene and elegant at his elbow, declared me the victor.

The duel was over. I loved a simple plan.

CHAPTER 18

IN WHICH I LEARN SOMETHING ABOUT DRAGONS

❧

Never meddle in the affairs of dragons, for you are crunchy
and taste good with ketchup.
~*Big Book of Fairyland*, "Flora and Fauna"
(and remembered T-shirt)

"PUT HIM DOWN, Darling."

The cat's lime-green eyes, the size of beach balls, gazed back at me in fierce disappointment. He shook Walt again, dangling him like a hapless mouse. Athena stalked over to stand between them and the audience. She wasn't as tall as one of his paws.

I sighed. Maybe not so simple. "You are an amazing and mighty hunter, Darling, but it's time to put the poor guy down."

"In truth, Lady Sorceress Gwynn, it's within your rights to kill him, as he would have killed you," the fae noble called out. The others enthusiastically agreed. For the enemy side, they seemed very much the same as our nobles—capricious and whimsically cruel.

"Isn't he your ally? Do it now, Darling."

He informed me that he wanted a new name. A battle name, now. *Then* he'd put the nasty Walt thing down.

"Well." The noble smoothed his elegantly embroidered sleeves, checking them for flaws. "He's not a terribly effective wizard. Really his death would be no great loss. Go ahead and kill him."

Walt moaned and I promised Darling we'd discuss the battle name in just a few minutes and to put the man down *now*.

"You've already declared me the victor, so it's not necessary." Exactly why I'd wanted Blackbird to make sure that happened, so I wouldn't have to kill poor stupid Walter. More for me than for him. My feline animus craved his blood, and that was a daunting enough feeling.

That part of me, along with Darling, wanted to taste his death and hesitated. The fae audience, much more excited now, began chanting for Walt's imminent demise. The staff in my hand took up the miasma of emotions and pumped it together into a powerful charge. Darling, sensing my change in intent, put Walt down and pinned him with a huge paw, giving me suggestions for various satisfying deaths.

Walter squirmed and wailed. I cast a wary eye to the sky for sign of dragons.

They did not arrive to save him.

"Kill him and you can have this castle," the fae noble said. "I have a proposition for you, Lady Sorceress. Something...tasty."

Tasty, yes. Like this death would be. Walter was a wart on

the world. He deserved to die. I formed a wish.

"Don't do it."

Starling's hand closed over mine on the staff and I started, surprised to see her there.

"Here, let me hold this for you, Gwynn. It's okay. I take care of things for you, remember?"

What did she mean? Of course I knew that! The savage desire for Walt's death fell away and I put an unsteady hand to my temple. "Whoa—that was intense."

Starling just nodded at me, somber.

"See? You ended up having a job after all. And tell you what, hang on to that thing for me, will you?"

She laid it over her shoulder, carrying it like a stick with a basket of apples on the end, and nodded her head toward Darling. "You might want to take care of that."

Darling, bored, was swatting Walt from paw to paw, a human cat toy. I gathered my skirts, jumped down from the pedestal and ran toward him. "Darling—no! Bad kitty. Stop that this instant or you don't get a new name."

Chagrined that I hadn't done it sooner, I poofed the spell, returning Darling to his normal size. Walt lay in a sobbing heap and Darling gave him one last swat, prancing up to me. "*Gigantor,*" he suggested.

"I am so not calling you Gigantor."

Starling stifled a giggle and Athena glared at her. "I think he should have whatever name he wants."

"I'm sure you think that, *Athena,*" Starling snapped back.

"Athena," I hastily interrupted their sniping, "hold the staff, please. Starling, check on Walt. See if he's suffered any...permanent damage."

Darling swirled himself around my ankles. *"Titanous."*

I rolled my eyes. *"No."*

"He seems to be okay," Starling reported. Walt had buried his face in her lap, sobbing into her skirts while she patted his head awkwardly.

"An odd choice, Lady Sorceress Gwynn." The fae noble peered at Walt. Blackbird, standing just behind him, had a funny look on her face. As if she felt ill.

"But my choice to make."

"He could be dangerous to you."

"I don't think so. Athena, I'm going to touch the staff for a moment, if you'll hold it out for me."

"I don't think—" Starling started.

"If I act weird, just move it out of my reach."

Athena balanced the staff, over twice her height, so I could just touch it and she could easily pivot it out from under my hand. I touched the globe with tentative fingers and looked at Walt. Away from the blazing light of the multiply magicked Darling, his native magic shone with dim light. He had some, but not a lot. The globe felt good under my hand. Too good. I recalled the way Walt had stroked it, an almost obscene lust.

I shook my head and turned to the fae noble. "I'm not concerned about ol' Walter, here. And you are?"

Blackbird, a warning in her eyes I couldn't interpret, stepped forward. "Lady Sorceress Gwynn, may I present General Fafnir."

He swept a bow. A light pattern of gray drifted over the right side of his face, like snowflakes. Or scales. His close-cropped hair echoed the color, giving him the look of an aged and grizzled soldier—unusual among his ageless kind.

My vision filled with a red haze of rage and the cat deep inside snarled. I reached for the staff and Athena danced back out of reach. Never mind. I didn't need it. Fafnir blanched and Blackbird's robin-dark eyes flew open in panic.

I took a step, fingers curving into claws, and Darling tripped me. Then Starling was slipping an arm around my waist, fake laughing. "Oops, Lady Gwynn! Watch your step there. What is *wrong* with you?" she hissed in my ear.

"That darn cat." I tried to smile, but my face felt stiff. Fafnir. Right in front of me. He gave me a cautious and curious look. I strained to wrestle the cat down and she fought me, hungry for this death. With enormous effort, I managed to contain her, and lock her in the cage of my heart.

"Perhaps we should take the wizard into custody—" Blackbird stepped in with smooth politesse, "—and give Lady Sorceress Gwynn an opportunity to rest from her great and terrible duel."

"Of course." Fafnir took my hand and bowed over it. I flinched, expecting his touch to be cold and scaly. He seemed not to notice, though he watched me closely. Undoubtedly sensing something. "How thoughtless of me. Still, I would like to discuss this proposition with you. And be sure to sentence the wizard appropriately—justice must be seen to."

"How about tonight?" Blackbird folded her hands, looking expectantly between us. "We shall have a victory feast, sentence Walter and you two can discuss then!"

I glared at her and she smiled sweetly, with steely determination beneath. The last thing in the world I needed—another fucking feast. And this one with a creature that made my stomach turn. Darling meowed up at me, lashing his tail.

"Colossus."

A snort escaped me and I picked him up so he could head-butt my chin.

"A brave and daring Familiar you have there, Lady Gwynn," Fafnir observed, then waved a gracious hand to include Blackbird, Athena and Starling. "Along with all your stalwart companions. I look forward to spending more time with all of you this evening."

He strode off, fae peeling away at his gesture to swarm around Walter, bundling him up to carry him to await his fate. I felt unutterably weary that it would again fall on me to make that call.

"Just confine him to his rooms," I called out. "Until we decide what to do with him."

"What is going on?" Starling demanded. Blackbird looked pained. "You asked me about Fafnir before and now you're acting strange."

Athena twirled her dagger through nimble fingers, holding the staff in her other hand, her face impassive.

The adrenaline and emotion from the fight were receding, leaving me drained. That, coming face-to-face with a monster and thinking about how to deal with Walter all combined to overwhelm me. Exhaustion stole my thoughts. I felt like a shell of myself.

"Leviathan," Darling suggested.

"Can we talk about this later?" I asked, my voice sounding plaintive to my own ears. The breeze had turned into a cutting wind, and dark clouds gathered darker overhead. Apparently the distant thunder had been more than surf. "Having a bit of rest sounds really good at the moment."

Thankfully they dropped the subject, Blackbird assigning her daughter a number of tasks designed to keep her distracted and busy. She wouldn't meet my eye, so she knew something about Fafnir for sure.

We got back to the rooms, everyone agreeing that a late lunch and a nap would be just the thing. With her easy authority, Blackbird arranged for real food, which we devoured. The wind truly howled outside, whipping the sea into a frenzy. I bolted the shutters, grateful for the warm fire now crackling away in the little fireplace. At least our quality of life had improved considerably. I lay down, Darling leaping up to nestle against me. *"Gigantor."* The name echoed in my head as I crashed into a dark and dreamless sleep.

THE CLATTER OF the shutters woke me with a start. Disoriented, I gazed blankly at the room, trying to remember where I was. For a moment I'd thought I was in my own bed, Isabel sleeping at my feet and I was my old self.

But no.

I heard soft snores from the other room and Darling half opened one lazy eye, then closed it again. Serendipitous if everyone was asleep, because I had an errand to run and I really didn't want to have conversations yet. Picking up my boots, I padded barefoot across the floor and slipped out into the hallway.

The place was such a maze that I wasn't sure I could find my way on my own, but it was worth a shot. Could I wish myself into knowing the route? I sat down on a stone step and pulled on my boots, lacing them up while I thought. The magic part of me still felt tired—though nothing like the time I'd pulled lightning. I'd probably used way more effort to zap Darling into Gigantor mode than necessary, but I'd wanted no mistakes. Dealing with my feline animus, too, seemed to strain my resources in some odd way. Something to experiment with. For now I needed a guide. Maybe I could wish up a little map that showed me where to go and that wouldn't drain me much more.

A gremlin popped its head over the edge of the next stair, making me jump. It chittered at me. Still no content. But Walter had communicated with them somehow.

"Can you take me to the dragons?"

It danced a little in place, then took off running down the steps and around the bend. Assuming that to be a yes, I followed. It came back into view, chattered and ran off again.

"Okay, Lassie," I called after it, "I'm following you."

With this method, it led me down, deep into the sublevels of the castle. I probably could have found the dragons myself, just by following the increasing heat. Brought a whole new meaning to the warmer/colder game.

Down below seemed to be a network of giant caverns similar to Walter's throne room. The gremlin, with a long, chittered explanation that still gave me nothing, pointed the way deeper in, then fled, climbing up a pillar and skittering across the ceiling. The floor heated my feet through the ankle boots, so I sympathized with the barefooted gremlin's plight. Although after that chilly wind in the arena today, the warmth felt pretty damn good to me.

I made my way cautiously through the shadowed cavern.

Not like I'd trip over a dragon or anything, but I wasn't at all sure of my welcome. Probably risking my fate to a dragon's mood wasn't the smartest move in my magic-depleted condition, but hey—opportunity had knocked and I didn't plan to stay in Walt's labyrinth of a castle beyond tomorrow morning. All I needed was a ride home. Oh, and magic wouldn't work on it anyway. Onward.

I heard the dragon before I saw it. The chain rattle of dry scales over stones made the angel hairs on the back of my neck stand up. There was an atavistic fear in confronting a giant reptile. Snakes and crocodiles and dragons should never be big enough to swallow one whole.

This one could do it without noticing.

It glittered even in the shadows, jewel tones catching some kind of otherworldly glow, shining like phosphorescence in a cave. An amber light spotlighted me, as if a great round window had opened. It took a moment for my mind to assimilate that the dragon's eye had opened, gazing at me with its own self-created light.

It took longer than that to persuade my frantic nervous system that fight or flight were not the only two options.

The dragon groaned a little, shifting into a more comfortable position, just as Darling would, enjoying a snug spot in the covers. The dragon lifted a taloned foreleg and shifted back a little more, showing me its belly in obvious invitation.

Either that or the enticement to get close enough to be easily munched.

Following my instinct—besides, who was I kidding? It could have gobbled me up any time it wanted to—I stepped close and scratched the tender and surprisingly soft scales. The dragon rumbled, sounding close to a purr. Using both hands, I redoubled my efforts and the lily earrings fell off, dropping to the floor.

"Dammit," I muttered, annoyed with myself for forgetting.

I felt around on the shadowed floor, then got on my knees in the hopes of seeing better. The dragon shifted, nuzzling my head with scorching hot breath and the amber light of its gaze illuminated the area. Snatching up the earrings, I tucked them in my pocket. The dragon's great snout followed my movement, then lingered over my hip, snuffling at my pocket.

Oh.

With a bit of trepidation, I pulled out the dragon's egg I'd taken to carrying in my pocket all the time. The amber light brightened and the dragon hummed a delighted sound. I held out the egg on the palm of my hand and the dragon's long tongue—dark purple and forked at the end—flicked out to lick it. Then wrapped around it and plucked it from my palm, setting it very carefully in the crook of its elbow.

"Well, I supposed that's fair," I told it. "My gift to you. If that even counts since it was likely stolen from your kind to begin with."

The dragon nuzzled my pocket again. This one might not go over as well. I pulled out the vial of dragon's blood though, and held it out for inspection. It sniffed, tasted and harrumphed in what I could swear was the dragon's version of a laugh. Pushing its snout against my hand, it indicated I should put the vial away again.

The tacit blessing pleased and relieved me. Though I would have given it that too. In that moment, I understood something more about the nature of worship. The creature so awed me that I wanted to give it anything at all. I wished I'd pocketed one or two of those poisonous apples from the orchard at Castle Brightness.

"Well, I'll leave you be." I scratched the itchy spot once more and the eye half closed in pleasure. "I just wanted to meet you. Pay my respects, that kind of thing."

The dragon nuzzled the egg and hummed happily.

"You're welcome." I hesitated. "Um. This feels forward and I know you have better things to do that cart people about, but if you're available to give us a lift back in the morning, that would be really great."

The dragon's tongue flicked out to brush my cheek, the barest kiss of heat. Somehow I couldn't quite envision Walt having the patience for this kind of conversation. Maybe I was wrong, since he'd clearly established some kind of connection.

"Okay. Well, see you in the morning, if that works out for you."

In the darkness beyond, I heard more rustling. Scales and leathery wings. More spotlights shone in the deep caverns as sets of amber and gold eyes opened, lighthouses in the distance. Despite the heat, I shivered a little at the sight.

Here there be dragons.

⟡

I MADE MY way back to the rooms feeling curiously restored by the encounter. The gang, however, was none too pleased by my solo excursion. Especially when I ducked telling them where I'd gone. For some reason the encounter felt special enough that I just wanted to hug it to myself for a while longer. Sometimes it seemed that telling someone else about an extraordinary event took the life and color out of it. I couldn't explain to myself my sense of awe and peace from being near the dragons.

Maybe I was just happy that something in this world had more power than Titania, for surely their magic-cancellation trumped anything of hers. Maybe that was just wishful thinking.

Fortunately Blackbird had arranged for me to interview Walter before the feast, so that he could be appropriately sentenced in front of everyone. That reminded me uncomfortably of my own sentencing banquet, which Blackbird likely understood—in particular that I would want to save Walter some of that anguish. This schedule had the added side benefit of thwarting Starling's efforts to dig hints about Fafnir out of me. She settled for giving me a doe-eyed look as Blackbird whisked me away.

Blackbird apparently knew where to find Walter, because no gremlins showed up to escort us. "Let's get this out of the way," she said, walking briskly enough that I had to step up my pace. "Yes, Lord Fafnir has been another player in this...scenario. I suspect you know something more of it and, worse, that there's something you're not telling me or Starling because you fear knowing it will create a wound too deep to be healed."

She smiled, tight-lipped, at my surprise.

"I am not without my own gifts, Lady Gwynn." She tapped her temple. "Understanding people's motivations goes a long way toward keeping them organized and happy."

It explained a great deal.

"I've told Starling to leave you alone about it, but I don't know that she will. Stubborn child." The exasperated affection in her voice touched me.

"She's no longer a child, Blackbird."

"No." She shook her head at herself. "But neither is she a woman-grown yet. I worry that what lies ahead for her will be painful."

"A philosopher where I come from said 'that which does not kill me makes me stronger.'"

Blackbird stopped and faced me. "Wise. And yet—of little comfort to a mother with a mortal child. That's not an easy thing to shoulder."

"The man who said that came from a world where all children are mortal, as was he."

She tipped her head a little. "Fair enough. I won't send her home. I considered asking you to do it, as a special favor."

"I can't. I promised."

"Fair enough," she repeated, more to herself. "As far as Fafnir goes—he remembers no more than I do. I feel quite sure of that. Your rage for whatever role he played is clear to me, so I won't ask you to go easy on him, either. Just…"

"I get what you're saying."

"But will keep your own counsel." She dusted off her hands and resumed her brisk march. "Just in this next tower here."

"No advice on handling Walter?"

She shook her head, completely neutral. "You, more than any other, know what he has faced in this world as opposed to your own. The laws you both understand likely will serve both of you best. I doubt he could face a more fitting judge."

"In our world, the person he offended would never be in a position to pass judgment." Mostly. Except maybe in politics. And the military. Reality TV shows too. "Never mind."

"Would you have Fafnir and the others pass sentence? You know what they would likely choose for him." A bristling squad of spear-laden gremlins guarded a pair of iron-braced wooden doors, stacked up an arm's length deep. I raised an eyebrow at Blackbird who looked amused. "Not my idea."

They parted for us, a spiky green sea, pulling the doors open as they did. Blackbird fell back, making me precede her into the rooms. Walter, wearing a silver collar and cuffs, sat in a mournful pile in a leather recliner. A platter of the same snack food he'd given us sat next to him and he drank from a hose attached to a silver samovar of yet more hot chocolate.

He glared at me. "You totally cheated."

I lifted my shoulders in a little mea culpa shrug. "I like to see it as thinking outside the box."

"I always hated that phrase. Success mumbo jumbo."

I realized he'd shifted into American English. "Yeah. What are we going to do with you, Walter?"

He fiddled with the cocoa hose. "I don't suppose you know how to get back? I mean, I wasn't much back home, but I had a decent job. Clearly my magic sucks here, compared to yours."

"Did you come right to this castle—when you fell through?"

His cheeks puffed out as he sucked on the hose, collapsed as he swallowed. "Came through a video game. I was playing Skyrim, you know?"

"I don't. Sorry."

"Heh. N00b. Anyway I'd Fus Ro Dah'd the thing and it,

like, sucked me in and boom! Here I was, facing a real dragon."

"That had to be something."

"No freaking kidding! Fortunately the thing seemed to take a liking to me and the rest is history. Until you came along."

I cleared a pile of soiled robes off a coffee table and sat, not pointing out that I wouldn't have come along if he hadn't kidnapped me. "That's really interesting. You must have a natural affinity for dragons. Were you by chance bleeding?"

He snorted. "Yeah—took an arrow to the knee."

"Someone shot you with an arrow in your living room?"

"No." He looked at me as if I was the nutty one. "It's a joke. There's this old guy in the game and—never mind. You wouldn't appreciate the meme. You're kind of a Debbie Downer, aren't you?"

"I meant, were you bleeding for real."

"Could be. You think that did it?"

"Partly, yes. And a wish to escape your old life."

"I had that. Stupid. This place is worse. And now I've really fucked myself over."

"Not necessarily, Walt."

He snorted and stuffed a cupcake into his mouth, pointing a pudgy finger at me while he choked it down. "Easy for you to say Miss Fancy Schmancy Sorceress. You have them all eating out of the palm of your hand. It took me all day just to wish up this recliner and that was with my staff. Now you have that too."

"That staff wasn't good for you, Walt. Trust me." I yanked the cocoa hose out of his hand. "And quit drinking out of silver. Are you an idiot? You know silver stops magic and you're drinking a hot, corrosive fluid out of it? Also, you live on top of dragons. No wonder you've barely got any magic left. You're amazing at quenching magic, so I think that if you simply get away from all these dampening influences and get some training, you'll be fine."

"You think so?" His beady eyes grew moist with longing. "Can I get the training you got?"

I nearly choked. "Believe me, Walt—you do *not* want that."

"Well, if it sucks, that would be a good punishment. You know, for kidnapping, attempted murder, pain and suffering, all that. It would be like rehab."

"Rehab from hell."

"Keeping it all to yourself, huh? That's not fair."

"Look. The things I went through I wouldn't wish on my worst enemy, much less on you. You have no idea what you're asking for."

He thrust his lip out mulishly, reached for the cocoa hose and stopped himself. "Well, my life is pretty damn shitty. I just sit here day after day and get fatter. No chick will ever want me and now you say I can't even learn what you did. Poorly played, Gwynnie."

I studied my hands, how even now I'd taken refuge in holding my wrist. "There must be other ways. I'll find out for you."

"Don't trouble yourself. I'll get Fafnir to send me there, for my sentence."

"If I think you're going to do that, *I* will sentence you to life imprisonment in this castle, for your own damn good."

"That's just cruel."

"No—what's cruel is what they'd do to you. It nearly killed

me, Walt."

"But you survived," he pointed out. "Now you're stronger than anyone. I'll find a way to get there."

Marquise and Scourge would have a field day with him. It would be turning a puppy over to a pair of bored and hungry lions.

"You have to negotiate terms if you do that. Good terms. Absolutely no loopholes."

"You do it. Sentence me and negotiate the terms."

"I can't do that to you."

"Then I'll go on my own." He watched me cannily, clearly perceiving I wouldn't let that happen. "You're a softie, Gwynnie. You won't lock me up here and you won't let me get taken in a bad deal."

"I'll think about it."

"You'll do it," Walt called after me. "You know you want to."

"I know I don't want to." I kept walking.

"Chicken!" His fake poultry noises followed me out the door.

CHAPTER 19

IN WHICH I TELL A
TERRIBLE STORY, TWICE

*The properties of crystal to enhance and expand the influence
of magic seem congruent with what I recall from New Age
thinking. Interesting.*

~*Big Book of Fairyland*, "Rules of Magic"

DARLING MET ME at the door of our rooms when we
returned, prancing with excitement. Athena lurked
behind him looking, of all things, a little guilty. "He's settled
on a new name," she informed me.

I tried not to wince and looked at Darling expectantly.

"Hercules."

"This is your influence?" I asked Athena.

She widened her large lilac eyes in effective innocence. "I
had nothing to do with it."

"Hercules, huh?"

*"Hercules. Hercules. Hercules. HerculesHerculesHercules-
HerculesHercules."* Darling danced about, chanting the name in
his head. He sent me an image of the young man he some-

times pictured to me, only tall and muscle-bound in this version.

"Fine." I stopped him and scratched his delightedly arched back. "Though I may call you Darling Hercules and Darling, for short."

I didn't think he'd bite on that, but he graciously agreed.

"Would you mind zapping me up something else to wear to the feast?" Athena gestured to her leather fighting outfit. "Something not too girly, but still nice."

"The Lady Sorceress Gwynn is not here to squander her magic making you new outfits," Starling called from the other room. "And she needs to get in here and take her bath or *she* won't be ready."

I rolled my eyes and Athena grinned. I wished her into a black-and-white tuxedo, with little tails and a top hat. "How's that?"

She looked in the mirror. "Spot-on, Lady Gwyn. Very nice."

I took myself into my room, where Starling had a brass tub steaming for me. "Oh bless you. I'm dying to get clean again."

She didn't smile at me. "You shouldn't indulge that fairy girl like that. She'll just take and take."

"I know how to say no. I'll make you a pretty outfit too, if you want," I coaxed her while I shimmied out of my now decidedly overripe dress.

"It doesn't really matter, does it? It's not like there will be anyone to dance with."

"I thought you were giving up on the love hunt for a while and focusing on adventure."

"Well, that's not going so well, is it? I'm just some silly

handmaid you're dragging along, kept in the dark, useful only for preparing baths for you."

If I'd known she was this mad, I wouldn't have undressed yet. I dunked myself in the water rather than stand there naked.

"I'd like to point out that I didn't ever ask you to be in charge of preparing baths for me."

"No, but gee—what else is stupid ol' Starling good for? I might as well be doing that." She plopped herself on the bed, folded her arms and gave me a mutinous look. "I want you to tell me what Fafnir has to do with all of this."

"It's an ugly, awful story."

"Do you think I'm not strong enough to take it?"

I opened my mouth to reply, then closed it, thinking of what I'd said to Blackbird. So I leaned my head back against the tub's rim, stared at the ceiling and told Starling Cecily's story, exactly as Nancy had told it to me.

"You think that happened to my brother." Starling's voice sounded thin, strained.

I wished the water warmer. "You know as much as I do now. Your mother has no memory of what exactly happened with the baby and Titania—it's weirdly blocked. She thinks Fafnir doesn't remember either."

"But you intend to try to find out."

"What I can, yes."

"He clearly recovered from being a puddle of melted goo," she pointed out. I cracked an eye open to check her expression and, while she looked a bit wan, she gave me little smile. "That immortality thing comes in handy, I guess."

"True."

"How can I help?"

"I don't think you can."

"Gwynn!"

"No, this isn't a *thing*. I don't think you realize that I just pretty much make stuff up as I go along. I play it by ear. I don't know how you can help with Fafnir because I don't know how the evening will go."

"Fine."

I washed my hair, thinking. "There is something you can do for me, but it might mean skipping the feast."

"I can do that."

"You could go talk to Walter for me."

Starling wrinkled her nose, but then smoothed her expression. "Okay. I will. What about? Just anything? Pump him for information?"

I dried myself with the towel she handed me. "He thinks he wants the training I had, from Marquise and Scourge." I hurried on before she could reply, unable to face her sympathy. "You know something of what I was like when I...got out of there. I can't talk to him—to anyone, really—about just how horrible it was. I want you to talk him out of it."

She began combing out my hair without a word. The quiet stretched between us while her thoughts hummed. "Does he need it—the training?" she finally asked.

"He needs training for sure, but without the torture part."

"Hmm."

"What? Don't *Hmm* me."

"I'm just thinking—you're always trying to protect people, Gwynn. Like you do with me, not telling me about Cecily's baby. You survived what they did to you. Maybe Walter deserves that chance too."

"It's not an opportunity, Starling! It's—"

"Shh." She put a soothing hand on the top of my head. "I'll talk to him and I'll be honest and tell him what I've seen of how much you suffered. Because I do know something of how much that wounded you. But I also think you don't realize how remarkable you are now because you did go through that. You have an enviable strength. I can understand how someone like Walter would look at you and want something of that."

"The price was too high."

"Was it? I wonder."

"And it doesn't feel like strength from the inside." I sighed. "Maybe I should try to talk to him about it."

She tapped me with the comb. "Trust me. I'll tell him the truth. You gave me this job. Now let me do it. Okay?"

"Okay. But remember to take some decent food with you. Otherwise you'll be eating cupcakes all night."

I THANKED MY lucky stars that Blackbird had gotten kidnapped with us because the feast was amazing. Feeling like I hadn't eaten for days, I stuffed myself. The gremlins happily followed Blackbird's directions, bringing in platter after platter of excellent meats and vegetables.

"Where did all the food come from?" I asked her. She sat between me and Fafnir—a thoughtful positioning on her part.

"The gremlins can conjure more than hot chocolate. You just have to know what to ask for. I think the wizard simply had no idea."

"He was never a very good wizard." Fafnir leaned over to address me. "That's why we negotiated a temporary peace treaty with General Falcon. Once I saw what you could do at the Plain of No Trees and then the Debacle of the Sirens—" he shook his head in admiration, "—I figured we'd better destroy you or recruit you."

"So you had Walter send the dragons to grab me on the Promontory of Magic?"

"It was worth a shot. I didn't expect it to work."

"So, Walter and the duel was the second attempt?"

Fafnir toasted me with his flagon and winked. "I bet on you."

Poor Walt.

"I didn't know about the peace treaty." But it did explain why Falcon hadn't summoned me and Rogue. A bit of luck, there. Or the magic, taking care of me.

Fafnir poured himself more wine. "Temporary. We can get the war going again as soon as tomorrow if you'd like to come over to our side."

"I'm afraid I've sworn service to General Falcon."

"Aha! But you're not with him now. Why is that, I wonder?"

I really didn't care to explain the whole sabbatical Rogue had wrangled for me. So we could go on our quest. My heart cramped a little, remembering how he'd looked with Titania. Was he under a spell? Faking it? Maybe he'd been faking it with me. I really wanted to look into the crystal globe again, and the strength of that desire bothered me. I could see how that thing would be addictive.

"Would you care to dance, Lady Sorceress Gwynn?" Fafnir

rose and came to stand by my chair.

"Excuse me?"

He laughed and swept a distinguished bow. "Grace me with a dance at least, if you won't join my army."

The fae musicians had struck up a sort of waltz on the dance floor below. Walter's ballroom was ironically much smaller than the throne hall. We all sat at tables on a raised dais that let us observe the dancers from above. Darling—I mean Darling Hercules—had already expressed his intention to help the dancing along with his anesthetic skills and the brightly colored couples, threesomes, foursomes and more whirled along in various enthusiastic tangles to the racing rhythm.

I did not want to dance. And not just because it was Fafnir asking. Though what I knew about him seemed so at odds with his demeanor. At least I understood why Cecily had believed she loved him. Somewhere in my own foolish heart, I'd imagined dancing at something like this in Rogue's arms. A silly fantasy I couldn't afford, especially not with Blackbird giving me a warning look.

Besides, I'd wanted a closer look inside Fafnir's head, didn't I?

"I'd be delighted, Lord Fafnir." I smiled and offered my hand. "Though I'm afraid I don't know the dances."

He kissed my hand with the barest brush of his lips, a studiously polite touch. "Then I shall teach you. Don't worry." His eyes went to the lily earrings I'd put back on. I'd made myself a blue gown to match, in a fit of nostalgia. "I shall observe Lord Rogue's claim to you."

He led me onto the dance floor, which allowed me to

refrain from commenting, and proceeded to show me the steps, which were intricate but repetitive. Rather like learning the newest line dance—once you got over the hump of the initial gimmick, the rest pretty much fell into place. Fafnir patiently explained, demonstrated and then started us out on slow turns. He made an excellent partner too, considerate of his much greater height and length of stride, adjusting his steps so I could easily match them.

"Lord Rogue is exceedingly lucky in having you for a consort. But then that bastard always has had the devil's own luck."

"And you, Lord Fafnir. Have you a consort?" I tried to keep the question innocent and neutral. Pain flashed through him, sharp, quickly hidden.

"Not at present, no."

I felt mean prodding him and reminded myself of poor Cecily's awful demise at his hands. "But you have had?"

"Certainly. Apologies to you, lady, but as long-lived as we are, we enjoy many consorts through our lives. Rarely are they as scintillating as you, however."

The man would have to be a skilled diplomat, expert at ducking sensitive issues. All of his thoughts that I could read, like his manners, flowed in a seamlessly polite and gracious order. If it hadn't been for that flash of pain, I would have started to think I had the wrong guy, despite the name.

"Seems that I heard you did have a mortal consort at some point—was her name Cecily?"

He stumbled over the next step, hissed in a breath and gave me a hollow look. I thought for a moment he might be physically ill, then remembered it wasn't possible. "How could you possibly know about her?"

He'd regained himself, spinning me through the dance with expert ease, not allowing either of us pause. His grip, though, tightened in a vise on me, reminding me of the fae's terrible strength. I readied a defensive wish, just in case. I still couldn't quite get past his surface mind. Not and keep track of the dance steps, dammit.

"Just something I heard," I got out and he relaxed his hold slightly, allowing me to at least breathe.

"Is that so, Lady Sorceress?" His flint-gray eyes searched my face and I saw the hardness in him now. "I wonder what game you're playing with me."

Might as well lay my cards on the table. "I seek to discover what became of Cecily—and her child."

His gaze dropped to my bosom and lower. "Is it true then? Do you carry Rogue's baby even now?"

"What happened to Cecily?"

Fafnir tipped his head, acknowledging the trade of information. "She died." He said it with bleak finality. "As you mortals are wont to do. She died birthing our child and I...I have never recovered from it."

"How very sad. Were you with her?"

He started to reply, stopped himself, frowning. And there it was—the oily black rope, the coil of a sea serpent showing through the waves and vanishing again. "Perhaps we need a breath of fresh air."

"Lead the way."

We pushed through the mad whirl of dancers and, as soon as we stepped through floor-to-ceiling doors out on to a wide balcony and out of Darling's influence, I became abruptly aware of my tired body and sore feet. We'd danced for hours already. I would have gone on too, never realizing the drain on my sadly mortal self. No wonder Starling had been so wiped out.

The sharp wind caught me as I stepped outside, tugging at my hair and gown, grasping fingers. I imagined I heard a howling laugh echoing through the roiling clouds that dashed in shreds across the moon. Like everything in Faerie, the moon glowed more luminous, larger and seemed to watch me with a certain awareness. The face of the Man in the Moon on one glance looked as always, on the next, fully intelligent with shrewd awareness. I shivered, wrapping my arms around myself, and wished up a cloak. Not the one Rogue had given me, which was presumably back with the wagon train.

Fafnir regarded the sky, eyes tracking something I couldn't see. Then a galloping horse flew across the moon, morphing into a fragment of cloud. I stared in wonder.

"The Wild Hunt gathers," Fafnir observed.

"Excuse me?"

"You don't know it? It rides through your world also."

"Um, we really don't have horses galloping across the sky—sorry to disappoint you."

He leaned back against the stone balustrade, seeming not to feel the bite of the wind. "You simply saw what you expected. With the dying of the year comes the hunt, gathering up stray mortal souls from your world and this. The autumn winds tear through the skies, now taking form, now vanishing again."

"How can the hunt move through both worlds—I thought no one could go back and forth through the Veil."

"The Veil grows thin this time of year and the worlds come closer together. Cecily came through around this time." He tipped his head back again, watching the sky. "Ah, I miss her still. It's an unnatural thing, for your kind to mix with ours. Only grief comes of it."

"Seems like you had some joy and love before the sorrow."

"What good is a sweet flavor if only the bitterness of regret lingers in your mouth?"

"What do you regret, Lord Fafnir?"

He laughed, a hollow sound. "So many things. Your life is so fresh and new. You cannot possibly understand how regrets pile up like stones, a tomb that crushes but never kills."

"You're not much like the other fae nobles I've met."

"No." He looked at me again. "I was there when Cecily died and yet I do not remember her death. What do you make of that, Lady Sorceress who knows more than she ought?"

"I don't know what to think of that."

"Liar," he said softly. "Who are you protecting—me? You cannot wound me, for I am already the walking dead. Tell me what you know and I shall owe you a favor."

"Any favor whenever I ask for it? That's an enormous thing to offer without caveats."

"I am not like the other fae you've met because I have nothing left to lose. There is nothing you could ask of me that it would harm me to give to you. I care for nothing, therefore I have nothing I cannot give up."

I didn't see a reason not to, though I believed it would hurt him more than he thought to hear Nancy's story. So, for the second time that night, I told the story. Funny how horrible images that haunt one's head lose their power when described aloud. The tale didn't quite drive me the way it had before, though I found myself hesitating when I got to the point where Nancy went upstairs to check on Cecily.

Fafnir had dropped his head while listening, gray hair like the shredded clouds overhead draping his severe face. He hadn't moved or commented, keeping his thoughts very close. When I paused, though, he spoke. "Go on. Finish it." A sound of a stone door scraping against rock.

I did, tucking my freezing fingers under my arms inside the cloak.

"She is buried there, at this inn?" he finally asked.

"I think so. Or nearby. And the favor I ask of you is that you will not take any form of reprisal against Mistress Nancy or anything she cares about."

He studied me then. "You'd squander your favor in this way?"

"I don't consider it a waste."

"Keep your favor. I will visit Nancy and reward her for the care she gave Cecily."

"She'll be frightened to see you."

His thin mouth twisted in a wry grimace. "That thought had occurred to me, Lady Gwynn—I shall approach the situation carefully."

"Okay, then I'll ask for something else."

"You are quick to exhaust this debt. Are you sure you don't want to save it?"

"I don't like open-ended accounts."

"Then what?"

"I'm taking Walter with me and will decide what to do with him. No public sentencing."

"You're within your rights to make Walter your slave if you wish. Keep the favor, open-ended or not. Though the crowd will be disappointed."

"My hearts weeps."

His brittle laugh whispered over me at that. "You remind me of Cecily. I think you would have liked each other."

"Did you love her?" I surprised myself by asking it. My bruised heart speaking for me.

Weariness creased his face. "We are not as you are. Do not experience the world in the same way and yet..." He smiled, a heartbreaking expression crossing his distinguished face. "I think I did."

We were quiet and I felt I should say something more. Anything. "But you don't remember any of what happened then?"

"Pieces. Fragments. Incandescence should not have been there and yet, now that I know, I see her face, that silver-clad bitch."

I realized then that what I'd taken for acquiescence and sorrow in him was instead a hugely bitter rage, tightly contained—and all the more explosive for it.

"Tell me." His face looked lean and haunted in the moonlight. Maniacal laughter drifted on the wind, howling through the towers. "Do you believe I killed her? Took my sword and carved our child from her still-living belly?"

"I don't know." I whispered it and he nodded.

"That time you told the truth. Tell me this one—do you carry Rogue's child?"

"No."

He cocked his head with a shade of doubt. "If that's so,

why does he not dance attendance upon you?"

"You mean, since the goal of the game hinges on impregnating me?"

Fafnir just gazed at me, inscrutable. Not that I thought he'd be able to discuss it.

"My Lord Rogue is currently dancing attendance on the Queen Bitch."

His gaze darkened. "Then she believes you to be with child. How very interesting. Does Rogue?"

My own memory blank haunted me. Surely I would have known from the evidence of my body if we'd done more than I remembered. More—I knew I would never agreed to intercourse and I couldn't believe he would have done so without my enthusiastic compliance. A great deal rested on me believing that.

"I think he knows I'm not."

"Even more interesting. Have a care, Lady Gwynn. Step carefully."

"I'm doing my best."

"And a word to the wise. Never think it's a game. Nothing is more serious."

§⁊₹

IN THE MORNING there was no sign of Fafnir and I felt quite certain I knew where he'd gone. Walter, however, joined us on the high tower where the glass coach still waited and I sighed at the sight of him. I'd hoped to drop him off somewhere, but Starling had told me he remained quite determined.

"You really don't have to do this, Walt."

He sneered at me, but his gaze went to the staff Athena carried. "I can handle anything you can, Gwynnie. I'll take my punishment like a man and then we can duel again. I'll win my staff back."

"What if I told you there's a way back through the Veil?"

"How?"

"The Wild Hunt. It's gathering now and they move back and forth between the worlds."

Walter laughed at me, holding his jiggling belly. "Odin's hunt? With carnivorous horses and the hounds of hell? No. Thank. You."

"You know something about it?"

"Hey, I read. Or did, when there were books."

A tornadic gust of wind warned of the dragon's approach and I hurried into the coach, with Darling Hercules in my arms. I didn't want to run the risk of him reverting to cat too soon and dashing off to hide. Walter's bulk made the interior of the coach a tight fit. To my surprise, Starling took the seat next to him without complaint. Blackbird settled herself next to me and Athena sat cross-legged on the floor, keeping the staff out of Walter's reach.

I'd experimented with it some the night before, with Starling keeping an eye on me for odd behavior, like a spotter standing by in case a weight lifter gets in trouble. I reconstituted the grimoire which, to my great relief, manifested carrying every last one of my notes, even what I'd written down moments before Walter's dragon snatched us. Using the crystal, I tried solidifying the spell. I decided against the one on my hair, since I could see permanence there being a real drawback.

Starling carried the grimoire and Walter looked over her shoulder in interest at it.

"Hey—is that a book?"

"My book. Yes." I answered for her.

"Can I see it?"

"No."

"Aww, come on."

"It's her grimoire," Starling explained. "It's full of super secret magical incantations."

Walter raised an eyebrow at me and I restrained myself from squirming. Who was the humbug now? "Nicely played, Gwynnie."

"Shut up or I'll negotiate you a bad deal with Marquise and Scourge."

"No you won't," he replied with confidence as the dragon's talons closed over the glass. "You don't have it in you. Hey—your hair looks like crap."

I thought of Fafnir's face as he considered whether he might have wielded the sword that ended Cecily's life. Did any of us really know what monsters lurked inside? Not always. Sometimes not until we faced ourselves in the mirror and saw the image, splashed with blood of the ones we loved most.

CHAPTER 20

IN WHICH I FACE THE MONSTER(S) IN THE DARK

The pattern of lines on fae faces seems to be an external manifestation of their internal state. A barometer of the "not self" within.

~*Big Book of Fairyland*, "Rules of Magic"

THE DRAGON TOOK us directly to Marquise and Scourge's castle—I suspect more at Walter's bidding than mine. Especially since I really *did not want to go.* At first, I told myself that I'd come a long way. I'd faced various trials and those two held no power over me. I could hand over Walt to his foolishly chosen fate and walk away. But, as we traveled, my calm thinned, giving way to a frost of fear. Though I tried to think of other things, flutters of terror cast shadows over my thoughts, scattering them. Clammy panic edged in with gnawing bites as the silent edifice came into view. What had possessed me to think I could do this?

I couldn't.

But however the dragon had known our destination, it

now did not hear my increasingly strident thoughts to take us somewhere else. Anywhere else.

Inexorably fast, we closed on the castle and, for a wild moment, I pictured myself clawing against the glass, scrabbling to escape like a frantic hamster trapped in one of those clear plastic exercise balls.

Not a pretty image.

Darling Hercules had once again abandoned me for Athena's clearly superior belly scratches, and Blackbird had her eyes closed in an apparent nap. Walter and Starling continued to chatter, as they had for most of the journey. I hadn't paid attention to their conversation, but looking for anything to distract myself from the shrieks bouncing around the inside of my skull, I listened in.

"But the dragons don't eat flesh—they only eat the apples," Walter explained.

"Then why do they carry animals off?" Starling pointed out.

"Probably because some wizard or sorceress commands them to."

"So dragons only do what they're told?"

"Definitely not. They won't do anything that doesn't sound like fun."

"Hard to imagine a dragon wanting to have fun."

"Really? Everybody likes to have fun, Star."

She pinked prettily and looked over at me, her forehead creasing. "Are you okay, Gwynn? You're looking like..."

"Like she's gonna hurl," Walter confirmed. "Shoot it the other way, chickie."

Blackbird's eyes snapped open and Athena studied me with

concern. This had to be the worst part of being the walking wounded. How everyone thought you were so great until you just collapsed into a broken heap of pitifulness.

"Just let me get through this," I told them, closing my eyes and concentrating on finding the protective nothing place.

"But Gwynn, maybe we should—" Starling started in.

"No, Star," Walt unexpectedly stopped her. "Leave her be."

I cranked one eye open to give Walter a stare of disbelief.

He shrugged, scratching his greasy chin. "Yeah, I know—I called you chicken and nagged you into this. I didn't realize you'd go this psycho about it."

"Then you've changed your mind."

"No. I can't." He glanced at Starling. "I know I'm a little shit. If I'm ever going to be more than that, then I need this Scared Straight deal."

I surprised myself by laughing a little. "Honey, you have *no* idea."

He nodded, fleshy jowls bouncing, looking more than a little afraid. "I figure as much. But I gotta do this. Do or die, right, Gwynnie?"

My lips curved into a rueful smile, cracking the chapped skin. I let out a long breath. "You're a fool, Walter."

"At least I know it." He grinned and gave me a little two-fingered salute.

Then the ground rushed up and we hit the emerald green grass with a solid thunk of reality. The dragon—I wasn't sure if it was the same one I'd "talked" to or not—labored aloft again. Stranded. And in my least favorite place in all of Faerie.

And there was some stiff competition for that honor.

"Athena, I'll take the staff now."

The fact that she handed it to me without hesitation and Starling didn't breathe a word of protest spoke volumes. Don't upset the unstable person. As if they'd planned it—who knows, maybe they had—they all climbed out of the glass coach and left me to come out at my own speed. Except for Darling, who sat quietly beside me until I was ready.

"What would I do without you?" I ran my fingers through his plush fur and he purred, sending a picture of me sitting there, bored and lonely.

"It's true."

He arched his back under my hand, then leaped like dandelion fluff to the floor of the coach and looked inquiringly from me to the door. The dragon had gone and I could hardly sit in here forever. Though, at the moment, that prospect seemed entirely possible and definitely more enticing. I might have done it, if only the glass hadn't been, you know, now totally transparent and worthless for hiding behind.

I decided not to fix my hair, to face them as I was. The small defiance shored me up, oddly enough. I had nothing to hide.

So I got out.

Sounded so simple. Took every last dreg of courage I could muster.

And they waited for me, Marquise and Scourge, my erstwhile masters, iridescently beautiful as ever. Arms wrapped around each other's waists, her bright head leaning against his dark one at identical angles, they smiled at me with sensuous warmth. They held open their free arms in invitation, as if I might join them in a three-way embrace.

I stopped right where I was.

"Lord Scourge. Lady Marquise." I gave them a bare and formal nod. "I've brought you a new pupil. I expect you to treat him well."

Marquise let go of Scourge and took a step forward, holding out lovely hands to me, her crystalline eyes like Christmas ornaments, sparkling with pleasure. "I thought perhaps you'd come back to play with us, little pet. We've missed you so."

"Indeed." Scourge followed her, laying an ebony hand on her alabaster shoulder. "Perhaps you'd like to stay for a while. The collar doesn't have to be silver. You can obey simply because you desire it." His voice dropped in timbre. "Because I require it."

I studied the grass, trying to keep my gorge from rising past the hard knot in my throat.

"Or—" Marquise clasped the hands I'd refused to touch, "—you could help train the new pupil. I think you might have a knack for it. The most submissive pets often make the severest masters."

I raised my eyes to their hopeful, seductive smiles, then made myself look at the others. Walter stared at Marquise with horrified fascination, unable to tear his eyes from her gorgeous body, fully displayed in a loose dress of copper net. Starling gazed at me with a stricken look, as if she might burst into tears at any moment. Blackbird kept a serene expression while Athena looked between me and the sadistic twins with calculation. Darling Hercules stood beside me, tail wrapped around my ankle.

"Definitely not, Marquise."

She tilted her head, sly and pouting. "I think you underestimate yourself. You have a new cruelty. Almost animal." She shivered in delicate, deliberate arousal. "I'd be your pet, if you asked me. Scourge would like that."

"Ah," Scourge rasped, "ecstasy incarnate. The new pupil will need to...stew...for several days, as you know. Come play with us. Perhaps you'll find your cure in the poison. There are many tricks we can teach you, if you'll let us. Ways to use your magical skills to drive a being beyond the edge of reason."

I'd been beyond that edge and I recognized the lure in what they offered.

"I have better things to do." Something tight broke inside me, in release and relief. The truth of it rang strong and true. Whatever else I might become, after all the ways they'd twisted and molded me, they had never touched the fundamental core of who I was. I had become someone with important things to do. Missions of my own making, perhaps, but all the more integral for that reason.

"So here's the deal. Walter here needs to learn to maximize his magic."

"Does he?" Marquise fastened her avid attention on Walt, who went bug-eyed with delighted terror when she ran her hands through his hair and used her inexorable strength to force him to his knees. It never paid to forget the strength of the noble fae. Their limbs might look spun-glass delicate, but that magically amplified superior leverage trumped everything.

"Gwynn!" Starling cried out and I shook my head at her. This would be the first of many humiliations for Walt, if he followed this path. Better he get a clear picture now.

Scourge had joined Marquise in her inspection, pulling Walt's head back to inspect his teeth. Marquise glanced over her shoulder at me. "He's not very enticing."

"He will be. He's been around dragons and drinking silver."

She wrinkled her pert nose. "That explains the stink. We'll have to sweat him for days just to get started."

Scourge twined black fingers in Walter's brown curls. "I have some ideas. A new regimen to try. It will be fun." He whispered something in Marquise's ear, running his tongue along the perfect white shell of it while Walter quailed at their feet.

"No permanent injuries." I called out. "No scars. No sex."

"Gwynnie!" Walt found his voice at last. He cast a significant look at Marquise and nodded. I pointed at Scourge with raised eyebrows and Walt's face fell almost comically. Why do so many guys breeze past the fact that they might not be the only ones doing the fucking?

"Not fair, Lady Sorceress." Scourge strolled over to me, lethal, looking me up and down as if he could see through my gown. "You know, from *intimate* experience, that we are in this for the side benefits. Why would we agree to such a travesty of a bargain?"

"You agreed to it with me." I made myself hold my ground, though I longed to back up a step—or fifty miles.

Scourge smiled, black tongue flicking out to moisten his lips and stroked hot fingers down my bare arm. "A special favor. And one I regret...so very, very much."

"Yes." Marquise joined us, hand on Walt's head, urging him to crawl beside her like a puppy dog. His eyes had glazed over with an uncertain combination of terror and titillation. "You'll have to sweeten the pot, Lady Sorceress."

That phrase again. I made myself unclench my jaw.

"I can pay you."

They looked insulted. "We're not poor," Marquise sniffed.

"Then what?"

They exchanged speaking glances. "A night in our bed—anything goes," Scourge said.

"Or a favor to be owed in the future."

"Or we get full use of this sweet boy."

The sweet boy in question was still on all fours, staring at the lush grass.

"What was the special favor?"

Scourge stroked his chin. "Lord Rogue promised to take my place, should it become necessary."

"Take your place how?"

Now he slid his thumb between his black teeth, ducking his chin coyly—an alarming expression on his severe face. "Oh, I think you know."

"He's with her because of you?"

"No," Marquise giggled, running a hand over my shorn hair, "because of you, sweet girl!"

I didn't even mind the chill her caress gave me, so tightly did my stomach clench. "Explain." It came out as a demand, which seemed to shock Scourge, but I didn't care.

"I don't answer to you."

"No?" Pulling on the crystallizing magic of the staff, I clamped down on both their minds, using a tweaked version of Rogue's mind spell. "How about now?"

Marquise stepped back, hiding behind Scourge and burying her face in his shoulder while his face twisted in a rictus of varying emotions as he tried to fight the compulsion.

"My, how we've grown," he snarled at me.

"Yes, your efforts to break me weren't as effective as you thought."

"We never meant to completely break you," Marquise's silvery voice was muffled by Scourge's shoulder. "We were to make you think we wanted to, so you'd find your own way to fight back."

"That was the favor Rogue asked?"

"He's soft. I warned him that you would be his weakness, not the strength he hoped for." Scourge put an arm around Marquise, brushing a surprisingly tender kiss on the crown of her head and eyed the lily earrings I'd reattached. "But he wouldn't listen."

"He won't listen to anyone." Marquise peeked at me through the fall of her hair.

"And he'd pulled in all of his favors. So he agreed to take my place with Titania, should that event occur. Apparently it did."

"What does that entail?"

Scourge shook his head. "Can't tell you what I don't know, Lady Sorceress. But I'll let you whip me to try to find out, if you want to. It could be fun."

"I would, if I thought you wouldn't get off on it."

"Pity."

Rogue had traded this to protect me from these two, to help me get the power and control I needed. By Titania, I planned to use it.

With a thought, I knocked them both backward into a heap, popping the truth spell as I did. Then gave Walter a hand up.

"Last chance to get out of this deal. You've seen what they're like."

He wiped his forehead, watching the pair roll against each other, laughing and obviously completely turned on by my magic wallop. "Is there any other way?"

"Not that I know of. But I don't know much."

"How long?"

"I don't know. I think they know when you're ready."

"Can you make it be sex with just the girl?"

"Maybe. But that won't necessarily be better—you have no idea how cruel she can be."

"I'm already nothing."

"That's not true. Walt. Listen to me—"

"No, I'm done listening to you. You can't stop me." He dashed over, prostrating himself at their feet while they reclined back, gazes hooded. "Please take me. I'll do anything you want. Just teach me to be as powerful as she is."

Scourge raised his black-on-black eyes to me and grinned. "Seems like we have a deal."

ʕ⟶ʕ

MARQUISE AND SCOURGE offered for us to stay the night, even winkingly offering me my old room, but I refused and none of my friends protested. Everyone seemed uncomfortable around those two.

Starling hugged Walter goodbye, a move that surprised me. Then, when I thought about it, didn't so much.

We were a somber group, though, climbing into the glass coach. Thinking of what awaited Walter, what he'd essentially condemned himself to, depressed us all. Blackbird gave the direction for us to rejoin the caravan and I wished the thing into motion. After a few hours, though, I ran out of steam. Apparently keeping something in motion required me to continually renew the wish. I toyed with making a perpetual-motion wish, but worried that it could lead to dire consequences, like rolling us off a cliff if I failed to notice fast enough.

Athena had pried the staff away from me after the confrontation with the monochromatic twins and only the realization that I wanted to smite her somehow, instead of giving it to her, made me release it. That traveling piece of the crystal cave carried a tremendous seductive punch. I really shouldn't use it too much.

Still, I suggested that, with the staff, I might be able to get us further. And was totally overruled.

"We all need a rest anyway," Blackbird announced, her gaze brushing over the left side of my face and darting away again. I rubbed my temple, wondering if the ache there indicated the spiraling out of my own silver pattern. The cat inside seemed quiescent, but that could be the exhaustion. My bones ached with it and, for once, I didn't mind that they all handled me.

We didn't have the tents or other supplies, but Athena handily built a campfire and Starling set out the food she and Blackbird had packed from the feast leftovers. As the sun set, the night grew colder, the wind picking up and rattling the brittle leaves of the trees around us. A faint howl echoed in the distance and I fancied a black horse dashed across the sky. A chill not entirely from the dropping temperatures sent a shiver down my spine.

I told the others to do their business in the woods for the night and that I'd put the force-field dome over us for warmth and protection. That kind of one-time wish I had it in me to do, I argued with Starling. It worked well too—letting out the smoke and carbon dioxide, allowing oxygen to filter in, but nothing else.

I confess I crashed immediately afterward, however. Never had I used so much magical energy—and gone so long without sexual stimulation—and the combination of the two took its toll. I hoped that was all it was.

Despite my exhaustion, I dreamed.

Instead of treading through the sand or climbing those impossible peaks, though, I lay in bed, weeping. And a hand with familiar long fingers brushed my cheek.

"Don't cry, lovely Gwynn," Rogue said.

He sat beside me on the bed, brushing his thumbs over my cheekbones, murmuring affectionate nonsense.

"I needed you with me today," I accused him.

The left side of his mouth turned up in a half smile. "No, you didn't. You did just fine without me."

"That's debatable."

He smoothed my hair back from my face. "So brave. Sometimes I think you don't need me at all."

"I do," I whispered. "And even if I don't, I want you, Rogue."

With a heartbreaking smile, he leaned over me, his inky hair curtaining us, and brushed his lips against mine. "I've missed you—and our kisses."

"Yes," I whispered against his mouth.

"So much." He deepened the kiss, his hand sliding down my throat to rest on my breast. With a little cry of longing, I threaded my fingers through his silky hair and clung to him while my clothes vanished. He kissed me, stroking my naked flesh with avid touches, now teasing, now painfully demanding, now gathering me against him so we slid, skin against skin.

I gasped at the intense pleasure of it.

Gasped again. "No. No, we can't."

Rogue pulled back, amusement quirking his lips, damp and darker red from kissing me. "Silly Gwynn, this is only a dream." He slid a hand between us and laid it over my belly. "This isn't about the child."

My heart lurched, picturing that little person and what could happen. "Am I pregnant? Tell me the truth."

He kissed me softly, a sweet, tender, seeking touch. "You would know, better than anyone."

"But I don't know."

He sat up and framed my face with his hands. "I made you a promise, my Gwynn. You, of all people, know I would never break my faith with you."

"Why did you leave me then?"

"I've tried to tell you—even I am constrained." A deep sorrow crossed his face. "Now more than ever."

"You could have told me. I would have helped."

"The details don't matter. You cannot save me. It's too late for that. Save yourself. Promise you won't look for me."

"No. I won't promise that."

His jaw flexed, betraying that he gritted his teeth. Perversely that pleased me.

"Stubborn."

"Back at you."

I woke up, blinking against the dark. Not even a hint of sandalwood in the air.

PART IV

MODIFYING THE VARIABLES

CHAPTER 21

IN WHICH I RETURN TO THE ORIGINAL PLAN, WITH A MINOR TWEAK

Rogue is an enigma. One I intend to solve.
~*Big Book of Fairyland,* "Rogue"

*C*LUNK. *CLUNK. CLUNK.*

Larch knocked on the force field again, repeating the noise that had awakened me. His earnest purple face peered in at me, comically distorted by the field. I collapsed it and the cool morning air rushed in, making me glad I'd gone to the effort to keep us warm.

"My lady sorceress—it's good to see you again."

"How did you find us, Larch?"

He shrugged, sticking his hands in the pockets of his little tunic. "I knew when you returned to our soil. Then I just had to run a little."

"And the rest of the caravan?"

"Waiting for your return."

"It's cold!" Starling wailed, poking her tousled blond head

up.

"Best get moving then." Blackbird was already standing and brushing out her skirts. "Get your juices flowing."

"Larch." Athena nodded at the Brownie, who gave her a little bow in return, taking in her changed appearance.

Darling Hercules ran his tail under Larch's chin, who steadfastly bore the indignity.

"Now that I've found you, the caravan can reroute to join us at the Port of Blue Mermaids."

I shook my head, the lilies in my ears swinging. "We're not going there. Or I'm not," I amended. "The rest of you can do as you like, of course."

"Why?" Starling stopped in the act of finger-combing her hair. "Where are you going?"

"To the Glass Mountains, specifically to the Queen Bitch's castle."

"You can't just walk into Titania's castle, dearie," Blackbird told me, in a tone that indicated she feared for my sanity.

One does not simply walk into Mordor. I would have said it, if Walt had still been with us. Funny that I could miss the little shit. At this point he'd likely be locked naked in that featureless cell and getting pretty damn hungry. Maybe, since he'd already submitted, they wouldn't spend so much effort breaking his will.

"I'll find a way."

"I thought we were looking for my dad."

"You can keep doing that, Starling—you and Blackbird should absolutely do that. It's as important as me rescuing Rogue. I respect that."

They all stared at me with expressions ranging from disbelief to dismay. From the tenor of their thoughts, most of them felt concern that recent events had been too much for me and I might be collapsing under the strain. Except for Athena, who simply spun her dagger in her fingers, waiting. She was getting quite deft with it. Darling sat beside her, eyeing it with bright interest.

"Lady Gwynn." Blackbird folded her hands, looking to Larch for support. "You must understand that Lord Rogue is not one who ever needs rescuing. He'll turn up when it's time." She didn't look at my belly, but the implication was clear.

"Indeed, it's true, my lady sorceress," Larch chimed in. "It's best that you look after yourself and your delicate cargo."

I unclenched my teeth. "Yes, he does need rescuing. You all heard what Scourge and Marquise told me."

Starling and Blackbird exchanged concerned glances. "Gwynn," Starling said in a gentle tone, "they said they had no idea where Rogue had gone."

I gaped at them. Athena shrugged a little and nodded, indicating she'd heard the same thing. Darling swiped at her dagger and she hissed at him. He flounced over to me and pictured Scourge talking with two faces.

Then I got it.

They'd deliberately spoken different words, knowing the others would hear one thing while I would understand the truth I'd compelled from them. Clever. And a nasty, undermining trick. One I'd have to remember.

"Okay." I surveyed them. "All I can tell you is that I understood something different. Something I know to be absolutely true. Rogue is with the Queen Bitch and it's due to a bargain he made to take care of me. I have to help him."

"If he did it to take care of you," Blackbird pointed out, "then you shouldn't undo the effort by putting yourself in Titania's clutches."

"I don't intend to be in her clutches. I plan to be smarter than that."

"How?" Larch asked.

"I'll know when I get there." I said it with as much confidence as I could muster. Darling Hercules pictured himself huge again, me riding him while he knocked the walls down and I smiled at it. "Besides—all the trails I follow lead there. I believe she's behind the baby-snatching game. It's foolish to do anything else."

"And what of your own child, Gwynn?" Blackbird demanded. "Will you risk its life so willfully also?"

"I am not pregnant."

"How do you know?"

I rubbed my left temple, which had developed an annoying twitch.

"It's not like I can drop by the drugstore and pick up an E.P.T. kit." My voice sounded tired. "But I'm 99.9 percent sure that I'm not."

They cocked their heads, not quite understanding. Interesting that none of them asked about my menstrual cycle and I wondered if any of them even had one. I hadn't had my menses since I'd arrived in Faerie. If I hadn't been assured in no uncertain terms that I would be fertile, I would have thought myself in sudden and abrupt, possibly magically caused, menopause. That could still be the answer, actually.

"I'm just...not," I added lamely.

Athena tucked her dagger away. "I'm in. Wherever you want to go. Not like I have anything better to do."

Blackbird shook her head. "No. After all this time, I must go after Fergus. That must take precedence for me. Starling, you'll come with me."

"No." Starling replied, staring at me. Then shook herself, as if surprised by her answer. And her mother's stern glare. "No, I won't. I serve Gwynn and I made her a promise. I'm going with her."

"Do you understand how impossibly dangerous this journey will be?" Blackbird asked in exasperation. "Do any of you? Nobody even knows where Titania's castle is."

"I do." They all looked at me in surprise. I pointed at the staff, tucked securely by Athena's feet. "That shows me."

"And are you willing to pay the price the staff exacts from you, my lady sorceress?" Larch asked, peering at me with shrewd blueberry eyes. "Already you tire."

"I'll use it sparingly."

"You have no supplies. No mode of transportation. No tributes for trade." Blackbird ticked the points off on her fingers.

"I can arrange for a supply chain," Larch told her.

"You can?" I hadn't expected that and he looked hurt by the implied insult.

"I would be terribly remiss in my duties if I did not," he reproached me. "Already I allowed you to be kidnapped. I can do this much."

"A dragon carried us off—there wasn't much you could do."

He held himself with stout dignity. "Nevertheless. I failed

to serve you properly. We have many villages along the way to the Glass Mountains. I will see to your comfort and protection."

"All right then."

"I'll arrange for horses immediately." He hesitated.

"Spit it out, Larch."

"It might be best if you ride instead of taking the coach. It won't do well once you reach the mountains."

"Makes sense to me. Blackbird—why don't you take the coach to the Port of Blue Mermaids?"

She sighed. "Fine. But I don't like this."

"I'll take care of Starling—I won't risk her."

"I'll take care of myself, thank you! I'm not a doddering idiot."

"No." Blackbird smiled sadly and brushed Starling's hair out of her eyes. "I can't help but worry for you. I can't lose you—" her voice caught, "—also."

Starling's brown eyes filled with tears. "I didn't think of that. I'm sorry. I'll go with you."

Blackbird shook her head briskly and wiped away a tear of her own. "That's not what I meant you to feel. You're right. Your place is with Gwynn. Just...be careful, would you?"

With a little hiccup, Starling flung herself into Blackbird's embrace, her golden hair a contrast to her mother's gleaming brunette, and her frame more humanly proportioned than Blackbird's longer limbs. Otherwise, they looked much the same, clearly sprung from the same seed. Athena toyed with the hilt of her dagger and caught me watching her. She gave me a little grimace for her fascination and busied herself lacing on her boots.

We decided to start walking while Blackbird waited for Larch to return with horses. He promised to catch up with us that evening. Or, barring that, the next day. She promised she'd be fine with her rapier and, besides, who would bother with her?

The four of us—including Darling Hercules—set off down the road Larch indicated. Athena promised that she knew the way also, with that enviable dragonfly girl hive-mind knowledge. I did feel keenly for Starling, that her mixed blood cut her out of that loop. I was foreign through and through, while she was cut out of a world that should have been hers.

As promised, Larch caught up with us by evening, bringing horses—including Felicity, who nickered at the sight of me—and a sack of tribute to trade. He wanted to trust Athena with that, as she would know the appropriate value of the things, but Starling thought Athena shouldn't have both the staff and the tribute items while Athena astutely pointed out that Starling had custody of the grimoire. Eventually they decided to trade the staff back and forth.

The one thing they agreed on was that I shouldn't touch it more than necessary.

I overruled them from time to time, however, ostensibly to practice with the staff. I grew my hair out permanently, just to prove I could, set the color and then left it alone. I stabilized a few other small spells. The staff didn't have the reach or resonance of the cave itself, but it amplified very nicely.

Taking a bite out of me every time. Little bleeding wounds I took care to hide from the others. Though Darling seemed to know, watching me with his inscrutable cat's eyes, thoughts quiet.

When I had enough energy, I checked the globe for Rogue's activities. Which were more of the same. Dancing, feasting, lolling about, fawning over Titania. Though I hadn't seen it directly—thank all the stars in the heavens—he seemed to be her lover. And utterly delighted with her.

Every night, I dreamed. Sometimes of the tender, ardent Rogue who visited me in bed and begged me not to look for him, even as he touched me like a starving man. Other times the bad dreams took over—me climbing up the glittering shards of the peaks, slicing my hands open.

I would have taken the lily earrings off, if I could have, just to stop the dreams. If I'd had the dragon's egg still, I would have. Several times I toyed with the vial of dragon's blood always in my pocket, considering if just a dab would do the trick. Always, though, I reconsidered. One doesn't squander a secret weapon on the way to the great confrontation.

The dreams—the good ones—were also the only source of anything remotely sexually interesting in my life. We rode all day, shoveled food into our mouths at night and fell into our beds, when we had them, dead to the world. If we slept outside, though we had blankets supplied by nearby Brownie villages, I invoked the force field. The Wild Hunt grew louder every night, so much so that I sometimes feared the pounding hooves would crash through the roof of whatever house we slept in. Though the others didn't seem to notice it as much, I didn't care to take any risks that the hunt might carry one of us away.

Otherwise, I grew parsimonious with my magic use. With every day that passed, I became aware that my reserves dwindled a bit more. Without Rogue's teasing and titillating presence, there was nothing to replenish me. Not even a convenient Officer Liam to charge my girly batteries. He was apparently trying to catch up with us, but wouldn't for some time, limited to nonmagical travel.

Not an ideal way to confront one's greatest enemy.

Finally, when Larch next made contact, I asked him to arrange for us to stay in a human village for the night. He gave me a dubiously blue look.

"Surely you can't be worried I intend to betray Rogue," I snapped at him, irritable. "Look what I'm already going through for his sake. This is something I need to do. Just trust me in this."

He slid his gaze off mine and on to Athena. "You'll have to play dumb," he told her. "The humans will expect it."

She widened her lilac eyes and rounded her little pink bow of a mouth, then giggled. Starling snorted and Larch just shook his head.

"Just set it up, Larch, please? We can handle ourselves."

We came upon the human village—a fair deviation from the road into the Glass Mountains—by early evening. As much as I'd longed to find a settlement of my kind when I first arrived here, now the miasma of purely human thoughts condensed into one place threw me off-kilter. More than I was already.

We rode down the simple main street, nowhere nearly as neatly kept as the Brownie towns. Many of the houses seemed ready to tumble in a heap of timber, and the people who looked out of unglassed windows, or emptied basins into the common sewer running down the center of the road, eyed us with suspicion.

This, then, was the third world of Faerie. And it belonged to my own kind.

The inn Larch had arranged looked similarly decrepit but at least glowed with the warmth of firelight—very welcome to me as the first fingers of the night wind slithered down my neck and the hoots of The Hunt drew near. An older man greeted us civilly enough, handing our horses over to a stable lad. He, too, cast a wary eye to the sky.

"Good night to be indoors, lady," he grunted. "Not fittin' for humans to be out, with that lot preying through the skies. My niece took ill with childbirth night before last and the Hunt took her. Left a wee bairn behind that Odin will likely take too, before the week is out." He looked Starling over and, seeing the high arch of her cheekbones and large eyes, dismissed her as one of us. Athena made a concerted effort to skip into the inn with an appropriately vacant expression and he looked right past her, instead focusing on Darling Hercules. "That one a good mouser?"

Darling Hercules stopped in his tracks, tail on high alert.

"An excellent one," I agreed, relieved by the change of subject. "And he'd love to."

"I got a corn bin infested with the critters. I'll give you all free lodging and board if we can borrow him overnight."

Darling Hercules pictured a heap of fat corn-fed mice in happy anticipation. The journey had been boring for him, riding along on his pillow, and I sent him off with good wishes. Up in our rooms, Starling set about getting a bath ordered for me while Athena sprawled on the bed, cleaning her nails with the dagger.

"Remind me why we're doing this?" Starling grumbled,

pulling a hopelessly wrinkled party dress out of my bags. It had likely been in there since we left Falcon's camp. "And can't you use just a little magic to fix this up?"

"I'm saving up for my special friend in the Ice Palace. Maybe there's something less wrinkled? Or I can mess with it when I get out of the tub."

"Oh here," Athena snatched it from Starling's hand, "I can do this. Titania knows I was good for little else most of my life so far." She put a kettle on the fire to start steaming.

"Thanks—it's probably the sexiest one, so that's a big help."

"Which brings me back to my original question. Why are we being sexy tonight?"

"*We* are not doing anything. You can have dinner up here and crash if you like. I'll be fine on my own."

"Doing what?" Starling wrinkled her nose in suspicion.

Athena heaved a sigh and glared at her. "Don't you get it?"

"What? What don't I get?"

"She has to go get her flirt on to pump up the magic. Hanging out with a bunch of girls and Brownies isn't doing it for her. She needs all the juice she can get and she's not getting it from us."

Starling came over to shampoo my hair for me, chagrin graying her thoughts. "Sorry, Gwynn. I didn't realize."

Actually, it surprised me that Athena had. "No reason why you would. It's not something I'm really comfortable discussing. I feel like a damn succubus or some such."

"Oh no." Starling shuddered. "You're nothing like those harpies."

An interesting mental image drifted through her mind and

I wanted to pursue it. But it also felt so nice to relax in the hot water with her deft fingers massaging my scalp. I must have dozed off, because I awoke to them whispering.

"Should she be this tired?" Athena's voice.

"Well, *I* am tired too!" Starling snapped back. "It's not easy going all day, sleeping in terrible beds. Not all of us are magic-fueled—some of us are human."

Athena made a derogatory sound. "Some more than others."

"Hey! That's just rude, you snotty little—"

"Girls, do I have to put you in separate rooms?" I dunked my head under the water to rinse out the soap and silence any petulant answers.

Starling stood ready to dry me off when I emerged. "Sorry," she muttered. She had dark circles under her eyes and I winced, remembering my promise to look after her.

I patted her arm. "Stay in the rooms. Rest."

"You shouldn't be down there alone."

"I can go with her. Magically fueled and all." Athena had the grace to look apologetic.

Starling wavered, clearly torn, but finally agreed. She had flopped on the bed and fallen fast asleep before we even left the room.

"I shouldn't be making us go so far every day."

Athena shrugged her slim shoulders. "You're worried for Lord Rogue. Every day he's with Titania, the tighter she binds him to her."

I stopped and stared at her. "Do you believe that?"

She considered. "Yeah. That's how these things work."

"What 'things'?"

"Possessions." When I frowned at her, she clarified. "Taking possession of another person. Deepens with time and proximity. Starling knows that too, even though she's not convinced that's what happened."

"What does she think happened?"

"That you're crazed with grief over your lost true love."

I sighed.

"That and she's worried about Walter."

"Yeah, me too. She has good reason to worry."

Athena seemed about to say something, then turned and headed down the stairs instead. "C'mon," she called over her shoulder. "Let's get you fed. Can't have our favorite succubus going hungry."

"Ha-ha."

The tavern rang with the gratifying sound of men's voices. I paused on entering the room, letting them take a good look at me. I'd never been the kind of woman who commanded much male attention—certainly not an entire roomful. But I'd gone to some effort, knowing something from what Liam liked.

My dress fell low across my bosom, revealing a fair amount of skin. My hair drifted long and loose down my back, something I knew would be unusual since, as I'd suspected, all the human women I could see had their hair tightly braided. My cocktail length hem showed off the better part of my legs, including the stiletto heels. I'd squandered a tiny bit of magic on "doing my makeup," adding shadows and colors to enhance what charms I possessed.

The women frowned at me and the men grinned in approval, salacious thoughts drifting my way like the scent of hot gravy. Oh yeah. I drank it in.

"Is this seat taken?" I asked as coyly as I could manage. The all-male table rearranged themselves, happy to accommodate me. Fortunately my meager flirting skills weren't called upon. The men competed with each other for my attention, all the while feeding me with fantasies of what they wanted to do to me. I only hoped I wouldn't have to draw on my newly replenished supplies to fend any of them off.

Athena, with an empty-headed giggle and bounce, brought me my meal and then plopped herself at my feet. I chatted with the men, answering their questions and embellishing freely—and without remorse—on the story of who I might be and where I was headed. I might have dropped Fafnir's name a few times and strongly implied Sugar Daddy status for him. A little misdirection never hurts.

All in all, I considered it a successful evening and, when I woke in the morning, the dredging exhaustion had at least eased. It had been a good dream night too, with Rogue dancing with me, spinning me around an empty ballroom, ardor in his dark blue eyes. Starling looked a bit better for the rest too, and we all counted ourselves lucky that no one had bothered us.

Of course, finding Larch sleeping on the floor outside our door tipped me off on part of the reason for that.

"Get what you came for, my lady sorceress?" He scrunched up one eye, surveying me.

"Yes. Thank you."

"No more human villages twixt here and the path into the Glass Mountains. You'll have to do without from now on."

"I'll have to."

We packed up and headed down for breakfast, where a lone redheaded man sat drinking a mug of beer.

Starling stopped on a gasp. "Daddy?"

CHAPTER 22

FURTHER UP AND FURTHER IN

Over and over it occurs to me that the Black Dog moves outside of the rules. I think this is important.

~*Big Book of Fairyland,* "The Black Dog"

I LOOKED FROM the grizzled man to Starling's wide brown eyes. Back to him. "Fergus?"

"In the flesh." He toasted me with his tankard, then winked at Starling. "No hug for your old da, Little Bit?"

She threw herself at him and he enveloped her in a bear hug, laughing when she squealed at the rough stubble on his face.

Athena and I sat gingerly on the other side of the table. Then she popped up again. "What am I thinking? I'll fetch breakfast."

I nabbed her sleeve to stop her. "Let the inn help do it. Who cares what they think now? I'd rather you stuck close."

Starling and Fergus finished their reunion just as the scowling maids brought out our food. Hopefully none of them had spit in mine. I certainly hadn't won any friends among the female population with my performance last night. I used a judicious wish to cleanse any germs or toxins.

"How are you here, Daddy?" Starling asked. Belatedly, I thought. Then the next thought occurred to her. "And oh no! You missed Mother. She went in the other direction, looking for you across the Endless Sea."

The guilt on his face told it all.

"Yes. How is it that you serendipitously just happened to turn up right this moment?" I inquired in a sweet voice. Starling gave me a sharp look and I hoped she'd be circumspect.

"I don't believe I've made your acquaintance, lady. Or your companion there."

"My fault." Starling jumped in. "Daddy, this is Lady Sorceress Gwynn, my liege lady. We're on a quest!"

So much for circumspect.

"A quest! Seems like my luck is with me, as I'm on a quest too. What is yours, Lady Gwynn. I tell you mine if you tell me yours." His Irish brogue rolled out thick and charming—and didn't take me in for one moment.

"I suspect you know exactly what our quest is, Fergus. Tell me this. How long have you been in the habit of lying to your wife?"

He scratched his bristly chin, white hairs peppering the red. I wondered how old he truly was. "Well now, a man sometimes tells his wife a pretty story or two to keep her satisfied. It hurts none. I didn't imagine she'd take it in her head to come looking for me, after all these years. Your turn—who's your little blue-haired servant girl there?"

"This is Athena. She's, um, a friend, not a servant."

Starling looked flustered, especially when Athena raised her eyebrows in feigned shock.

"Athena, eh? Companion of heroes. Seems apt." Fergus winked at me.

Wow. Put like that it sounded really…egomaniacal. "I hadn't thought of it that way."

"I like it," Athena countered firmly and Fergus nodded.

"See? The lass knows it's right. What with you on your own odyssey."

"You're remarkably well-read for a poor Irish farmer."

"Yes, that. You can't farm at night and those right bastards close the pubs at two—have to pass the time somehow."

"Sleep?"

He shook his head. "Never was much good at that."

"What are you good at, Fergus?"

"Rescuing pretty maids and not a hell of a lot else, as it turns out." His tone turned bitter and he turned a canny eye on me that belied his drunken Irishman guise. "You came through with magic, it seems."

I nodded, not willing to confide much else.

He drank deeply, set down the empty tankard. "I came through a hero. Obstacles crumble before me. Castles fall. Princesses throw themselves at my feet." He seemed to recall Starling's presence and patted her knee in apology. It seemed the drunken Irishman bit might be entirely too real and not a counterfeit at all.

"So, yes, gossip travels," Fergus said around a forkful of eggs. "I've been round this area for a while. I think you know why." He gave me a little nod of confidence, winking on the side away from Starling.

"I do. So does Starling. And Athena."

He looked a little taken aback, not meeting his daughter's gaze. Darling leaped up on the table just then, walking regally between our plates.

"This is Darling Hercules," I told Fergus. "My Familiar."

Fergus made a noncommittal noise while I offered Darling some breakfast. He started to tell me about all the mice he'd eaten and I asked him to please stop.

"The thing is—" Fergus cleared his throat, "—knowing where you're going and all…I'd like to come with you, Lady Gwynn. I can be of help perhaps. And I have a vested interest."

"That would be entirely up to Starling. I trust her judgment in this."

"It is?" Starling twisted her fingers together. "You do?"

"Of course." I stood. "Athena, let's go see that the horses are ready."

Starling looked pale and more than a little panicked, but I gave her a cheerful grin and herded Athena and Darling Hercules outside. The horses were, of course, saddled, loaded and stamping in the chill morning air with puffs of eager, steamy breath. My team handled things far too efficiently for anything less. Like Larch delivering my black cloak with the green ribbons that Rogue made for me. I needed the warmth.

Athena leaned against her brown mare, her tufted blue hair a match for the clear morning sky, and tilted her head in thought. "Why did you leave it up to Starling?"

I checked my saddlebags for the grimoire, even though I knew it would be in its usual spot, and resisted the urge to look in the sphere to see what Rogue was up to. Probably tangled in Titania's lush arms. Not that I was bitter. "It's family stuff. He's been lying to Blackbird—ironic, since he clearly had no idea she didn't remember what he told her anyway—and by default lying to Starling, as well. He's been pretty much absent from their lives because of this obsession and now he wants in, not to spend time with his daughter, but because he thinks we'll get him closer to his goal. If she doesn't want to give him the time of day, that's okay by me."

"Families seem like complicated things. Like an intricate dance."

"That's probably an apt analogy. And, like a dance, when it goes right, it can be a joyful thing."

"Until someone gets their foot stepped on."

"My mother broke her elbow while dancing once—extremely painful."

"You know," Athena plucked a bit of brittle leaf from her horse's mane, "before I...changed, I never thought about family. Now I feel this absence of something I never expected to have, like maybe I was better off not knowing I didn't have it."

"Blessed are the lilies of the field, for they grow in blissful ignorance."

Those pretty lilac eyes flashed. "That was me. A happy flower—is that what that means?"

"Yes. Though I think I butchered that quote. It means that they're happy because they don't know any better. Being aware of the world means knowing suffering too."

She pulled out her dagger while she thought, spinning it absently. "You're obsessed with your quest too."

"Yes. But I like to think I'm not hurting anyone else. And maybe serving a good cause."

Starling and Fergus came out the doors. She fussed with tying her cloak. Then met my eyes. "I said he could come along—mainly because I think we could use his help."

"Good enough for me. Let's get going."

Fergus brought round an impressive stallion. Exactly the kind you'd expect the fairy-tale hero to be riding. He saw my dubious expression. "Goes with the territory. There are certain tropes I seem to have to conform to." A sword that could have played Excalibur in any movie was strapped prominently near the pommel.

Interesting.

We rode out of town, looping back to the road Athena pointed us to. On the horizon, something glittered, reflecting the light of the rising sun. I squinted at it.

"The Glass Mountains," Athena told me.

To my dismay—and just as in the dreams and visions—they did seem to be actual glass. As we rode closer, the peaks grew taller, jagged edges gleaming sharp, catching passing clouds and shredding them. The smaller, slightly more rounded foothills became more clear over the course of the day. But even this mountain girl didn't see how anyone could travel through those intimidating sharp valleys.

"Do people really manage to traverse these mountains?"

Fergus snorted out a laugh. "Only the crazy ones. And the heroic types. Same thing, really."

I gave him a sour look. "You did it."

"Guilty on all charges."

"Is there any other way to reach Titania's palace?"

"I've been trying for years—that's why I'm riding your coattails, Lady Sorceress."

Just great.

We stayed at a Brownie village that night, in the foothills of the Glass Mountains. Staying with the Brownies meant lots of cheerful singing, brandishing of the light-up pillows I'd invented, and being left pretty much alone. Larch joined us with a pack mule loaded with supplies and said he'd stick with us from then on.

"Did Blackbird make it onto the ship for her voyage?" I asked in an innocent tone over dinner. Starling bit her lip, staring at her plate, and Athena looked amused. Fergus visibly flinched. Go me.

"She did, my lady sorceress."

"I think she won't find what she's looking for."

Larch rolled a blueberry eye in Fergus's direction. "It appears not."

"Any way to get her a message, do you suppose?"

"No, my lady. Quite impossible."

"I hate to think of her, all alone, undertaking such an enormous journey, all for a lie."

Fergus glared at me over his tankard. "Come from a Catholic family, do you, Gwynn? You're quite expert with the guilt."

"I like to think I come by it naturally."

He sighed. "What would you have me do? We've just established there's no way to get her a message."

"Make it right."

"How am I to do that?"

"You could go after her," Starling said to her plate.

He glanced at her, surprised. "I can't do that."

"You can," I pointed out. "You choose not to."

Fergus clamped down on the words he had been about to say, pressing his lips together and shaking his head. "You don't know how things are. What she did."

"Actually, Daddy—" Starling tossed her hair back and stared him in the face, "—we do know."

"Do you then?" He breathed and reached out to touch a shining lock of her hair, faltering when she pulled back. "Then you understand, Little Bit, that it was never about you."

"It is about me. You can't parse out who gets hurt when you make choices like that." Starling sounded surprisingly calm. Not the daughter Fergus remembered, by the look on his face. "I'm here to find my brother too. This quest belongs to all of us. You could let us do this and go find Mother."

Fergus looked pained. "I can't."

"She loves you."

"I know that. And sometimes it's just not enough. One day you'll understand." He heaved himself up and took himself off to his room.

"I already do," Starling said to the space he'd left behind.

"We can kick him off the team," I told her.

"Make him go away so I don't have to deal with him, like you did with Officer Sean?" She rolled her eyes at me. "Yes, of course I knew about that. It's sweet of you, Gwynn, but I end up feeling like you think I can't handle stuff for myself."

"I didn't mean it that way."

"I know, which is why I'm not insulted. Yet. My decision stands. If he chooses to come with us, he can."

꿍ㅠ꿍

THE NEXT MORNING we began the climb into the Glass Mountains. It had been a bad dream night for me and I felt as thin and brittle as the razor-edged peaks rising above us. Starling had shaken me awake at one point, saying that I'd been shouting so loudly, a few Brownies had rushed to our defense. Darling Hercules slept beside me for the rest of the night, his purring soothing me, but not loud enough to cover the sounds of the Wild Hunt shrieking through the treetops. I could only hope they didn't prey through the mountains. As it was, I lay awake for the rest of the night, listening and wondering what the hell I was going to do when we reached Titania's palace.

We rode on narrow paths through steep-sided ravines, the horses' hooves sometimes slipping on the slick surfaces. The terrain wasn't truly glass—at least, not this low down—but more rocky with glassy inclusions. Obsidian rocks jumbled up against boulders of clear crystal. Loose pieces of what seemed to be precious jewels sometimes showered in minor landslides, set loose by unknown creatures following us from their vantage along the ridgelines.

Larch, sure-footed and tireless, led us through one valley and into the next. Each night I touched the globe as lightly as I could, rose up and traveled the distance to Titania's palace and back, then pointed the way to him.

I avoided looking inside. It only seemed to make things worse.

And each night we camped under worse circumstances, on flat diamond surfaces that no pile of blankets could soften. Larch and Athena took turns standing guard, though I assured them that no one could get through the force field. I hoped. I hit my store of magic for it every night, sure that Starling, Fergus and I would not withstand the cold. Darling took to sleeping *on* me, which I didn't mind that much, since his distracting weight kept me grounded in my body, breaking through the nightmares to remind me that they weren't really real.

Or, at least, not real enough that I'd actually sliced off my hands. I breathed a sigh of profound belief to awake in the morning—or move from the one reality to the other—and see that my hands remained attached.

One morning we awoke to muffled light, and my heart lurched me out of drowsiness with a great thump. Snow had fallen, clinging to the force field instead of sliding off, shrouding us from the world. The air inside felt thick and close, making me worry for what might have happened if enough carbon dioxide had built up that we wouldn't have awakened at all.

I used a bit of magic to heat the field enough to slide the snow off before I popped it, saving us from a dousing of snow—something Darling thanked me for, as he rarely did. I fretted as we rode, wondering if I dared protect us again that night. Perhaps Larch or Athena could alert me if it began to snow, but then what? Maybe I could heat it enough to keep the snow from sticking, but that would be a constant energy drain I couldn't afford. Unless I stabilized it with the globe, which exacted its own toll.

"My lady sorceress?" Larch's voice broke through my reverie. I'd been riding dully along, immersed in my thoughts, Darling on the riding pad behind me, under my cloak. Starling, Athena and Fergus all looked at me questioningly, which meant it wasn't the first time Larch had tried to get my attention.

I was getting really tired of people giving me worried looks. "What?"

He pointed. The path before us, already no wider than my arms outstretched, narrowed and began to climb up a sheer-sided peak, brilliantly clear and cold blue in the center. Above, Titania's palace glittered, lethally lovely.

"We'll have to leave the horses here and walk up."

"They can't stay alone." Not like we could turn them out to graze in this sterile wilderness of stone.

"I'll stay with them," Larch agreed. "Someone of my kind would stand out among Titania's crowd."

I realized he was right—in all the visions, I'd never seen a Brownie among Titania's jeweled throngs of admirers. Spoke well of the Brownies, I thought.

"We're all going to stand out," Athena observed. "Unless Gwynn can magic us up some disguises."

"Maybe so."

"We'll see," Starling put in firmly. "Let's get up there first."

Fergus, eyes glued to the palace looming above, dismounted and strapped his sword to his belt. He pulled out various other tools and supplies, fitting them into various pockets of his cloak. Abruptly he looked more like a champion and not the drink-sodden Irishman oozing bitter regret.

"Hold up there, Prince Charming," I told him. "We can't just charge up there and storm the castle."

He flashed me an impatient and arrogant glance. Did he look younger and slimmer all of a sudden?

"You may do as you wish, lady sorceress," he sneered,

making it clear he didn't think much of my abilities. Given what he'd seen so far, I hardly blamed him. But the attitude seemed way out of line. "The end of my quest is in sight. I must reach out and grasp it."

"Nice line and it all sounds terribly heroic, but how exactly do you plan to get into the castle?"

His russet hair glinted with gold when he tossed it and a handsome smile in my direction. "I have my ways."

And with that, he ran up the trail and out of sight.

"So much for him being helpful."

"I can't believe he did that." Starling gazed after him, then held up a hand at my incredulous look. "Okay, I can. But still…"

"The one advantage," I speculated, staring up the narrow trail, envisioning what stood at the top, "is that anyone watching the trail or guarding the gates might be distracted by his arrival. Could we sneak in after him?"

Athena laughed outright. "You really think you can sneak into Titania's palace? When she knows exactly who you are? She'll know you the moment you walk inside her doors. Fergus is not enough of a distraction, especially if he gets himself captured right away. We need a diversion. An inside man."

"We have an inside man," I pointed out, "except I can't really assess whose side he's on at the moment. If what you say about possession is true…"

"We need someone to talk to him and find out," Athena agreed. "I can do it."

"No," Starling interrupted. "I can."

"You?" Athena sounded dubious, but I stopped her.

"You're right. You're perfect for it."

Starling nodded, looking oddly pleased for someone taking on a potentially dangerous mission. "If I know how to do anything, it's visit the fancy folk and suck up to them."

"I can wish you a gown, jewels."

"And I'll be your brainless servant girl," Athena added in an admiring tone. "Well thought out, Starling."

"I'm not an idiot," Starling replied, a bit too tartly but Athena just grinned at her.

I scratched Darling Hercules's back and he complained about being cold. "Take Hercules with you. I'll change his coat, just in case anyone recognizes him. He can take messages back and forth, if it comes to that."

I made Starling's traveling gown into a party dress of bronze that flattered her shining hair and soft brown eyes. With plenty of jewels lying about, I wished her up dazzling necklaces and earrings. With a grimace of resignation, Athena let me restore her long, powder blue ringlets and insisted that I "dress" her again in the typical dragonfly girl outfit of a sheer little dress and nothing else. When I worried about her getting cold, she wryly noted that no one worried about her sort being uncomfortable and it would be out of character for Starling to have dressed her any other way.

Darling Hercules grumbled, but agreed to the plan, letting me give him an elegant fluffy white coat and blue eyes. He looked rather magnificent, we all thought.

"No," I told him, "you do not look like a girl. There are plenty of white male cats. And you do not want *her* attention, do you?"

It was a low blow, but he stopped complaining. Even Darling Hercules had the sense to be very afraid of Titania.

With that, they stood poised at the bottom of the path, ready to go.

"Tell Rogue…if you can get close enough to talk to him, find out if—"

"I know what to say, Gwynn."

"I know you do. I just worry that he won't believe you. Wait. Larch, do you have that dragon's egg still?"

He bowed with grave courtesy and dug it out of his tunic, from who knows where, since the thing had no pockets.

"May I borrow it for a moment?"

"Anything that is mine is yours, my lady sorceress."

I ignored that one and took the egg, holding it up to my ears. As I'd hoped, the lily earrings fell off, releasing my flesh with small sighs. I handed them to Starling and she nodded solemnly and tucked them into her dress.

I hugged them both goodbye. Darling Hercules, still sulking, wouldn't let me, and I felt more than a little bereft, watching them go up the hill without me. Larch and I took the horses back down the trail a ways, to a wider, semi-more comfortable spot.

And settled in to wait.

CHAPTER 23

IN WHICH I GO TO THE BALL

ꞗᵗꞔ

Titania appears to be less a goddess or queen than a very powerful sorceress, with a far-reaching mental hold on just about everyone in Faerie. Other than that...

~*Big Book of Fairyland*, "Flora and Fauna"

I TRIED TO enjoy the respite from traveling, the sunshine in our little canyon alcove. But it was exceedingly difficult to relax when people were off risking their lives for your project. This wasn't something I'd encountered in my old life, really ever. The most I could have hoped for then was that someone would rescue me from a stultifying conversation at a department party. That had been heroic enough, given that they often risked being trapped themselves. I felt like a different person now. Older. Hopefully wiser.

Certainly more tired.

After we ate, I settled in to meditate on my reserves. I could wish that I had a better sense of my fuel reserve, but I just didn't yet. I'd only ever run it completely down once. I'd hated it enough not to let it happen again.

Rogue's comment that he had resources outside himself niggled at me. Why had *that* had to be a future lesson? If ever I needed resources outside myself, now would be an ideal time to discover them. I wondered again about the Black Dog. Was he a source of power for Rogue, along with the curse of his existence? Did Titania hold that aspect in thrall, also? If indeed that was what was going on. It seemed that, from what he'd told me, that elemental aspect of himself couldn't be contained or controlled, by anyone at all. Except that it listened to me.

Something to exploit, perhaps.

What I didn't get was, that first time, my natural energy had come back fairly quickly and in full measure. Why did I feel as if something were constantly draining me?

I eyed the staff, now safely in Larch's keeping. That thing could very well be it. Yet it was my most valuable tool for the time being. What else did I have? The vial of dragon's blood. I'd given the egg back to Larch. After seeing how tenderly the dragon had treated it, I felt wrong thinking of it as an anti-magic hand grenade.

If I thought to exploit the Black Dog, then I should consid-er my own elemental beastie. The itching throb in my temple had subsided, and her ghostly presence in my heart had quieted. Very likely because I'd been using so little magic. A heartening thought for me—I could retire somewhere quiet, use no magic and perhaps escape the fate in store for me that way.

It seemed impossible to contemplate, a life without magic. Ironic, since I'd lived most of my life without it. But I'd had work. Perhaps I could study magic, tucked away in some tower, and grow learned and eccentric.

The image held a certain appeal.

At any rate, waking my inner big cat seemed prudent, so I began making tiny, very low-energy wishes, like running water through the pipes, priming the pump. I changed bits of gravel into popcorn, just for the whimsy. Larch's tunic went from red to polka-dotted—and back again when he scowled at me. I nursed my anger, which she seemed to feed on best, using it to heat the magic. I imagined throttling Titania's flower-stem of a throat, and the cat purred in agreement.

As the afternoon waxed on, several conveyances passed overhead. A couple of dragons went by and then some sort of fancy flying coach. Where could a sorceress get one of those? Then the ever-alert Larch moved us farther off the trail, hiding us just in time for a laughing party of noble fae to ride past without seeing us.

"Big party at Bitch Palace?" I wondered out loud.

"It is All Hallows' Eve," Larch observed. "Titania often performs rituals when the Veil is thin."

"It's Halloween?" I wanted to smack him. "And you didn't think that was important to mention before now?"

"My lady sorceress has heard the Wild Hunt growing louder each night. As you are not a fool, I presumed you knew such a simple thing."

"What kind of rituals?"

He shifted. Looked away. "Horrible ones," he whispered. And refused to say more.

I waited with increasing impatience, which at least served to fuel the cat, who paced to match my internal restlessness. The sun began to set, and the howling neigh of horses echoed on the wind.

At last, a glowing light came down the narrow path, which so many had gone up. Carrying a little lantern, Athena bounced along, curls blowing in the wind, skipping without a care in the world.

I grabbed her in my excitement and relief. "Thank goodness! What happened? Where are Starling and Hercules? Tell me everything!"

"Geez, Gwynn, I will if you'll stop talking long enough."

"Sorry."

"Understandable. So, it turns out that it's All Hallows' Eve, which is a stroke of great good luck."

"So, I've been recently informed." Apparently not everyone knew. I threw a glare at Larch, who steadfastly fed the fire. "Why is it good luck?"

"Titania is hosting a costume ball. Full masquerade. They swept me and Starling right into the guest suites without a single question."

"And Fergus."

She sighed. "Subterfuge is not his forte. Apparently he stormed the gates and is now languishing in a cell."

I rubbed my temple. "I suppose we'll have to rescue him now."

"We made a plan. Darling Hercules found him and will set him loose in case we need his heroic assistance."

"Very nice."

"So, you just need to dress up and come to the ball. Make it a good costume, so *she* won't recognize you. But there will be so many new faces and outlandish costumes there that Titania is highly unlikely to see you talking to Rogue. Get a dance with him, if you can—that's your best bet."

"Did Starling talk to him?"

A shadow dimmed her pixie face. "She did. Acted like he had no idea who she was. No trace of his normal self. He might be lost to her. You'll know when you see him, but we want you to brace yourself for the possibility that he's gone, okay? He may never again be the fae he was."

My heart fell through my belly at the thought. All of Rogue's brilliance, mischief and sensuality snuffed out, leaving only Titania's plaything behind.

"Did she give him the earrings?"

"Of course, but he barely paid attention, just commented that they were lovely and gave her a gift in return—usual protocol."

I tensed. Afraid to hope. "What gift?"

She looked at me oddly. "A piece of jewelry. Nothing of note."

"Describe it."

"A little gold thing. Kind of shaped like this." She held up her thumb and forefinger in a U-shape, and a sob of emotion escaped me. "What?" she demanded. "Is that a bad or good sound?"

I wrapped my arms around my ribs, uncertain myself of what feelings poured through me. "It's good. I think it's good."

She grinned at me. "Two pieces of good news. That means number three will be our lucky charm. Now get dressed. We have a ball to go to."

᚛᚜

I WENT ALL out. Style-wise, not magic-wise. With Athena's

coaching, I dressed myself entirely in black, with a dark green sash at my waist. I created a hoop and petticoats of matching green. Then studded the gleaming black overskirt with green silk bows that held the fabric up in swoops. I was the anti-Scarlett.

The neckline hung seductively over my shoulders and I changed my hair to a deep green that matched my eyes. Athena piled it high on my head in an elaborate style, using pins I wished up for her from the bits of gravel and popcorn.

I gave myself above-the-elbow black satin gloves, something Athena hadn't seen before. We debated over the actual mask. Seemed tradition dictated that one wore an animal, insect or flower face. I decided to take a risk and wished up a mask worthy of Venetian Carnivale. Both Athena and Larch were taken aback by it, but agreed that it would be exotic and in keeping with the competition for the unusual.

With reluctance, I left the staff behind. It might come in handy, but with my reserves so depleted, I couldn't really afford the bite it took out of me. Also, if the worst happened, letting Titania get her multi-jointed paws on it would be a bad idea.

I turned my shoes into Keens for the trudge up the hill, Athena lighting my way and diligently skipping. When we crested the top, we entered a wide, polished glass courtyard. Torches ringed the low walls and fae guards in uniform stood at even intervals, here and on the walls. As one, they saluted me, swords flashing silver.

Fergus had stormed this setup? I shook my head to myself. And changed my shoes into something prettier. Glass slippers were really tempting but so impractical.

Inside, I was ushered to the ballroom by a page, who also swept my cloak away and asked for my name. Athena gave me an imperceptible shake of her head, as if I needed it, and I told him to announce me as Lady Mysteriouso, with a wink.

As Cinderellaesque as this all felt—though I liked that I'd been my own goddamned fairy godmother—if I'd thought the room would come to a halt, gasping at my loveliness while I posed at the top of the stairs, I was dead wrong.

I don't think anyone could even hear the announcement of my arrival over the sweeping music and the roar of conversation.

Besides, another party rustled up behind me, all dressed as lavender lizards, which creeped me out enough that I scooted out of the way like a golfer who'd lingered too long at the tee. Unfortunately, my haste plunged me into the crowd before I scanned the room for Rogue.

"What is he dressed as?" I hissed at Athena, who cupped her hand to her ear. I had to shout the question from close quarters, only to be disappointed by her palms-up gesture showing she had no clue.

A fae lady dressed in bronze wearing a mask shaped as a lion crashed into me, giggling wildly. I tried to sidestep her, but the white cat with a baby lion mask, yanked along on her leash brought me up short. Darling Hercules sent me a pointed complaint that none of this was in our original bargain. I sent him a rush of affection and gratitude, promising a grander role for him soon.

"*Goliath,*" he replied.

Heaven help me, I agreed on the spot.

Starling nearly put my eye out with one of the spiky mane

things on her mask when she embraced me and shouted in my ear to follow her. Taking my hand, she dragged me through the spinning dancers, threading us through the tumultuous crowd with easy expertise. Starling in her element—who knew?

And then.

There he was.

I stopped, breath harsh in my throat, barely an arm's length from where Rogue lounged against a wall, head turned away to watch the dancers. He wore all black, of course, but tight, molded to his long, lean body like a loving glove. When he turned to look my way, as if sensing my regard, a mask with the face of the Black Dog stared at me.

Only the eyes were cobalt blue instead of amber.

Did he recognize me? I couldn't tell. His gaze dropped to my exposed cleavage, drifted down to survey the rest of me and rose again with easy lust. Those dianthus-edged lips curved in a sensuous smile that could have been for any woman. But the look floored me. Arousal flooded me, my nipples hardening and my vulva spiking with a sudden ache as the tender tissues surged turgid with blood. With it, came the magic.

Oh my Lord Rogue. He sure did it for me like no one else.

He held out an elegant long-fingered hand and I took it. Leading me onto the dance floor, he slipped a familiar arm around my waist and pulled me close, pressed tight against him so my nipples chafed against the dress as we danced.

And danced and danced.

Expertly, he waltzed me around the dance floor, the throb of the music matching the three-four beat of his heart, which thundered through me, a foghorn penetrating the night. I sent a brief, heartfelt thank-you to Fafnir, ironically enough, for teaching me the steps, then gave myself up to Rogue's embrace.

He stared into my eyes through our masks, never looking away, even as we spun in circles. I was hot and wet just from this much, but now I knew to embrace it, pulling the magic to me with the sweet desire. He smiled, a half twist of the lips on the left side of his face, as if he could feel what I did, but otherwise...

Otherwise, there was no indication that he knew me at all.

Except the cord between us. The moment he touched me, it reeled in tight, gluing me to his arms. It felt like home, being with him again, and I confess that for a while I simply reveled in it.

Then it occurred to me that he held me with both hands, our bodies pressed together, in violation of our agreement. Just as with all the agreements he'd broken. I imagined those just added layers to Titania's hold on him.

I reached out to find his thoughts and met a blank wall. No, not blank. A thick, ropy and oily barrier. The now-unmistakable stamp of Titania's interference. I searched Rogue's eyes, looking for some hint of the man I knew inside.

Nothing nothing nothing.

If he hadn't given Starling that horseshoe ornament, I would have despaired in that moment.

"Rogue?" I had to say it loudly, over the hubbub, but he seemed not to hear me. I leaned up closer to put my mouth nearer his ear, but he turned his head and, like a snake striking, captured my mouth with his.

The kiss held all his usual devastating power, but with a certain remoteness. He never stopped carrying me through the steps of the dance, even as he plundered my mouth with a remote and ruthless lust he'd never—even in his darkest moments—shown me before.

I managed to wrench my lips away, but he held me still with that alien strength, smiling at my futile struggles to escape him.

Then he released me and I nearly stumbled. His renewed grip around my wrist steadied me. He turned and, dragging me along by the hand, pulled me through the teeming crowd and to foot of Titania's throne.

With a little shove, he pushed me to the floor and swept a bow to Titania. "Look, my queen, I've brought you a present."

PART V

BREAKTHROUGH

CHAPTER 24

IN WHICH I AM CORNERED

𝆕

*The longer I am around magic, the more it becomes clear that
it manifests with as much unpredictability, complexity and
sheer variety as any organic system.*

~*Big Book of Fairyland*, "Rules of Magic"

THE ROOM DIDN'T go silent or anything, so I barely heard
what Rogue said. Fortunately our little drama was but a
small piece of the larger play. I clamped my thoughts down as
tightly as I could, pushing as much of myself behind that wall
of silence I'd learned.

I knelt at Titania's feet demurely—submissively, even—not
allowing myself to reflect on the irony that this skill too, came
in handy. If we'd worried about her recognizing me, the
moment pointed up how silly that had been. She barely
glanced at me, far more interested in some display across the
room. Naked, as always, she wore only a mask. An elaborate
living mask that I quickly realized had been the face of some
unfortunate fae, borrowed for the night. The ripped edges of
flesh bled freely, dripping blood over her voluptuous breasts

and running in rivulets down her sweet flesh.

Knowing the owner of the face likely couldn't die, I imagined him screaming in agony somewhere locked away in her beautiful palace of glass and light, waiting for her to return his face. If she ever did.

Thankful that playing meek meant I didn't have to look at it anymore, I sank myself into submitting. Biding my time.

Rogue stroked my hair affectionately, trailing long fingers along the nape of my neck. The touch, so familiar, so very *him* and still nothing. Finally Titania shifted her attention. I felt it in the change in Rogue's demeanor.

Titania sighed loudly enough to be heard over the tumult. "Really, Rogue. Aren't you tired of playing with humans? I thought you'd gotten enough from your little mortal tart."

"She's tasty. I thought perhaps you'd like to share her."

"No. Go slake your thirst if you must, but be back by midnight. If she survives your attentions, you can display her later. A little whipping before she's passed around to the others, perhaps."

"Thank you, my queen." Rogue tugged me up by the wrist and towed me from the room. In an act of supreme faith I let him, praying to the gods I'd never believed in that this was the right thing to do and not my last night alive before the fae gangbanged me to death. Walking briskly, he dragged me down a hall and into another wing, into a set of rooms made entirely of clear glass and set out over a drop to the chasm below, brightly lit by the moon.

Rogue tossed me onto a bed and pounced on me, pinning me with his long body, and holding my wrists together in one hand above my head. He kissed me breathless, yanked off the

Dog mask—thank goodness—and kissed me again. Then he pulled off my mask and stared long and hard into my face.

I'd wondered, back at that first feast, what it would be like to see his face above mine in the night, the black thorns spiking around his mouth and eye, the mask of a predator more than the Dog's had been. Now I hovered in an aching space between one thing and the next, poised above a figurative abyss as much as the literal one.

Would he try to rape me and would I be able to stop him? Or was he still in there?

He closed his free hand over my throat and I gathered the magic, calling the cat to the surface.

Poised.

"By Titania's rotten womb, idiot Gwynn—I expressly told you not to look for me."

A bubble of the sweetest relief bubbled through me, and I pulled my wrists from his slackened grip and wrapped my arms around him, sobbing out his name.

He rolled onto his back, bringing me with him and stroked the back of my neck. "I didn't think you'd forgive me."

"For which thing?" I teased, giddy with seeing him again.

"I hope you have a plan for getting out of here."

"Not so much," I said against his chest. "I was kind of winging this."

I wouldn't have heard his sigh, but I felt it in the deep rise and fall of his chest, the falter in the rhythm of his heart.

"Can't you ever just do as you're told?"

I raised my head to look at him, the dark sorrow creasing his face. "As I've told you lo, these many times—not my forte."

He sat up, tumbling me to the side, and stood, gazing

down at me. "Well, I hope your strength is in escape because you'd better get out of here immediately. I won't be able to help you. If you're incredibly lucky, she won't make me stop you."

"She has that much control over you? I find that hard to believe."

He laughed, short and bitter, folded his hands behind his back and began pacing. "You'd better start believing and fast. Midnight looms. I don't think you or that fool Starling could survive what happens then."

"All right. Then we'll escape before that. Let's get cracking on a plan."

"Don't tell me what it is."

"But you have to know—you're coming with us."

He spun on his heel, staring at me as if I'd completely lost my mind. "Do you understand nothing at all, foolish Gwynn? I cannot come with you. That's why I warned you not to look for me. I'm trapped with her forever. Think of me as dead."

I scooted myself off the bed, not easy when your recently crushed hoopskirts are springing back to life around you, and faced him. "You are not dead. Who's being the idiot here? There must be a way out of this mess. I know perfectly well you got into it over me, and I won't let you just take the fall."

"You're wrong, Gwynn." He ran a hand over my hair, unsmiling, but with that tinge of sad affection. "You got into all of this over me."

"I thought we got swept into it together."

"That may well be," he agreed. "But none of it really matters now."

"Probably not, but we're certainly not going to win the

game with you stuck here sucking up to the Queen Bitch instead of the whole impregnating me thing."

"You really don't know?"

"Know what?"

Something flashed in his eyes. He cupped my face in both hands, frustration and despair tingeing the air like burnt milk. "Don't you get it? The game is over. We lost. *I* lost. This is it. The aftermath. This is what it looks like."

I searched his face. "How can that be? We had seven years."

"*You* thought you had seven years. You may recall I pushed for less. Did you think I had no reason for it?

"I've never understood your reasons, Rogue. If you could explain them to me, that might make all the difference."

"Would it?" He dropped his hands and paced to the clear wall, gazing into the abyss. "What about your list? Even if you've resolved points one and two, as I recall, points three and four have not changed. Even if it is all moot now."

I struggled to recall exactly which points I'd reeled off to him. The man had an eidetic memory. Impossible for a mere mortal to keep up with. "I'm not saying I'm ready to have a baby with you—and geez, this sounds like a conversation from a Harlequin novel—but we can't debate it when you're locked up here. Come with us. We don't have much time left."

"Actually, you don't have any time left, Sorceress." Titania oozed into the room, bringing a wave of scorching heat with her. She pulled off the living mask and tossed it to the floor, where its mouth worked like a dying fish, shaking her head at Rogue, making a little disappointed moue. "Did you really think I wouldn't recognize your mortal pet? You are not clever enough to defeat me, Lord Rogue. You never were. Chain her to the bed."

In two strides he had me locked in those arms of steel, his face an impassive mass, the oily rope snapping through his mind. I screamed and fought, lashing out with spells that Titania neatly shattered, one after another before they could fully form. The cat rose up, snarling, but my flesh caged her in. I slashed at Rogue's face, the pitiful human claws causing little damage. Then my hands were fastened to the bedposts with cuffs of silver and the magic faded to a distant chime, my hoop skirt belling up ridiculously.

Until Titania vanished my dress also, leaving me naked.

With ruthless strength, Rogue spread my legs, fastening my ankles to the bedposts, while I thrashed and fought, bowing my body in an effort to free myself, the emerald hair coming undone and spilling everywhere. The cat drove me as much as my own fear and panic, the silver cutting into my skin. She howled, desperate to be free. The ethereal entity solidified, hurling itself against the wall of my flesh.

And broke through into the real world.

Gleaming metallic claws split through my fingers, shredding the flesh, the agony piercing me. Helpless to stop it, I writhed with the pain, with the terror and hopelessness of facing my own death.

But the claws stopped there.

Leaving me panting, broken. Trapped.

Titania slid an arm around Rogue's waist, extra-jointed fingers sliding open his tight shirt so she could toy with his chest, watching with avid interest. "She has a certain appeal, I suppose. Perhaps she'll last a little while, entertain the guests for a time. In the meanwhile, would you like to have her again?"

I fought the rolling pain from my hands, struggling to understand. Again? And the leaking emotions from Rogue— guilt, remorse, desolation.

"Again?" I managed to grit through my teeth, begging for it not to be true.

Titania smiled, sweetly, and rounded the bed to trail burning fingers down my sternum, resting her hand over my belly. "Don't you remember?" Then she giggled, a carefree, happy sound that pounded through my skull. "Oops. That's right. I made you forget. Silly me." Her eyes narrowed into cruel slits. "Let's fix that, shall we?"

I gagged when she slid into my mind, that oily rope of her presence so palpable. I hid myself behind silent walls, but she pursued me, an anaconda gorging itself on all my thoughts until she reached that knot she'd left behind.

And undid it.

The memories of that night spilled out and all those dangling threads of unease rearranged to form images, full color and fleshed in despair.

We were back in the high-ceilinged bedroom at Castle Brightness, in that bed of spiraling gold vines, drunk on lovemaking and liquor. Rogue lay beneath me, tied with the green ribbons he'd promised not to undo until dawn, letting me have my way with him. Putting himself at my mercy.

And Titania is there. Standing by the bed, watching me milk Rogue with my mouth, raking his body with my nails. He's calling my name, but I don't listen. She has a hand in my hair and I'm her willing puppet. He thrashes beneath me, but I mount him easily, riding him though he tries to buck me off. Titania and I laugh at his protests. It's me, taunting him, stealing his seed.

She passes a hand over my forehead and I fall asleep, giggling to myself, as she unties him and takes him away.

Rogue watched me with anguished eyes staring out of the cruel set to his face, seeing me live it again. I groaned, shaking away the agony of the memory. I almost wished I didn't remember now.

Almost.

I clenched my fists, digging the sharp claws into my palms, clinging to the pain as an anchor of the here and now. In some ways, I hated her most for planting that false memory of lying in Rogue's arms, feeling sweetly safe and cared for. When I had raped and destroyed him.

"Rogue," I choked out. Asking for something. Forgiveness. Understanding. Solace.

Titania looked between the two of us, yellow eyes glittering. "So charming. There's nothing so sweet as a dog's love for her master and his sense of responsibility for her. Of course he knows her life is a brief flicker compared to his. That's why he breeds her." Titania traced the shape of my womb. "Too bad this puppy won't survive the night."

Something cool tapped against my thigh, penetrating the roiling haze. Before I formed the thought to wonder what it was, I knew. The vial of dragon's blood. Immune to magic and not vanished. My only weapon. And as out of my reach as my home world.

What had Rogue said? *This is the aftermath.* Somehow I'd lost without ever fighting.

Fuck that.

I took all the agony, emotional and physical, and hurled it behind the walls of my mind. The cold silence left behind calmed me. I took a deep mental breath.

"You won't kill me. You want this baby." I threw the words at her. A challenge. Rogue flinched but I had nothing left to lose at this point. I intended to fight as the cornered animal I was.

It caught her a little by surprise. Then her eyes narrowed, burning magic rising in tangible threat. "Why would you think that?"

"I saw what you did to Fafnir and Cecily's baby. What made it inadequate? What are you searching for?"

Titania's eyes blazed like noonday suns. She grabbed one of my nipples and twisted hard.

I screamed.

She leaned down and placed her mouth over mine, drinking it in, all my trapped magic and life force pouring into her.

I bit down.

Now she shrieked, releasing me and stumbling back, pink blood pouring out of her mouth, the same sticky sweet stuff choking me. I spit it out as best I could. Rogue stood still at the foot of the bed, a statue of himself.

"Rogue, help me!" I screamed at him.

He didn't move, his mind thick with ropy blackness. But Titania came back at me, power boiling out of her.

And a fluffy white cat leaped on her back, raking her with Herculean claws. The sight tore through me—exhilaration that Darling Hercules had come to my rescue, and utter terror that I'd suffer through his death on top of everything else. My heart froze waiting for Titania to shatter him.

But she wailed, fighting him off with her hands, never quite connecting as he moved in a blur of speed and feline flexibility, never quite there by the time she reached him, snarling in her long hair and scratching like a dervish. Why she didn't use magic on him immediately, I didn't know, but I yanked in desperation on the silver cuffs, hoping against hope that I might wrench myself free.

"Hold still!" Starling hissed, brandishing a set of keys. With smooth efficiency, she tried them one by one, as if she had all the time in the world while Titania struggled with Darling.

"Hurry," I urged her.

"Not helpful," she snapped back, crawling over me to unlock my ankles.

The final cuff clicked open just as Titania hurled Darling across the room, rage contorting her features. She spun to me.

Starling dove off the bed. I seized the vial at my side, the stab of pain from my ruined hands barely registering, and sliced off the seal with one of my new claws.

Titania hurled herself at me, power boiling out of her in a supernova and I dashed the dragon's blood distillate in her beautiful face.

Oh. My. God.

It ate at her like a living thing, gnawing into her face with acid speed, growing and proliferating like the worst flesh-eating bacteria. The smell of hot plastic filled the room. Her howls turned into demonic roars, then contorted as the concentrated anti-magic corroded her vocal chords. At the same time, her own immense immortal magic battled it, reforming her bones, skin and muscles in a convulsing amalgamation of meat. She fell to the floor, writhing.

Rogue pulled me off the bed, breaking my trance of horror. A drop of the distillate fell on my calf and I hissed at the burn, dropping the empty vial.

"Run." He clothed me with a thought—oddly in my old Ann Taylor dress, the one I'd worn into this world—and pushed me toward the door, where Starling stood, poised to flee with a limp Darling in her arms.

"No." I dug in. "Not without you."

Confusion broke across his face, leaving fragments of tortured dread and splinted hope behind. The ropiness in his mind had receded. "How can you—"

"Is Darling Hercules all right?" I called to Starling, cutting him off.

"I think so—just unconscious."

"Where's Athena?"

"Guarding the door."

"I love you guys so much. Give me Darling Hercules. Rogue, push Titania onto the bed with your magic—don't touch her."

I cupped Darling against my chest, pinning him with my forearms, making the curved platinum-silver claws of my ruined fingers stand up so the blood ran down my hands, soaking into Darling's fur. Hopefully he wouldn't be too angry about it.

"Starling—be my hands. See if you can lock her into at least one of the cuffs. Don't get any of that shit on you, if you can help it. But I think your human blood will protect you."

She set her mouth in a determined line and managed to grab a foot from the flailing body Rogue floated onto the bed, locking it down.

"That's good enough," I told her.

"No, it's not," Starling snarled. "I want her where she had you. And I want free of her." She fought the other foot into place and reached for one of the hands Titania had clapped to her melting face.

"No! It's too dangerous."

"Then protect me." She gave me an even look. "I'm going in either way."

Wishing I'd thought of it before—which was the kind of wish that never came true—I created nitrile gloves right on her hands. She jumped a little then grinned at me, a maniacal baring of teeth, and wrestled Titania into the wrist cuffs. The Queen Bitch's melting and reforming hands turned into cold lumps of gristle when the silver touched them, creating a kind of stasis.

No time to find it interesting. I turned to Rogue.

"You're on. Get us out of here."

He wrenched his gaze from Titania's shuddering form. "I can't. She holds my leash, Gwynn. Even now. I can't escape her."

"The Black Dog can."

His stunned expression gave way almost instantly to a shout of inhuman victory. Seizing my head in his hands, he kissed me with bruising force—but arching his body not to touch my broken hands. "I love you, brilliant Gwynn."

As abruptly as he'd grabbed me, he released me, throwing straining arms up to the ceiling and unleashing the wild animal within.

My cat shrieked to join him and I clamped down, hoping

she wouldn't tear me apart now.

Rogue's transformation went better than the last time I saw it—perhaps the difference between him yielding utterly instead of battling the beast.

The Black Dog shook himself, fastened me with gleaming amber eyes and flashed white fangs. Starling muffled a little shriek.

"It's okay," I told her, "he listens to me."

I hoped.

CHAPTER 25

MIDNIGHT

۶ᡁ

If the loss of memory feels like a wormhole, then its return
feels like having an amputated limb sewn on in the
wrong place.

~Big Book of Fairyland, "Memory Inconsistency"

"GET US OUT of here, please."

The Dog flashed white fangs in his canine grin and ran to the door, looking back at us to follow. Starling, bless her, mastered herself and edged around him to lift the latch. Athena spun around, her face blanching, little dagger thrust out. "Thrice damned Titania!"

"A friend. Let's go."

The Dog dashed down the hall and I ran after, each jarring step amplifying the throbbing in my hands. The cat inside me relished it, using that opening to push at me, to escape the cage of my body.

"He's headed for the ballroom!" Athena shouted behind us. "Don't follow him there!"

"He's our way out. We have to trust him." I called back.

She snarled some kind of obscenity in reply.

We burst into the ballroom like a cannonball rocketing through a flock of parrots. Brightly dressed fae flew in all directions, scattering before the Dog with cries of excited terror. Except the partygoers already fastened to various sadistic machines in various states of undress and bloodiness. Apparently the festivities had been well underway.

I tried not to look as the Dog gleefully plunged through the crowd, seizing and tossing aside bodies. Athena touched my arm gently, gaze fastened on my grotesque hands. "Gwynn…"

"Later."

The Dog had cleared a path and we ran after him, climbing the grand staircase and hurling ourselves outside to the wide glassy courtyard.

Something shifted in the air, an abrupt change in barometric pressure. The ground moved under my feet, a minor seismic shift. The Dog scented the air, giving an excited yip. Starling gasped and Athena whispered, "Midnight."

With the screeching sound of claws on glass, magnified through the mountain range, the Wild Hunt arrived.

Giant bearded men and vicious blonde Valkyrie creatures pounded through the air on horses made of night and bloodthirst. Hounds poured between their hooves, living ink. The guards scattered and we cringed back, ready to join them, to run from this fire back into the frying pan.

But the Black Dog leaped forward, baying a challenge. The hounds, now visible, now a thread of fang in the dark, circled him. I must have cried out and started forward, because Starling and Athena now held me between them.

The Dog and the Hounds engaged in a snarling fight,

shimmering in and out of sight. The Veil had thinned and they moved between worlds. Now in this one, now in another.

A massive hunter shining with ancient power waded into the fray, swinging a broad-bladed sword and bellowing. Kicking the Hounds aside, he lifted the sword, bringing it down in a merciless arc toward the Dog.

"I challenge you!" A voice rang out. A man, bold in shining armor, stepped out of the shadows. The hunter answered on a shout, turning to face the new foe with relish.

"Is that...Fergus?"

"I got him out with the chatelaine's keys while Athena watched to see what happened with you." Starling's fingers dug into my arm. Fergus had flung back his helm and engaged the mighty hunter with surprising ferocity, shimmering with heroic magic.

Amazing.

The Black Dog barked with urgency, now standing king among a pack of cowering Hounds. The other hunters galloped through the night, wheeling in circles.

"They'll hold off until the challenge is complete," Athena tugged me forward. Starling dropped my other arm and ran beside us.

"But Fergus!"

"No." Starling was shaking her head, blond strands flying in the wind. "This is what he wants. He made me promise."

The Dog was already rocketing down the glassy path. I stumbled some, trying to keep up, and Athena took Darling from me. The cold numbed my feet until I thought to wish up my cross-trainers. Stumbling through the dark, I felt the adrenergic response pumping through my system begin to ebb and then crash.

The horror of it all leaked through the edges of the silence I'd created in my mind, worming through the edges with whispers of insanity. I wanted to flee from the images, what I'd seen and done. What I had done to Rogue.

That I was pregnant.

The tiredness, the constant drain on my energy, that feeling of being attenuated—I had denied what they all knew.

I fought the red-black edging in around my vision, knowing my blood pressure must be dropping, shock setting in.

I turned my head, to warn Starling, but the dark overcame me.

CHAPTER 26

AFTER THE AFTERMATH

ᘓᕤ

Sometimes the fae seem to have no emotions at all. Other times, I think their frame of reference is just so wildly different that it only seems that way.

~Big Book of Fairyland, "True Love"

I CAME TO slowly, aware first of the aching pain in my hands, of their frozen rigidity.

Almost against my will, I flexed my fingers, crying out at the stab of agony.

Darling Hercules brushed against me and the pain receded, washing away again. He sent me loving thoughts, to my gasping gratitude. He slipped away again, but stayed near. I became aware of the cadence of a horse and that I was cupped in someone's arms. And the scent of sandalwood and Stargazers.

"Rogue."

My voice came out creaky, mouth dry. I cracked my eyelids open, flinching at the bright light of day. He looked down at me, the left side of his face full of winding thorns, the right impassive.

"You're awake now?" he asked.

Hello, Captain Obvious. Rogue smiled a little, clearly hearing the thought. But it didn't move past his lips. He, ever the perfectly powerful one, looked exhausted.

"You've been talking since you passed out." He looked off into the distance. "Calling my name. Sometimes screaming it."

Oh.

He shifted me in his arms and I realized he had me cuddled on his lap as we rode, held in a grip that would never break. My hands were wrapped in mittens of fabric, curled up against my chest.

"We'll fix them," he said. "You'll be okay."

"Everyone else?"

"Fine. Riding ahead since I must go slowly with you."

"But Darling is here."

"Yes. Insisting on being called Goliath now."

"Oh yes. Long story." An uncomfortable silence settled. "I'm amazed the Queen Bitch didn't kill him."

"She can't. That's why he's a cat. He used to be a powerful wizard, with certain immunities to her magic. Trapping him in this body with his minor abilities was the worst she could do to him."

Darling Hercules sent the image of himself as a handsome young man, looking glum.

"Why didn't you tell me that before?"

"With your attack on her, certain…restrictions have lessened." He shifted as if uncomfortable.

"Do you need to rest your arms?"

He raised an eyebrow at me, some of his usual supercilious

self showing through. "No."

No. Of course not.

"Are you uncomfortable?" The thought seemed to occur to him and he scrutinized me with unusual solicitude.

Warmth fluttered through me, a furry feeling that faded when I realized what must be behind it. "Are you asking because of the pregnancy?"

His face hardened and he looked down the road again. "I'm sorry for what happened. That I didn't protect you from that."

"Protect me? Aren't you the wounded party here?"

His lips quirked, a little bitter, a little amused. "I can't escape that I wanted this—no matter how it came about."

"You tried to stop me and I—"

He squeezed me gently. "I tried to stop you because I knew how bitterly you'd regret it. I don't want you to hate the child. Or me. Or yourself."

"Lots of hate to go around."

"Yes." His cobalt blue gaze scanned my face, his mind brushing mine. "Will you ever be able to forgive me, do you think?"

"Again—I should be asking you to forgive me."

He stopped me with a shake of his head. "No. You were forced as surely as I. Ultimately it's my fault that you're here."

"Why is that, Rogue?" I asked softly.

"Because I wished for you." He said it with a light tone, but I felt the depth of emotion beneath it. The way he held me gave me a different perspective, the way the black lines climbed down his jaw and neck, his sharp profile etched against the impossibly brilliant blue sky. A sweet relief filled me to know that. That he truly had wished for me. It made everything better. Not logical, but there it was.

"What's done is done. No sense dwelling on the past."

"Your reasons for not wanting this baby still stand."

"Yes, but we've gone from hypothetical to real. As you pointed out, that particular battle is over. This is the aftermath."

"True." He shifted again and I thought he'd rather be pacing. "I can feel that you're angry."

"Oh, yes. Yes, I am." I took a moment to let it simmer down again, push the cat down, my fingers throbbing anew. Darling Hercules sent an inquiry from where he must be riding behind Rogue and I reassured him that I didn't need another dose. "But I think it would be a mistake to be angry at you. *She* raped us both."

"I feel ever so much better now," Rogue replied in a dry tone, but the relief coursed through him strongly enough for me to taste, like fresh snowmelt. Like mine.

"You know what pisses me off?"

He looked wary. "What?"

"I finally got to have sex with you and it sucked."

"I was attempting to break Titania's compulsion, not pleasure you," he retorted, clearly stung. "Besides, you were in charge, as I recall."

"Well, it still sucked. First I couldn't remember it and then when I did..." An involuntary shudder racked me. Rogue halted the horse and pulled me up, embracing me carefully, burying his face in my hair.

"I'm sorry, lovely Gwynn," he murmured against me. "So very sorry for what happened."

JEFFE KENNEDY

"I was the weak one. I failed you."

"You've never failed me. Some things are beyond even you, my powerful Gwynn."

"Yes, well, I got her this time."

"For the time being, anyway."

"I kind of hoped I'd killed her."

He cast his eyes to the heavens, just shy of rolling them. "If only it were so easy."

"Hey—the dragon's blood extract was a brilliant weapon!"

"Yes. We'll have to discuss that."

"If you come up with a suitable gift in exchange, I might teach you how I did it," I replied in a lofty tone.

He stroked a finger down my cheek. "Oh, I believe I can come up with something. And I promise you, this time the sex won't suck."

"I'm already pregnant," I pointed out. "The deed is done."

"Don't tell me your people think that's the only reason for sexual intimacy."

"Well, some do, actually."

"And you?" He held my gaze as he asked the question, as if he truly wanted to know me.

I flushed a little. Such a strange, backward relationship we had. "I've always been rather the opposite."

"Why doesn't that surprise me?" His quirk of a smile softened into something more serious. "I want to be with you. Let me do that. Believe that what is between us can be more."

"What is between us?"

"You came after me—that's everything. All along I knew I needed you. Or the Dog knew. Now it's clear why."

"You said you loved me."

He cocked his head, that indicator that something didn't translate exactly right. "Is that important to you?"

"I don't know. Maybe." I relaxed against him, savoring the feel of his leanly muscled body. "I don't know anything right now. Do I have to?"

He laughed a little, under his breath, and kneed Felicity to continue. "No. We'll get to my castle and take time to discuss."

"What about Falcon?"

"What *about* him?" Irritation crept into his tone, though his grip remained gentle.

"I still owe him service. As do you, for that matter."

"I'll deal with Falcon."

"How?"

He raised an eyebrow in casual arrogance. "I told you. Falcon's rules don't apply to me. I'll handle it like I do everything."

"With obfuscation, tricks and underhanded manipulation then."

"Gwynn, you wound me—I am never underhanded."

I laughed and he seemed pleased, grinning at me.

"We have time to settle Falcon. Titania won't come after us for a while, anyway."

I tensed and he tightened his arms to steady me. "She will, won't she? Her game isn't done. She'll try to take this child."

"As surely as the sun rises and the Wild Hunt rides."

"What will we do about it?"

"Do? I'll take you home. We will heal, rest, recover and make love. There will come a day when we'll face war. Until then, we enjoy what life has to offer, lest we forget the very things we fight for. Is that acceptable to you?"

"Thank you for asking." I let my head fall back to rest on his shoulder, letting him support me for a little while. "Yes, that sounds pretty damn wonderful."

The story continues in

Rogue's Paradise

Want a sneak peek? Flip the page!

CHAPTER 1

IN WHICH I AM ATTACKED BY FLYING MONKEYS

※

The only thing the stories seemed to agree on was that the fae were capricious beings who delighted in disrupting human lives, awarding their magical favors according to a system of ethics known only to them.

~*Big Book of Fairyland*, "Flora and Fauna"

THE FLYING MONKEYS attacked just before sunset.

Swear to God, that's exactly what they looked like. I even looked for a smoke trail warning "Surrender Dorothy!"

"I have no idea what that means." Rogue, as usual, had read my thoughts as clearly as if I'd shouted them. "But now would be an excellent time for you to focus and possibly assist."

I struggled to clear my fatigued brain and sit straighter on his lap—not easy on horseback, with our steed Felicity breaking into a panicked run over the glassy black rocks as the sky overhead darkened with throngs of winged primates.

"I thought you said we'd have some time before the Queen

Bitch would be strong enough to come after us." I gasped as the mare whipped around a narrow curve.

Fortunately Rogue needed no reins, guiding her with the grip of his muscular thighs and likely his mind, leaving his hands free to hold me tight against him. As a fae noble, Rogue possessed many skills, and apparently superb horsemanship ranked high among them.

"What makes you think it's her?" He sounded arrogant—something that once would have grated on me—but I felt his anxiety beneath. Rogue had suffered far more at Queen Titania's hands than I. We hadn't discussed yet what had happened to him as her puppet and slave, largely because he'd been letting me sleep off the exhaustion from battling her.

Also, Rogue was far from the type to confide. He might never tell me.

His gorgeous face was tense, creased with the torment of his captivity, the winding black lines that covered the left side of his face and body stark against his skin. Apparently even immortals could look the worse for wear.

I wasn't in much better shape, perilously drained of my magic reserves, my hands a crippled mess—and unfortunately pregnant, just to top it all off.

Neither of us was fit to fight. Nor could we afford to be recaptured by Titania.

We barreled into a narrower canyon that forced Felicity to slow her headlong rush and fortunately limited the angles the monkeys could come at us.

"Whether or not this is Titania's doing," Rogue said, "these creatures are more like guard dogs. It wouldn't require much of someone to send them. However, it may require much for us to deal with them."

"What do you want me to do?" I asked.

"How much power do you have?"

I wished I knew how to answer that. Rogue had been teaching me more about my abilities to work magic and how to draw energy from outside myself, but we hadn't gotten far before Titania snatched him. It was a bad sign that he, the ever-and-all-powerful—far more magical than I, though I hated to admit it—had to ask me for help.

"Some. I don't suppose you have my crystal staff tied to the saddle?"

Rogue looked grimly amused. Then ducked when a flying monkey, clawed fingers outstretched, dive-bombed his head. Monkeys shouldn't have curved talons, but pretty much anything goes in Faerie. A burst of magic from Rogue, his signature feral black and blue, whooshed past me, and the monster chimp dissolved in a puff of sparks.

"Your girl, Athena, took it. She seemed to think you couldn't be trusted with it."

And Athena had ridden ahead with the others, since Rogue had been burdened with unconscious me. Annoying of her as the thing would augment my abilities, even if it was danger-ously addictive. Compared to my current alternate fate, that sounded like giving up caffeine when starving to death.

"You can't nuke them all, like with that one?"

"No. Not enough power for so many." He hated admitting it too. Quite the pair we were.

"Tell me what you want and I'll do my best." How little power was "not enough"? No delicate way to pose the question so it wouldn't impugn his male ego. Asking Rogue if he had no magic left and no access to those outside resources he'd bragged of seemed akin to asking a guy whether he thought he could get it up or if he was done for the night.

A trio of monkeys swarmed us, a talon raking Felicity's hide. The horse screeched and put her head down, bucking with terror, which Rogue barely managed to control, his steely strength keeping me from being thrown. My cat Familiar, Darling Hercules, riding behind Rogue on his special saddle pad, sent me a startled image of him digging in claws and holding on for dear life.

Whatever we were going to do, we needed to do it fast. The trio of monkeys wheeled back on us. One went up in sparks, but the other two seemed only singed around the edges and one managed to sink talons into Rogue's shoulder before he got it on the second try. Not a good sign.

Darling Hercules let out a yowling wail and swiped at one of the monkeys that tried to grab him. To all appearances a humble tabby cat, he had grandiose ideas about his size and battle readiness.

"*Goliath,*" he nudged into my head, insistent on his new battle name.

"*Later,*" I answered. "I suppose wishing them away won't work?"

Grimly, Rogue shook his head. "Too many. They'll just keep coming."

Already the evening sky looked dark as night with their bat-winged bodies blocking the last of the light. Only the narrowness of the canyon we were tearing down kept them from simply dropping on us like an immense cloud of hairy locusts. As it was, they came at us singly or in small groups, scratching a cheek here or slicing an arm there, before Rogue could blast them.

"However, if—" Rogue's words came in puffed bursts of effort. "If I can pull power from you...I have an idea. So I need to know how much you have."

I couldn't answer that—not as if I had a little gauge warning me I was at less than 20 percent battery—but I did know how to charge myself up pretty fast. Just lucky that my favorite catalyst happened to be holding me in his arms.

"Ow—dammit!" I screeched as a talon tangled in my hair, taking some of my scalp with it. "Can you keep them off of me? And slow Felicity down, if at all possible."

"For a time, yes. Be sure to hold on." He freed one arm and his gleaming blue-platinum sword appeared in his hand. A major magic for me, a parlor trick for him. Apparently easier than frying monkeys, however. The monkeys came thicker as Felicity slowed, but they stayed farther back, wary of that sharp edge.

Turning myself around in the saddle wasn't easy by any stretch, but I trusted Rogue, even one-armed, and his uncanny long-limbed strength to keep me from tumbling off. I maneuvered to straddle Rogue's lean hips, while Darling Hercules complained bitterly in my head that I'd better not kick him. I told him to make himself useful and deaden the agony flaring up from my fingers as I clumsily slid my bandaged hands behind Rogue's neck. Thankfully the cat did, removing the pain with his oh-so-useful gift of magical anesthesia.

"Gwynn, what in Titania's name are you doing?" Rogue flicked his sword and a monkey fell in two pieces, spraying white blood on the black rocks.

"Kiss me." I pressed my groin against his, the sure rise of his cock making me giddy with a flood of strength and the hope that this might work.

With a grunt, Rogue split another diving monkey and glared at me. "After all this time of dreaming that you'd finally ask me for that, *this* is the moment you choose, contrary Gwynn?"

"You want power from me. You're the one who pointed out that sex energy is my shortcut. So shut up, pucker up and keep an eye on those monkeys."

He barked out a laugh, but wasted no more time. That seductive mouth of his fastened on mine with a ferocity that belied his weariness. His deep blue eyes stayed open and I felt the contractions of his chest as he swung the sword. Holding me pressed against him, he kissed me with all the fierce desire I could wish for. My own longing for him welled up, hot and needy—all the more so for our long separation—so ready for him. A monkey raked claws down my arm, and I flinched but focused on the kiss.

Not sure how to do it, I tried linking with him as we'd done once before, mentally putting myself in his hands and pouring the energy into him. Rogue hummed deep in his throat and pushed the hard ridge of his erection against me, sending a bolt of electricity through me that ricocheted between us. The sexual heat built between us, the magic wild and potent, overwhelming in its intensity. He ran his hands over my back, cupping my bottom and pulling me even closer to the lean length of his body while he stroked his hips, driving me into frenzy.

Wait—both hands?

I became aware that Felicity had stopped and stood head down, breathing in great gusts. Starting to pull back, I gasped when Rogue nipped my lower lip. "No, don't stop, lovely Gwynn."

I managed to tear my mouth away. The skies were clear, if rapidly deepening into an ultraviolet dusk. A luminous silver behind the edge of one canyon wall hinted at moonrise. A few early stars, spinning with kaleidoscopic color, pierced through, like wormholes to other worlds. For all I knew, they were.

"What happened to the flying monkeys?"

"They're gone." He cupped the back of my neck, tilting my head so he could nibble the sensitive underside of my jaw. I melted, moaning a little. "You are delicious, powerful Gwynn. That was far more than I needed. I'm glutted with you."

With a flick of a disgusted thought, Darling Hercules jumped down from the saddle, mentally muttering about there being no mice in this prey-forsaken place.

"What did you do? How do we know they won't keep coming?" I asked, my breath coming unevenly.

"I...reversed them in a way. Instead of finding us, they go backwards."

"Clever."

"I'm flattered you think so." He found my mouth again, kissing me long and sweet and deep, rocking against me.

So help me, I wanted him like nothing I'd felt before. As if all the months of buildup, all that teasing and torment, had layered on, fueling my desire just a bit more with every encounter. This close to him, to his deeper thoughts and emotions, I knew Rogue felt it too. The unbearable need to bury ourselves in the other.

"Gwynn," Rogue murmured. "Say it can be now."

All those times I'd said no. All those arguments and my determined resistance. I might have paid my life debt to Rogue by promising to bear his child, but I'd at least been able to forestall those consequences by refusing his seduction. All come to nothing.

I'd never agreed and I'd still lost that battle. I hadn't quite assimilated that I was truly pregnant. Titania had forced us— tricked, manipulated, however you wanted to split the hairs— into doing the deed, but then she'd removed the memory afterward. It had happened weeks ago. Or months, as time in Faerie flowed in a different way. Titania had restored the memories and informed me of the pregnancy in a neat double whammy meant to lay me low. I was still reeling from the rawness and violation of the rape. Technically I'd done it to Rogue, but I counted Titania as our true rapist, as she'd pulled the strings.

I could let that go now. No more defending myself from the embryo I already carried. I could say yes, finally.

"If you say no again, it might kill me," he growled, biting my lip again, then laving it with his tongue.

"Even though you're immortal?" I teased.

"Even so."

"Then yes."

Something inside me released at that moment, old scar tissue breaking open, finally yielding up that tight, binding pain. A rush of gladness followed. I didn't have to fight this anymore.

Not letting me go, raining kisses on my upturned face, Rogue swung down from Felicity, in a feat of strength and grace that had me gasping. He smiled, the fanged lines around his beautiful mouth twisting with the movement, loving that he'd impressed me.

His magic swirled and he laid me down on a bed of velvet he'd wished into existence, stretching himself beside me.

"Doing magic left and right now?" I asked him in an arch tone.

"Yes. I am overflowing with you. And still you feed me more. Let me have more."

"It's yours."

With a choking sound and some incoherent emotion I couldn't discern, he fell on me, fingers twining into my hair, holding me in place while he kissed me in that drugging way that swept all thought aside.

I meant it too. For the time being, at least, I just wanted to enjoy him. Savor the moment without worrying how much I might lose to his magnetic personality. He'd said he loved me and, though it might not mean to him what it did to me, I wanted to believe in that. Even if it had been in the heat of battle and the crushing aftermath. I only wished that I could touch him in turn. At least loosen the band that tied back his hair.

But I couldn't use my hands. Thanks to the handy anesthetic magic of Darling Hercules Goliath—I was trying to remember, though the name chain was getting ridiculous—I mostly didn't feel anything. The makeshift bandages swaddling my hands, however, both mittened me and hid from view the lethal claws that had made a ruin of my fingers. The feline spirit that had recently taken up occupation in my soul had helped defeat Titania, but it also wanted out and needed my flesh to do it.

Nothing to do about it at the moment. Rogue had promised we'd fix it and we would. For now I wanted not to think about it, to simply seize the moment and savor Rogue.

Besides, I had other means at my disposal. A lowly scientist in my previous mundane life as a university professor, I'd become a sometimes distressingly powerful sorceress, with even my least notion coming true until I learned to control it. A hair tie was far more easily dealt with than, say, an army of flying monkeys. I vanished it, and the black silk cloak of Rogue's hair fell around us.

"I am looking forward to the moment," he commented in a wry tone, "when I manage to sweep your thoughts away in truth."

"You'll just have to work harder."

"Oh, sweet Gwynn, I fully intend to." He untangled his hand from my own hair and put it on my bare leg, raising my skirt. I stared into his fulminous eyes, riveted.

At last.

"Oh no!" Starling's startled exclamation shattered the moment. "Turn around, you guys."

Athena's and Larch's voices protested. Rogue and I stared at each other, sharing the same frustrated annoyance. For once we were in perfect sync. His hand flexed on my thigh, as if unwilling to let me go, then relaxed and smoothed my skirt back down. He sat up, drawing me with him.

Larch, Athena and Starling stood a short distance away, black-and-silver shapes in the moonlight, Starling wringing her hands together and clearly kicking herself for the interruption. My half-fae, half-human maidservant and friend had been hoping so hard for me to give in to Rogue that she no doubt deeply felt the irony of interrupting us. Larch, a Brownie stolid as the blue fireplug he resembled, looked into the distance. Only Athena, a petite fairy girl with a diabolical brain, seemed unperturbed, spinning her glinting dagger in her fingers, a salacious grin on her face. Darling wound around their feet in greeting and I glared at him. He could have warned us they were close.

"*Goliath,*" he replied in a grumpy mental tone, tinged with more than a little jealousy. Great.

"Looks like you're feeling better, Gwynn," Athena observed. "We thought we'd better come check on you two to see how you fared against those nasty chimps, but you seem to be doing quite fine without us. Brilliantly, in fact."

"We should go!" Starling announced. "Come on, everyone. Back on your horses. We can, um, go find a place to camp."

"No, don't go." I levered myself to my feet awkwardly, Rogue assisting me after a moment's hesitation. Dark and broody irritation rolled off him, but I could hardly dismiss the people who'd accompanied me on this quest—and who probably were the making of it. Especially with another attack possible. What had I been thinking? About sex, clearly. "Are you guys okay? No one is hurt?"

"A pair of those things grabbed Larch and nearly carried him off, but Athena threw her dagger and hurt one, so they dropped him," Starling said, looking between me and Rogue. She produced a bright smile. "So we're fine! We'll just see you and Lord Rogue in the morning."

With night truly fallen, and without Rogue's intense body

heat to warm me, I shivered. He slipped an arm around my waist and drew me against him, a casual intimacy I'd never before been able to allow and I leaned my cheek against his chest. The 3/4 rhythm of his heart pounded under my ear, reflecting all that aroused desire I sensed, but didn't show on his impassive face.

"There should be no stopping for the night," he declared. "It's likely only a matter of time until something worse is sent after us. More distance is better."

"That's not what you said a few minutes ago," I said for his sharp ears only.

He looked down at me, eyes bright as if lit from within, and cupped my face, thumb running over my cheekbone. "I lost my head."

I leaned in to the touch, impossibly moved by that simple declaration.

"I'd tell you two to get a room," Athena cracked, "but I don't think there *are* any for leagues in any direction—besides Titania's castle, that is."

I laughed, amused that the idiom existed in the fae culture, too, but Starling rounded on the petite fairy girl. "You will not speak to Lord Rogue and Lady Gwynn that way!"

Athena spun her dagger for a moment, eyeing Starling. "Why don't you make yourself useful and get Gwynn's cloak for her?"

"Oh!" Starling took the bait immediately and dashed to the saddlebags, rummaging wildly, as if to make up for her lapse with speed. I would have told her not to worry, but having the cloak sounded really good. The cold seemed to be eating into me.

Starling brought it over and Rogue took it from her.

"Allow me." He shook it out and held it for me to step into, his long fingers brushing my neck as he settled it over my shoulders. Fastening the green silk frogs at my throat, he bent down and whispered in my ear. "I'd planned to have you naked by now, not wearing more clothes. You owe me."

Owing Rogue anything generally led to very bad bargains for me, but this time the demand rocketed through me, full of sensual promise. The cloak felt heavenly—hopefully it would soon warm me up.

A hound bayed, the bone-chilling sound eerie in the night, quickly joined by more wolfish howls and shrieks from humanoid throats. Horses thundered in silhouette across the face of the moon.

"Another excellent reason not to be caught sleeping. The Wild Hunt rides—and they appear to have slipped their leash," Rogue said in a dry tone. "Let's be on our way. My Lady Gwynn?"

At least he made a semblance of asking before he swung me up in his arms and strode toward Felicity, who'd managed to find a few tufts of grass growing between the black rocks. Mounting with no hands and the same fluid grace, he continued to hold me, like a bride carried over the threshold.

"I can sit astride," I protested.

"This way you can sleep. Your mortal flesh needs it."

"Starling is half-human—she needs rest too."

"Lady Starling," he called out, and the others clopped up to join us. "Shall I bespell you to stay in your saddle, so you can sleep without fear of falling off?"

"Oh, Lord Rogue, that would be lovely, but I fear I couldn't pay for such a generous gift."

408
J E F F E   K E N N E D Y

"On the contrary," he replied. "I am in your debt, for your great services in rescuing me."

She fluttered, embarrassed and pleased, then agreed. Athena and Larch, fueled by magic, could continue indefinitely. Larch never even rode, just ran beside us, his squat, Brownie body moving at uncanny speeds. We set off down the canyon, moonlight bouncing off the opaque glassy surfaces of the rocks.

"You could have spelled me to stay in the saddle. Hell, I could have done that, too," I said.

He adjusted his arms around me, my hip pressed against the hard line of his cock, obvious even through my thick cloak. "Indulge me. If I can't have everything yet, I can at least enjoy the feel of you in my arms."

"You could also let me ride Felicity and you could poof yourself elsewhere, like you do. You have enough power now, I'll bet."

"True." He sounded thoughtful. "But you are forgetting something. I'm not leaving you behind, ever again, my Gwynn."

His words had the power of a vow. Not lightly done in Faerie, where crazy-ass goddess and queen Titania played enforcer and executioner. "You're being awfully sweet and romantic. Prison changed you, man." I reached for the joke, shying away from the intensity of it all, but Rogue went still, pulling his thoughts deep where I couldn't hear them.

"Yes," he finally said. "Yes, it did."

క్̃

Buy *Rogue's Paradise*

TITLES BY JEFFE KENNEDY

༗

FANTASY ROMANCES

BONDS OF MAGIC

Dark Wizard
Bright Familiar
Grey Magic
Familiar Winter Magic (In Fire of the Frost)

HEIRS OF MAGIC

The Long Night of the Crystalline Moon
(also available in *Under a Winter Sky*)
The Golden Gryphon and the Bear Prince
The Sorceress Queen and the Pirate Rogue
The Dragon's Daughter and the Winter Mage
The Storm Princess and the Raven King (May 2022)

THE FORGOTTEN EMPIRES

The Orchid Throne
The Fiery Crown
The Promised Queen

THE TWELVE KINGDOMS

Negotiation
The Mark of the Tala

The Tears of the Rose
The Talon of the Hawk
Heart's Blood
The Crown of the Queen

THE UNCHARTED REALMS
The Pages of the Mind
The Edge of the Blade
The Snows of Windroven
The Shift of the Tide
The Arrows of the Heart
The Dragons of Summer
The Fate of the Tala
The Lost Princess Returns

THE CHRONICLES OF DASNARIA
Prisoner of the Crown
Exile of the Seas
Warrior of the World

SORCEROUS MOONS
Lonen's War
Oria's Gambit
The Tides of Bára
The Forests of Dru
Oria's Enchantment
Lonen's Reign

A COVENANT OF THORNS
Rogue's Pawn
Rogue's Possession
Rogue's Paradise

CONTEMPORARY ROMANCES

Shooting Star

MISSED CONNECTIONS
Last Dance
With a Prince
Since Last Christmas

CONTEMPORARY EROTIC ROMANCES

Exact Warm Unholy
The Devil's Doorbell

FACETS OF PASSION
Sapphire
Platinum
Ruby
Five Golden Rings

FALLING UNDER
Going Under
Under His Touch
Under Contract

EROTIC PARANORMAL

MASTER OF THE OPERA E-SERIAL
Master of the Opera, Act 1: Passionate Overture
Master of the Opera, Act 2: Ghost Aria
Master of the Opera, Act 3: Phantom Serenade
Master of the Opera, Act 4: Dark Interlude
Master of the Opera, Act 5: A Haunting Duet

Master of the Opera, Act 6: Crescendo
Master of the Opera

BLOOD CURRENCY
Blood Currency

BDSM FAIRYTALE ROMANCE
Petals and Thorns

Thank you for reading!

ABOUT JEFFE KENNEDY

Jeffe Kennedy is a multi-award-winning and best-selling author of epic fantasy romance. She is the current president of the Science Fiction and Fantasy Writers Association (SFWA) and is a member of Romance Writers of America (RWA), and Novelists, Inc. (NINC). She is best known for her RITA® Award-winning novel, *The Pages of the Mind*, the recent trilogy, *The Forgotten Empires*, and the wildly popular, *Dark Wizard*. Jeffe lives in Santa Fe, New Mexico.

Jeffe can be found online at her website: JeffeKennedy.com, on her podcast First Cup of Coffee, every Sunday at the popular SFF Seven blog, on Facebook, on Goodreads, on BookBub, and pretty much constantly on Twitter @jeffekennedy. She is represented by Sarah Younger of Nancy Yost Literary Agency.

jeffekennedy.com

facebook.com/Author.Jeffe.Kennedy

twitter.com/jeffekennedy

goodreads.com/author/show/1014374.Jeffe_Kennedy

bookbub.com/profile/jeffe-kennedy

Sign up for her newsletter here.

jeffekennedy.com/sign-up-for-my-newsletter

www.ingramcontent.com/pod-product-compliance
Lightning Source LLC
Chambersburg PA
CBHW030547020726
47494CB00005B/1519